THE
ATOMIC EXPRESS

Richard L. Miller

Also by Richard L. Miller

Under The Cloud

Dreamer

THE
ATOMIC EXPRESS

Richard L. Miller

An author's edition was published in hard cover in January, 1997.

Published in the United States by

Two-Sixty Press
P.O. Box 7888
The Woodlands, TX 77387-7888

Library of Congress Cataloging-in-Publication Data:
Miller, Richard L.
The Atomic Express/Richard L. Miller 1st ed.
p. cm.
ISBN 0-9669414-0-3

First Edition

Book Design: Words & Graphics

Printed in the United States of America

For Kim

1

The Nevada Test Site

April 1956

An atomic bomb, just before detonation, makes a slight humming noise. No one knows when the sound actually begins, but it becomes audible about ten minutes before the actual shot. To anyone sitting next to the device, time in those final ten minutes becomes a plastic, slippery flow of discrete instants. Each second lasts an eternity, an eternity saturated with visions of the bomb casing's dull gunmetal, the rusty gray of the shot tower, the purple window of storm-filled, early morning desert sky. And that sound, that *hum*. Subtle, like a persistent scrap of memory that would neither go away nor reveal itself completely.

Carl Rhinehart stood for a moment to stretch his legs, a six-foot-two insect atop a 400-foot steel tower. The first time he'd heard the hum, he thought it was from somewhere else, either from inside his head or from the desert outside the shot cab. Perhaps from another dimension. It had reminded him of no other sound on earth and had frankly scared the hell out of him.

Rhinehart now understood the hum had a more pedestrian origin; it was simply the routine vibration of atoms inside some electrical gadget located deep within the bomb. Probably a timer. Whatever it was, it was damn annoying. It reminded him of the low whine heard near the State Street subway rails on cold winter days in Chicago. Rhinehart yawned, leaned against the bomb, and checked his watch. Ten minutes.

Eleven miles away at the Camp Jupiter Control Point, the test manager, Milt Henderson, was probably running around, checking the circuits, barking orders to the scientists, engineers, assistants, congressmen and other flunkies who came to see the big firecracker go off.

Looking out the shot cab window through the light drizzle, Rhinehart could barely make out a blurry riot of headlights lining the nearby ridge. Troop trucks. Sergeants were probably saying, "Men, what you are about to witness is an *atomic fireball. .*"

The night before, in a blinding rain storm, Rhinehart had stepped off the train, waved goodbye to his friend Pliney and climbed the tower. "Say hello to whoever you meet over there!" the old engineer had said.

"*Whom*ever you meet," Rhinehart had corrected him.

One hour and 538 rungs later, he was at the top of the shot tower, sitting next to a 38-kiloton something called *Boxcar II*. Something he was partly responsible for.

By 3 a.m., the golfball-sized raindrops had been replaced by a weak drizzle, and the murky desert below had become like a Friday night football game at the fairgrounds: headlights, flashlights, flares, spotlights, beams of undetermined origin. The gentle plonk of rain on the tin roof of the shot cab had been replaced by the raucous roar of mud-stuck flatbeds, growling tanks, whining helicopters, yelling sergeants and squawking loudspeakers.

Standing in the cab doorway, Rhinehart had seen jeeps, tanks, flatbeds, two-ton pickups, even a Greyhound bus, all scattered across the desert floor like toys from a child's play chest. And parked at a discreet distance from the tower, almost invisible through the mist, was Pliney's train engine, the Atomic Express. Behind it were nine railcars, waiting patiently as soldiers filed out and started toward the trenches. Some had climbed into the foxholes, others into the slit trenches, still others into "shelters," cement-reinforced tin cans buried under ten feet of desert alluvium.

Now, an hour later, the train and the trucks were gone; the desert was quiet. Except for an occasional metallic crackle from the loudspeakers and, of course, that annoying hum from the bomb, the place was almost peaceful. Rhinehart turned away from the window and surveyed the inside of the shot cab. Despite the gloomy darkness, he could make out pulleys, chains, electrical gizmos, batteries and cables surrounding the bomb. And the television camera. The expensive automatic-exposure, automatic-focus television camera was the contribution of Security Officer Fogler. He wanted to make sure communists didn't sneak up the tower during countdown, steal the bomb and run away with it. Rhinehart had effectively compromised the million-dollar system by turning off its light source, a hundred-watt bulb. Now it sat there in the dark with him, zipping and zooming, stupidly trying to focus on the cab's corrugated metal north wall.

Thoroughly bored, Rhinehart looked back at the nuclear device, with its familiar rectangular bump on one side. The radar clock. Deftly yanking off the cover, he saw a single red lamp flashing at one-second intervals. From eleven miles away, someone at the Camp Jupiter laboratory was aiming a radar pulse gun at the cab. And the little clock on the side of the bomb was counting the pulses, nice as you please.

Suddenly the background humming sound changed to a higher pitch. Won't be long now, Rhinehart thought. He knew that when the humming stopped, it would be replaced by a single loud click.

It was a sound only a few people had ever heard—this close anyway. But Rhinehart and the other atomic scientists knew about it. Some thought the click came from a tiny black ten-ounce switchbox riveted onto the bomb next to the radar lamp. Others claimed the click was the result of neutrons passing through one's ears. Rhinehart preferred to think it was the sound of the universe splitting in two. Others thought it might be linked to the *precursor pulse*, that mysterious blip of electro-magnetism that always appeared on the oscilloscopes at the Control Point a millisecond *before* the light reached them.

No matter. Rhinehart knew that after the click that would be *it* for the noise. It would drown in the blur of radiation, pouring out through the bomb casing like water through a sieve, 20,000 tons of energy from a 500-pound box.

From the far end of the metal bomb cab came a soft chirping noise. "A damn cricket," Rhinehart shrugged. "All this noise is starting to get on my nerves."

Then he became aware of a new sound, this one a low whine. Within seconds two dots of light popped into view over the ragged southern horizon. It was an airplane. A civilian airplane.

Rhinehart peered at the approaching object and shook his head. "Wonder what we'll have up here next," he mused, "a blasted five-piece band?"

"Is that it, Bobbie Jean?"

"Is that what?"

"The tower, dammit, what do you *think* I said?"

"Oh, yeah, sure, Suze."

"Well, are we gonna miss it?"

"I think so."

Susan Colter felt a shiver ripple down her shoulders and settle into her lower back. Strapped into a big, fat airplane over the Nevada Test Site at zero hour. Perfect.

"Got your camera?" the pilot asked.

"Well, yeah, Bobbie, but—"

"There's the tower," Bobbie said, pointing into the darkness ahead of them. "Take your picture."

"It's dark out there." Susan stared at the opaque blackness outside the windshield. "I can't see a damn thing."

"Me neither, Suze," Bobbie Jean nodded, "but I know we're in the right spot. There's a whole string of cars and junk back there on the ridge."

"What's our altitude?"

"Can't tell. Got the lights off."

"Well, now, *damn!*" Susan yelled. "What if we smack into the tower?"

"Don't worry about that." Bobbie Jean squinted at the instrument panel. "Just get your flash ready. It'll be on your side."

"You sure? It's pitch dark out there."

"Kick that window loose," Bobbie Jean said, pulling back on the throttle. "I'll switch on the landing lights, brighten things up out there."

"Okay." Susan pushed against the right front window. "Just give me a minute."

Suddenly the darkened cockpit became a roaring cacophony of dust, sand, paper and rain. In the cold, wet 90-mile-per-hour blast, Susan felt the rain sting her face like birdshot, felt her hair first go damp, then wringing wet, and then stream straight back behind her. It was like flying seven hundred feet over the desert on a motorcycle.

"Ya look like *hell*, Suze!" Bobbie Jean yelled over the roar of the wind.

"Just give me the lights!" Colter yelled back. Trying to keep her eyes open against the onslaught of the slipstream, she could barely make out the blurry shape of an approaching cabin. A cabin perched atop a tower. The shot cab. "Now, Bobbie! Let's see it!"

The Cessna's twin landing lamps came to life, clearly defining the dark shape at the top of the tower—a huge squarish object, big as a semi truck, rushing almost directly toward them.

"All right, bomb," Susan said, aiming her camera at the approaching shot cab, "smile."

Rhinehart watched the plane close in on his position, its twin headlights illuminating the interior of the shot cab, bringing the bomb and the cluttered cab into sharp relief. At the last minute, with an accompanying burst of light, the plane pulled up and thundered past, not fifty feet overhead, its twin shafts of phosphorescence extending away into the mist.

As the whine of the airplane faded in the distance, Rhinehart sat down and stretched his legs. He again became aware of the fibrillating red radar lamp, the cricket's chirp, the gentle hiss of rain on the tin roof and the soft hum of the bomb.

The theorists who had designed the first bomb believed time itself is composed of discrete packets, a string of "nows" like frames in a movie, which, when speeded up, went to compose microseconds, milliseconds, seconds, minutes, years. Get close enough to an A-bomb, and time stands still; packets of neutrons stop mid-space and things turn into an energy-packed eternal "now," as in a movie where the film has jammed in the projector. Look close enough and you can see the searing around the edges. Just before the film catches fire.

Rhinehart jumped. Two brilliant red flares broke the darkness outside, hissing into the sky not 200 feet from the shot cab.

In the distance the loudspeaker squawked. "One minute to detonation," the voice said. It was Don Hendrix. Probably wearing his red suspenders, bow tie, red socks. And gnawing on a Clark Bar. Hendrix, Rhinehart decided, was responsible for the Clark Bar candy wrappers littering the floor of the shot cab.

"Thirty seconds. Take your positions."

In the distance a dust cloud puffed as 6,000 soldiers—in perfect unison—placed their forearms over their eyes, then dropped to one knee. At his back, Rhinehart heard the hum-m-m-m, increasing in pitch, getting louder. Then, suddenly, it stopped.

"Ten, nine, eight. . ."

Last thoughts. Rhinehart scratched his head. Hell, *everybody* should have some appropriate last thoughts.

"Six. . .five. . .four. . ."

What to think about? Let's see. The first time with Judy Trembly?

No. Inappropriate. Has to be more spiritu-

Click.

━━◦◦━━

The sudden noise jolted Will Perkins from his best nightmare in days. There he was, ten years old, his girl cousin next to him screeching like a banshee. He was gripping the fright rail of a Ferris wheel seat, looking *up* at the ground, nickels, dimes, pennies, pencils—falling away toward the open-mouthed adults around the cotton candy booth.

It had been a great nightmare. Now all that was left was this . . . roar. Then, from behind it, came a man's voice. "Ha! You okay, Lieutenant?"

Perkins looked up at a short, chubby, red-headed man in a Hawaiian shirt. "I was having a nightmare."

"Looked like it," the man said. "For a minute there, I thought you were going to fall out of your seat. Quite a scene."

"Yeah." Perkins rubbed the sleep from his eyes.

"This place is really something, I love it," the man continued. "I never can wait to get back."

"Do you work here?" Perkins yawned.

"Used to," the man smiled. "Well, actually still I do. Ever watch *The Big Picture*?"

"Huh?"

"Television show," the man said, nodding furiously. "Comes on right after *Sky King*. On Saturday afternoons. Army Signal Corps Pictorial Center. That's me."

"You?"

"I shoot film for *The Big Picture*. You know. Bombs. Mushroom clouds. Soldiers. That kind of thing."

"Really?" Perkins smiled. "And you work for the army?"

"I'm *in* the army!" The man extended his hand. "Captain Hugh Duffel. As in *duffel bag*, get it?"

"Yeah, uh, my name is Will Perkins. Good to meet you."

"Gonna be in General Umber's Atomic Brigade?" Duffel asked.

"Yeah," Perkins nodded.

"Great!" Duffel grinned. "Umber's a friend of mine. Personal friend. Even lets me ride in his helicopter. Big sonovagun. Has its own latrine. I talked to him just last week. He told me they're bringing in some Navy blimps."

"Blimps?"

"He thinks the Russians might use them to sneak in over the pole." Duffel paused to scratch under the Hawaiian shirt. "It's possible, you never know. Anyway, blimps make great targets. Easy to hit."

"Yeah. I guess," Perkins nodded slowly.

"Well, I'll let you get back to sleep," Duffel said. "That was some nightmare."

"Yeah," Perkins smiled.

"Say Lieutenant," Duffel turned back. "If you ever want to *really* see a bomb blast, you know—close up —let me know. I've got connections. I know everybody at Camp Sagebrush. Because I'm a journalist. Sort of."

Perkins closed his eyes again. It was still dark outside. Maybe he would have time for another nightmare before morning.

He trusted his nightmares. Always about falling from great heights, the dreams were reliable as a good Bela Lugosi movie. In his nightmares he had fallen off roofs, out of planes and tall trees, from the top of the Empire State Building and, of course, out of the Ferris wheel. He had fallen naked and clothed, with his siblings, friends and army buddies, with Harry Truman, Joe Stalin and Churchill. And most recently with the little monster who'd started it all. His wretched girl cousin.

"Hey Willie," she'd always yell. "Watch me turn this sucker upside *down!*" And he would always try to protest, but nothing would come out. Then he would be falling, headfirst, toward some sharp-looking object on the ground.

Perkins felt the bus slow down and lurch to the side. Through the window he saw a guard waving the bus through the gate and into a parking lot glowing bright orange beneath a battery of street lamps. Camp Sagebrush in the southern Nevada desert. Where the tall mushrooms grow.

As the bus rumbled into the parking lot, the other passengers slowly came to life. Rumpled soldiers groaned, sat up and stared blearily out the windows. A few seats ahead, a ball of crinoline sprouted feet and almost rolled to the floor. Probably a senior officer's wife coming in from Vegas.

Wiping the last traces of sleep from his eyes, Perkins looked into the darkness past the parking lot. The scene was a uniform black. It might be the Mojave Desert or some unnamed southern Nevada ridge—in the daylight, a mixture of light tan and bleached white, as far as the eye could see. Just like the poster in the recruiter's office.

The sergeant had told him Camp Sagebrush was the healthiest spot in the country. Wide open spaces, "located in the scenic basin and range country—where the sky is blue and the air is fresh . . . a place where aspiring leaders will not only learn about tactical combat in the modern environment, but will also witness some of the most beautiful and awesome displays of aerial ordnance that modern science can offer. Just the place for that all-important training *so necessary for advancement* in the new *atomic army.*"

Back at Fort Ord, his commanding officer had asked him about his assignment. "You sure you want Camp Sagebrush, Lieutenant?"

"Yes, sir," Perkins had said, standing ramrod straight.

"No, I don't think you want this," the old man said. "How about Fort Sam Houston? Fort Riley, maybe."

"I really want to go to Camp Sagebrush. The atomic brigade is there. I understand it's a good assignment."

"Still believe the recruiters, do you?"

"Sir?"

"Recruiters lie. Most of them are assholes. Did you know that?"

"No sir, I didn't know that."

"Well, they are."

After an awkward, silent pause, the old colonel had pulled the orders across the desktop and scratched in his signature.

Suddenly, the bus door opened and a stocky sergeant entered. "Welcome to Camp Sagebrush," the man snapped. "Enlisted men assemble by the guard shack . . . officers in front of the bus. Any questions?"

Stepping off the bus, Perkins scratched his side and looked down at his shirt. The ride from Fort Ord had reduced his normally well-pressed uniform to the consistency of a bag. His tie looked like a black dishrag and his sharpshooter medal was sticking into the skin of his chest. Perkins pulled on his tie and imagined himself six years hence, a major, no a *colonel*, leading his brigade through its paces, steely-eyed, casually mentioning his training "back at Sagebrush" where he first got his ticket punched on the long road to his general's star. An atomic Marcus Aruelius, taking no account of mushroom clouds or neutrons or gamma rays or anything else before dishonor.

In the distance, a dull red flash suddenly illuminated a purple cloud deck. Heat lightning? Another flash, nearer. A flare.

Looking around, Perkins noticed he was the only one standing in the officer's area. Wasn't the man in the Hawaiian shirt a captain? Scanning the parking lot, he saw no trace of the man from the Big Picture. Maybe he had already caught a ride somehow. Things happen like that in the army.

Twenty-two miles due north of the Camp Sagebrush parking lot, Joe Bob Ramey brushed away the desert sand until he saw the latch, a simple steel lever lying flat against the surface of the lid. "Here it is, Art."

"And here's the Geiger, Joe Bob." The taller man, his radiation suit gleaming white in the sun, handed Ramey the small, clicking instrument, then backed away.

"Damn ground's hot enough." Ramey lifted the heavy lid back, exposing the dark interior of a vertical steel culvert. "What was the yield on this one?"

"Nominal—twenty kilotons."

"Bet it was more'n that," Ramey said softly, easing himself into the hole. "Bet it was twice that."

"It was only twenty," the tall man said. "I checked it before the shot."

"Hell, Flagmeyer," Ramey snorted, descending the ladder into the hole, "you can't figure the yield of a bomb *before* it detonates. Unless ya got a crystal ball or something." He stopped a third of the way down and switched on his belt lamp. The bomb shelter looked stable; probably wouldn't cave in. The radiation meter only read a few millirads. Probably didn't even need the gas mask. Stepping onto the corrugated steel floor, he shined his flashlight on the green walls, then around the room. Despite its proximity to ground zero, the shelter seemed remarkably intact. The pressure wave had squeezed it in only a few places, denting the sides. The monster's thumbprints.

The other shelter—the one directly beneath the shot tower—had been crumpled like a beer can in the hand of a big Irishman. Inspecting the damage had been like trying to walk through a wrecked car. But this shelter looked good. A soldier could survive here.

Suddenly, the radio crackled. "How's it look down there?"

"Everything's pretty much intact," Ramey replied.

"Do you see the neutron monitors?"

"Yeah," Ramey said, retrieving the small rectangular boxes. "Nobody stole 'em this time."

Shortly after the soldiers at Camp Sagebrush learned that the monitors contained gold foil, the little boxes had started to disappear. Ramey figured the soldiers had something to do with it, taking little detours during their maneuvers under the cloud. Later they'd drop the loot off at pawn shops. Probably a third of the wedding rings sold in Vegas were radioactive.

"Come on up," Flagmeyer's voice crackled over the speaker, "I see the train."

"Okay." Ramey took a last look around the interior of the shelter and quickly climbed back to the surface.

"We can make it if we hurry," Flagmeyer said, pointing to a flicker of light on the horizon.

Ramey brushed himself off. "Hell Art, it's only half a mile to the siding. Besides, Pliney knows we're here."

"I just don't want to be stranded. This place gives me the creeps."

As the two scientists walked toward the tracks, they saw the dusky-red hue and familiar hammer shape of a late-model diesel locomotive, its beacon flashing relentlessly, even in the scorching brightness of the Nevada desert at mid-day. The twin yellow marker lights high on either side of the hood and the gaping engine coupler fronting the steel fender skirt reminded Joe Bob of the expressionless face of an Indian warrior. In contrast, the downslanted windshield behind the rotating headlight beacon added a sorrowful, almost comic appearance to the massive engine.

"You sure Pliney will let us in the cab, Joe Bob?" Flagmeyer asked. "Last time I was out here, he made me ride on the flatcar."

"That's 'cause you had George Linneman with you," Ramey chuckled. "Ole Pliney doesn't much care for our boss."

The train approached with a familiar screech of brakes. Even with no rail cars in tow, the heavy diesel required about a hundred feet or so to come to a complete stop. The engineer, a heavyset red-faced man with thin white hair, leaned out the window. "Hi, boys. Enjoyin' the sun, I see."

"You should be wearing your respirator, Mr. Pliney," Flagmeyer said. "It's hot out here."

"Hell yes, it's hot out here!" the engineer snorted. "It's the goddamn desert!"

"He meant radioactive, Pliney," Joe Bob said, swinging up into the cab. "Got any passenger room up here?"

"Shore, come on up," the engineer said. "Watch yer step. Had a senator out here yestidday slip an' bust his ass. Funniest thing I ever seen."

"Was he with Marienfeld?" Ramey asked.

"Yep," Pliney nodded, "I was hopin' ole Stanley would break somethin' too, but he didn't. That sonovabitch does have an exceptional sense of balance, I'll give him that."

"That's about the only sense he's got," Ramey said, glancing at his radiation meter. "Looks like we're down to a few millirads. Guess we can take the masks off now."

"I'm leaving mine on till we get back," Flagmeyer replied, settling into a corner of the engine cab.

"That's up to you, Art." Joe Bob unzipped the cotton rad suit and felt a hot breeze against his sweat-soaked undershirt. "Warm enough for ya, Pliney?"

"Nope." The old man sent a bullet of tobacco juice within inches of Flagmeyer's head. "I could stand another few degrees."

"I don't see how." Ramey shook his head. "I bet it's ninety-five out there, and you're duded up in bib overalls, long-sleeved shirt—engineer's boots . . ."

"Hell, Ramey, I'm an engineer!" Pliney pulled the striped trainman's cap down over his white hair. "Lemme tell ya, I spent years and years on the ol' North Shore line outta Chicago—damn near frooze up I don' know *how* many times. Just got *real tired* of it. Nah, I like this place. Warm."

"Yeah," Ramey nodded.

"Ya out here inspectin' the terlet tanks again?" Pliney asked, easing the throttle forward.

"Underground shelters," Flagmeyer corrected him. "They're *underground shelters.*

"Okay, shelters," the engineer said. "I saw 'em puttin' some of them goddamn shelters in up at the old north target. I thought they wasn't gonna do any more testing up there."

Ramey glanced up at Flagmeyer, then down at the floor.

"Shore hope they don't have any plans for no A-bombs at the north target. That's where my rail yard is. Where I keep my *engines.*"

Ramey shrugged and squinted out toward the horizon.

"Yeah," Pliney continued, "I *saw* them cement mixers and metal culvert and all that business up there. They're gonna set one off up there, ain't they, Ramey?"

"Haven't heard," he replied, wiping dust from his face.

"Yeah, *shit.*" Pliney hammered the horn button with his fist. "You two know what's goin' on around here sure as a cat's got climbing gear! They're plannin' to melt those trains—an' you guys know it!"

"Come on, Pliney," Ramey said evenly. "We're civilian employees, just like you. The director calls all the shots around here. If you want to know what's gonna happen to your trains, ask *him.*"

"Uh huh. Shore," Pliney nodded. "I'll just call him up on the phone tonight. Mebbe he'll invite me over for dinner or somethin'. Mebbe I'll bring him a bottle of *cabernet.*"

"I don't think Demming drinks," Flagmeyer offered.

"Don't make no difference." Pliney pushed the throttle foward. "The sonofabitch still wouldn't tell me nothin.' Davis Demming would lie even if it was easier to tell the truth. Now *you* two are guys I can trust."

"Come on, Pliney," Joe Bob shrugged, "I can't tell anybody 'bout where they're gonna do the tests. My boss'd cut off my water and take out the meter."

"He's right," Flagmeyer said. "George Linneman is very strict about security."

"Yeah," Pliney nodded, "Linnemen's another sonofabitch for sure. I just wanted to know if they was gonna melt my trains. Just curious."

The low rumble from the thousand-horsepower diesel rattled through the cabin, momentarily precluding conversation. The train reminded Joe Bob of his days growing up in San Antonio and the hours he had spent near the railroad tracks, watching the different trains come through. He especially liked the diesel limiteds—great red and yellow engines pulling miles and miles of silver passenger cars on their way to New Orleans or Dallas or Phoenix. Ramey felt sort of bad about being partly responsible for having trains vaporized at the Test Site.

"Well, Mr. Pliney," Flagmeyer said after a pause, "the reason they brought the trains here to begin with was because of the civil defense experiment . . ."

"Yeah, uh-huh. You guys *know*, doncha? They're gonna melt 'em all right." Pliney paused to tap a cracked engine gauge. "You know why they laid all this track past the target? They just wanted to see what the goddamn atomic bomb could melt. That's the only reason. You know that well as I do."

Joe Bob glanced at Flagmeyer. He had heard the story before.

"Awhile back they had me bring in an American Railfan from the Bangor and Aroostook. Real good looker. Droopy windows, just like the Express here. Had me park it right underneath the tower. Looked like it was, you know, *mournful* or somethin'. I sure hated to see her go. Damn bomb drove that engine in the ground and *then* melted her. All's that was left was this little tin foil *blanket.*"

Flagmeyer adjusted his respirator and looked at his watch.

"I remember when they called me out of retirement," Pliney continued. "Said all I had to do was ferry a bunch of soldiers to the trenches. Then, before you know it, they had me takin' things to the display zone in front of the towers. Washin' machines, cars, howitzer cannons, teevees. Just to see what the bomb would do."

"I don't know," Joe Bob said evenly. "We just check the atomic devices when they come in. We don't have anything to do with the experiments—"

"Ain't your job, is it?" Pliney asked stiffly.

"Nope," Joe Bob frowned. "It ain't."

2

Sagebrush

"Y our name, sir?" The tall, morose corporal behind the desk looked bored beyond tears.

"Lieutenant Will Perkins. I just arrived from Fort Ord."

"You seen the commanding officer yet?"

"I've, uh, been at the gate for the past couple of hours," Perkins answered. "The truck was late."

"Just as well," the corporal shrugged." Our CO has been missing since the last bomb test. Probably dead."

"Excuse me?"

"Captain Wanker. Our commanding officer. He was taking over for our *other* commanding officer, Captain Stein, who was *almost* dead." The man paused to scratch his nose. "Do you have an appointment?"

"Uh, I'm checking in . . . uh, corporal . . ."

"McCorkle." The man scratched his nose again. "PFC McCorkle. Actually, I'm getting my promotion any day now, so Captain Stein let me wear the stripes. I run the company quarters while the officers are missing. Of course, *one* of them should show up sooner or later. I mean, there's a test scheduled tomorrow morning."

"A test?" Perkins asked.

Suddenly the hallway door burst open and a tall, bald man strode through the lobby past the startled Perkins and into a back office. "You're in luck," McCorkle said. "There's Captain Stein right now. Go on in."

Perkins quietly walked into the tiny, cramped office and closed the door behind him. The man behind the desk looked up for a moment, silently motioned him to a chair, then returned to signing his name to a sheaf of papers. "I'll be with you in a minute, Lieutenant," he said, without looking up. "I've been away for a while and it looks like I have some catching up to do."

Perkins nodded. In contrast to his own baggy appearance, the captain seemed all sharp angles and creases. His khaki shirt appeared as stiff as cardboard, while his arms looked like bundles of steel cables moving beneath smooth leather. The face was built of granite cheekbones with obsidian eyes behind rimless glasses and a prominent nose that obviously had been broken more than once. Barely healed scars spread from his collar to the left side of his face like an angry, corrugated mask, the obvious remnant of a horrible accident.

Suddenly, the man looked up and fixed Perkins with an intense stare. "Now, how can I help you?"

"I'm uh, Lieutenant Will Perkins, just in from Fort Ord. . ."

Without smiling, the man extended his hand. "I'm Captain Jake Stein. Welcome aboard."

Despite his unnerving appearance, the man's grip was warm and strong. Solid. "I'll have McCorkle take you to your quarters," Stein said. "Your room will be across from mine. There's no air conditioning, but don't worry, you'll only be in there at night. And it's cool around here at night."

"Uh, okay," Perkins nodded. "Is there anything else, uh, I should know? Orientation or something?"

Stein paused. "Didn't they give you that information back at Ord?"

"Well, they told us that radiation can be lethal, and to stay in the trenches until, I don't know, after the initial burst."

"That's good advice," Stein said, returning to the papers on his desk. "Don't ever forget it."

"Yes, sir. Thank you, sir."

Later, as he followed the tall enlisted man toward a group of wooden barracks, Perkins was astonished at how hot it had become. In the few hours since sunrise, the Nevada sun had turned into a fierce, pure white disk in a lethal blue sky. Beyond the wooden and brick structures of Camp Sagebrush, the landscape was a paper-white glare. White sand, white dust, white mountains. A white that attacked the eyes, burning them like film that had been exposed too long, erasing the images until only the outlines remained. Squinting at the ground, Perkins saw that the white glare was actually cream-colored earth dotted with blue-tufted cactus. The ones growing near the camp fence looked singed.

"Is this where the bombs are set off?" he asked finally.

"No," McCorkle replied, "that takes place about eleven miles north of here. Fourteen targets in all. Some we maneuver, others we just watch."

"Oh."

"Sometimes we get to ride the train out to the trenches. Other times we go on foot. It's no fun, I'll tell you." McCorkle shook his head. "There's things out there that you don't *want* to know about."

"Coyotes?"

"Worse," McCorkle shrugged. "There's scorpions, spiders, milli-pedes, centipedes, decipedes and just plain *pedes*—beetles, horseflies and little black ants that prefer your shoes, pants and anus to their own deplorable homes in the desert. You'll see cactus, Joshua trees, birds, lizards and the occasional Gila monster. And, of course, there's the helicopter."

"The what?"

"General Umber's helicopter." McCorkle opened the door to the barracks. "It's black. Equipped with fifty-millimeter cannons. He likes to shoot up the Joshua trees."

"I see."

"And of course there's the mushroom," McCorkle continued, leading the way upstairs. "Sometimes it leans east, like a poplar in the wind. Other times it just goes straight up like a brocolli from the pit of hell."

"I've always thought it looked like a *cauliflour* from the pit of hell," said someone behind him. Perkins turned to see a fat man in a tee shirt lounging on a nearby bunk, his feet propped on a stack of olive drab army blankets. "The color's right, anyway—kind of an off-white with *sparks*."

Perkins turned and surveyed the huge room. It resembled all the others he had seen in the army—twin rows of about two dozen bunks, each with a metal wall locker at one end, a wooden, olive drab foot locker at the other. A breeze puffed through the open windows carrying with it a fine dust that accumulated on the lineoleum floor. Perkins noticed a round wall thermometer, its red needle aimed at the 100 mark.

"Your room's in here," McCorkle called from a hallway at the end of the bay. "Sorry about the climate."

"It can get kinda' *warm* some of the time," the fat man said, running his hand over a thatch of shiny black hair. "Of course, leaving the window open helps, especially on the ground floor. Second floors, being closer to the sun, are definitely more *sultry*. Now, on the positive side, the floor fans do help to control the swelter, but at night it's like trying to sleep in a dust storm."

McCorkle opened a small door at the end of the bay. "Here's your officer's quarters."

Perkins stared at the room, a tiny cubicle hardly larger than a closet, covered from floor to ceiling in a melancholy shade of light green, and furnished with a single bunk bed and a single window—closed. "Well, guy," he muttered to himself, "welcome to your career."

3

Rhinehart

"**D**amn it, Rhinehart," Linneman yelled from behind his desk, "why did you do it? Are you trying to get me fired?"

"I was inspecting the switches." The tall, gangly man slouched in his seat, a shock of black hair hanging in front of his face. On the end of his nose was a prominant patch of sunburn, the only spot of color in a uniformly pale complexion. The hazel eyes, deep set beneath bushy black brows, slid from side to side like bubbles in a carpenter's level, first eyeing the floor, then the wall, then the bookshelf, then the floor again.

Despite his 31 years, Rhinehart looked like a teenager who had just been caught with a bra in the back seat of his father's car. To make matters worse, he was wearing one of the brown World War II Eisenhower jackets he had bought at the army surplus in Vegas. It served no purpose in the hot Nevada desert; he obviously wore it to infuriate the military.

"You were inspecting the switches?" Linneman asked.

Rhinehart's long fingers absentmindedly drummed on the mahogany arm of the chair. "And I forgot to come down."

"You *forgot* . . .?" Linneman leaned across the desk, eyes wide.

"Okay. I'll tell you the truth, George," Rhinehart shrugged. "I went to sleep."

"Why is it you want to blow yourself up?" Linneman asked. "If it hadn't been for that lunatic pilot buzzing the tower you'd be vapor right now! *Fallout!* Does that concern you at all?"

Rhinehart reached into the Eisenhower jacket and produced a cigar.

"Do you know what Demming said to me this morning?"

"No." Rhinehart reached into the rolled-up cuff of his faded denims, then began searching through his pockets. "What did Demming say to you?"

"He said the next time this happens . . . the next time any of those tests are halted because of you, *I'll* have to pay for it. Fifty thousand dollars! Right out of my pocket!"

"Hm," Rhinehart said. "Can they do that? I really don't think they can do that, George . . ."

"Yes!" Linneman exploded. "Hell, I don't know!"

"Could I trouble you for a light?" Rhinehart asked, holding up his cigar.

"Now you listen to me." Linneman's eyes narrowed into angry slits. "I have an ex-wife. A very expensive ex-wife who likes to watch television all day. Just to keep her amused and off my back, I'll have to dole out alimony as long as I live. If Demming starts charging me for delays . . . it will substantially jeopardize my ability to *do that!*"

"At fifty grand a pop, I would say so," Rhinehart agreed. "But I really don't think Demming has any *legal*—"

"Rhinehart," Linneman growled, "I'm sending you over to the infirmary. I want Dr. Bartholomew to examine you."

"Oh, come on, George," Rhinehart said, putting the cigar away. "I'm not crazy."

"Quiet!" Linneman stood up and came around from behind his desk. "First Wiggers, then Jeffrey and now *you*. . ."

"Now, of course, Wiggers and Jeffrey *are* a little—" Rhinehart began, sitting up in his chair.

"Quiet! I don't want to hear it!" Linneman interrupted. "Do you know what people are saying? They say I have a bunch of arrogant lunatics working for me."

"Who said that?" Rhinehart appeared genuinely hurt.

"Everybody says it!" Linneman shouted. "Demming, Marienfeld,

Henderson, those officers over at Sagebrush. And they're right!"

"You should tell them I'm just eccentric."

Linneman stopped cold, then leaned forward. "Climbing up a detonation tower and sitting on top of an A-bomb is *eccentric*? Word around the lab is that you were trying to kill yourself."

"Not true, George," Rhinehart replied, "I was just trying to leave the test site."

"If Hendrix hadn't pulled the safety switch—"

"Hendrix didn't pull anything," Rhinehart said. "The bomb went off on schedule and here I am. Sort of."

Linneman shook his head incredulously. "The bomb *didn't* go off and that's final."

"Maybe it did. Maybe it didn't." Rhinehart picked up his cigar. "The sad fact is, with quantum mechanics, there's no way to tell for sure."

"Rhinehart," Linneman said, grinding his teeth, "I don't want to hear anything more about any raisin-brained, crackpot quantum crap . . . from now on. Got that?"

Rhinehart shifted uneasily in his chair.

"No more early morning hikes around the desert during a countdown . . . no more checking the tower at the last minute . . . no more suicide attempts *of any kind* involving our atomic devices," Linneman said. "If you want to kill yourself, why don't you use *pills* or something . . . like *normal* people? Not an *atomic bomb*!"

"It's not the same thing, George," Rhinehart answered calmly. "You see, with the bomb you can jump to a different universe. Elmore Wiggers proved that if you're close enough to the detonation —"

"Wiggers? *Wiggers?*" Linneman interrupted. "You know where Elmore Wiggers is?"

"Well . . ."

"He's *dead*, that's where he is!" Linneman barked. "Lot of good quantum mechanics did him!"

"I'll admit there are some difficulties," Rhinehart mused. "But once the bugs are ironed out—"

"That does it!" Linneman picked up the phone. "I'm sending you to the shrink. He's been after me to send you over, and by God, I'm going to do it."

"Uh, George . . ."

". . . I can't have my men running around trying to kill themselves during this test series . . . hello, Carol? Put me through to the infirmary . . . Dr. Bartholomew's office."

"George—" Rhinehart said, tapping his shoe nervously.

"Yes, Carol, it's for Rhinehart. And send over a guard, please, just to make sure he doesn't get sidetracked. Thank you." With a deep breath, Linneman hung up the phone. "There."

"Uh, George."

"What?"

Rhinehart held up the cigar. "Mind if I smoke this first?"

Later, after Rhinehart left, Linneman settled back in his chair and stared at the wall. Of all his subordinates, of all the weapons specialists, Rhinehart was the worst—an arrogant madman trying to sell everyone at Camp Jupiter on his personal quantum-crackers philosophies. Riding exploding bombs like they were subways. From universe to universe.

Linneman didn't know beans about quantum mechanics and he liked it that way. An electrical engineer by education, he was interested in *whether* the electricity would flow in a given circuit, not *why*. In his old job of connecting wires in the shot tower junction boxes, he had never given a thought to electrons, waves, particles or flaky subordinates. Now he was a manager, in charge of seven crazy weapons specialists. He opened his desk drawer and retrieved a bottle of Old Feather. "One thing about quantum physics I do understand," he said, unscrewing the cap, "if a scientist doesn't see me drink this, then I'm not really drinking it."

In a way, he understood the lure of quantum philosophy. To his way of thinking, it allowed a scientist to invent anything he damn well pleased, then sidestep the consequences. Because if he didn't see the consequences, then, by God, they didn't exist. Take Emil "Megaton" Meghalty, for example. Two days after arriving at Jupiter, the little scientist had begged to add the deadly H-bomb fuel lithium deuteride to one of the conventional atomic devices. "We can load it on the train, in the hopper car! Take it to ground zero and set it off! It would make a wonderful bang!

"Sorry, Emil," Linneman had said. "No H-bombs in Nevada." Meghalty then went into seclusion in a corner of the lab and, two weeks later, presented Linneman with his own hand-crafted thermonuclear device. Linneman responded by shipping the damn thing off to the

Pacific, where the army used it to vaporize an entire island.

For weeks after the incident, Meghalty pouted like a grounded teenager. He had wanted to watch the blast himself. When he didn't get to see it, he wasn't sure it had really happened. To him, the second the H-bomb left the lab it no longer existed. And since he never saw the island—allegedly dissolved—perhaps his bomb never existed either.

How did a person *manage* people like that and still keep things on an even keel? Linneman shook his head in bewilderment. His immediate superior, Test Site Director Davis Demming, was deathly afraid of fizzles, misfires and delays—anything that gave Washington the impression things were not perfect at the Nevada Test Site. If the devices worked consistently, if the lab sent up fireball after blinding fireball and reduced rows of 400-ton steel towers to ash and vapor, then everything was wonderful. If *nothing* worked, it was another matter entirely.

First the memos would come. Then visits from the whining Public Relations Officer, Stanley Marienfeld. Then the requests to visit the Administration Building. Then the phone calls from the chief of the Atomic Energy Commission in Washington, the fearsome Dr. Anna Faye Trumbo. The thought of a call from Trumbo sent chills through Linneman's entire body.

Taking another drink, Linneman thought about the early years. The easy years. When he first took over as head of the Weapons Lab, its primary function was to inspect weapons from Los Alamos. The scientists under his charge would heft the big metal objects onto a table, dissect them into their component parts, and reassemble them with a little tag marked "OK." Then the sullen devices were placed on the lab train for their trip to the target where they were detonated. Simple. Easy.

In those days, Linneman's office had remained completely in the shadow of the Los Alamos bonanza, protected from the erratic breezes and eddies of office politics and public sentiment. Both responsibility and blame seemed to flow past, leaving him and his office unscathed. At one point, during a lull in the testing, Linneman thought he had achieved bureaucratic nirvana, where all the organizational lines seemed to pass through his office like neutrinos through warm beer, never leaving a trace, not even a bubble. It was a wonderful time.

Then it all ended. Linneman ran his hand through his thinning hair, and glanced out the window. He remembered the awful day when Los Alamos decided to phase out pedestrian A-bombs in favor of the Big Guys—nerve-jarring, attention-getting thermonuclear devices. Suddenly, no one was making A-bombs anymore.

While Test Coordinator Demming protested that America *needed* bombs for the Nevada Test Site, Los Alamos explained that if even one of the multimegaton bastards were ever detonated at Camp Jupiter's chintzy targets, it would turn Nevada into America's *lowest* state. No, they said, if you want to stay in business, you'll have to design and build your own damn bombs, and thank you very much.

The next day, a memo arrived from Dr. Trumbo. Henceforth and immediately after the stockpile of Los Alamos devices ran out, the Nevada Test Site Weapons Lab would begin doing what it should have been doing all along, i.e., designing, building and detonating its *own* atomic bombs.

The day of the memo, Linneman had taped a cautionary reminder on his wall—a drawing of a flounder. He thought it was only appropriate; not only was the flounder the lowest, flattest creature on the planet, it was also blessed with both eyes on one side of its head—the better to watch out for shit from above. Since then, Linneman had consciously emulated that style. Settling back into his chair, he looked at the drawing and took a final drink. Wouldn't it be great, he thought, if Rhinehart and his quantum theories were right—that if you didn't directly observe something, it didn't exist? If that were the case, there would be no overbearing Dr. Demming, no Dr. Trumbo, no Atomic Energy Commission. And no recalcitrant, sensitive bombs to make and test.

At this quiet place in time, bottle on the table, fish on the wall, these were the only real things—Linneman, his flask and his flounder.

"Dr. Bartholomew," the voice over the intercom squawked, "the security guard is here with that scientist from Camp Jupiter, Dr. Rhinehart."

"Yes, yes. Rhinehart," Bartholomew said, loosening his bow tie. "That fellow on the tower. Tell him it'll be a few minutes."

Bartholomew hated this. Of all his patients, Rhinehart was the most insulting, the most troublesome. The man had no respect for physicians, the military, *anybody*. It was a shame he was so valuable to the weapons program. Retrieving a thick file, Bartholomew switched on the intercom. "Tell him I'll see him now."

"He says he'll be there in a minute. He hasn't finished reading."

"Pardon me, nurse?"

"He'll be there in a minute. He's reading the newspaper."

Bartholomew carefully clicked off the intercom, drummed his fingers on the desktop, then glanced again at Rhinehart's file. PhD. Mathematics. Quantum physics. That was it, Bartholomew thought to himself. Quantum physics. The root of the problem.

Early in the twentieth century, atomic theorists claimed that an electron could be either a wave or a particle, depending on what the person measuring it expected. Later, when they discovered that an electron might not even exist unless someone was watching it, all sorts of metaphysical hell broke loose. If an electron behaved that way, why not an entire atom? If an atom, why not the whole *world*?

But that idea was *routine* next to Rhinehart's view of things. The way he figured it, if things existed only while he was observing them, then he must be *responsible* for everything—the creator of all he viewed. Keeping up with this patient was getting to be a pain in the ass.

"Dr. Bartholomew," the voice over the intercom squawked.

"Yes, nurse."

"Dr. Rhinehart says he's finished with the sports page and he's ready for his session."

"Then send him in," Bartholomew ordered, stiffening himself for the battle. It wouldn't be quite so bad, he thought, fighting with an unalloyed solipsist—but a solipsist wanting to abandon his own world? I'll have to be tough, Bartholomew decided. There'll be none of this quantum physics nonsense.

"Mind if I borrow the sports page?" Rhinehart strolled through the door, his Eisenhower jacket unbuttoned to reveal a ragged denim shirt. "I'm proud of how my teams are doing."

"Please sit down," Bartholomew said. "Your supervisor, George Linneman, asked me to speak to you. I understand you had a little problem earlier this morning."

"Uh, no," Rhinehart said after a pause. "Everything went fine."

"Of course, the bomb didn't go off," Bartholomew smiled, steepling his fingers.

Rhinehart shrugged and looked absently around the room.

"Now, Carl, I assume you wanted the bomb to detonate because you were up there on that tower. And if it didn't then, that must have been a problem for you."

"Well, actually, *Norm*," Rhinehart smiled genially, "there *was* no problem, because there *was* a detonation. And now I'm here and everything is fine."

Bartholomew winced. Okay, he thought to himself, don't let your ties to reality get sucked into this lunatic's personal whirlpool. "But the detonation was *after* they brought you down from the tower, Carl. An hour later."

"That was the second burst," Rhinehart said. "I ought to know. Both of them were my bombs. The whole thing was mine. In fact, I'll bet *you're* just something I cooked up on a bad day."

"No, no, no." Bartholomew struggled to retain his smile. "You had nothing to do with my existence."

"Suit yourself," Rhinehart said, picking up the paper. "You sure you don't mind if I borrow this?" He snapped the page. "Heck, why am I asking you?"

"Carl, Carl," Bartholomew said smoothly. "You're getting into that old quantum physics jalopy again, I can tell. Let's get back to why you tried to kill yourself."

"I wasn't trying to kill myself."

"Yes you were."

"I'm here, aren't I?"

"Okay then." Bartholomew said irritably. "Have it your way. But why do you think you can use *our* atomic bomb as your personal . . . *transportation*? That's not what it's supposed to be used for!"

"Beats any other use I can think of," Rhinehart said.

Bartholomew closed his eyes for a moment. It was a shame Rhinehart wasn't in the military. That bastard would find himself sitting at ground zero, and it wouldn't be to travel to some other *planet*.

"Okay, okay." Bartholomew took a deep breath, then shuffled a few loose memos. "On to some other things. When you were sitting up there—in the bomb cab—did you, ah, see anything?"

"See anything?" Rhinehart looked up. "Which time?"

"The last time. Just before they brought you down."

"Before detonation?"

"Okay. Yes. Have it your way. Before detonation."

"An airplane," Rhinehart mused. "It tried to knock over the tower. I don't know *how* I came up with that."

"An airplane," Bartholomew nodded. "Anything unusual on the ground?"

"Standard stuff," Rhinehart said. "Helicopters everywhere. People running around, hiding in holes."

"Anything at the military instrument bunker?" Bartholomew asked. "The general tells me there have been some thefts of equipment there recently. Neutron sensors, I believe."

"I didn't take them," Rhinehart said, reaching for the newspaper. "Pawn shops won't buy them anymore. Too radioactive."

"So you didn't see anyone trying to *break in* or anything?"

"During an atomic test?" Rhinehart laughed. "Norm, only a *lunatic* would do that—er, do you have the want ads?"

"Get out." Bartholomew glared.

"It's only been a minute or so," Rhinehart whined, dropping the paper. "Ramey bet me you'd last at least half an hour."

"Get out!"

"Then you don't mind if I take the sports page?"

A few minutes later, alone in his office, Bartholomew picked up the phone. "Get me the colonel."

"Colonel Myrmidon." The voice on the line was cold, flat.

"This is Dr. Bartholomew. I've just finished interviewing that fellow on the tower. . ."

"And?"

"Well," Bartholomew paused, "I don't think he saw anything."

4

Spies

The alien object hung in the air over Perkins' head, big as a factory, its moving parts going this way and that, shimmering and blinking in the diffuse twilight. Perkins knew it wasn't real— no sun was visible. All his dreams seemed to take place at some impossible time, a twilight noon. The moon showed up often in his dreams, but the sun never did.

In the distance, Perkins could hear the soft buzz of reality, like the sound of a beehive filtered through the static of an old radio. Someone was talking about bombs. In response, Perkins saw the storm clouds, their shapes distinct against the purple sky. They emitted an occasional bolt of lightning, striking the tower, a thin antenna projecting from the sandy earth.

From some point above, Perkins looked down on the antenna. Around him, gears and pulleys, treads and tracks rumbled away into themselves, disappearing, then reappearing. Suddenly, they were directly above the tall, thin structure. The buzz in his ears grew louder. To his surprise, Perkins saw that the tower was surrounded by dark concentric circles. He was staring into the center of a target. Then the floor dropped away and he felt himself falling into the bulls-eye. As the ground approached, the buzz increased, becoming louder until it was almost deafening.

Click.

". . . The hallmark of an atomic burst is the emission of extremely bright light . . ." The tall man on the stage was pointing to something drawn on a chalkboard. A mushroom cloud.

There was no tower, no bulls-eye. Just a lot of soldiers listening to some scientist talk about bright lights and radiation.

It was almost five in the afternoon. The orientation session had gone on now, without a break, for almost three hours. In that interval, great rolling clouds of sleep had overtaken Perkins any number of times. In response to the thick heat and boredom, random playful signals from his cerebral cortex had coalesced into rampaging daydreams. First they had drowned out signals from the outside world, then they had chased him down like great storm fronts, stripping his body of conscious activity and leaving it in the questionable care of his autonomic nervous system.

In the few instances he managed to stay awake, he did so by comparing the various speakers on the podium to celebrities, animals or even food. One man—a short, thick AEC official named Demming— reminded him of an overstuffed link of kielbasa sausage. Another guy— someone named Marienfeld—resembled a large slick amphibian that someone had first trained to bark, then dressed in a shiny, dark blue suit.

One of the scientists looked like Einstein, white hair exploding from his scalp. Another resembled a huge rumpled bear with glasses. The current speaker—a Dr. Flagmeyer—resembled someone out of a WWII movie: thick, rimless glasses, rectangular, serious-looking face, long blond hair combed straight back. Watching him snapping the wooden pointer against his pressed cotton trousers, Perkins thought he looked like an earnest but misguided Luftwaffe officer. Humorless, but apologetic. "I'm sorry, but the bomb *is*, after all, designed to blow you to bits . . ."

After Flagmeyer finished speaking, the Einstein-scientist scrambled to the podium and began lecturing in some foreign accent: "Zo you zee, za blast vave reflects from za surface of za earth to create za *mach stem*. . ." Within minutes the man was bouncing across the stage, jabbing the air with his wooden pointer, then slamming the chart on the blackboard with his fist as though *it* were the target to be destroyed. "And zis *radioactive* base surge, can cruuuuusssshhhh even za most solid entrenchment, fracturing za metal und concrete into tiny particles und zen DRIIIIIVING zem into za *dirt*."

"I saw something like that once," one of the soldiers observed. "My cousin had this pet lizard—acted just like what you see down there."

"I'd have to disagree, Robert Wayne," said a burly man with a greasy wave of slicked-back hair. "As a species, the lizard has a more *casual* personality."

"Not if you give them coffee." McCorkle mumbled. "What time is it?"

"Almost five," the fat man responded.

Shading his eyes with his hand, Perkins decided the hot air billowing in from nearby Yucca Flat had somehow cooked time itself. The very seconds had become calcified. Perkins yawned the heated air into his lungs. He was tired, starving and felt as though someone had driven a roofing nail into the back of his neck. On stage, the little scientist had been replaced by the a tall, scowling officer admonishing everyone to keep quiet about what was going on at the test site: "I would stress that you are prohibited from saying anything at all about what you do here. This is a top-secret operation, you know. Spies for the various foreign powers will do anything to learn what is taking place here. They will tour the site posing as civil defense officials; they will overfly the area in chartered light planes. And they will try to get information from you— any way they can."

"I would certainly hope so," one of the soldiers mumbled.

"Now, if there are no questions," the man concluded, "I'll turn the microphone over to Captain Spaulding for a few closing comments."

A young, smiling blond-haired man bounded onto the stage. He reminded Perkins of a college cheerleader at a football game. "All right!" he gushed, slamming his fist into the palm of his hand. "You soldiers out there may think you're tough. You may think you're smart. And I know some of you have been to West Point—"

Perkins looked around. The crowd was absolutely silent, some appeared to be just waking up.

". . . But just because you're here at the test site doesn't mean you're an atomic soldier, no sir!" The man's blue eyes sparkled. "While General Umber would like to have all of you in his brigade, he can accept only the very best."

"I think I'm starving to death," McCorkle mumbled.

"—If you're good, if you're tough and if you can accept responsibility—then you've got a chance to be in the best fighting organization in this man's army—the Atomic Brigade! So for those of you new to the Test Site, I'd like to take a few minutes to tell you what this place is all about!"

An hour later, as Perkins slowly made his way down the grandstand, he realized that he didn't remember much of the orientation. Except, of course, for the most important things—that only the best made it into the general's elite brigade—and that tomorrow morning he would see his first nuclear detonation, up close. It would be his first big test on the way to becoming an atomic soldier. Pausing for a moment at the foot of the grandstand, he looked north, toward the testing area. On the jagged horizon he could make out the eye-blinding expanse of white sand, and beyond it the dark beginnings of a Nevada thunderstorm.

Suddenly, someone slapped him on the back. "Hey, Peekers! Fancy meeting you here!"

Turning, Perkins saw a grinning man dressed in a garish Hawaiian shirt and khaki trousers. From beneath the standard issue army cap exploded clumps of orange fuzzy hair, cut a shade too long for anything military. Yet perched on each shoulder were the unmistakable captain's bars.

"It's me! Hugh Duffel! Remember? Signal Corps Pictorial Center. The *Big Picture!*" Duffel grabbed him by the shirt. "Good thing I ran into you."

"Look, I really have to meet up with my commanding officer—"

"Nah, this won't take a minute!" Duffel dragged Perkins toward a large red building. "I'm shooting some footage inside the cafeteria. Civil Defense stuff. You know, the Russian blimps *could* come over the pole any minute. People wanna know what to put in their fallout shelters—"

"Uh, look," Perkins stammered, trying to break free, "I really don't have time . . . "

"—So I figured I could kill two birds with one stone." Duffel flung open the door and pulled Perkins into the corridor. "I rounded up the camp dietician and had her bring in the four basic food groups. Yeah, right through this door here."

Perkins found himself in a hot, damp area behind the kitchen. Before him was a substantial brunette holding a can of vegetables over her head. "Canned peas," she said, smiling sweetly.

"Wait until I get behind the camera, kiddo," Duffel commanded, scrambling behind a small tripod-mounted camera. "I can't believe it," he said, turning to Perkins. "She's been holding those peas all this time."

"I, uh—" Perkins looked around for an escape.

"Shh!" Duffel hissed. "This is a take! All right, sweetheart, that's a can of peas, not a *torch*. Bring it down a little bit. Hold it about the level of your face."

She brought the can close to her right ear.

"Is it saying anything important?" Duffel asked acidly, his face against the viewfinder.

"Not yet," she giggled.

"All right. Take five." Duffel shook his head. "Last week I was shooting 'duck and cover' footage for the Civil Defense Agency. Had a ball. I'd yell, 'hey kids, here comes the Russians! Duck and cover!' And they'd fall outta their chairs, dive under their desks."

Perkins scanned the room for an exit.

"I even got some film of a little league baseball team diving into a manhole—one by one. You have to see it to believe it." Duffel turned back to the brunette. "You can drop your peas now, sweetheart."

"Thank you," she chirped.

"When those kids grow up, anytime someone yells 'duck and cover' they're gonna fall down," Duffel said, adjusting the camera. "I'm no psychologist, but there's great potential for harm, don't you think? I'd rather shoot soldiers any day."

Perkins eased back toward the door.

"Of course, radiation fogs up the film, that's the only problem. You ever work a Bolex camera, Lieutenant?"

"Uh . . ."

Without waiting for an answer, Duffel turned back to the girl. "Let's try it again, okay? If we have to adjust the light, my assistant, the lieutenant here, will be doing that." A second later, Duffel threw a switch on the camera and a motor inside began to whirr. "Now!"

"Canned peas." The dietitian smiled at Perkins and winked. "Is a member of the four basic food groups and deserves a place in your Civil Defense shellout falter pantry—"

"Fallout shelter pantry," Duffel said, then turned to Perkins. "I didn't write this script. But you know, even for someone who's not an actor, these are *not* demanding lines."

The brunette set down the can and picked up something else. "Meat," she chirped, holding up a huge slab of steak, "is another member of the four basic food groups."

Suddenly a sad-faced corporal stepped between the dietitian and the camera. "Uh, excuse me, Captain Duffel, we finally located him for you." The man motioned toward the door, and a rhinoceros of a man in a tee shirt and apron walked into the room. The man's clothing was stained all the way from his neckline to his dusty army boots. From the corner of his mouth dangled a cigarette that looked like it had gone through at least one other owner. There was absolutely no question about the man's occupation.

"Ah," Duffel smiled, "the cook. I guess you actually fix up what this lovely dietitian here suggests."

"I don't know nothin' about diets," the man growled in a deep bass voice. "I cook what I want."

"Then you two haven't met," Duffel smiled.

"Nope." The cook warily eyed the brunette holding the steak.

"I see." Duffel rubbed his hands together. "Fine. I'm glad there's a *system* here. Would you like to be in a movie?"

"Nope."

"Well, good," Duffel nodded, the smile still on his face. "You can go back to your mess then."

"Commissary." The cook appeared hurt. "It's called a commissary."

After the cook left, Duffel turned back to the girl. "Shooting's over for the day. Start up bright and early tomorrow. Or maybe the next day, I don't know. Okay?"

"Okay." The dietitian smiled and winked at Perkins on her way out.

"Look, if you're not going to film anything else, I really have to get over to the company headquarters." Perkins started for the door.

"Not so fast, Lieutenant." Duffel clapped a pudgy hand on his shoulder. "How would you like to be my assistant?"

"I doubt if I can do that," Perkins said. "I've just started training for the Atomic Brigade. I don't think my commanding officer would let me—"

"*Sure* he would!" Duffel said, tightening his grip. "You'd be fine! No problem at all! And—" Duffel leaned closer and winked. "You'd get your name on television. Part of the *Big Picture*. Wouldn't that be nice?" Duffel leaned even closer. "Do you know how many generals watch television? A *lot*, I'll tell you. And the important thing about that is—when your name comes up for promotion . . . they'll say, 'Hm. Perkins.' Why *sure*! We know him! He's the guy that helped out with the *Big Picture* at the test site. Why hell *yes*! Let's give him his promotion!'"

"I don't know—"

"You'll be well-known in all the right circles! Think about it! A lieutenant, treading into the homes of most of the generals in the army. In their goddamn *living rooms*! On Saturday afternoon. Just after *Sky King—*"

"I don't think so." Perkins backed out of Duffel's grip.

"You're missing the opportunity of a lifetime," Duffel said, his eyes wide. "The army now, the big time later! You might even be on *Beat The Clock*!"

Perkins gulped and backed anxiously toward the door. Maybe it was the heat and humidity of the kitchen, but *last* place he wanted to be was in the back of a cafeteria on the nuclear test site, with a wild-eyed army captain in a Hawaiian shirt.

A second later, he found himself hurrying down the narrow, darkened hallway, bumping into hard-faced soldiers and civilians, rushing against the flow of dinner traffic, drowning in a crowd of strangers.

━━◦◦◦━━

Joe Bob Ramey took a drink, then gazed through the window at the dark bomber, glistening in the late afternoon rain. The huge plane was parked across from Ethel's Bar at the Yucca Flat runway. Probably it held the bomb for tomorrow's test.

"Another beer, Joe?" Ramey turned to see the bar's proprietor, wiry as a desert rat, eyeing his empty glass.

"Yeah, Roy, I suppose." Joe Bob reached into his pocket for another fifty cent piece. "When you gonna drop the price of a beer?"

"When another bar opens up on th' test site," Roy replied, setting down a Carling Black Label.

"It'll be a cold day in hell when that happens—an' you know it," Joe Bob growled, handing over the fifty cents. "Over at the Pig 'n Bun, I can buy the same beer for a quarter."

"Uh, huh," Roy nodded, scooping up the money. "But th' Pig is about forty miles away, now ain't it? Like I said, when another bar opens up around here, I'll drop m'prices. Maybe."

Joe Bob sighed. If ever there was a monopoly, this was it. Somehow, back in 1949 when the place was just getting started, Roy and his wife had set up shop near the air strip, paid off a few politicians and never bothered to leave. When army camp and the weapons lab came in two years later, Ethel's Bar had a captive and thirsty clientele. As a result, prices were usually twice to three times what anyone would pay at a conventional saloon.

To be sure, Roy had turned a lot of the money back into the operation. He'd put up the biggest sign outside of Vegas: a huge glowing neon mushroom cloud proclaiming *ETHELS BAR The Only Restaurant At Ground Zero.* Proud of his unique place on the map, Roy had also spent a respectable sum decorating the bar with an extensive collection of atomic bomb memorabilia. There were atomic bomb lamps, signs and ceiling fans; atom bomb chairs with backs in the shape of the mushroom cloud. Even atom bomb swizzle sticks. On the ledge surrounding the dining area there were mushroom-shaped ashtrays, whiskey bottles, salt-and-pepper shakers and statues.

And, of course, there were the games. Roy had somehow figured out that weapons scientists were suckers for flashing lights and nearly naked women, so he installed an entire wall of pinball machines. Most of the playing boards were overflowing with images of impossibly voluptuous females. By pressing the side buttons at exactly the right moment, the lonesome soldiers and scientists could send the steel ball hurtling toward the high-number aperture, which in turn elicited an immediate response in an appropriate section of the display.

Joe Bob poured beer into his glass. The place *was* expensive, but it could be a lot worse. Besides, it wasn't anywhere near as tacky as Las Vegas.

"Hey, Ramey," Roy said, approaching the table again, "you look *hongry*. Want a menu? Got a special runnin' today only. Neutron Ham 'n Eggs, just three bucks."

"Three bucks?" Ramey looked up. "Hell, Roy, that's highway robbery!"

"I had to pay for the menu," Roy nodded. "That leetle sketch here cost me a bundle."

Ramey looked at the menu in Roy's hand. On it was a caricature of an unshaven cowboy holding a Geiger counter, glowing in the dark, and cursed with lightning bolts jumping from his hat, eyes and rear end. In the background the artist had sketched an assortment of sage, juniper and cactus—as well as the all-important atomic detonation.

"Ain't that somethin'?" Roy asked proudly. "That mushroom cloud is just big enough I can write in the special of the day. Whatcha think?"

"Roy, that cowboy's got a lightning bolt shootin' out his ass."

"Yeah," Roy nodded. "Yer friend Rhinehart's idee. You sure you ain't hongry?"

"Not anymore," Joe Bob shook his head.

"What you boys gonna blow up tomorrow morning?" Roy asked, sitting down. "Another train?"

"Don't know," Joe Bob replied. "I don't have anything to do with that. I just inspect 'em."

"I heard you boys're gonna be makin' your own pretty soon," Roy said. "That's th' word around here, anyway."

"Nobody's told me anything."

"I hear yer old buddy Stein is back."

"That right?" Joe Bob looked up.

"Yup. He was in here about two hours ago." Roy scratched his head. "Had some of his boys with him. Foolin' around with the pinballs, gettin' ready for that thing tomorrow mornin', I guess."

"Probably." Ramey paused for a moment. "How did he look?"

"Well, y'know that damn fireball marked him up some, but other'n that, he don't look none the worse for wear. Now if that'd happened to me, I'd a' *quit*. Tell 'em take the nu-cleer dee-vice and shove it up their ass *sideways*."

"Tough to do when you're in the army, Roy."

"Yeah, Ramey, I forget you done some time in the service, too. You know all about that stuff." Roy walked back behind the bar. "Yeah, ol' Stein was in here, lookin' mean as ever. An' it looks like he's goin' out to them trenches again. Ain't that somethin?" He shook his head. "The man's got more balls'n a truckload of elephants."

"Guess so," Ramey said, getting up from the table. "Well, I'd better get on out of here. It's a long drive home."

"Yeah," Roy laughed. "It's all of 20 miles down t' Indian Springs. Watch ya don't get lost on that ol' Jupiter Highway now, Ramey."

A minute later, Joe Bob stepped off the front porch of the bar and into an unseasonably cold spring rain. With any luck it would clear before morning.

===⊸⋓⊸===

"Tarnation, I don't know why in the hell you women wanted to meet here—especially when there's a storm comin' up." The old man, his face a leathery rug, stared at his coffee. "You tryin' to punish me for things I ain't done yet."

"Come on, Frye," Bobbie Jean said, settling into the booth, "the Pig 'n Bun is halfway between our places and yours. Besides, you practically live here."

"There's a storm comin' up, dammit. I oughta be home right now. I don't like flyin' in th' rain."

"What about those tourists you flew into Reno last week, Harold?" Susan asked. "Right through the middle of that thunderstorm—"

"And I caught a cold out of it, too," Frye groused. "Been sneezin' my damned head off. What'd you ladies want to talk about?"

"We got a few pictures this morning," Susan grinned.

"And we never got caught," Bobbie Jean said. "Slicked that plane in at four hundred feet, did what we had to do, then got the hell out."

"When I heard they stopped the test, I damn sure *knew* you two had a part in it," the old man grinned. "How'd ya do it?"

"In from the south," Bobbie Jean replied. "Guess they thought it was a military flight."

"There's no radio communication allowed just before the shot," Susan said. "To them we were just part of the operation. By the time they figured what had happened, we were skating out over the Syncline Ridge. Worked like a charm."

"Did you fly Albert?" Frye asked.

"As always," Bobbie Jean smiled.

"Shoulda' took a faster plane." The old man shook his head. "That damn helicopter's gonna catch you one of these days. Knock that big fat ol' bird of yours right outta the sky."

"Albert did real good," Bobbie Jean said. "Got us in, and got us back out."

"Jus' dumb luck," Frye snorted. "Didja see what you was lookin' fer?"

"Didn't see any sign of wreckage—'course it was night so we really didn't expect to." Bobbie Jean patted Susan's shoulder. "But m'copilot here got some shots of the tower—

"Th' tower?" Frye grinned.

"And she thought she saw somebody up there! Standing in the door of the shot cab."

"The hell you say!" Frye looked at Susan. "Was he all tied up or somethin'? Handcuffed, mebbe?"

"I couldn't tell," Susan replied. "It seemed like—"

"Probably *was* handcuffed," Bobbie Jean shrugged. "Might even have been *chained* to the bomb."

"Well, I'll just be damned!" Frye leaned back in his chair. "Them bomb scientists have to be the *meanest* race of people on the face of this earth."

"I said, it *seemed* like it," Susan said. "I didn't say I was absolutely sure. It was hard to see."

"Hard to *see*?" Frye snorted. "All you's had to do was jus' *look*! Hell, next time you go up ya oughta' take a *professional* observer—"

"Now, stop it, Frye," Bobbie Jean said. "You're just peeved it wasn't *you* making that flyover."

Frye leaned across the table. "I'll tell you ladies what—you let me fly in there'n we'll do more 'n just take a buncha *snapshots*. Snapshots ain't gonna tell ya what happened to yer daddy."

"It's the best we can do for now," Susan shrugged.

"Naw! I'll tell you what ya oughta' do." Frye dropped his voice conspiratorially. "Sneak up that damn tower and just get ya an A-bomb."

"We're not interested in their bombs, Harold," Susan said. "We're interested in what they're doing at ground zero."

"Yeah," Bobbie Jean nodded. "Particularly in that bunker."

"Well, now, hell. We'd have time to look at that, too! You could get out and walk over to that bunker like you was walkin' up the sidewalk to yer house. Knock on the door. Ring the doorbell. Ask if anybody's home. You two just ride with me next time an' I'll show ya how it's done. Shoot, we can go tonight—soon as this storm blows over."

"Oh yeah," Susan said. "Fine. I can see that. Steal a bomb. Two women and a seventy-year old man in a . . . what? A *Piper Vagabond*? Does that plane have an engine or a rubber band?"

"Now, you leave Lucille out of this," Frye groused. "She's a Vagabond DELUXE."

"Oh, *Deluxe*!" Bobbie Jean said. "That changes everything. That black helicopter better look out!"

"Is that how it works, ladies?" Frye huffed. "I go twenty miles outta' my way—into a damn cold front—jus' so's I can listen to two women make sport of my ideas an' insult my airplane—"

"I'm sorry, Harold," Bobbie said hastily. "Lucille's a fine airplane."

"*Fine* plane," Susan agreed.

"And, you're a fine pilot . . ."

"*Fine* pilot . . ."

"Hey! What is this?" Frye exploded. "A testimonial *dinner*?"

"Listen, Harold," Susan said. "We think your plane is fine and your flying is fine too. We even think your idea for landing near the tower and stealing a bomb is fine."

"*You* think it's fine." Bobbie Jean looked at Susan. "I think it's crazy."

"Well, it's *interesting*," Susan said. "And we'll think about it. Really. But the fact is, for now we want to keep taking pictures of ground zero. And that means we want to keep flying over. So, we think we might need—"

"Your airstrip," Bobbie Jean smiled.

"My *what*?" Frye asked, squinting across the booth with his one good eye.

"Your airstrip," Bobbie repeated. "The one southeast of Warm Springs, the one just a hundred yards outside the test site."

"The one the government doesn't know about," Susan said.

"It's not on the sectional chart, Harold," Bobbie Jean said. "And the test site borders your property. Isn't that interesting? I can't imagine how you fly in and out of there without breaking *some* federal law."

"—So you two want ta use my personal landin' strip fer yer little midnight runs on th' test site? Ya want to lead a whole goddamn *flo-tilla* of jets an' helicopters back to my ranch. Is that what you're askin' me to put up with?"

"Only in the worst emergency," Susan smiled. "We'll probably be able to lose 'em first."

"Probably," Bobbie Jean agreed. "We just want your permission to use your airstrip. Once in a while."

"Emergencies only," Susan nodded.

"Lemme think about it," Frye said, standing up.

"How long?" Bobbie Jean asked.

"About five minutes."

"Five minutes?"

"I have to use the can," the old man said, shuffling away, "an' five minutes is about how long it takes me to bleed th' lizard."

"Five minutes?"

"Takes awhile," Frye cackled, closing the rest room door, "it's a big lizard."

"I swear," Bobbie Jean said after a moment, "one of these days I'm gonna beat that old coot."

"Don't beat him until after we use the strip," Susan laughed as the rest room door opened.

"Back so soon, Frye?" Susan smiled. "What happened to your lizard?"

"Probably couldn't find it," Bobbie Jean whispered.

"You girls're in luck," Frye said, returning to his seat. "I decided to make a deal with ya."

Later, as the plane lifted off into the grey haze of the rain squall, Susan leaned her head back and closed her eyes. It had been a rough day. "What did you think of Frye's deal?" she asked after a few minutes.

"Deal?" Bobbie Jean snorted. "He said he'd let us use his sorry old runway if we'd help him steal a bomb? What kind of a deal is that?"

"Aw, that's just talk," Susan said. "You know him."

"I don't know, Suze, he's ornery enough to try it. God, wouldn't it be awful to have to bail him outta jail for theft of an A-bomb? Isn't that a federal offense?"

"I'm sure it's illegal *somewhere*," Susan nodded.

"Yeah," Bobbie Jean said, "and so is trespassing on restricted government property. But we do it all the time. And nobody's said anything yet."

"Yeah, but they will," Susan sighed. "I think that general knows it every time we fly over. One of these days our luck's gonna run out. We sure can't fly out over the Syncline Ridge anymore."

"Yeah, we're gonna need Harold's airstrip," Bobbie nodded.

"Maybe we *could* take him along," Susan grimaced. "To ride shotgun."

"We will *not* take that old man over the test site," Bobbie snorted. "My insurance won't allow no seventy-year-old tail gunner."

"Aw—"

"No, I mean it!" Bobbie Jean scowled. "I don't want Harold and his .44 Buntline taking down any military aircraft. I *do* know *that's* against the law."

"Well, these flights over the Test Site are probably a waste of time anyway." Susan sat up in her seat. "The general knows we're not gonna see anything down there. By the time we fly over, the bunker's all sealed up. And if we did catch them doing anything, that black helicopter would be on us in a minute."

"Prob'ly," Bobbie agreed.

"I was thinking, maybe we ought to go back to the photos again . . ."

"I don't know, Suze," Bobbie said. "They really don't show anything. I think your scientist friend is just wasting our time."

"Maybe," Susan said, looking out the window. "But he seems to know a lot about the *Windstorm* shot. And he's given us some good leads—"

"And he could be working for the general, too," Bobbie Jean said. "I can see it now—wake up some morning and my house is surrounded by guys in black suits wantin' to search th' premises . . ."

"I trust him, I don't think he'd turn us in."

"I don't think ya oughta' trust *any*body," Bobbie grumbled.

Susan settled back into the seat and listened to the roar of the engine. While the front windshield was a blurry pattern of rain, the side window offered a patchy view of the ground below—a few houses, the thin, grey line of highway.

"Well," she said, "we could join the army. Maybe ask for Camp Sagebrush."

"Don't think so," Bobbie Jean replied. "Besides, we're too old. When was the last time you saw WAC recruits in their mid-thirties?"

"*Early* thirties," Susan corrected, wiping fog from the windscreen. "But you're right, we're just not army material. No talent."

"Our talents lie elsewhere," Bobbie Jean said, puffing her rain-soaked hair. "Intelligence. Glamour."

"Femme fatales. Spies." Susan yawned, rubbing her nose on her denim jacket.

"Uncovering dark secrets at the atomic test site," Bobbie Jean said.

Closing her eyes, Susan listened to the steady drone of the engine mixed with the hiss of rain hitting the windscreen. "I just want to know what happened to my Pop," she said quietly. "That's all."

5

H-Hour

Perkins looked around the crowded barracks, then at his watch. It was 9 p.m. In just five hours everyone here would be transported north into the black desert and into trenches a few miles from ground zero. Yet everyone in the room seemed, well, *relaxed.* Some were reading, some were sitting crosslegged on their bunks, probably writing letters to girlfriends back home. In the center of the bay a group was even playing cards.

"Hey, lieutenant!" one yelled. "You want to join the game? A little blackjack—"

"Uh, no," Perkins shook his head. "I'm not real good at that." In fact, he *was* a fairly good card player. But he wouldn't be able to keep his mind on the game. Besides, his commanding officer, Captain Stein, was due to arrive any minute to take him to the military briefing for the scheduled maneuvers. Stein probably wouldn't approve of an officer playing cards with the enlisted men.

Perkins's mind shifted to the upcoming briefing. What kind of maneuvers would take place? Would they stand and watch the fireball from some safe distance or would they have to get closer? One of the enlisted men, Corporal Doggett, said they would have to march *toward* the mushroom cloud itself, stopping just short of the base surge. Perkins had always wanted to get close to an atomic mushroom—but not close enough to *touch* the damn thing. He felt his stomach begin to knot up.

"Hey, Sergeant Quaak!" one of the enlisted men suddenly yelped, "you got ashes in my coffee! What'd you do that for?"

"Henh!" the white-haired sergeant grunted. "You won the last round. Wot ya expect?"

Perkins studied the gruff, iron-jawed little sergeant; his corduroy-leather features and unruly thatch of white hair reminded him of Spencer Tracy. Perkins was a big fan of Spencer Tracy. Back in Missouri, he had seen *Captains Courageous* four or five times.

Perkins shook off the thought. Here it was, just seven hours before an atomic test and he was thinking about *movies*.

"You asleep, Wobey?" Sgt. Quaak asked, the folds of skin above his eyes forming two quizzical chevrons on his forehead. "It's your draw."

"Lessee," Wobey said, with a wide grin, "I'll just take *one*. I can hear the cash jinglin' in my pocket already!"

"Is that right?" Corporal McCorkle leaned his lanky frame against a bunk and studied his hand. "Flamboyant tonight, aren't we, Jimbo? If this were played on a stage, I would condemn it as an improbable fiction . . . Rico?"

"Gimme two," snapped a short, intense-looking teenager, his eyes narrow like the ports of a machine gun emplacement. He had twin tattoos of snakes on both biceps.

"Ah," said McCorkle, "Mr. Rico, the prince of Las Vegas, the scourge of Monte Carlo—wants two cards. That makes five doesn't it, my good man?"

In response, the scowling Rico stabbed the air with his middle finger.

"Table for one, Mr. Rico? Certainly," McCorkle shot back. "A man of few words but many cards—Sarge, you're next."

"Henh." Sgt. Quaak tapped the ashes of his cigar smartly toward McCorkle's face. Perkins suspected that if the old geezer didn't already have a perfect hand, he was darned close.

"Well?" McCorkle asked after a moment.

"I give up," Wobey said, throwing down his cards.

"Me too," Rico growled.

After a pause, McCorkle turned over his two cards. "Ace, queen. Twenty-one. Guess I win." With that, he reached for the small pile of money in the center of the table. Suddenly, a wooden cane appeared across his wrists.

"Henh," Sgt. Quaak said, "I got twenty-one with *three* cards. Guess *I* win."

McCorkle smiled broadly. "I was just pushing this money to your side of the table, Sergeant. Very good hand you have there. Don't you think so, Corporal Puhl?"

"Very good indeed." The fat enlisted man leaned over the table. With his huge belly and shiny black pompadour, Vincel Puhl resembled a small-town, gas-station version of Elvis.

Quaak stuffed the money in his shirt pocket. "Now it's time everybody was turnin' in. Big day tomorra."

Perkins shivered.

"Have you been appraised of the plans for tomorrow, Sergeant?" Vincel asked, pulling a comb from his pocket.

"I dunno." Quaak shuffled the playing cards, then placed them into his pocket. "Won't know until after Captain Stein and th' lieutenant here get briefed."

"Do we *have* to attack ground zero again, Sarge?" McCorkle asked. "Every time we do that somethin' bad happens."

"Nobody tells me nothin'," Quaak responded, heading for the door.

"Uh, Sarge," one of the men asked," I don't suppose they found Captain Wanker yet—"

"Nope. Henh." Quaak's face wrinkled into a sly grin. "He's still out there—lights out in five minutes."

Perkins stood up shakily. Maybe it was his the way he had been sitting, but his legs felt weak. For a moment he felt as though he were in a car racing downhill—without brakes.

"Lieutenant." Looking up, Perkins saw the hard face of Captain Stein. "Get your notebook. We're late for the briefing."

"It's one of the last bombs designed by Los Alamos," the dour colonel told his audience of officers. "Its yield will be the standard 20 kiloton. About the size of the Nagasaki device."

The tall, brittle man at the blackboard spoke in a wavering, singsong voice like the drone of an unsympathetic physician delivering bad news.

"Your infantry battalion commander, Colonel Thorne, will direct the frontal assault on the objectives. At the same time, I shall direct two companies of tanks—two platoons each. As always, armor will begin the assault, then break away to allow the infantry to advance to the objectives. Any questions?"

No one spoke.

"Now on the last maneuver," the man continued, "some tank commanders became lost in the haze. Therefore, as with any conventional conflict, I will expect the turret hatches to be up and the tank commanders to have their heads *outside*, directing the drivers. Just remind them to keep their heads down at detonation. Any comments or questions?"

Silence.

"As usual, I remind you to keep your distance from the equipment bunker. The scientists at Camp Jupiter are performing some very sensitive experiments there." The man paused and surveyed the audience. "So, if there's nothing else, I will yield the floor to the commander of the infantry battalion, Colonel Thorne."

A stocky, fireplug of a man approached the podium. "I just got a few things to say," he growled. "Every time we have one of these things, some jackleg troop gets *hurt.*"

Perkins felt the knot in his stomach tighten.

"Now, that thing that happened to Stein's platoon, we can't control that. The lab boys screwed up, an' I don't think the army oughta be held responsible. But there's things go on we can do somethin' about." He paused to scan the audience. "Men fallin' down on the way to the objective, or once they get there, slippin' all over the glass. Now listen, you men been *through* this before, you know there's *glass* at th' GZ. An' glass is slick. So watch yer step."

"Yessir," everyone said, almost in unison.

"An' another thing," Thorne said, moving around in front of the audience like a bulky prizefighter, "when you get to the GZ, *ya got to remember not to touch the tower!* Damn! I don't know *how* many times I had to send some damn fool peckerwood PFC over to the infirmary 'cause he just *had* to touch that tower. Wanted to see if it was hot. Well, I can tell you from personal experience it *is* hot. It's just like touchin' a hot iron!"

Thorne held his hand aloft, showing a red, scarred area across the palm and wrist. "See that? I got that bein' stupid. Burnt like a piece of red meat. Just remember, what's left of that shot tower can stay hot for days. I don't want anyone gettin' hurt out there tomorra! Everybody got that?"

"Yes sir!" everyone said.

"Guess that's all," Thorne growled, sitting down.

"Well," Stein said, looking at his watch, "we'd better get back to the barracks. Morning is only three hours away."

"But what are we supposed to do?" Perkins asked, his face flushed. "All that colonel said was—be careful, don't touch the tower—what am I supposed to *do* out there—?"

"Very simple, Lieutenant," Stein shrugged, "you're supposed to face a 20-kiloton atomic bomb. *That's* what you're supposed to do."

"But—"

"And if you're careful—and lucky—" Stein paused, the trace of a smile on his scarred face, "you might get a promotion out of the deal."

Back in his tight, stuffy room, Perkins kicked off his shoes and tried to remember the scenario: The Russians had landed at San Francisco and were rampaging east, crossing the Sierras at Yosemite. Hours away from Camp Sagebrush. The Atomic Brigade would engage the enemy, deploying tactical atomic weapons. Well, *one* weapon. Supposedly, the sight of 2,000 soldiers running through the ground haze would be enough to scare the Russians back to where they came from.

Perkins placed his shoes beneath the bunk, then began slowly unbuttoning his shirt. By the third button, he was asleep.

The sharp electrical patterns behind his eyes coalesced. Like images on a wavy, liquid screen, the patches and fragments of vision circled slowly, condensing into a world of sight and sound and touch. Gradually Perkins regained his bearings. It was late at night and he was back home again, behind the grain bins at the fairgrounds, reaching beneath the fuzzy pink sweater of his dark-haired high school girlfriend. No army, no Stein, no atomic bombs.

Behind the grassy hill, the ferris wheel at the carnival roared and clanked amid the late-August whine and saw of countless cicada. Lying in the grass, he placed his hand across her back, feeling the goosebumps.

Suddenly, they were in the spotlight.

"Jus' keep yore clothes on, girl," the owner of the flashlight said. Flat, dull, the voice of doom.

"Oh, my God."

"You get back to the car. I'm gonna have a talk with yer boyfriend here."

Suddenly the girl was gone and Perkins was running through the grass toward the hill, over it, down into the weeds and onto the track. Despite his agility, the overall-clad man seemed to be closing the gap. Only inches to go. "I gotcha now, boy!"

Running headlong over the ties, Perkins felt the grip of a huge hand on his shirt, heard it rip it down the back.

"You're a dead man!"

"Huh?" Someone was holding a flashlight in his face. "I'm sorry about your daughter," Perkins stammered. "Look, we weren't gonna do anything. Really."

"What are you talkin' about?"

"Then, who . . ."

"Anyway, you're dead," the voice rasped. Somewhere close by, Perkins heard a click. Blinking away the sting and blur of sleep, he looked above the rim of brilliance to see two shining eyes, their surfaces so viciously bloodshot they resembled tiny spherical roadmaps.

"What's going on?"

"I just killed ya. Just now," the man growled.

Then Perkins noticed something else, hovering motionless just to the left of the flashlight, a dark, blunt metallic surface with a hole in the center. With a blood-pounding start, he realized he was looking at something from an entirely new and lethal perspective. "That's a .45 isn't it?" he gulped.

"That's right," the man said.

"Did you kill me with that?"

"Nah, too loud," the man said. "I used piano wire."

Perkins slowly reached up and felt his neck.

"Made it into camp about an hour ago. Came through the motor pool, got right past that stupid guard," the man said, lowering the gun. "He was from D Company."

"*Was?*"

"Scaled the outside wall, cut open yer screen. Now here I am. If you'd a been a communist agent, you'd be dead by now."

"Why don't I turn on the nightlamp?" Perkins blurted. "Might keep your flashlight batteries from running down."

"Yeah, that's a good idea." The man flicked off the flashlight. Reaching for the lamp, Perkins glanced toward the window. A big ragged hole had been cut from the center of the wire screen.

"Now the mosquitoes will get in," Perkins mumbled, switching on the light.

"I'll get ya a new one," the man said, placing the weapon into his belt holster. In the incandescence of the small lamp, the intruder's face was a haphazardly chiseled, off-white geography of scars, three-day-old whiskers and salt flat alkali. Beneath multiple layers of dust, dirt and green paint, his clothing vaguely resembled military issue desert fatigues, the same kind worn by the various army ordnance engineers Perkins had seen wandering about the test site. Wondering what time it was, Perkins began searching for his watch.

"If yer lookin' for your gun, forget it. I already killed ya."

"I haven't been issued one."

"Why not?"

"I didn't ask for one."

"*Every* commissioned officer should have a sidearm," the man said. "What if the troops don't want to follow orders—refuse to find and fix the enemy?"

"I don't know."

"Yer a sorry excuse for an officer. You know that?" the man sneered.

"He's new here, Ratney," someone said. " Leave him alone." Perkins looked up to see a tall shape in the doorway.

"You're dead, Stein" the intruder growled, aiming the gun.

"No, I'm not," Stein replied, gently easing the barrel aside, "but I heard you were."

"The security here is shit, you know that?"

"I'll try to do better in the future. Where have you been?"

"Out." Wanker put the gun away. "North of here. Been living on lizards and spiders."

Stein nodded. "Find any spies roaming around out there?"

"Not this time."

"Too bad. There's another test in the morning. You plan to be there?"

"Damn straight!" Wanker grinned. Perkins noticed that the man even had a coating of dust on his teeth. "You gonna take the first line of trenches?"

"I don't think so."

"'Fraid you'll get burned again?'"

"No."

"Well, I told ya you shouldn't listen those damn lab clowns," Wanker said, his voice softening. "Now, me—I don't listen to nobody—except, of course, the general—"

"Look, Ratney," Stein interrupted, "if you want to take part in this thing tomorrow morning, you'll have to go over the plans. At least you should know where the target is."

"*The* target? You mean there's just *one*?" Wanker looked hurt.

"Just one," Stein said, putting his arm on Wanker's shoulder. "Come on, let the lieutenant get some sleep. It's past midnight and we've got a 2:30 reveille. I need some sleep myself."

"Yer a pansy-ass, Stein," Wanker growled, walking into the hall. "Been away from this too long. Got lazy—"

"Right. And you need to shave and brush your teeth." Stein's voice trailed off. "You look like hell."

Perkins set his alarm clock for 2:30, turned the light out, then collapsed. It was one nightmare after another.

———※———

Shivering in the cold night air, Joe Bob Ramey stepped back from the concrete door of the Control Point, pressed the buzzer and waited for someone to let him in.

From its position atop the eastern slope of Syncline Ridge, the building afforded an excellent view of most of the test site. Standing at the front door, Joe Bob could see a brightly glowing dot of light to the northeast that was the 400-foot-tall shot tower. Ramey liked the towers, thought they resembled a cross between oil derricks and radio antennas. He enjoyed looking at them, enjoyed riding to the top of the damn things, wiring up the detonators, then sitting down on the edge of the bomb cab platform, 400 feet in the air and feeling the big towers sway in the breeze.

The purpose of the towers was simple—keeping the atomic fireball as far from the ground as possible should theoretically result in less fallout. Of course, it rarely worked that way. The damn towers themselves usually evaporated—and instead of radioactive dirt, the countryside was pelted with hundreds of tons of radioactive welding fume. But according to the experts from Washington, the stuff usually landed within about fifty miles of the test site anyway, in places where few people lived.

Joe Bob ran a calloused hand across his burr haircut, then looked up at the flag, slowly undulating in the gentle breeze. The wind was out of the southwest; this morning the fallout would land northeast of the target. Away from the trenches. Pulling up his collar against the chill, he wondered how close the soldiers would get to the target. As close as the last time? He hoped not. At least this time it wouldn't be his fault.

Suddenly he heard the familiar click of the bolt behind the concrete-and-steel door. A short, stocky man in a lab coat and an engineer's short-brush haircut peeked out. "You Dr. Ramey?"

"Yeah, I'm Ramey."

"Are you sure?" the man asked skeptically, peering over his thick hornrims.

"I'm never sure of anything," Joe Bob replied, "and I left my I.D. at home."

"Sorry," the man said, pushing the door closed, "you'll have to go back and get it."

"C'mon, Hendrix." Ramey squeezed his compact frame through the door. "I didn't *want* to come out here this morning. Anybody else here from the Lab?"

"You and Rhinehart are the only weapons men on this test," the man said, following Ramey down the corridor.

"Carl's here?" Ramey asked.

"Yeah," Hendrix said, adjusting his glasses. "George Linneman brought him in two hours ago, handcuffed his leg to a chair, then left. Has him watching a television monitor."

"Least he's not up on the tower this morning," Joe Bob chuckled. "I heard you were the one that stopped the shot."

"Just lucky," Hendrix said, scratching his flattop. "If that stray plane hadn't buzzed the tower, I wouldn't have caught it. I took a quick look through the scope—to see if they'd damaged the bomb cab or something—and there he was. Milt Henderson was the one who actually pulled the plug. Demming just raised hell."

"I can imagine," Joe Bob said, entering the Control Room.

For several years the Control Point had been under the command of two persons—Test Manager Milt Henderson and his sidekick, Deputy Test Engineer Don Hendrix. Both were as short as Joe Bob, and like him, both sported exceedingly short hair. There, however, the similarities ended. While Ramey tried to keep his weight at a wiry 145 pounds, both Henderson and Hendrix appeared to be on the far side of 200.

Both men usually wore expressions of plodding determination mixed with abject resignation. This, coupled with their choice in clothes— plaid jackets, rumpled shirts, mismatched socks and horn rimmed glasses—conveyed the impression of two distracted, bumbling bureau- crats. Thankfully, nothing could be further from the truth. Joe Bob knew they were capable, tough professionals, the kind who would kill a countdown if the test was in the slightest jeopardy.

While everyone respected Henderson's expertise, Ramey held Hendrix in particularly high regard. Don Hendrix's specialty was the misfire, the unexploded atomic device. Countless times, Joe Bob had seen him squeeze his bulk into a radiation suit, march through the door—usually humming some damn silly ditty—then drive to one of the target areas to defuse something. Misfired missiles, bombs, satchel charges, warheads, canisters, land mines. All nuclear. All deadly beyond redemption.

"Where are the soldiers gonna be?" Joe Bob asked, walking past a bank of glowing television monitors.

"Fourth circle," Hendrix replied, "three miles from the GZ. Shouldn't be any problem."

"Still pretty damn close if you ask me."

"I can understand your being nervous about it," Hendrix nodded. "Did you do a yield calculation on this one?"

"Nope. I quit doin' that after the accident. Linneman might've given the job to Art." Joe Bob scanned the room. "Where's Rhinehart?"

"Over next to the wall," Hendrix said. "Oh, by the way, if you see a reporter, let me know. Henderson invited one up here and he got away from us. He's wearing a black suit and a fedora. His name is Batman or something."

A moment later, Ramey found the sullen, unshaven Carl Rhinehart. Surrounded by equipment, he was blearily watching a bank of closed- circuit television monitors, one hand twirling a contrast control, the other holding a huge cigar. For the occasion, he had chosen to wear faded denims and a torn tee-shirt under a leather jacket with an "I Like Ike" sticker on the back. On the top of his head was perched a pair of black Wayfarer sunglasses.

"See anything at ground zero, Carl?"

"Nary a soul," Rhinehart yawned. "Say, do you think you can bum a cigar off Henderson? I'm almost out."

Joe Bob pulled up a chair. "Hendrix says he's busy lookin' for a fugitive reporter—say, what happened to your foot? Looks like there's something attached to it."

"It's a handcuff," Rhinehart answered.

"How do you go to the rest room? Take the chair with ya?" Ramey grinned.

"Nah, I just do this." Rhinehart reached down with one hand and deftly popped the cuff open. "Don't tell George."

"Nice trick."

"I *did* invent all this, you know," Rhinehart shrugged, turning back to the monitors. "Well, it looks like the troops are arriving."

———◦◦◦———

Perkins gripped the canvas strap of his field pack and looked out the window into the darkness. The test site's diesel locomotive was taking them through the most desolate countryside he had ever seen—a black, empty place in the middle of nowhere. As the train rounded a turn into the darkness, he saw the faint beam from the rotating headlight and the twin rails shimmering into the void. Alongside the track, he caught an occasional glimpse of some almost-familiar object—an abandoned artillery piece, a fragment of metal, an occasional set of tire tracks. It was like descending to the bottom of the ocean, where only darkness and wreckage exist.

"Uh, how long do you think it will be?" Perkins heard someone ask.

"Ten minutes maybe," came the reply. "You can see the staging area already."

Perkins looked out the window again. The horizon was now ringed with a diffuse glow.

Ten minutes later the glow had coalesced into dots and fields of light, its reflection against the desert creating a dull haze that extended sixty or a hundred feet into the sky. Looking more closely, Perkins could see that the cloud was composed of dust, kicked up by scores of vehicles.

As the train slowed and penetrated the area, the image became a glittering, glaring cluster of headlamps, portable spotlights and beacons, all scattered among an aggregate of mortars, howitzers and tanks. In addition to the chaos of vehicles and armor, the place was strewn with an amazing variety of radar receivers, small concave dishes mounted on truckbeds, rotating bar-shaped devices on tripods. Planted at the periphery of the staging area were four immense swimming-pool-sized saucers, slowly bobbing up and down as though nudged by some invisible wind. And though the angle varied, all were aimed in one direction, north, toward a thin, fragile object surrounded by a tiny pool of light. From a distance, it looked like a radio station antenna.

Suddenly, the train creaked to a halt. "Roma locuta," Perkins heard McCorkle say. "La causa finita est. This is it."

Minutes later, Perkins found himself thumping along in the desert after a clump of shuffling soldiers—toward a thin, illuminated antenna looking no larger than a toothpick stuck in the ground. Somewhere up ahead, presumably between them and the tower, were a series of trenches. There they would wait out the detonation. Perkins began to wonder if someone had made a mistake. What if there *were* no trenches ahead? What if they ended up in some flat, unprotected area beneath that damn deadly tower?

Suddenly, a chill came over him, a tightening in his chest. It was the same feeling he had experienced at the top of ferris wheels. The same one he felt inside his nightmares. Shuffling over the alkali surface of the desert, dodging the scattered stands of cactus, he decided to try to change the subject in his mind, tried listening to the rhythmic clang-clang-clang of the utensils inside his mess kit, then to the gentle thump of the galoshes hanging from the back of his field pack.

Nothing worked.

Up ahead, the dark aggregate of soldiers seemed to move away, forming a single vibrating mass of canvas and leather. Leaving him behind. Perkins broke into a run, his boots hitting the ground, soft, dusty explosions in the night. Then the movement stopped. Alongside them was a single black line. The trench.

"All right," Stein's voice rang out, "at the two-minute siren, I want those respirators in place . . . cotton in your ears. Goggles on. Anybody forget to bring dosimeters?"

"They weren't issued dosimeters, sir," someone said. "Radiation officer never showed up."

"Thank you, Corporal Wobey," Stein growled. "Now, I don't care how hot or *stuffy* it gets down there, no one takes off his utility jacket. No one removes his helmet. No one. Understood?"

Silence.

"Now," Stein continued, "this is Lieutenant Perkins's first nuclear test, so I'm going to ask Corporal Wobey to be second in command...at the next shot, you'll be taking orders from the lieutenant. Understood?"

"Yessir," the group mumbled.

"Good. Now, the first red flare means three minutes to detonation. At two minutes you will hear a siren and there will be a second red flare. I want your eyes covered by then. If you look at the detonation without dark goggles, you can be blinded permanently. Any questions?"

Shivering, Perkins rolled his eyes skyward. At the staging area, the glow had blotted out the stars, but here, halfway between the tanks and ground zero, the constellations shone brightly, ice crystals on black metal.

"Immediately after the detonation, we will rendezvous in front of the trench, then move forward to link up with Delta Company. From there, we move to the objective, 1500 yards west of the GZ. "If you get lost," Stein continued, looking directly at Perkins, "the marker lines are a few yards either side of us. Just move until you reach the cable and then follow it south. It will lead you to the staging area. Got that?"

Perkins felt another rush of fear. What if he missed the rendezvous point *and* the cables? What if he got lost out there? No. He wouldn't think about it. It was an irrational fear and—

Suddenly, a green flare blossomed in the sky above the shot tower. As it slowly dissolved toward the ground, the loudspeaker came on: "It is H minus twenty minutes. H minus twenty minutes. Troops and observers are requested to enter the trenches. Get into the trenches, gentlemen."

Seconds later, Perkins looked around and realized he was the only one left standing above ground. After a quick glance at the shot tower, he dropped to his knees on the desert, then slid into the dusty, murky trench. In the darkness, Perkins felt the trench wall nearest ground zero. Sandbags. What if the shock wave caused them to collapse?

"Hey, Lieutenant Perkins!" someone said. "Welcome to the party!"

"Yeah," another voice said, "Doggett is our official greeter to the trenches. He understands holes in the ground better than anybody."

Perkins switched on his flashlight. Nearby were Puhl, McCorkle and Doggett. They looked bored. "As a veteran of these gatherings," McCorkle said, "I recommend leaning against the dirt wall. It's easier on the back." Despite the cramped quarters, the tall McCorkle had somehow managed to turn his field pack into a sort of chair, while the sandbags near the top of the trench served as an improvised foot rest.

After settling into the trench, Perkins stood up and looked around. The sky had turned from pitch black to deep purple. A mile to the north, the single dot of light had been replaced with glowing gridwork. Then he saw something move on the desert, heading toward them from ground zero. Perkins felt a shiver run up his spine and vibrate his shoulders.

"Hey, anybody down there wanna be a movie star? Get your face on television. Right after *Sky King*. Whattaya say?" The voice was familiar. Eyes wide, Perkins looked up just as the glare of a flashlight hit his eyes.

"Whattaya know! Peekers! They got you right out here on the front line, huh? Real cannon fodder. Mind if I join you?"

"Get *down*!" Stein yelled.

"Woah! Hey!" The man tumbled into the trench, landing with a thud near Perkins. The flashlight illuminated a disheveled, perspiring man with curly red hair. Instead of the regulation army boots, he wore scuffed brown broughams. The front of his army field jacket was undone, revealing a palm tree and some parrots. "Remember me? Hugh Duffel. You helped out in the cafeteria with that dietitian. Look, I think you should reconsider my offer."

"Yeah, I—uh—"

"You gotta admit, Perkins," Duffel looked him in the eye, "anything beats *this*."

"Good morning, gentlemen."

Ramey looked up at a small man in a black suit. "Yes?"

"I'm Lester S. Battmund, from the *BOSTON DAILY NEWS. .*"

"Go away," Rhinehart growled, staring at the monitors. "We're busy."

"You're watching television," Battmund said, sitting down. "I don't want to take up much of your time, but I have a few questions—"

"*Five minutes to H-hour,*" Hendrix's voice crackled over the Control Room speakers. "All personnel on the test site take cover immediately. Repeat, take cover immediately."

"Uh, is this how you normally dress on the job?" Battmund asked, staring at Rhinehart's ragged Eisenhower jacket and torn tee shirt.

"I always dress this way when I watch TV, Mr. Batman," Rhinehart replied.

"We're monitoring the television cameras at the test site," Joe Bob explained. "We use them to make sure nothing unusual happens before the bomb is detonated."

"So I guess it's a very important test, then," Battmund said, producing a notebook. "Maybe even classified, huh?"

"Maybe." Rhinehart lit a cigar.

"H-hour minus four minutes!" the radio crackled again. *"All Control Point personnel planning to view the detonation should have protective goggles—"*

Battmund reached into his coat and produced a pair of cheap sunglasses. "Do I put them on now?"

"You probably should use these instead." Joe Bob handed the reporter a pair of dark goggles.

"I understand the Camp Jupiter Weapons Laboratory is planning to design its own bombs . . ." Battmund paused, then leaned forward conspiratorially. "Could you let me in on some of the plans? Off the record, of course."

Joe Bob glanced at Rhinehart. "Sorry. Top secret."

"Oh, come on, Joe," Rhinehart said after a moment, "I'm sure we can trust *Batman*. Besides, what could it hurt?" Rhinehart looked over his shoulder, then leaned forward. "What we're planning now," he whispered, "are smaller bombs."

"Smaller?" The reporter looked skeptical.

"Smaller," Rhinehart nodded. "Loaded with just a few *grains* of plutonium. Something that will produce a ten-inch-wide fireball. It might not be spectacular, but its purpose would be to *annoy* the enemy."

"Annoy?" Battmund looked confused.

"Annoy." Rhinehart puffed on the cigar. "Done right, you could have a whole battlefield covered with little tiny fireballs. Little mushroom clouds going up, oh, maybe a couple of feet."

"That's something."

"Sure is," Rhinehart nodded, "and the bombs'd be so small you could carry 'em in your pants pockets."

"Like jawbreakers," Ramey nodded.

"Of course, those neutrons would *roast your lil' weenie—*"

"Three-minute flare!" Hendrix's voice blared. "All planes begin radio silence!"

"There it is!" Doggett pointed toward the north. Perkins turned to see a bright red flare streak into the purple sky.

"H-minus three minutes," the loudspeaker intoned.

"*The Big Picture*, huh?" Perkins asked. "And I'd be your assistant?"

"Sure," Duffel nodded. "And like I said, all the generals watch television. You have television where you came from?"

"Uh, sure—"

"Well, give it some thought. It might change your whole perspective on things." Duffel aimed a small movie camera at the line of red fire in the sky.

"Yeah, guess so," Perkins nodded.

"Say, do you mind if I mosey down this way?" Duffel pointed into the darkness. "Might get a better angle on this thing."

A second later, he was gone.

"Who was that?" Doggett asked.

"Guy from the *Big Picture*," Perkins said, staring into the darkness.

A vicious siren whine broke the stillness. "H minus two minutes. H minus two minutes," the voice over the loudspeaker crackled. "Face right. Attach goggles and respirators. Kneel down, place your right arm over your face."

"Interesting thing about respirators," Vincel Puhl said, "they make a person look just like a collie."

Perkins fumbled with the catches of the respirator bag. With a finger-pinching tug, the bag finally snapped open and the flimsy rubber face mask fell to the ground.

"*H minus one minute thirty seconds.*"

Nothing was going right. The rubber straps were knotted up. His hands shaking furiously, Perkins tried to disentangle the straps but succeeded only in dropping the filter cartridge from the end.

"Here," Wobey said, calmly taking the mask. "You have to screw it on like this. There."

"Thanks," Perkins said. He tried to fit the mask on over his face, but even that wouldn't work.

"*H minus one minute. H minus 59 seconds.*"

From somewhere outside the trench, he heard the rumble of the approaching tanks. Suddenly, a spotlight beam arced across the sky above his head. Why wouldn't the respirator fit?

"*58 . . . 57 . . .*"

His heart pounding, he loosened the straps of the mask, trying to get them to go over the helmet. To his horror, one of the rubber ribbons came free of its serrated buckle.

"Take off your helmet first, sir," Wobey said. "Then you can fit the respirator over your head."

"I don't *want* to take my helmet off," Perkins said, his voice shrill with fear.

"You'll have to, sir. It's the only way you can get it on your face."

"H minus fifteen seconds."

"You better get it on your face right now, sir," Doggett whispered.

Ripping the helmet from his head, Perkins slapped on the facemask. Then, reaching behind, he grabbed the loose straps, *tied* them together, pulled hard. The mask gripped his face. Perfect. He settled in to await the shot.

"Nine . . . eight . . . seven . . ."

"Your helmet, sir . . ."

"What?"

"Your helmet." Wobey pointed to his head.

Perkins looked down to see his helmet lying at his feet.

Click.

And the world disappeared.

⸻

Captain Spaulding's face pressed the Control Point window. "God, it's beautiful. Even with dark glasses—"

The early morning darkness had given way to a blinding glare as a star formed 400 feet above the desert floor. By the time Joe Bob made it to the window, the star had expanded into a glowing, turbulent cloud of orange flame, twisting and roiling on the ground like some captive demon from the pit of hell.

"That's odd," Henderson murmured, puffing on his pipe. "No ballistic rise. It's just sitting there on the surface."

"It's expanded to a thousand feet," Hendrix said, watching the radar scope. "It *should* have risen already. What have we got out there—?"

In the fading glare of false dawn, Ramey saw the approaching pressure line, stretching across the horizon, rushing toward the Control Point.

"Here's the shock wave!" someone yelled. With a dull thud the pressure in the room increased perceptibly, then decreased again. From outside the building came a sharp clang, followed by the sound of breaking glass.

"Somebody forget to close the door downstairs?" Henderson asked. In response, one of the technicians hurried toward the stairs.

"Ah, now we're getting some rise," Hendrix said, staring at the chaos. "That was beginning to worry me. Thought it might go big on us."

"Did that thing have any lithium, Joe?" Henderson asked, looking away from the window.

"Dunno, I didn't inspect it."

"Los Alamos deserves a pat on the back for that one," Captain Spaulding said, walking away from the window. "Think you guys'll make one that good?"

"Prob'ly." Joe Bob watched the mushroom cloud roar skyward, surrounded by a purple glow of ionized air. At the base of the stem was a boiling wall of dust ten stories high.

"That thing *had* to have lithium in it." Hendrix shook his head. "Hope those troops had enough sense to stay back."

"The troops are safe." Spaulding folded his arms. "They know what to do."

As the mushroom rose into the sky, the fiery torus was clearly visible, a cylinder of yellow flame circling the dark, roiling stem. Then, as it neared the cloud deck and cooled, the stem pushed up through the center of the smoke ring and spilled down over the side as sheets of salmon-colored ice.

To the west of the cloud, Ramey watched the rocket trails, thin ribbons extending from the ground, bent and pushed askew by the force of the blast. Without looking at the neutron measurements, he knew the detonation had been exceptional—far more than the estimated 20 kilotons—perhaps twice that much.

Turning back to the television monitors of ground zero, he saw only static.

———❦———

The glare seemed to last forever, turning the world a searing white. Reaching for his helmet, Perkins saw its outline slip from his fingers, touch the ground, then become airborne again in a helpless ballet. All in absolute, profound silence.

Above him the glare poured across the roof of the trench, then slammed into the opposite side, dissolving even the outlines into a uniform sheet of solid light. He knew he should close his eyes, knew that the light would stream through, burning everything it touched. Yet his eyes *were* closed. Squeezed tight.

Perkins covered his face with his arm and the glare diminished to a red-hued negative of itself, glowing like the inside of a furnace. Then the trench itself became the furnace, as if someone had placed a hot iron across his exposed ears and neck. At the same time, he noticed two rivers of darkness coursing, beating across his field of vision, one small, the other larger. With a shock, he realized he was looking *through* his own forearm. And still there was absolute silence.

"Well shone bomb!" From somewhere in the red haze came a voice. "Truly the bomb does shine with a good grace!"

Then it hit. The noise and its attendant pressure wave slammed into him with a force he could feel inside his chest. And slowly, sickeningly, the trench began to move. As the thunder from ground zero rattled through the air above him, it was met by a dark, clanking, whining mass of machinery. Opening his eyes for the first time, Perkins saw a nightmare world of orange haze and metal objects passing directly overhead, trailing curtains of dust.

"Cave-in!" someone yelled. Perkins tried to move but couldn't.

"Let's go!" another voice said. "C'mon!"

By now, the all-consuming brilliance of the haze had dimmed to a uniform orange glow. It was like being inside a dying ember. There was no way on earth he would make it out of here alive. It was better to be buried here and now.

"Gotcha."

In the gloom, Perkins felt his field jacket tighten across his armpits. Something was lifting him from the earth.

"Thought you might need some help," someone said. It was a huge creature in army fatigues with a dark, dog-like muzzle protruding from beneath the steel helmet.

Perkins looked back at the trench where he had been. It was no longer there.

Suddenly, a tall figure appeared from the haze. "This most excellent canopy of air, why, it appears no other things to me than a foul and pestilent congregation of vapors."

McCorkle.

"The trench caved in." Stein's voice. "Everyone accounted for?

"They're all here," McCorkle said, panning his flashlight across the troops.

"Good," Stein nodded. "Let's move north to the rendezvous point."

Following the soldiers north through the gloom, Perkins noticed a distinct smell in the air—a sweet, acrid odor, such as after a heavy lightning storm. At the same time, his mouth registered a sharp metallic taste like he was coming down with the flu.

It had been several minutes since the blast, but the air still reverberated with a dense, deep rumble like distant, constant thunder. It seemed to be coming from some point in the sky. Looking up, he saw an eerie halo of light flickering at the zenith of the gloom. It seemed to be right over his head. Staring at the glow, dust clouds swirling around him, Perkins felt a curious mixture of awe and fear. He wondered if those at Hiroshima and Nagasaki had seen the same thing.

Then he remembered. The man from the *Big Picture*. The chubby, red-headed guy from the *Big Picture* had been in that trench with them. Turning to look at the trench line, his flashlight illuminated only a gray haze over a featureless white surface. There was nothing to show that a trench had even been there. No footprints, not even his own. The constant wind from the blast had erased them even as they formed.

His heart racing, Perkins panned the flashlight across the scene. There was nothing except an amorphous gray haze. Then he noticed something unusual crossing the light beam. Clouds. Small patches of vapor, tiny clumps of white cotton blowing across the sandy ground. It was like watching a speeded up film of a cumulus cloud field from above. Only it was on the desert floor. No one had told him the bomb could produce this sort of thing.

After one last glance for any sign of Hugh Duffel, Perkins turned back to join the platoon. To his horror, he saw that the soldiers were gone, vanished amid the dark, churning clouds of dust and ash.

He was alone.

=〰=

"You really should see this!" Captain Spaulding handed the binoculars to the reporter. "The base surge extends all the way to the first row of trenches!"

"Huh. I'll bet it's hot out there." Battmund squinted through the binoculars. "How hot do you think it is?"

"Hot *enough*, mister!" Spaulding beamed, retrieving the binoculars.

"Hot enough to melt a rhinoceros," Rhinehart said, blowing a stream of cigar smoke into the air.

"Yes," Spaulding nodded. "This is an *amazing* shot. A perfect shot. Awe-inspiring!"

"Yeah," Joe Bob nodded, "unless you're *out there*."

After ten minutes of walking through the thick cloud, Perkins noticed for the first time how unbearably warm things had become. It was like walking through a dust bowl inside an oven. Rivulets of sweat began at his hairline, then coursed down his face to sting his eyes with salt. Even with the respirator, the thick dust made visibility—and breathing—impossible. Resisting the urge to rip off the mask, Perkins reached for his walkie-talkie, then thought better of it. How would it look, yelling for help when he probably wasn't ten feet from the clearing? Instead, he reached for his flashlight.

Clicking the light on and off several times, he began to calm down. Earlier, Stein had said that there was some sort of cable running between ground zero and the staging area. All he had to do was find it and make his way back. In the last few minutes, the gloom had lightened considerably; perhaps the sun was coming up. Soon he would be able to see the staging area itself.

Suddenly, a few feet ahead of him, he saw two steel cables, crossing each other, forming a taut X on the surface of the desert. Was this the cable Stein had mentioned? And if it was, which way was the staging area? Perkins thought for a moment, then decided to follow the cable to the right. He hoped it would lead to a clearing. The heat was becoming unbearable and the metallic taste in his mouth made swallowing almost impossible.

Then he noticed that the cable was gone. Vanished without a trace. Was he heading in the right direction? He thought he saw soldiers moving through the dust cloud toward him, but the shapes were only a stand of charred cactus. For a moment, he thought he heard something. A helicopter? No.

Moving ahead, he found himself staring at the ground again. He hadn't noticed before, but the ground was littered with tiny dark metal spheres, surrounded by what looked like big flat snowflakes. Bending to pick one up, Perkins discovered that the flakes were particles of ash. What was ash doing in the Nevada desert?

Slumping along, Perkins became aware that the soles of his feet were burning. It was just like summertime, walking across hot sand without shoes. No, it was like crunching along over hot glass. He stopped and tried to listen past his own labored breathing. *Something* behind that curtain of dust was making a noise, a cross between a whine and a roar. Nodding to himself, he recalled hearing it before, just after the blast, when something moved over the trench. Then, peering into the fog, he saw movement. Maybe a hundred yards ahead, a huge black shape was hovering over a hill in the center of a flat area. On top of the mound were figures dressed in white. As Perkins watched, the black object settled to the ground, paused briefly, then rose into the sky with a deafening roar.

A search party. Probably looking for him and the missing man from the *Big Picture*.

Suddenly, *another* huge, rectangular object roared over a hill directly behind him, growling and clanking inside the haze. It was a Chaffee tank.

As Perkins stared, the tank stopped, the top hatch opened and a head popped up. "Well, they radioed, said you'd be out here. And sure enough, here you are!"

"Uh, yeah. Here I am," Perkins nodded lamely. The voice was familiar.

"You're one gutsy sonofabitch—we're only about a hundred yards from the tower! The man climbed out of the tank and balanced on the turret. "Takes *balls* to march to ground zero, yessir! Ain't many besides me that would do it! Pansy-ass troops are scared of a few neutrons! Scared it'll poach their *oysters*!"

"What?" Perkins squinted into the haze.

"But here you are!" he shook his head. "Right up here at the GZ itself! The general's gonna just *love* you! Huh!"

Perkins peered at the man on the tank. Though the man wore a respirator, he could make out the scabrous, alkali complexion, the wild look in the eyes—

He had been rescued by Ratney Wanker.

6

Suze

Joe Bob Ramey felt like he was drowning in a river of hot dry air. The only breeze, from a single ceiling fan above the stage, just increased the heat load.

"Why don't they put air conditioners in this place?" Flagmeyer groused, tugging at his shirt collar. "I feel like a roasted duck. I really hate these meetings."

"Keep smiling, Art," Joe Bob said. "Don't let 'em know you're afraid."

"I'm *not* afraid." Flagmeyer pulled off his jacket. "I'm having a heat stroke."

Ramey grinned at the audience. *They* didn't seem to mind the temperature. To a person, the grizzled ranchers, lean, frowning house-wives, a few pilots and the occasional mean-looking newspaper reporter all seemed cool as cucumbers. Maybe they were used to this.

"Why do we have to do this, Joe?" Flagmeyer loosened his tie and stared at the hostile audience facing them. "Why not Rhinehart? Why is it *we* always have to represent the Weapons Lab?"

"Carl's a little too eccentric for *scientists*, much less a bunch of Nevada ranchers," Joe Bob replied. "They'd probably lynch him."

"Then why not Meghalty?" Flagmeyer asked. "Or maybe Eduard Uborka?"

"Ed and Emil are from Budapest. Nobody'd understand 'em. Besides, when they get nervous, they forget English."

"Yes, but they *talk* like scientists," Flagmeyer said, glancing across the stage at the other speakers. "I don't know why Marienfeld always wants us to do this."

"Guess we're the only ones dumb enough to do it," Ramey chuckled.

"We should be inspecting bombs," Flagmeyer insisted. "I mean, that's our *job*."

"So's this," Joe Bob replied. While he never liked attending these public relations exercises, Ramey figured the least the government could do was try to ease tensions with the locals. Thing was, Art Flagmeyer was right—it never seemed to work. Folks usually left the meetings madder than when they showed up.

"Where's Marienfeld?" Flagmeyer asked, looking at his watch. "He was supposed to be here...I heard he was going to bring his wife along."

"Hope so," Joe Bob said.

"I can't believe he got her on the payroll," Flagmeyer whispered after a moment. "How did he *do* that? I thought it was against the law to hire your own relative . . ."

"It is," Joe Bob nodded. "But you forget, Stanley didn't hire her. *Demming* did."

"Yeah, that's right," Flagmeyer nodded. "I just wonder why he did it. I mean, it's not fair—"

Just then a scowling man in a shiny blue suit entered the room. He was followed the short, precise AEC physician, Dr. Bartholomew, and by a tall, curvaceous blonde dressed in a short green outfit that came to just below her knees. The response from the crowd was a chorus of low grumbles.

"There's *part* of your answer," Joe Bob said, watching Marsha Marienfeld stroll past him to her chair on the dais.

"Think she'll say anything today?" Flagmeyer asked, straightening his tie.

"Nope. Too smart," Joe Bob grinned. "Another reason why Demming hired her."

A moment later, Stanley Marienfeld stepped to the microphone and forced a shapeless smile. "Ahem. Good to see you could make it to this month's meeting. As you know, the Atomic Energy Commission, in its effort to be a good neighbor to the citizens of southern Nevada, holds these meetings to clear up any questions about our operations."

"Get them scientists up there, Marienfeld," an old man in the front row barked. "An' quit wastin' our time."

"Moreover," Marienfeld continued, "I hope our presence here will quiet any suspicions that the detonations are ejecting anything into the air that is the least bit hazardous to anyone's health . . . "

"Get on with it!" a wiry housewife commanded.

"Certainly." Marienfeld cleared his throat. "Now, is there anything you might like to say before I introduce our experts here—any problems or questions that may be on your mind? Any *concerns*?"

"Yeah!" a cowboy sitting in the back of the room called out. "We're concerned about those damn atomic bombs!"

"In what way?" Marienfeld smiled.

"We're concerned 'bout their affects on our health!"

"We at Camp Jupiter are concerned about your health too," Marienfeld answered.

"Then *why* do you keep settin' 'em off?"

"Allow me to explain," Marienfeld smiled. "Ahem. We at the test site are concerned about your health. But you're probably more concerned about your health than, well, *other people* might be. And in the same way, I know you're more concerned about your health than you are about, say, *my* health—"

"I don't give a damn about *your* health," the cowboy said. "I want to know what them mushroom clouds are *doin' to us*."

"Well, Dr. Bartholomew will answer your health questions," Marienfeld said. But, first, I'd like to turn the microphone over to our army representative, Captain Spaulding."

"Good afternoon, ladies and gentlemen," Spaulding said, a wide grin across his boyish face. "I guess you know we had another test last week. Probably *saw* it from where you lived. A beautiful shot."

"That fallout turned my sheep blue," someone said.

"That test was momentous in that it was one of the *last* devices produced by Los Alamos," Spaulding continued. "From now on, the atomic devices will be made by our own Camp Jupiter Weapons Laboratory! From now on, the Nevada Test Site will produce its own nuclear devices, to be used by the new Atomic Brigade!"

"Tell us about that army captain you fried out there, Spaulding," a short blonde in the front row said.

"I'm afraid you have your facts wrong, Miss Barnett." Spaulding smiled. "The soldiers are not allowed to enter the ground zero area until it's absolutely safe."

"Then I guess it was just a bad case of sunburn, right?"

"I don't know what you're talking about," Marienfeld said. "Anyone else have a question?"

An old man stood up. "Yeah. I was wonderin' why th' hell don't you set them bombs off somewhere's else? Like mebbe *California*."

"That's a real interesting idea. I'll take it up with the President," Spaulding nodded soberly.

"You *do* that."

"I'm sure you will all be proud to know that your fine state will continue to be the first line of defense against the Russian invasion. Now, I guess, I'll turn it back to Dr. Marienfeld." Spaulding left the microphone and returned to his seat.

A pretty, dark-haired woman in the front row raised her hand. "Before you sit down, Captain Spaulding, I have a question about the atomic soldiers."

Marienfeld stood up and approached the microphone. "Maybe another time, Susan. Our next speaker is our health care chief, Dr. Bartholomew."

With that, the dapper Bartholomew leaped up from his chair and strode to the lectern.

In the audience, a tall man wearing a white shirt and string tie stood up. "Doctor, lately there's been some talk of an increase in cancer around here. Would you say it might have to do with the atomic tests?"

"Absolutely not," Bartholomew responded. "There has been no increase in cancer. As a matter of fact, with the clean desert air, low humidity and abundant sunshine, this county is one of the healthiest in the nation. Lots of vitamin D. Any other questions?"

The dark-haired woman in the front row stood up again. "My name is Susan Colter and I'm a reporter with the *Beatty Gazette* . . ."

"I know who you are." Bartholomew forced a smile.

". . . I'd like to know what you are doing about the hepatitis cases at Camp Sagebrush?"

"Hepatitis?" Bartholomew eyes widened in astonishment. "Miss Colter, there *are* no hepatitis cases at Camp Sagebrush."

"Yes, there are," Colter said, looking at a small notebook. "I understand there are ten soldiers confined to a quarantine ward of Loper Infirmary with hepatitis."

"That's nonsense!" Bartholomew glared at the woman. "Where did you hear that?"

"Then those soldiers *don't* have hepatitis?" she bored in.

"Now, you listen to me." Bartholomew aimed a long finger at her. "Before you begin spreading rumors like this you had better be *very, very* sure—"

"Well, time's up! Thank you doctor," Marienfeld said, grabbing the microphone. "Now, in the interest of time, I think we can only hear from one other speaker, weapons specialist Dr. Joe Ramey."

Joe Bob slowly unfolded himself from his chair and stepped up to the microphone.

"So, Dr. Ramey—" The woman reporter was still standing. "Do *you* know anything about the hepatitis?"

"Nope."

"Okay." She flipped a page of her notebook. "Now, I understand that Camp Jupiter has rounded up a number of diesel locomotives at one of the targets. Rumor has it they will be involved in some sort of giant nuclear test. Any truth to that?"

"No truth whatsoever," Marienfeld said quickly, taking the microphone again. "In fact, there *are* no trains anywhere on the Test Site."

"What about the lab train?" the woman asked. "The one you call the Atomic Express?"

"Well, there's *that* one," Marienfeld shrugged. "But it's not really a train in the true sense. It's more of a locomotive that occasionally ferries railcars around the desert. Purely transportation for the troops. And the other locomotives there are just for replacement parts. Strictly routine."

"Glad you could clear that up, Stanley," Colter smiled humorlessly. Then, turning back to Joe Bob, "Six months ago, in an interview with a Las Vegas reporter, one of your co-workers, a Dr. Jeffrey Christopher, claimed that he and his associates were going to 'pinch off the world'. It seems an odd choice of words. Can you tell us what he meant?"

"Nope," Joe Bob replied.

"Would he be available for an interview? Perhaps to clear up--"

"Miss Colter," Marienfeld broke in, "Dr. Christopher is busy working at the test site and certainly doesn't have time for interviews."

"Perhaps some of his associates might be able to tell us what he meant?"

"No one has the time for interviews," Marienfeld shrugged.

"Stanley," Colter said, "even *you* will have to admit that 'pinching off the world' is strange talk coming from a nuclear scientist. Now, I'd like a reply from Dr. Ramey about this." She turned to Joe Bob. "Dr. Ramey, don't you think that's a strange thing to say?"

"Well . . ."

"Would you characterize either Dr. Christopher as mentally unstable?"

"No, of course not." Joe Bob glanced back at Flagmeyer, who had his hand over his eyes.

"Then do you have any idea what he meant by the phrase 'pinching off the world?'" Colter's slate-blue eyes bored in on Ramey. He was in the crosshairs.

"Susan," Marienfeld stepped to the microphone, "Dr. Christopher obviously meant it as a *joke*. That's all."

"Excuse me, Stanley," Colter replied. "Is this the Howdy Doody show? I direct my questions to Dr. Ramey, yet I hear *your* voice. I know it's you because I can see your lips move. Now, if you're going to answer all his questions for him, I would like to know what he's *doing* up there? *Modeling clothes?*"

Joe Bob stepped back from the podium. Away from the line of fire.

Marienfeld's smile hardened. "I realize you haven't been a reporter very long, Susan, but you should know the rules anyway. Dr. Ramey is not allowed to answer questions of a sensitive nature. For example, questions about his job. Or his colleagues. But you can certainly ask him anything *else* you like."

"Like what he had for lunch? His favorite color? That sort of thing?" she glared.

"Well," Marienfeld shrugged, "I suppose that would be all right."

"I see," she said acidly. "Thank you, Stanley. And thank *you*, Dr. Ramey. Thank you very much."

"If there are no further questions," Marienfeld said, easing Joe Bob away from the microphone, "we'll see you again in a few months."

After waiting for the surly audience to leave the room, Ramey stepped off the stage and eased his way toward the door. Then he caught sight of the dark-haired woman reporter, standing amid a group of people, listening to a tall, talkative man in a string tie. As he made his way past her, he noticed that, despite the crowd, she seemed to be looking away into the distance—totally oblivious to everything around her—the heat, the crowd, the other reporters, him.

7

The Copenhagen Interpretation

J oe Bob leaned back in his wooden office chair and stared at a newspaper, mumbling the words aloud. "Camp Jupiter representative Dr. Joe Ramey discounted reports of mental instability among scientists at the weapons lab. Ramey refused comment on persistent rumors of unusual activity at the test site—dammit!" He threw the paper down, nearly knocking a coffee cup to the floor.

"Mentally unstable . . . unusual activity . . ." he growled, looking out the window. To the north a black cloud formed a neat "Z" in the air, the result of an early morning nuclear test. No doubt one of the scientists in the weapons lab had inspected the device —opened it up, looked at the detonator, examined the wiring harness, checked the configuration of the nuclear capsule—done all the things to make the device work. And the proof was in the cloud, that Z shape in the sky.

Loonies couldn't do that. Wise-ass lady reporters *sure* couldn't do that. It took education, experience and skill. And dedication. Why else would anyone want to live in the desert *and* work for the government? Of course, the job paid well. And you got to fool around with the world's biggest firecrackers.

And just because Dr. Jeff tried to jumpstart his own religion at a Las

Vegas casino doesn't mean the whole weapon lab is loaded with crazies. Where in hell did that lady reporter get off calling all of them crazy? She'd probably never even *met* Rhinehart.

Joe Bob reached into his desk drawer and extracted a thermos of cold coffee. Maybe it was the way the weapons specialists looked that gave them a bad reputation. While he dressed pretty much like the standard guy from San Antonio—blue jeans, khaki shirt, boots and baseball cap—the others *did* reinforce the mad scientist image. Emil "Megaton" Meghalty had wild hair bushed up all over his head and thick glasses that magnified his eyes to where he looked like a deep sea creature. And at times he would seize up—go absolutely stock still—when he was thinking about something complicated. Meghalty wasn't crazy, he was just *so* smart that his brain drained the current from everything else.

Then there was Uborka. While Meghalty reminded Joe Bob of a sea creature, Uborka resembled a big, friendly bear, plodding along, black hair piled like a haystack atop his head, one fist wrapped around a slide rule, the other around a cup of black tea. And while Meghalty locked himself in his office and talked back to his radio, Uborka would be over at Ethel's Bar doing his robot impersonation. It was funny as hell.

Uborka and Meghalty were always planning end-of-the-world-strength bombs. Bombs that, as Rhinehart put it, "could blow apart the planet Neptune." But for weapons scientists, that wasn't crazy, that was just their *job*.

Joe Bob took a drink of coffee. Fact was, if that reporter had met *any* of them she probably would wonder about their sanity. The atomic scientist's view of reality *was* different. To understand how the atom worked, one had to understand quantum mechanics—the theory that the universe is just so many particles and waves. Foam on the surface of the Big Pond.

Joe Bob remembered when his college professor clotheslined the whole physics class on the subject of reality—talked about electrons disappearing in one place and reappearing someplace else—without going through the space between. About a world where two different things can happen at the same time.

At first, everyone balked, citing common sense, the Constitution and the Bible. But within the year, driven mostly by the requirement for grades, everyone was thinking in terms of waves, ripples, probabilities and the fact that nothing exists when you're not looking at it. It was like the world was just a big television set. And Somebody was always changing the channel.

Joe Bob remembered the day he went home to tell Mary Jane Sweeney, his high school sweetheart, that when he was away at college, she didn't exist. Fine, she had said, and ran off to marry some asshole football jock.

Then, last year quantum physics was hit with Everett's Interpretation—the weird proposal claiming that each time an electron snaps, cracks or pops, the universe branches off like a mesquite tree. And since an electron is always making *some* kind of noise, there must be a hell of a lot of universes. All running alongside one another, like a thousand-lane highway at rush hour. Hearing about it, Joe Bob remembered thinking: (1) Huh. Maybe ol' Mary Jane *does* exist after all, along with that damn Jock, and (2) it's not so bad, 'cause in some next-door universe he and Mary Jane are happily married and maybe he's even seein' her little sister on the side. Heck, maybe in *some* universe a couple of lanes over, he's even married to *both* of them!

Of course, while quantum theory was necessary to designing everything from bombs to television sets, it *could* jangle up a man's personal life. Take Carl Rhinehart, for example. Quantum theory had dealt him a bad hand, for sure.

When the great Danish physicist Niels Bohr first cooked up his quantum theory, he wanted to know why electrons were particles when he tested for particles and waves when he tested for waves. Bohr finally decided that you get from electrons what you expect. Or more to the point, nothing can happen—or even exist— unless you happen to be watching for it.

This peculiar idea was called the *Copenhagen Interpretation*, and Carl Rhinehart bought it lock, stock and barrel. In fact, he figured that nothing existed *at all* except Carl Rhinehart. Everything was a product of his overactive imagination. "You guys are just a bad dream," he would tell the other scientists at the test site, who in turn, would talk about him behind his back—proof that he was wrong—and called him *Copenhagen Carl*.

Then Rhinehart modified his thinking to include the dual-lane-reality stuff and came up with the idea that, while he was still alone in this particular universe, he could switch worlds by getting juiced up on enough quantum energy. Like from atomic bombs. It led to some real peculiar behavior.

No, Ramey thought, it was a good thing that lady reporter had never met Carl Rhinehart. Then they'd *all* be under investigation.

"Joe," the intercom crackled. "Are you there?"

"Yeah, George," Joe Bob sighed.

"It's 8:15. You're late for the meeting. The man from the army is here. Everybody's waiting on you."

"Be right there." Ramey looked at his watch. It had stopped at seven thirty.

"Where have you been?" George Linneman asked as Ramey walked in the door.

"In m'office," Ramey replied, taking a chair next to Flagmeyer.

"Well, okay," Linneman said, running a hand nervously over his thinning brown hair. "Fine. Is everybody here? Where's Jeffrey?"

"He's still in the hospital, George." Joe Bob pulled a notebook from his pocket.

"Now then." Linneman nodded and looked at his schedule sheet. "Where's Wiggers?"

"Still dead, George," Rhinehart replied in a bored voice.

"Oh. Yes. Of course." Linneman glanced around the room, a nervous smile on his face. "As you know, our stockpile of Los Alamos bombs has been nearly depleted. And as you also are aware, we have been waiting for the go-ahead to design and construct our own nuclear devices here at Camp Jupiter."

"It's either that or we're out of a job," Flagmeyer said under his breath.

"I'm pleased to say the funding has been authorized!" Linneman held up a memo. "Signed yesterday by the Director of the Atomic Energy Commission, Dr. Anna Faye Trumbo."

"Great!" Joe Bob slapped the table with his hand. "When do we start?"

"Can we make some thermonuclear devices?" Meghalty asked.

"Only low-yield tactical weapons," Linneman said. "No thermo-nuclear."

"I don't see why not," Meghalty said testily.

"We could use them to dig holes," Uborka added, his eyes wide. "It would save jobs."

"The Atomic Army doesn't need thermonuclear in a ground war," Linneman replied. "And since the army is writing the check for this, we go along with what they want."

Joe Bob leaned back in his chair. So they had the army to thank for their new status.

"When do we start, George?" Flagmeyer asked.

"We start right now," Linneman replied, looking around the room. "And since Eduard and Emil are the ones here with the most experience at weapons design, they're in charge of the first project."

In response Uborka and Meghalty smiled broadly.

For his part, Joe Bob was relieved. No way on earth did he want a hand in designing the very first Camp Jupiter atomic bomb. Too much responsibility.

"Eduard," Linneman continued, "I'd like you to submit your design by next week. I'll send it along to Dr. Demming for approval—"

"Next week?" Uborka asked, a shocked expression crossing his face. "Next *week?*"

"You want us to draw up an atomic bomb for one week?" Meghalty gasped. "Impossible! It would work us too much!"

"One week," Linneman snapped. "As soon as the design is approved, we'll send it to Livermore Labs for construction. Any *other* questions?"

Joe Bob looked at Uborka. By now, the initial elation on the big Hungarian's face had melted into the most heart-breaking frown imaginable. As for Meghalty, he stood motionless in front of his chair, frozen in space, the eyes behind his thick spectacles registering brainlock.

Have fun, fellers, Joe Bob thought to himself. The army's countin' on ya.

8

You Bet Your Life

Perkins opened his eyes and stared at the off-white plaster ceiling. The cobweb was still there, an abandoned piece of dust-coated filament, hanging directly above the glass IV bottle next to his bed. As he watched, a breeze from the ceiling vent caused the cobweb to balloon and wave and snap in the stream like a thin flag.

After a moment, he turned his gaze out the window, through the thick wooden slats of the venetian blind. Although they had taken his watch away from him—they said it was a radiation hazard—he guessed it was probably ten in morning. For one thing, the street fronting the hospital was empty. No marching troops led by barking sergeants, no convoys of jeeps from the motor pool. No lines of enlisted men policing the lawn. Just bright mid-morning in a hospital room in the middle of the Nevada desert.

"You awake?" A freckled-faced young man with reddish-blond hair was standing in the door. "I heard you were in here."

"You did?" Perkins sat up in bed.

"Sure. Everybody in the ward is talking about you, Lieutenant Perkins," the man said, smiling. "How you hiked all the way to ground zero and saluted the tower."

"I don't remember doing that," Perkins said, uneasily eyeing his guest. With his oversized hospital pajamas draped around him like a blue shroud, the visitor looked like a country boy in a Greek toga.

"My name is Corporal Andy Sloan." The man extended his hand. "I'm getting out of here tomorrow. At least that's what Dr. Bartholomew says—are you with Captain Stein's outfit?"

"Yeah," Perkins nodded, "training for the Atomic Brigade."

"Me too," Sloan said, easing into a chair. "I was getting real close to getting accepted into General Umber's Brigade—had my interview and everything. But then this happened."

"What?"

"Got in the wrong trench, too close to the bomb," Sloan shrugged. "Didn't Captain Stein tell you?"

"No."

"He was the one that got me out. If it hadn't been for him, it would have been a lot worse." The boy scratched his head absentmindedly. "It was really something. Like a wall of fire that kept on coming, rolled right over my position. Never seen anything like it. Good thing I had my wires on."

"Wires?"

"Yeah," the boy said, pointing to a bare patch on his scalp, "they had me wired up, so's they could tell if I was in trouble. Guess it worked, 'cause I'm still here." He paused for a moment. "You know, I'm leaving the hospital tomorrow."

"Are you going home or something?" Perkins asked. "Sick leave maybe?"

"Nope," Sloan shook his head. "It's against the law to go out in the public with radiation hepatitis. Anyway, Dr. Bartholomew's gonna send me back to my outfit—see how I do before they test me again."

"Good luck," Perkins said. "Hope you make it."

"Just keep trying," Sloan smiled. "That's my motto."

As the door closed, Perkins slid deeper between the sheets of the hospital bed. Despite the brightness of the morning sun, he felt a slow, soft drowsiness settle in.

—⚓—

"Listen, Lieutenant, you can tell me. I'm your *doctor*." The man's face was so close Perkins could see the row of teeth beneath the clipped salt-and-pepper mustache. "How did you manage to get to ground zero? Were you lost?"

"I was looking for the Big Picture."

The man leaned even closer, darkening Perkins's field of vision. "Lieutenant, I'm trying to *help you*."

"I want to be a general," Perkins heard himself say. "In the atomic army. In the Atomic Brigade. That's what I wanted to do. Then I lost the guy from the Big Picture."

"Captain Wanker says you were found at the tower. Said you could almost reach out and touch it."

"That's what I was gonna do. They all said so." Blinking the clouds from his eyes, he watched the room hazily take form. In front of him, leaning over the bed, was a small man with a mustache. Behind him was a tall figure in dark green.

"So you did this on your own?" the small man asked.

"That's right," Perkins said. In response, the small man's eyebrows arched up. It reminded him of someone he had seen on television. That's where he was. This was a dream and he was on television.

"*You Bet Your Life*," Perkins heard himself giggle stupidly.

"Excuse me?"

"This is *You Bet Your Life*. What's the question?"

"Why were you at ground zero?" the man asked.

"I was looking for the fat guy with the Hawaiian shirt. He was with the *Big Picture*. Do I win?"

"Did Captain Stein send you to the tower?"

"I did it myself," Perkins heard himself say. "Do I get a second chance?" The dream was taking on the qualities of a nightmare. His voice and his thoughts seemed to be separate. He seemed to be his own audience, watching himself on a screen in his mind.

"So you didn't see what you were looking for."

"Nope. Didn't see anything. Just the tank. And Captain Wanker. Captain Wanker's tank." Perkins stared at the screen. What was going to happen next? What was he going to *say* next?

"All right." The small man sighed and shook his head. "We'll keep him another two days, then send him back to his company."

Then the curtains began to move. The television show, the movie—whatever it was—was about to be over. "No!" the Perkins on the screen said. "Wait a minute! Not so fast!"

"Is there something else?" The man turned and stared into the camera. "Are you going to tell us something else?"

"I answered the questions, didn't I?" Perkins asked, watching the curtains converge across the screen. "I want my prize."

"Oh, don't worry, Lieutenant," the man said, moving away from view. "You'll have another opportunity—"

"Well, I hope so," Perkins said as the curtains closed. "I really—"

Then the screen went dark.

⟶⟵

"Good afternoon, Donna, is Dr. Demming in?"

"Hi, George," the woman said, not looking up from her magazine.

"He's expecting me," Linneman said, studying one of Demming's dog-with-pheasant paintings.

"Yep." In the awkward pause after her reply, Linneman looked down to see what she was reading: an advertisement for Clorets.

Linneman tensed up. He could never understand why he looked forward to these terse, abbreviated conversations with Demming's secretary. But he did. For, despite her terrible personality and her difficult boss, she was the most appealing thing on the Nevada Test Site. Except, of course, his bi-weekly paycheck. "Marienfeld's with him right now," the woman said, finally turning the page. "Take a seat, okay? He won't be long."

Linneman found a metal chair at the corner of the room and sat down. For some reason, he found Donna's standoffish manner fascinating. Although Rhinehart had characterized her as "beady-eyed, muscular and ratlike," Linneman thought she was, well, *attractive.* Donna's terse demeanor and short black hair reminded him somewhat of his ex-wife. In fact, just six months after his divorce, he had phoned the receptionist for a date.

"Donna? This is George."

"George who?"

"George Linneman. Director of the Weapons Laboratory. I see you about every day . . . I was wondering if you had any plans this weekend?"

"Depends. What do you have in mind?"

"Uh, I thought we could go out and visit the test site. They're putting the finishing touches on Doom Town—you know, that fake village they're going to blow up?"

"Doom Town."

"Right. I thought we could drive up there this weekend and look around. Sixteen houses and five stores. All empty. They even have a water tower!"

"George, I'm busy this weekend."

"You are? But it's really a great place, you should see it. Looks just like a real town. It's a Civil Defense test and—"

"Call me in a few months."

"It may not be here in a few months, Donna. They're going to blow it up with an atomic bomb."

"Guess I'll have to wait until they build another one. 'Bye."

The intercom suddenly squawked, bringing Linneman back to the present. It was Demming's voice. "Donna. Send George in, please."

"Well, George! Come in, have a seat!" Demming smiled broadly, brushing long strands of gray hair over his bald spot. "I'll be with you in a minute. Stan and I are having a conversation about a little public relations problem."

"Of course." Linneman took a seat and glanced over at the nattily attired Stanley Marienfeld—his long, fat fingers folded over his bulbous vest.

Months before, when it was first rumored that the Nevada Test Site would close down, Marienfeld and Demming had abandoned their comfortable khakis for vests, suspenders and dark, thick suits—all in the hope that it might make them look more *managerial* and thus employable. Safety Officer Deckman even gave up donuts for a while and tried to lose weight. When it became clear that the test site wouldn't close after all, many went back to their old ways, but Demming and Marienfeld kept their suits—even on the hottest days. Joe Bob Ramey said they looked like a pair of small-town morticians.

"Er, George," Demming said, "Stanley here has a problem with the locals again. They want us to cancel the tests during rainstorms. They say they're concerned that the rain will wash the radioactive dust out of the cloud and contaminate their crops. *I* didn't know they grew anything out here, did you?"

"No," Linneman shook his head. "I know they raise sheep—"

"I haven't even seen many *weeds* since I've been here." Demming shrugged. "Just cactus. I can't imagine how a little radioactive dust could hurt a *cactus*, can you?"

"Well—" Linneman began.

"I know what to say, Stanley." Demming turned back to Marienfeld. "Tell them that a thunderstorm during a test is actually *helpful*. Tell them fallout is going to fall to the earth anyway. That's why it's called fallout. The rain just helps it happen quicker. Clears the air, so to speak."

"I like that," Marienfeld said, making notes.

"You know, once the fallout hits the ground, the rain will almost immediately wash it away to, uh, storm sewers. Rivers. Lakes. Where it won't do any harm. Of course, it's not harmful anyway . . ."

"Of course not," Marienfeld said, writing furiously.

"Besides, we have to know our bombs will work in the rain. I've heard it rains all the time in Russia." Demming turned back to Linneman. "Tell me, George, what are we going to do if the Russians invade Austria on a rainy day in April? Hm?"

"I don't know, sir."

"Ask Bulganin or Khrushchev to please wait for a *sunny* day?"

"Yes, I like it," Marienfeld said, flipping a page in his notebook. "These are really good points you raise."

"Thank you," Demming smiled. "Now, is there anything else?"

"Well," Marienfeld said, scratching his head, "some of the grocers in St. George are complaining that the fallout makes the local milk taste like *iodine*. Now, personally, I think they're just trying to stir up trouble—"

"Why, there's nothing wrong with iodine," Demming said. "Iodine's a very good antiseptic—physicians recommend it for all sorts of things. I used it myself on a scratch just this morning. And I'm still sitting here. I don't know what's wrong with these people."

"One other thing." Marienfeld looked at his notepad. "I've been receiving calls from people wanting rides in the blimps."

"Blimps?" Linneman asked.

"They're bringing in some Navy blimps from San Diego, George," Demming said. "They want to see how well they stand up to an atomic bomb."

"Some people saw them heading for the test site," Marienfeld said. "Now they're calling—begging for a ride. Of course, I say no."

"Absolutely no rides," Demming nodded, leaning back in his chair. "Unless it's someone important. A congressman, maybe."

"Of course," Marienfeld smiled broadly. "Good thinking, *Davis*."

"This fallout nonsense," Demming turned to Linneman and shook his head, "isn't that the darndest thing you ever heard? After all, God approves of the bomb, don't you think, George?"

"Well, I really don't know," Linneman shrugged.

"If He didn't want us to have it, He wouldn't have let us build it. Don't you think?" Demming raised his eyebrows like an old, bewildered steer. "I mean, He *could* have smote them all down with lightning. Oppenheimer, Szilard, all of them. But he didn't. Now, doesn't that tell you something?"

I really don't know for sure."

"But He didn't smite them, did He?" Demming asked, his hands on his vest. "So He must think it's okay to build bombs. And test them, of course."

"It certainly makes sense to me," Marienfeld nodded.

"And I'm sure if He has anything to do with it," Demming paused, staring at the ceiling, "fallout would be *anything* but harmful. Don't you think so, George?"

"I'm really not a theologian, Dr. Demming," Linneman replied.

"Don't you go to church, George?" Marienfeld leaned forward.

"No."

"You don't?" Demming clouded over.

"Theology's not my field, actually," Linneman squirmed. "I was trained as an electrical engineer."

"You should go to church, George," Demming said. "You might learn a thing or two about why we're here."

"On earth?"

"At the test site, dammit." Demming's brow knitted up. "Now, George. I suppose you know the reason I called you in today." Demming steepled his fingers on his vest. "I'd like you to tell Stan and me about Camp Jupiter's first A-bomb design."

"Ah, it's coming along," Linneman said nervously. "I gave the assignment to Meghalty and Uborka—they have the most experience. I'm sure they'll do well."

"Hm . . ." Demming paused for a moment. "You know this is a

crucial test. Frankly, everyone wonders whether your men can cut the mustard."

"Excuse me?"

"*Do the job*, dammit," Demming snapped. "People wonder if they're capable. After all, the most they've done since they've been here is just *inspect* the bombs."

"And kill themselves," Marienfeld sneered.

"You know, George, all eyes are on us now," Demming warned. "Especially with those Navy blimps coming onto the test site . . . do you think your first device can knock them out of the air?"

"Well," Linneman shifted in his chair, "Uborka and Meghalty have always clamored for big weapons. They've always wanted to add lithium deuteride to the Los Alamos devices. Turn the little bombs into H-bombs—"

Demming nodded.

"And, uh, well . . . if anything, their first device will probably be, um, *too* big."

"No bomb is too big, George," Demming smiled. "Dr. Trumbo likes big tests—and so does the American public."

"Atom blast rips desert—troops maneuver!" Marienfeld said, spreading his hands across an imaginary headline.

"Balls of fire soaring into the air," Demming chuckled, "soldiers running around beneath that big mushroom cloud—tanks clanking along—towers melting—blimps exploding. It's very dramatic. And darn good publicity."

Linneman wiped his brow. "Well, I'm sure we can knock a *blimp* out of the sky."

Demming peered over the top of his glasses. "Can you do it by next week?"

"Next *week*?" Linneman's jaw dropped.

"The general wants the blimps destroyed next week," Marienfeld nodded. "I heard him say so."

"Er, well, next week. *Ahem*." Linneman cleared his throat. "I really don't think Emil and Eduard are going to have their bomb ready by then. First they have to come up with a design, then send off to Hanford for the plutonium, and then get the other components—why, it might take a *month* at least—"

"Okay then!" Demming interrupted. "We'll use a Los Alamos

device next week. There's a few left in the stockpile—but after that one I want to see some *progress*."

"Of course."

"Listen." Demming leaned forward ominously. "There's a lot at stake here. I happen to know the director of the Atomic Energy Commission has some very big plans for the test site. And I want to make sure they're *fully realized*—with no fizzles. And no embarrassments."

"Of course," Linneman nodded.

"Just remember that." Demming leaned back in his chair and smiled.

9

Marienfeld's Wife

C'mon, Marsha, try it. *Please!*"

"Stop it, Rhinehart," Marienfeld's wife commanded. "You're worse'n a kid begging for a pony."

"*Please!*"

"Forget it, Rhinehart. I've changed my mind and that's that." Marienfeld's wife exhaled a pale blue stream of smoke in the direction of the pinball machine. "That tower was scary enough. I will *not* screw you inside a balloon. Especially during an atomic test."

Rhinehart grabbed her sleeve. "You said you wanted excitement. Besides, it's not a balloon, Marsha. It's a blimp. We'll be inside a blimp."

"Blimp, balloon, what's the difference?" Marienfeld's wife tapped an ash into one of Roy's mushroom-shaped ashtrays. "Look, it's almost three o'clock. I gotta be in Vegas in an hour. And don't you have a meeting or something?"

"I'll be late," Rhinehart declared. "I'm always late. They don't care anymore."

For the past hour he had been sitting at Ethel's with the luscious Marsha Marienfeld, crying, wheedling, *begging* her to go somewhere and trade clothes. Nothing seemed to be working. Not only had the recent refusals played havoc with Rhinehart's libido, they had also called into serious question his solipsist view of the world. Part of his creation wasn't cooperating.

"Listen, Rhinehart." Marienfeld's wife turned back to him, her blue eyes hard as marbles. "That damn tower made me so sick I almost threw up . . . and there wasn't even a test going on."

"It was the wind," Rhinehart said. "A 500-foot tower will sway in the wind—"

"And being in the cab with that, that *thing* looking over our shoulders—" She arched an eyebrow. "You call that romantic?"

"It was exciting," Rhinehart shrugged. "You said you wanted excitement, not romance. Besides, the device wasn't armed."

"I don't care," Marienfeld's wife said. "I didn't have a good time. And I don't want to do anything like that again—look, I really think we should call it off."

"Returning to the back seat of Deckman's Ford, huh?"

"Deckman?" Marienfeld's wife stopped cold.

"Deckman," Rhinehart said, waving smoke from his face. "Goofy guy with the crew cut—the one who walks around covered with radiation dosimeters. The one who lives on donuts and coffee . . ."

"Are you saying I screwed Deckman?" she barked, sending a solid kick to Rhinehart's leg.

". . . and eats—ow!— pickled eggs at the bar and tells everybody about your Schnauzer-shaped birthmark."

"Liar!" Marienfeld's wife snarled.

Rhinehart leaned closer. "He said you've tried out every bed in Doom Town."

"I'm am *not* going up in that blimp with you."

"Okay. Forget Deckman," Rhinehart said, shaking his head. "Forget the tower. The blimp will be better. It'll be safe, it'll be dark and it'll be fun. Just think—gently floating a few yards above the desert floor, rocking in the breeze, back and forth, back and forth, until—"

"Stop it, Rhinehart, I'm getting airsick already."

"I thought you told me you liked blimps."

"I do. I rode in one once and it was fun. But there wasn't any atomic bomb going off at the time."

"Look. We've been through this before," Rhinehart said. "I know what they're going to do. I know the plan. They're going to tie that blimp out there about ten miles from the target. It's perfectly safe."

"Ten miles huh?" She took another drag from the cigarette, then looked at him. "You're *sure*?"

"Absolutely." He crossed his heart. "When the device detonates, all the blimp will do is wiggle a little bit. Very exciting. Very safe. Believe me, I know."

"You know, huh?" Marienfeld's wife eyed Rhinehart suspiciously. "They've never had blimps here before. This better not be another one of your delusions! I mean if you're going up there to try to kill yourself—"

"No, no, no, no, no," Rhinehart shook his head. "That was just an ugly rumor started by your husband or something. I swear, I don't know why I invented him."

"Dammit, Rhinehart . . ."

"Just kidding, just kidding!" Rhinehart said quickly. "Please tell me you'll do it, Marsha. It'll be fun. Exciting—and *safe*."

"Safe, huh?" she asked. "It had *better* be safe."

"Oh, it'll be safe. Very, *very* safe. Much safer than the tower. Safer than fooling around at Doom Town even."

"Well, it had *better* be."

"Very safe," Rhinehart said, patting her hand. "And exciting. Please think about it."

"Okay." She pulled her sleeve from his grip. "But if anything goes wrong, Rhinehart—it'll be your ass."

10

Super Chief

J oe Bob eased back on the red metal lever, and the tower elevator emitted a loud grinding screech, then jolted to a stop. They were on the upper mezzanine, the last stop before the bomb cab itself, a corrugated metal shack perched 500 feet above the desert. "Here we are, George. Now don't go gettin' dizzy on me."

"I'm fine," Linneman said, unhooking the latch. "I wish they'd put railings on this thing."

"Nobody's fallen off yet," Joe Bob said, stepping out on the grating. "Just don't look down." Even a quick glance down through the thin metal grid was, he had to admit, a scary proposition. The trick was to watch the most immediate surface—the fragile wirelike latticework that served as a floor—and ignore the kaleidoscope of concentric triangles falling away into the distance.

"Stay away from that edge, Joe," Linneman said, looking up at the square platform of the bomb cab.

"Heights don't bother me much, George. I used to do this all the time."

"I want to get this thing over with." Linneman shivered visibly. "It's not safe up here."

The damn place *wasn't* safe, Joe Bob had to agree. The ladder rigging had been placed at the very edge of the mezzanine; a man had to actually swing out over empty space to begin the climb. On the earlier shots, the elevator had gone all the way to the bomb cab, but for some reason the last few towers had been designed so the lifts stopped at the mezzanines. The equipment, including the bomb, had to be lowered into the cab using a helicopter.

"You want to go first, George?" Joe Bob pushed his cap back on his head. "This is your idea."

"It's *your* performance evaluation," Linneman said, his back flat against the tower's frame. "*You* go first."

Joe Bob swung from the mezzanine out onto the ladder rungs. "Okay, but ya better let go of that crossbar there— I wouldn't want you to *break* it." Pausing for a moment on the ladder to watch Linneman's progress behind him, Ramey glanced out at three Navy dirigibles, huge silver fish floating in the cloudless Nevada sky.

A slow, deliberate minute later, they reached the narrow corrugated metal ledge facing the bomb cab. Above them, a section of the roof had been removed and sunlight poured through, dappling the metal floor. With rhythmic creaks and whines as the structure swayed with the wind, the place seemed peaceful, a cross between a sailboat and a south Texas repair shop on a Sunday morning. Except for one thing: the object in the center of the room—a menacing teardrop-shaped device four feet in diameter and exactly six feet from its blunt nose to its box-finned tail.

"Is this it, George?" Joe Bob stepped over a length of cable to the device. "The thing that's supposed to take out those enemy blimps?"

"Art Flagmeyer already looked it over, Joe," Linneman said, removing a clipboard from his belt. "Detonators are in place, everything's here except the plutonium. So be careful."

"Looks like one of the old 1951 models." Joe Bob rested his hand on the bomb's cool surface. "What's Los Alamos doin' now, sending us jalopies?"

"It still holds a lot of plutonium," Linneman said. "Why don't you check the firing circuit? That shouldn't take us long."

Ramey removed the voltmeter from his belt, knelt next to the device and opened the side hatch. Inside, he saw the wiring harness, the complex net of multicolored cables that connected the detonators. Expertly tracing the harness back, he located the black box-shaped firing circuit. And sitting atop it, like a transformer with a tiny red lamp, was a smaller but equally important device, the radar clock.

Few tactical weapons were detonated by impact; most were fired by remote control, timed radar signals beamed at the device from the Control Point—setting things in motion that would result in the detonation of the explosive charge. The firing circuit, with its attendant radar clock, counted the pulses of energy reaching the antenna. Then, when the firing circuit reached the right number, it sent a charge of electricity from the capacitor to the detonators. If the plutonium core was the heart of an atomic bomb, the radar clock with its tiny red light bulb kept the beat.

"How's it going?" Linneman asked.

"Red light hasn't started flashing yet," Joe Bob grinned, clamping the voltmeter cables on the firing circuit.

"I don't know why they leave that thing on there," Linneman growled. "It doesn't serve any purpose."

"Well, it lets you know if the thing's gonna blow up."

Linneman backed up to the wall. "Is the circuit okay?"

"Looks fine to me." Ramey reached in to disconnect the voltmeter cables. "Heard anything about what they're gonna do up at target 14?"

"The *Vulcan* shot?" Linneman asked. "No, Demming hasn't told me anything."

"Well, Pliney's been all fired up lately," Joe Bob said. "Wants to know why all them trains are bein' parked up there. He's afraid you and Demming want to melt the old Super Chief."

"Those plans come from Washington," Linneman shrugged. "Straight from Dr. Trumbo. I don't have anything to do with it."

Joe Bob closed the side hatch and stood up. "Want to hear what Hendrix told me last week? He said there's a load of lithium deuteride comin' in. That wouldn't have anything to do with the *Vulcan* test would it?"

"Hendrix is always spreading rumors."

"Yeah. But it don't mean he's wrong." Ramey paused and looked at Linneman. "Lithium deuteride is fusion fuel, George. It doesn't have any other purpose I know of. Is this place gonna start settin' off H-bombs now?"

"You'll have to ask Demming." Linneman started down the tower.

Twenty minutes later, Joe Bob steered the Camp Jupiter pickup truck onto a small concrete slab near the railroad crossing. In the distance, a yellow dot shimmered on the southern horizon. "Here it comes, George. Right on time."

"I think we should drive over to Target 14." Linneman wiped a layer of desert dust from his forehead. "That train cab is too hot inside."

"You just don't want to face Pliney," Joe Bob said. "He knows you're fixin' to blow his trains all to hell."

Within minutes, the yellow switch engine slowly rumbled toward the truck. As the diesel slowed down, Ramey waved his hand and the train responded with a short blast from the horn. Brakes screeching, the locomotive ground to a halt.

The red-faced engineer peered out the window and shook his head. "The things you find in the middle of nowhere! What the hell you doin' out here, Ramey? Hidin' from work again?"

"Couldn't today," Joe Bob yelled back. "Th' boss came along— mind if we hitch a ride to th' railyard?"

"Come on up!" Pliney motioned toward the open door of the switch engine. "You two gonna set up a bomb out there or somethin'?"

"Not today," Ramey answered, swinging up into the cab. Behind him, Linneman grasped the yellow railings and carefully followed him up the metal steps.

"Hidey, Linnement," Pliney nodded soberly, then spat a stream of tobacco out the window. "What brings you out to the target today?"

"Oh, George and I are just doin' a little field work," Joe Bob said. "Lookin' at towers, that sort of thing."

"I see Linnement's got his wire cutters," Pliney said, staring straight ahead. "You sonsabitches are gonna bring a nu-cleer bomb up to my railyard, ain't ya?"

"Where's your other diesel, Pliney?" Ramey asked. "You know, that red one you usually run through here. The old Super Chief."

"The *Express*?" Pliney squinted one eye. "She's up there at 14. Sittin' right next to the tower. Think they'll put the bomb on her? I heard tell they was gonna load her up with some kinda' chemical before they did it. Seems a shame. I ain't even greased her yet. Why, that old diesel—"

"Theose switch engines," Linneman broke in, "are the single biggest expense at the test site, involving hundreds of maintenence personnel. If it wasn't for them, we could probably afford all kinds of *useful* equipment here."

After an awkward silence, Pliney leaned forward and whispered to Ramey. "That Linnement is one *tight-fisted* sumbitch, ain't he?

Joe Bob grinned but said nothing. A sharp clacking noise filled the cabin as the engine passed over a junction. Outside, a set of rails veered off east toward another target zone.

"I ain't dumb." Pliney spat another stream of tobacco juice out the window. "I saw yer buddies puttin' in them underground tanks all around the tower. I know what they're gettin' ready to do. They're gonna set one off up there."

"Sounds to me like you're gettin' *attached* to those diesels, Pliney," Joe Bob said.

After a slow, bumpy ride through a cleft in the hills, the train entered the test basin at target 14. Looking out over the yellow switch engine's long nose, Joe Bob saw the thin shot tower reaching up to the blue sky. Around its base were an assortment of dark rectangular objects, strung out in thin lines across the desert floor. Diesel locomotives. And with them, the shiny, silver passenger rail cars. Empty, awaiting vaporization.

Several minutes later, the engine passed over a dark ring painted on the ground, the outermost circle of the target zone. The train was entering ground zero. To the northwest, Ramey scanned the lines of railcars, motionless in the desert, their shiny aluminum sides reflecting the noonday sun. Pliney's railyard.

As the yellow switch engine slowed down, it passed a silver-and-orange engine parked on a sidetrack. Joe Bob could make out a word scarcely visible beneath the coating of Nevada dust: HIAWATHA. Behind the silent engine stood five silver cars and a single wooden caboose, its red paint dulled by the desert grit.

The diesel passed another smaller circle, then another, until they were just fifty yards from the tower at the bulls-eye. Directly to the east, a windowless concrete bunker rose a few feet from the ground. To the north, beyond the track's endpoint, lay the display area, a hazy line of battlefield emplacements, tanks, trucks, mortars and artillery. Not far away, past the bunker, a line of thin pipes jutted from the ground, marking the location of the underground bunkers outside the one-mile line.

Pliney idled the engine, then applied the brakes. Within a minute the switch engine came to a stop directly beneath the square shadow of the bomb cab.

"Suppose there's any radiation here, George?" Joe Bob asked, stepping to the ground.

"I don't think so," Linneman said. "Deckman was out here yesterday and didn't find any."

"Deckman couldn't find his ass with both hands," Joe Bob laughed. "We goin' up on the tower?"

"No, I just have to connect the switchbox." Linneman nodded toward a small, square pedestal about a hundred yards away.

"Need any help?"

"No. I'll get it." Linneman drew his cap down over his head and stalked away toward the switchbox.

"That's Linnement's a real horse's butt, ain't he Ramey?" Pliney said, scratching his head.

"Aw, I don't know." Joe Bob looked at the ground for a moment. "He was a good engineer before Demming made him a manager."

Pliney watched Linneman open the grey door of the switchbox. "They're gonna have a damn military test out here. Ain't they?"

"Yeah," Joe Bob nodded, "kinda' looks that way. All that equipment north of here—tanks, cannons. And, there's the bunker." Ramey looked at the long, flat, concrete building, its composite roof shining pure white against the desert. Also present were the earmarks of a classified experiment: the perimeter of electric fence and the heavy black television camera attached to the roof.

"When d'ya think they're gonna do it?" Pliney stepped down from the train.

"Don't know. I think they're supposed to blow up some blimps first."

"Rhinehart said it was set for early next week," Pliney said. "That what you heard?"

"Could be," Joe Bob shrugged. "Looks like George is gonna be a few minutes. What say we take a look at those trains again?"

The old engineer sent a bullet of tobacco juice to the ground. "C'mon—I got one over here you ain't seen yet."

Joe Bob followed Pliney across the tracks, between a gleaming set of hopper cars toward the group of locomotives. He enjoyed coming to target 14 and walking among the trains. It relaxed him—took his mind off the bombs and the tests and the experiments. Though he couldn't admit it to the old engineer, he knew that in just two months the *Vulcan* device would turn the big diesels into metal fume.

Pliney stepped up to a gleaming silver dining car, paused for a moment, then opened the door. "After you."

Entering the car, Ramey was surprised to find the interior decked out and ready for service, ready to take paying passengers across the country in high style. The walls, covered in a dark wood veneer, fairly glowed beneath a mirrored ceiling. Drapes covered the oversized windows and muted the sunlight, removing its desert harshness and giving the interior a soft brown cast. Along one side of the dining car were six full-sized tables, each covered with a wrinkled but clean white tablecloth. Surrounding each table were four chairs covered with smooth red-orange fabric. Smaller tables, with two chairs each, lined the opposite side. At the rear, a passageway led past a buffet table and an unidentified, shuttered compartment.

"These railcars, you know—" the old engineer looked around, "—they came from the *Chief*. Sure hate to see her go."

Joe Bob looked at the tables. Each held a large, rectangular menu. Picking one up, he shook his head and smiled. "California select prunes. Steamed salt mackerel, club style. Little pig sausages with buckwheat cakes."

"I did that," Pliney said, his voice barely audible. "That atomic bomb'll probably be set off on a morning—I suppose—well, I just thought I'd set out the *menus*. Got 'em from the Super Chief."

"Breakfast," Joe Bob read from the paper, "being a record of the victual along the trail . . ."

"Nice, huh?" Pliney smiled.

"They're not gonna set it off *tomorrow*, ya know," Joe Bob said replacing the menu on the table.

"Mebbe. Mebbe not," Pliney shrugged. "Can't plan for nothin' anymore."

From the diner, Joe Bob followed the engineer into the Pullman lounge car, with its thick blue carpeting, overstuffed sofas and armchairs covered in blue plush. The large rectangular windows were blocked by thin, wooden venetian blinds, shielding the fragile interior from the harsh desert sun. Ramey wondered how long the blinds would protect the car from the glare of the atomic burst.

"You oughta' see the section-sleeper." Pliney thumbed toward the rear of the train. "Got brown curtains. Green carpet. I can almost imagine crossin' the country in somethin' like that . . . with, you know, Veronica Lake or Jean Simmons or Bette Page."

"Who?"

"Or *all three* . . . whooeee!" the engineer chortled. "Now, that'd be a time!"

"They'd probably fight to get off the train."

Halfway back to the switch engine, Pliney stopped to look at the little diesel *Hiawatha*. "That's the one I was tellin' you about," he said, motioning toward the engine. "She's got droopy windows. Looks kinda' sad."

Joe Bob stuffed his hands in his pockets. In the distance, a cloud of dust billowed briefly. Soon it would cross the target zone and fill the air with a fine brown grit. He hoped Linneman was finished with the switchbox. "You know, Pliney," he said, "if they *do* use this place as a target, it might be an air drop. If the bomb explodes at 20,000 feet, why—the fireball might not even touch the train."

"Don't lie to me, Ramey. They're gonna put an atomic bomb on top of that tower. And they're gonna do it real soon. That's why Linnement is out there wirin' up the box. Ain't that right?"

Joe Bob shrugged.

"'Course, it wouldn't matter all that much," the engineer muttered, looking at the sky. "Prob'ly the best thing. Just turn everything into so much *dust*—send it away with the mornin' breeze. All that's gonna be up there is just the ghosts of these old girls . . ." Pliney kicked a clod of alkali. "Let's see if that sonofabitch Linnement is finished wirin' up the place."

Following Pliney back toward the switch engine, Joe Bob was stuck by an odd vision: a brace of diesel locomotives, racing along through the clouds, far above the earth, pulling lines of silver railcars, gleaming and flashing in the sun.

11

Symphony

Y ou sure you're right about this, Harold?" Susan asked, staring squarely at the old man. "They're going to explode one on *Monday*?"

"Monday mornin', bright and early," Frye responded, settling onto his front porch swing. "Roy and Ethel Lemeur both told me. Said they heard them army colonels talkin' about it. Said they was gonna blow them blimps clean outta the air."

"Did they say anything about the death bunker?" Bobbie Jean asked.

"I doubt if Roy and Ethel would know about anything like *that*, B.J.," Susan said.

"Well, the guy *you* talk to over there hasn't been much help either," Bobbie Jean replied. "He didn't even tell you about this thing Monday."

"Ya need a new *informant*, ladies," Frye chuckled.

"He *did* tell us about the photos," Susan said. "That's something we didn't know before."

"Yeah, but ya ain't seen 'em, have ya?" Frye leaned forward. "Sounds to me like he's just stringin' ya along. Mebbe he figgured there's *compensation* of some sort down the road—"

"Why you old reprobate—" Susan grinned.

"Frye's right," Bobbie Jean interrupted. "We can't really trust anybody. 'Specially if he works for the government."

"So what choice do we have?" Susan asked. "How are we going to find out about the death bunker if nobody will *tell* us? And they won't let us onto the test site." She shook her head. "It's either fly over and take pictures—or find somebody else on the inside who'll talk to us."

Bobbie Jean slammed her fist into her hand. "I got it. Let's *kidnap* the bastards! *Make* 'em tell us what they're doing out there."

"Great idea, B.J.," Susan said, leaning back against the porch rail. "But kidnapping is a federal offense."

"Damn it all!" Frye barked. "What kinda vigilantes are you two anyways? In my younger days we woulda' snuck out there, waltzed right into that damn bunker—mebbe even kicked in the door!"

"With a bomb on the tower ready to go off," Susan smiled.

"Huh!" Frye looked around, his eyes wide, "we'd a climbed that tower, unwired that thing and just *carted it off*!"

"Who's this *we*?" Susan asked. "What kind of people did you run with in your youth, Harold—*Vikings*?"

"Just what we need," Bobbie shook her head. "The world's oldest juvenile delinquent."

"Go ahead," Frye snorted, "sit on my porch, use my landin' strip, drink my beer and then give me a lotta guff. Tryin' to pull my leg or somethin'."

"We're drinking your *iced tea*, Mr. Frye," Susan corrected him. "And I assure you neither I nor Miss Barnett here would ever try to pull your leg."

"Ever." Bobbie Jean nodded.

"Oughta' try it sometime," Frye grinned, raising his foot from the floor. "Might get a surprise 'r two."

"You come up with just one good idea, you ornery old coot, and I might consider it," Bobbie Jean said.

Frye took a drink of beer. "I got a lotta good ideas."

"Let's go, B.J." Susan stepped off the porch.

"Watcha' gonna do?" Frye prodded. "Buzz th' tower again? Take a few snapshots?"

"Come on, B.J."

"Careful ya don't hit one of them damn blimps! They ain't real easy to spot—'specially in th' dark!"

"He's right, Suze," Bobbie Jean said finally. "It'll be too dangerous. I don't think I'd want to risk flying Albert out there."

Susan stopped, then turned back. "Fine, fine. What else have we got? Nothing."

"Oh, I don't know." Frye carefully dropped his empty beer can into a cardboard box. "Mebbe you could cozy up to one of them bomb boys. Mebbe even show 'im a little—"

"You old buzzard!" Bobbie Jean exploded.

"Only a suggestion." Frye raised his hands in defense.

"Wait, B.J.," Susan said, "maybe he's right. The informant we have isn't very reliable—maybe we need another one. Maybe even *more* than one—"

"Suze!" Bobbie Jean's eyes widened. "Are you serious? I can't just go an' cozy up to any of those damm people!"

"Maybe you won't have to," Susan shrugged. "It's my fight anyway."

"Suze—"

"We have to find out about the bunker *some* way," Susan sighed. "And I've run out of ideas."

Sloan paused at the foot of the stairs, hefted his canvas bag and slowly began the climb to the barracks bay. It was the middle of the afternoon and the bay was empty. The guys were probably out at the test site, getting ready for the next shot.

Reaching the top of the stairs, he lowered the bag and took a deep breath. The empty bay reminded him of his second grade classroom back in Seattle, especially the time he'd been sick and had to stay inside during recess. Switching on a floor fan, he dragged the canvas bag to his bunk. The dark green army blanket covering the mattress looked a lot more inviting than the sterile white hospital bed he had put up with for weeks. Unzipping the bag, he searched for his notebook. He had some time. He would kick off his boots, stretch out in the wake of the fan and write a letter to Cathy. Maybe tell her about the scenery here. Maybe about his dreams.

"Good to see you're back, Andy."

Sloan looked up. It was Captain Stein. "Afternoon, sir."

Stein sat down on a nearby bunk. The burns across the officer's face had been replaced with new skin, giving his face a mottled, angry appearance. Sloan wondered why the medics never sent Stein to the infirmary—they had both taken the same amount of radiation.

"How are you feeling?" Stein asked after a moment.

"Dr. Bartholomew said I was well enough to come back to the company. Still got a problem with my tooth." Sloan pointed to his cheek. "Had a gold cap. The bomb made it radioactive, so they had to pull it." He paused. "How about you?"

"Took some leave time, went back home for awhile, drove around the countryside." Stein smiled. "Everybody commented on my sunburn."

"Yeah?"

"I told them I'd been to the ocean," Stein chuckled. "Stayed in the sun too long. They usually don't see burns like that in New England."

"Or in Seattle." Sloan paused. "Sir, will I be able to go back to the testing? I heard there's one set for Monday and I just wondered if I'll get in on it."

"I don't know, Andy." Stein studied the floor for a moment, then looked up. "I was planning on your staying back here. Or maybe with the observer group—"

"Look, sir," Sloan interrupted, "I know what you're trying to do, and I appreciate it. But I really am well enough to go out there. You know, every day in the hospital, I've been wonderin' if I'd ever get out, you know?"

Stein nodded.

"Now that I'm getting better, I was wondering, well—" Sloan paused, his throat dry, "Look, I don't want to be transferred out of atomic training just because of one accident. I really like being in the Atomic Brigade."

"Andy, the observer post is eleven miles from the target. After the maneuver you can just come back here until you're feeling better."

Sloan's throat was still sore, like he had swallowed broken glass. "I'd rather be in the maneuver—with the rest of the guys."

Stein took a deep breath. "Corporal Sloan, I'm *not* going to put you on the ground for this one. But there's a tank formation leading the infantry advance. Maybe I could talk Colonel Thorne into finding room for you there."

"Really?"

"*Maybe*," Stein stood up. "Either way, I'm sure the army would count you as a full participant in the shot."

"Thanks, sir. I really appreciate it."

"Report to Sergeant Quaak this evening before lights out. We should know something by then."

After Stein left, Sloan stretched out on the bunk. Though it was hot in the bay, the breeze from the fan brought a chill, like wind blowing across a mercury sea. Maybe he was catching another cold.

⊰⚜⊱

"I don't like this, Joe Bob," Flagmeyer said, staring at the dour group of people sitting opposite them. "Somebody's going to be fired. I know it."

"Relax, Art." Ramey took a sip of coffee. "We got our funding and nobody's gonna get fired. It's your standard pre-shot conference. Just try to look serious."

"But there are so many managers here." Flagmeyer looked around the room. "Even Marsha showed up!"

"Prob'ly to add some *class* to th' place." Ramey watched Marienfeld's wife carefully twist the cap from a recalcitrant inkpen.

A moment later five army officers strolled in, clanking across the hardwood floor like a brace of tanks. Captain Spaulding and a grimy, mud-splotched Captain Wanker marched stiffly over to the wall, while the blocky Colonel Thorne and the lean, precise Colonel Storax took seats next to Linneman. The tall, expressionless Colonel Myrmidon walked up behind Linneman's chair and surveyed the room.

"This is really unusual," Flagmeyer shook his head. "The army *never* shows up at these meetings."

"They want to be sure we will knock the blimp from the air," Uborka whispered. "That's their reason."

"There *is* no reason," Rhinehart mumbled from behind a pair of dark sunglasses. "It's all an accident. I should know."

"I wish the hell that man would *clean up* once in awhile," Flagmeyer grumbled, staring at Ratney Wanker. "I'll bet he's radioactive."

Joe Bob nodded. "Stein claims he glows in the dark."

"How *is* Stein?" Flagmeyer whispered. "I thought he'd be here."

"Ain't seen him."

"Good morning, gentlemen—and Mrs. Marienfeld." Demming smiled broadly from the podium. "Tomorrow morning we will detonate one of the last Los Alamos devices. And after that, Dr. Linneman's group will begin overseeing the manufacture of *our very own* atomic designs. We're here to discuss a few things regarding tomorrow's test, but before that, I'd like to introduce a very special friend of the AEC and of the Nuclear Test Site. The chairman of the Joint Commission on Atomic Energy, Senator Hodel Curry!"

A ruddy-faced man in a thick brown suit stood up. Joe Bob applauded half-heartedly as the senator waved at the group, his wide, perfect smile directed at a vague space about a foot above everyone's heads. After scanning the crowd, the senator finally rested his gaze on the smiling Mrs. Marienfeld, who responded by tapping the end of her ball-point pen against her lower lip.

"It was Senator Curry here who persuaded Congress to increase the funding on nuclear testing," Demming said. "I think we all owe him a debt of gratitude."

"I think he owes *me*," Rhinehart commented.

"Now to the business at hand." Demming glanced around the room. "I assume everything is ready for the test Monday—there'll be some troop maneuvers. Correct?"

"That's right," Colonel Myrmidon nodded. "We're ready to go."

"Good, good," Demming smiled. "Now, does anyone have any last-minute questions?"

"Yes, I have one," Colonel Storax said, rising from his chair. "Are there going to be reporters?"

Demming looked at his notes. "We've allowed one reporter in—a fellow named Battmund. But he's assured us that he'll clear his copy with us prior to publication."

"I don't like reporters," Storax said gruffly. "They get in the way."

"Anyone else have something to add?" Demming smiled.

"Yeah, I want to say something." Captain Wanker leaped to his feet. "You know how long it takes to *get* to ground zero when you're a mile from the blast? A damn long time, I'll tell you. And you know why?"

Demming stared at Wanker.

"It's the cactus. They're all over the place and they're always on fire—especially right up next to the GZ." Wanker looked around the room. "Now when you're runnin' across the desert and your damn uniform is *already* smokin' from the heat, an' you're tryin' to stamp *it* out and find the enemy at the same time—bam! You run into a *goddamn burnin' cactus*. Get fire and sparks all over everything."

"And?" Demming asked.

"And I just thought, if you guys're so damn smart, maybe you can come up with a big lawn mower that'll, you know, *trim up* the place before the shot. It'd make it damn site easier on the troops that have to charge though there, I can tell you that."

"We could set them off in a parking lot," Rhinehart suggested. "No cactus there."

"And something else." Wanker pulled a tiny notebook from his shirt pocket. "There's way too much *fog*."

"Fog." Demming cocked his head to the side like a confused parrot.

"Up close to the GZ there's so much crud in the air you can't see your hand in front of your face. How in the hell can we take the objective when we can't *see* it?" Wanker looked around. "Now, a big enough fan would *blow that stuff right outta there*."

"We could attach the fan to the big lawn mower," Rhinehart offered.

"And one more thing," Wanker glanced at his notebook. "You need bigger bombs. The ones you got won't finish off the shot towers! We march to the GZ and there's that damn shot tower—splayed out over the desert, glowin' like a poker and hotter'n the hub of hell. Step on that an' it'll cook your foot!"

"I—uh—I'm sure we can do something about that . . ." Demming seemed to be trying to smile, but the corners of his mouth merely jumped back and forth between a frown and a terrified grin.

"Seems to me the least you could do is blow that damn tower *outta* there so the fightin' man doesn't have to *trip* over it!" Wanker continued irritably.

"I think Captain Wanker has a point, Davis," said Senator Curry in a deep, pear-shaped voice. "The fighting man is crucial to this nation's defense."

"The way I see it," Rhinehart joined in, "it's either bigger bombs or thicker boots."

"Yeah, yeah," Wanker nodded agreeably. "Thicker boots would help. I've gone through three pairs of 'em now. Had the soles burned right off the bottom. Like walkin' across a hot iron out there."

"Why don't you just wait until the sand cools down?" Hendrix asked.

"*Wait*?" Wanker barked. "If we had to wait for *that*, we'd be waiting all day!"

"I recommend asbestos boots with lead uppers," Rhinehart said. "That should do the trick."

"Yeah," Wanker nodded, sitting back down. "That'd work."

Rhinehart leaned back in his chair. "See? All the man wants is good, reliable footwear."

Demming shuffled some papers irritably. "We'll look into it, I assure you. Now, as many of you know, when the very first atomic bomb was detonated near Alamogordo, New Mexico, the local radio station played *The Nutcracker.* Well, the senator here has come up with the wonderful suggestion that we continue that tradition. And I agree wholeheartedly. To facilitate his suggestion, the senator has even earmarked a portion of the funding for the purchase of a broadcast booth—complete with microphones and loudspeakers."

Ramey rolled his eyes toward the ceiling.

"Now," Demming smiled, "any suggestions for the music?"

After a moment of awkward silence, Captain Spaulding raised his hand. "I suggest a march. John Philip Sousa."

"That's *circus music*," Wanker snarled.

"How about . . ." Henderson gazed at the ceiling. "Something by Rimsky-Korsakoff? *Procession of Nobles*, maybe."

"That's a good one you seldom hear," Hendrix nodded. "We could set up a row charge and fire a bomb on each beat."

"I know that song," Thorne growled. "It's either a fast two or a slow three. Nobody can march to it."

"Or dance to it," Joe Bob added.

"How about Tchaikovsky's 1812 overture?" Hendrix offered. "In place of cannon shots we could have *three* separate ground zeroes—with three detonations in sequence."

"That's a lot of pomp and circumstance, Don," Henderson said, wagging a finger. "A nuclear row charge is *very* expensive. Maybe something by Rachmananoff."

"You two guys seem to like *Russian* composers," Colonel Storax glared suspiciously.

"*You* try finding a place for an atomic bomb in anything by Handel or Bach," Hendrix replied.

"How about the Brandenburg concerto?" Flagmeyer suggested.

"Gentlemen," Meghalty said with great gravity, "I would like to make not one suggestion, but *two*."

Joe Bob was astonished. It was the first time the wild-eyed little scientist had ever shown any interest in music.

"Ahem. I suggest *Kenge Djepi* and *Avazi I Dy Motrave.*"

"Albanian music?" Rhinehart replied testily. "*C'mon*, Emil. Besides, *Kenge Djepi* is a lullaby and *Avazi* is too oriental-sounding. No beat."

"Wait, I know!" Uborka stood up, waving his hands. "We could have the bomb *itself* make the music! Wire up instruments that would record the energy spectrum—and convert it to musical notes!"

"What the hell is that man talking about?" Thorne growled.

"Of course, if you want the beautiful high notes, say, like a violin," Uborka continued, "you will need a thermonuclear device."

"Gentlemen," Demming interrupted, his smile waning. "let's stick to *conventional* methods of making music, shall we?"

Captain Spaulding raised his hand. "If the Camp Jupiter personnel can provide some microphones, I can provide the army band. We'll place them on either side of the shot tower—at a safe distance of course."

"Can the band play *Ghost Riders in the Sky*?" Hendrix asked.

"Anyone else have an idea?" Demming asked sourly.

"*Sixty-Minute Man,*" Mrs. Marienfeld suggested, smiling demurely.

Rhinehart suddenly rose to his feet. "Okay. I've thought about this at great length, and I have the perfect piece of music for the test: Berlioz. *Hungarian March Opus 24.* Beautiful piece of work, very short and to the point. And, considering the presence of our esteemed guest," Rhinehart smiled at the senator, "appropriate for the occasion."

"Hungerian Opus?" Demming asked.

"Very beautiful. Very dignified," Rhinehart said. "I have the sheet music in my office."

"Well, er, I guess that's fine." Demming looked befuddled. "If you'll send the music to Captain Spaulding, he'll forward it to the army band. Now, if there is nothing else, I'll see everyone at the Control Point in the morning."

12

Clipper of The Clouds

Dammit, Rhinehart, I don't think I'm going to like this," Marienfeld's wife said over the whine of the jeep's engine.

"Nonsense." Rhinehart aimed the vehicle over an embankment and into a gully. "It'll be great."

"It'll be scary. I don't know how I let you talk me into this."

"You were the one that suggested it," Rhinehart said, narrowly avoiding a dense patch of sagebrush.

"Me?" Marienfeld's wife asked angrily. "*You* were the one."

"Okay, maybe we *both* came up with it."

Marienfeld's wife was nervous, angry and a little scared. It was probably her fifteenth time on the test site in the middle of the night, but it would be her first time in a Navy blimp. During an atomic test. Riding along in the borrowed military jeep, she wondered what it would be like up there. Probably scary. And cold. She scrunched up on the seat, burying her chin against her chest. "How much farther?"

"Another two miles," Rhinehart said. "We're cutting through Achera dry creek. Nobody knows about this place except me."

"Is this how you managed to sneak out to the tower last time?" she asked.

"Sure is. Hendrix discovered this short cut last year."

"I thought you were the only one who knew about it."

"Well, besides Hendrix." Rhinehart turned the wheel sharply, barely missing an enormous boulder. "Anyway, this will take us right to the blimps."

"Tell me something, Rhinehart." Marienfeld's wife cocked her head suspiciously. "Were you *really* trying to kill yourself up on that tower?"

"Why do you ask?"

"Well, you *were* sitting on an atomic bomb, you know," she shrugged nervously. "It just seems—"

"Look, Marsha, it was all a big misunderstanding." Rhinehart's voice oozed confidence. "It has to do with quantum mechanics. Lots of mathematics—say, is your husband working at the Control Point tonight?"

"Yeah, he's always at the Control Point," she said sourly, "even when there's no test scheduled." She turned toward Rhinehart. "How far away are we gonna be from the blast?"

"The shot tower?"

"Yeah. The blast. The fireball. How far are we gonna be from it? I'm not going up in any goddamn balloon just to get my butt scorched off."

"Sensible."

Marienfeld's wife grabbed Rhinehart by the neck. "That being the case, *how far are we gonna be from the blast?*"

"A long ways." Rhinehart pried her hand loose. "A very long ways. Besides, I've made some calculations. There's no way an A-bomb can destroy a blimp. The silver coating reflects the heat, and the shape keeps it stable."

"What if they try to, you know, *shoot* it down? What then?"

"They wouldn't do that," Rhinehart said. "Hendrix said they'd be aiming for the shot tower."

"Look, Rhinehart," she growled, "you're not gonna try anything funny up there, now are you? Like maybe *suicide*?"

"Me? Ha!" Rhinehart laughed. "What a joke!"

"Well, if you *are* planning to try it, you better hope it works, " she said, "because if it doesn't, I'll finish the job."

The headlights illuminated the dusty creekbed ahead of the jeep and flickered off the towering walls of the gully. Here I am, she thought, out in the middle of nowhere, in the middle of the night, zipping through a dry gulch with the looniest scientist at Camp Jupiter. Heading for a gasbag motel floating in the air ten miles from ground zero. At least it would be interesting. Even her in-laws admitted that life with Stanley required momentary jolts of electricity to keep from falling into the terminal blahs. She figured an interlude with Rhinehart might be good for a few hundred volts, might keep her awake for a week. Her metabolism had always been a little *fast*.

As a teenager on vacation with her parents, she had crawled into the back of the family camper and flashed the motorists following them. The effects had always been interesting—old men would honk their horns in approval, farmers would grin and wave, women would express shock and outrage. And then there were the teenage boys. The sight of bare female chest always made adolescent males go absolutely crazy. They would honk their cars' horns. They would honk *their* horns. They would weep, scream, bark, tear their hair and rend their clothing. Regardless whether their vehicle was a convertible or a sedan, they would try to stand up. They would drool, lick their windshields, expose all sorts of things. Ten or eleven Fords, DeSotos, Hudsons, Packards, Plymouths, Nashes and assorted jalopies would tailgate her father's camper, all jockeying for position.

She remembered that time in Nebraska, just east of Kearney when she yanked down her shorts and actually mooned an entire chapter of Future Farmers of America returning home from a county fair tractor pull. That bit of excitement lasted her almost a whole year— until she was eighteen. Then the airship *Shenendoah* came through town on a promotional tour and unwittingly offered her the opportunity to flash the entire population of both Minneapolis and St. Paul. Fifty thousand people all at once.

Now, ten years later, she was going to do it again, sort of. And while the blimp floating over the test site certainly wouldn't be seen by many people—a few hundred soldiers maybe— these Navy dirigibles had something going for them that the Shenandoah lacked: an atomic mushroom in the neighborhood. It might not be cushy, she thought, but it would sure be *different*.

Suddenly the jeep sprang up the side of the ravine and vaulted out onto a smooth expanse of salt flat. Rhinehart turned out the lights. "This is it. Area 10."

Marsha Marienfeld looked out through the windshield. In the moonless night, the surrounding area was pitch black, while a brilliant spot of light in the distance marked the location of the shot tower. She had never been this close to a real ground zero. Oh, she had sneaked out to Doom Town with Bill Deckman a few times, but she had never really considered that a real bomb target. With the houses and sidewalks and things, it was just too civilized. Looking at the distant circle of light, she said to herself, "Marsha, now, *that* is a ground zero." She felt a shiver run up her back.

"Where is everybody?" She pointed at the light. "There's no one there. No cars, no trucks, no jeeps, nothing."

"You're right," Rhinehart said. "Now watch out for the blimp. It ought to be around here somewhere."

"Listen," she said, grabbing Rhinehart's shirt, "I thought there was always a bunch of people hanging around. I remember Stanley telling me that. He said there's usually a hundred people standing around at the GZ until just before the test."

"We're coming in from the northwest," Rhinehart explained. "Everybody's on the other side of the tower. Do you see that blimp anywhere?"

"I don't know about this," Marienfeld's wife whined, looking at the eerie point of light. "How far away is that tower? It doesn't look very far away to me."

"It's a good five miles."

"Doesn't look like any five miles. It looks like it's—I dunno—*closer* than that."

"It looks closer because it's dark," Rhinehart said. "This blimp we're looking for was moored at the five-mile circle. Don Hendrix told me so yesterday."

"What if you got the wrong one?" She pulled nervously at his shirt. "Maybe one that's closer to the tower? Like a *mile* or something?"

"Never happen," Rhinehart said. "I know this place. Look. Here we are."

As Rhinehart brought the jeep to a stop, Marienfeld's wife saw an enormous dark shape obscuring the stars.

"This is it!" Rhinehart said, training a flashlight on the object. "The five-mile blimp!"

The dark shape hovered over the desert like a huge rubber sausage, smooth, gray and benign. The finned tail section, big as several barn doors, made it resemble a torpedo, or perhaps the business end of a Buck Rogers ray gun. Beneath the ship, attached to steel cables, was a silver and blue gondola. The rear section was composed of metal while the front section—probably the pilot's cabin—consisted only of a row of windows. To either side of the cab, perhaps a foot from the windows, were the propeller blades from the twin engines.

"Navy ZSG-3," Rhinehart said admiringly. "Two hundred and fifty feet from bow to stern. Gondola is 43 feet long, seven feet wide—with most of the amenities of home. Our very own rubber motel."

"Looks more like a big hot dog," Marienfeld's wife said. "I don't know how I'll feel about screwing inside a hot dog."

"It'll be great." Rhinehart switched off the flashlight and climbed out of the jeep. "If we time it right we can climax just as the bomb explodes."

"Climax? *Climax?*" Marienfeld's wife asked irritably. "What kind of word is that? I'll bet you've done this before. I'll bet you've had all *kinds* of bimbos up here."

"Believe me, you're the first," Rhinehart said, looking up at the blimp. "Now, to get up there, we have to climb this rope ladder here."

"You go first." Marienfeld's wife stepped out of the jeep. "I'll wait here. I want to see if it's safe."

"No, you go first," Rhinehart said. "It's safe. Besides, if you fall, I'll be able to catch you."

"Uh huh." Marienfeld's wife started up the ladder. "I bet you just want to look up my dress."

"Of course not." Rhinehart switched on the flashlight. "Here. This'll help you see the rope ladder."

———※———

"Anyone home?" Sloan asked, peering into the tank.

"Yeah, sure." The tank commander, a short blocky sergeant, swiveled his chair around to greet the newcomer. "But aren't you gonna be on the ground for this one?"

"M'name's Corporal Sloan. Captain Stein assigned me to the tanks. I really wanted to be out there in the trenches, but he thought I'd be more useful here."

"Yeah, Colonel Thorne said you'd be along," the tank commander said. "My name's Sergeant Romero. Climb on in."

"Thanks." Sloan squeezed himself into the front hatch. The only other person visible in the front of the tank was a morose, enlisted man surrounded by levers.

"Ever use a gunner's telescope?" the sergeant asked, peeking down from the turret housing.

"No."

"Ever been in a tank before?"

"No."

"Well, you can be our assistant driver. Maybe help out loading shells. We're supposed to blow hell out of ground zero this mornin'." The sergeant pointed to a metal rod running the length of the cabin. "Watch yer step. That's the drive shaft. Prob'ly take a leg off. Now, like I was tellin' these reporters here, this old Chaffee's been modified for nuclear combat, so things are kinda' mixed up in here."

"Reporters?" Sloan asked, bumping his head on the ceiling.

A hand reached out from the darkness beneath the turret housing. "Lester Battmund. Washington Daily News." To Sloan's surprise, the man was wearing a black wool suit and a fedora.

"Captain Hugh Duffel," the other man said, also extending his hand. "Producer for *The Big Picture*. It's on Saturday afternoons, right after *Sky King*." The man pumped Sloan's hand. "Great show. Army stuff."

"We didn't have a television," Sloan smiled, "just radio."

"This tank has one-inch plate on the front," the sergeant continued. "Permanent grousers on the tracks, twin Cadillac engines. We can get to the GZ in five minutes. That's after we blow the hell outta—er, the objectives—yer gettin' this down aren't ya?"

"Oh, sure," Duffel smiled, tapping his forehead. "Keep it all up here."

"Well, *I* have to take notes," Battmund grumbled, clambering over a section of metal shaft. "Anybody got a light in this place?"

"Watch yer step, Batman," the sergeant said. "That's the drive shaft yer knee's up against. We start up an' you'll lose a leg."

Battmund backed away from the driveshaft.

"Yeah, gotta watch these babys when you start 'em up. Sometimes they catch fire. 'Course, that's not the big problem. When them shells come outta that chamber they're hottern' a blue blaze. Gotta keep yer collar buttoned up. And th' smoke's so bad ya can't get yer breath. Say, are you gonna print our names?"

"Sure," Battmund said, looking at Sloan. "I heard you tell Sergeant Romero you wanted to be in the trenches with the rest of the men. So what are you doing in this tank?"

"My CO put me here," Sloan said, trying to get comfortable. "The doc says I caught some kind of flu virus at the last test. I guess he wants me to get better before I go out there again."

"You caught the flu out there?" Battmund stared.

"Yeah," Sloan smiled sheepishly. "There's all kinds of flu bugs out there. Radiation doesn't affect 'em at all, I guess. Did you know a cockroach can stand all sorts of radiation and nothing will happen to him?"

"There's roaches at ground zero?" the tank driver asked.

"This thing has not one but *two* hydramatic transmissions—" the sergeant patted the engine cover. "And without the coolin' fan, this ol' Sherman'll get up to, I bet, 150 degrees."

"Task Force Zipper? Come in."

"Jeez!" The sergeant picked up the phone. "I thought we had radio silence—Romero here. Captain Wanker is that you? Yeah. He's here. The reporter too. Do what? Hell yes, we'll knock it down! What do you think we are, *amateurs*?" He put the phone back in the cradle and shook his head.

"What's up?" the driver asked.

"That was Wanker," the sergeant replied. "He wants us to make sure we knock out the objective. Wants us to throw everything at it. Cannons, howitzers, machine guns—everything."

"Objective?" Battmund asked. "What's the objective?"

"The objective is top secret," the sergeant said crisply. "I can't talk about it."

"Bigger than a breadbox?" Battmund asked.

"Oh, yeah." Romero reached up and closed the hatch, then dimmed the interior lights to almost total darkness.

"Is it bigger than a house?" Battmund pressed.

"No. Well, maybe. I'm not sure."

"Bigger than a blimp, then?"

"Same size," the sergeant replied. "*Exactly* the same size."

Rhinehart climbed up the ladder, past the single tire hanging beneath the gondola and into the cabin door. Inside, Marsha Marienfeld sat huddled on a bench seat next to the open window. In the distance was the bright, steady glow of the shot tower. Rhinehart squinted for a moment, then held out his arm.

"Whatcha' doin?" Marienfeld's wife asked.

"Uh, nothing. The tower—"

"The tower *what*?"

"I guess it's taller than I thought. Bigger ground zero, maybe."

"Taller? Bigger? What are you talking about?"

"This blimp might be a little closer than five miles. Four maybe." Rhinehart said. "Yeah, I'd say four miles."

"*Four* miles?"

"This blimp can take it. The fuselage is designed to deflect the shock waves and the skin has a heat-resistant film on it—"

"What?"

"It's a coating, like you see on Juicy Fruit gum wrappers. Real thin, lightweight. Works great—even deflects neutrons. Darndest thing. You know if you're ever in an atomic attack, just go to the grocery store—"

"I want out of here. I want out of here *now*!" She stood up, almost bumping her head on the low ceiling.

"Look." Rhinehart patted her on the shoulder. "There's nothing to worry about. I've been a lot closer than this before."

"You *have* been out here with other women!" Marienfeld's wife growled. "How close have you been?"

"I forget exactly," Rhinehart said. "But don't worry. We're still safe as can be, I'm sure of it."

"Well, okay." She relaxed. "Wait a minute. Is that music?"

"It's the army band playing Berlioz," Rhinehart said, looking at his watch. "Hungarian March Opus 24 . . . in honor of Senator Curry."

"What?"

"It's from an opera—*The Damnation of Faust.*"

Marienfeld's wife sat down on the bench and looked around the cabin. "Well, here we are. We gonna do anything or not?"

"Well, first, I'd like to do a few calculations." Rhinehart glanced nervously at the tower. "You happen to bring a pencil?"

"Did I bring a pencil? Look, I didn't even bring underwear. I *sure* don't have a pencil." She removed her dress, folded it and placed it on the bench beside her.

"I need a pencil." Rhinehart tried to think: there were three airships on the test site—two at two miles and one at five—*or was it five airships at three miles*—no, there were only three to start with. He needed a pencil. A slide rule. Damn.

"C'mere," Marienfeld's wife said. "I'm getting goosebumps."

Rhinehart started over. According to Hendrix, there were three blimps positioned at various distances from the shot tower. One at the one-mile circle, one at the four-mile circle and one at the five. The blimp at the five-mile position would probably remain intact, while the one at four miles might break loose from its moorings. He didn't want to think about the third blimp.

Rhinehart scratched his head. There were only two safe places around an exploding A-bomb—at least five miles away or *right* on top of it, with your bags packed and ready to go. And now, inside the gently bobbing blimp with the naked Marsha Marienfeld, he might be some-where in between. "Would you like to go to ground zero?" he blurted suddenly.

"No," Marienfeld's wife said. "Of course not."

"Well, it might be safer."

Suddenly, from far away, a loudspeaker began droning the familiar: "Take your battle positions. Zero minus two minutes—"

Grabbing a piece of paper and a pen from the map compartment, Rhinehart hastily sketched a right triangle.

"What are you doing?"

"Ratios. I'm doing ratios," Rhinehart replied, scribbling furiously. "From here, the tower *looks* a half-inch tall. But it's really five hundred feet tall. So that means we're . . . lessee. ."

"Look," she said scooting down the bench. "There's a comfy place back here behind this big box—"

"Whew." Rhinehart looked at the sketch. "No problem. By my calculations, the airship is four miles from ground zero."

"Good. Now, c'mere and get your clothes off."

With a huge smile, Rhinehart removed his shirt and trousers. Then he stopped. "Wait."

"What *now*?"

"If that tower out there is only a hundred feet tall . . ."

"What?"

"It means we're in the blimp *closest to the tower*."

"Fine. Okay," Marienfeld's wife purred. "Now, c'mere."

Outside the loudspeakers blared, "Thirty seconds to detonation. 29—28—"

Inside the blimp, Rhinehart decided to dispense with foreplay.

"UmmmmMMMM." Marienfeld's wife wrapped her legs around Rhinehart's waist. Soon, the blimp was rocking back and forth, bow to stern, creaking like an old sailboat on a choppy lake.

"Hmmm!"

"Hmmmmmmm!"

"Oh! Oh!

OH!

Click.

In the darkness, Battmund tapped the tank commander on the shoulder. "Do we have to put on dark glasses, Sergeant?"

"Nope."

"Here," Duffel said. "I brought along some extra Ray-Bans."

"Won't need em," Romero said. "We spent three days sealing this tank. Tape's on everything. Ain't no way light can get in." The sergeant's voice was calm, confident. "The first we'll know about it is the shock wave. 'Course, it might turn out to be just a damn dud. Why I remember—"

Suddenly shafts of light pierced the tank's interior, brilliant white needles extending from the walls, the control surfaces, the floor. All in perfect silence.

"Jesus Christ," the driver mumbled.

To Sloan, the beams seemed solid enough to touch. It was like being inside a pincushion.

"What the *hell* is going on?" Battmund whispered.

Then, the sound of an approaching stampede. The tank bucked and shook, sending dust, notebooks and shell casings flying through the air.

"There's—a *train*—running through here!" Battmund screamed.

Marsha Marienfeld opened her eyes. A few inches above her, everything had gone absolutely white as the glare coursed through the open windows in solid, opaque sheets. Curled up on her back on the bench seat, her knees just inches from her ears, she suddenly realized she was swimming in a shallow pool of relative darkness, protected from the intense light by a cheap metal cabin heater.

Rhinehart was not so fortunate. Caught in pushup position, arms straight out, butt high, he took the full force of the glare, rendering him translucent. As a result, Marienfeld's wife was presented with the unpleasant vision of being screwed by a skeleton.

"I don't like this," she growled.

"It's great!" said the skeleton.

"I really don't like this."

"Oh! Wait! Oh! Oh! Oh!" said the skeleton.

"I really hate this," Marienfeld's wife said. "I'm not having any fun." The sun had come up just fifty feet outside the window, then somehow expanded to cover half the sky, turning it a fiery red. And there was the roar—like a freight train running between her ears. Oddly, it brought back an image from her childhood. As a little girl, she had once climbed inside an empty 55-gallon drum with her neighbor, a greasy brat named Eddie Smye, and then rolled down a hill. After being scratched terribly by the rusty insides of the barrel, Eddie Smye had suggested adding quilts as padding. That worked fine, and then Eddie had suggested rolling in the barrel *naked*.

This was a lot like that stupid barrel. It was bad enough getting screwed by a skeleton, but now the walls were moving—caving inward, puffing back out. This wasn't fun anymore and that damn fireball *sure* seemed a lot closer than five miles.

"I don't like this one bit," she said amid the chaos.

"This is great," said a now completely transparent Rhinehart. "This is the best one ever!"

Suddenly the entire airship tipped up on its tail, sliding maps, navigation equipment, coke bottles, to the rear of the cabin.

"You *have* been up here before, I just knew it!" Marienfeld's wife yelled, thoroughly angry. Suddenly a metallic crunch from the rear of the blimp joined the roar of the fireball. The tail section slammed into the ground. An instant later, a cable tore past the open window and slapped against the rubber skin of the blimp.

"Our mooring line!" Rhinehart yelled, "we're loose!"

The airship, propelled upward by the bomb's base surge, climbed like a fat angel, nose in the air.

"That was great!" The now-opaque Rhinehart slid to the floor, then tumbled into a clump of maps and charts at the end of the cabin.

"I want my clothes," Marienfeld's wife demanded. "I want out of here." Through the open window she could see the immense, boiling mushroom cloud, now turning several shades of purple and gray. Occasionally the cloud parted briefly to expose a flash of orange fire. Then she noticed how stuffy and hot the interior of the gondola had become.

"Turn on the fans," she ordered. "This thing has fans, I saw them."

"I can't believe it!" Rhinehart struggled to his feet, bewilderment across his face. "The skin on the blimp must have deflected both the heat *and* the shock wave!"

"I'm hot." Marsha Marienfeld crawled on her hands and knees toward the control panel. "I want the fans."

The airship bucked and lurched, bobbed like a ship on the Atlantic as each successive blast wave hit, then slid away. Reaching the panel, she turned a key, then grabbed the first set of levers and pulled hard. In response, the airship's engines roared to life, and the blimp slowly aimed itself straight for the smoking, churning stem of the mushroom cloud.

***

"Start movin'!" Sergeant Romero yelled at the driver.

"Right!" Hugh Duffel slapped his leg. "Get this buggy movin'! Let's have some *lethal symmetry*!"

"But the fireball hasn't even cooled yet," the driver said, peering through the viewing shot. "It's just sittin' up there, rollin' around over the top of the tower."

Peering out the smaller observation window, Sloan saw the huge orange and yellow fireball, an angry sun hovering over the horizon. Beneath it, and approaching their position, was a furiously boiling river of dust and grit, made liquid by the bomb's heat.

"You heard me! Go!" The sergeant squeezed behind the huge gun. As the tank lurched forward, Sloan banged his face against the cannon barrel, then bumped his helmet on the turret housing.

"Bear left, ten degrees," the sergeant ordered. "Still can't see them goddamn blimps—left! I said *left*!"

"Yes, sergeant," the driver mumbled. Through the window, Sloan watched the scene as the driver guided the bouncing tank toward the rumbling base surge.

"Go!" the sergeant yelled. "Next turn, hold that throttle down—you're gonna lose the slack! There ya go! That's better—"

"Great job!" Duffel yelped. "Wish I'd brought my camera. This would make a great movie!"

"What's the driver doing?" Battmund asked, trying to hold his pencil to the notebook.

"Gotta hold the throttle or the track'll come off the idler," the sergeant replied. "That happens at ground zero, we're dead—hey! There's one!"

"What?" the reporter asked.

"It's a blimp!" the sergeant yelled excitedly. "I can't believe it! It's just floatin' out there—jus' *askin'* for it! Gimme a shell!"

Sloan looked through the window for the cannon target. Then he found it, a small grey dot bobbing crazily near the stem, halfway between the ground and the roiling mushroom. The stem itself looked like a stream of water from a faucet, except that it seemed to be flowing up instead of down, drawing the blimp up into the mushroom itself.

"Get it before the cloud does!" the sergeant ordered. "Ready—fire!"

Suddenly Sloan's ears imploded, and the interior of the tank filled with the sharp odor of ammonia.

"Hot shell!" The sergeant slid the bolt on the cannon and the fiery hot brass cartridge case flew out and slammed against the wall of the tank, ricocheting just inches above Sloan's head. "Gimme tracers! I wanna see where I'm aiming!"

Sloan pressed his face to the observation window. Outside, the dusty gloom was punctuated by lines of tracer fire, all converging toward the small object bobbing near the stem. Then it was gone.

"Veer to the right ten degrees!" Duffel commanded, waving a map. "Maybe we can take prisoners, ha ha."

"We're in the dustcloud, Sarge," the driver yelled. "Want me to turn off the fans?"

"Yeah," the sergeant said. "An' get yer gas masks on."

Sloan looked out the window. Darkness. Turning, he was startled to see the reporter holding his fedora tight to his face.

Rhinehart, wearing only his shoes, leaned out of the open gondola window amid the lightning, smoke, ionization glow and fireworks. Only seconds before, two blimps floating not a mile away had suddenly shivered and fell to earth. For some reason, there appeared to be tanks, howitzers, mortars and God-knows-what-else out there shooting *real bullets*.

Luckily, the inadvertent starting of the twin engines had moved them out of the immediate area, saving them from a similar fate. And while the blimp had been momentarily aimed toward the atomic cloud, the shock wave had propelled it backwards. The dirigible was traveling atop a huge wave of air moving perhaps eighty miles an hour. With any luck they would soon be out of range.

"You think this is funny, don't you?" Marienfeld's wife screamed, running up and down the bruised and dented cabin. "We're going to die up here and you think you're Captain Nemo!"

"Nemo had a submarine," Rhinehart said, waving at no one in particular.

"You crazy bastard!" Marienfeld's wife, her face pinched in anger, punched his arm smartly. "I *demand* you land this thing right now." She turned to the window, her arms folded angrily across her breasts.

Rhinehart noticed that the red glare from the tracer shells was casting an appealing glow on her otherwise humdrum behind. That— along with the lightning flashes and the purple aura of ionized air—

"All this commotion is too demanding on our eyes," Rhinehart said, "I suggest we lie down."

"*What?*"

"Or risk blindness," Rhinehart put his arms around her. "Those howitzer tracers are bright enough to put out your eyes—"

"They can put out our *lives*, you moron!" Marienfeld's wife screeched.

"You look terrific in the morning," Rhinehart said, smoothing debris from the bench seat. "Have I ever told you that?"

"How are we gonna get down?" Marienfeld's wife wailed. "Just tell me that? We'll be trapped up here forever! Or shot down—"

"Too far away," Rhinehart nuzzled her ear. "Don't worry about a thing—"

"All this lightning up here!" she said. "What if we get hit?"

"We're not grounded," Rhinehart mumbled from somewhere south of her neck. "Besides, the blimp is filled with helium—I think."

"You think!"

"I'm sure of it!" Rhinehart said from between her breasts. "Helium . . . nonflammable . . . nothing to worry about. Mmmm—"

"Make a hard right, twenty degrees," Duffel commanded, peering at the map. "We should be able to see something in a minute."

"I want a piece of the gondola," Battmund said. "If it isn't too much trouble."

"Step on it, driver," Sergeant Romero growled. "I don't want Wanker getting here before we do."

"Yes, sir, I—oh, swell . . ." The driver paused as the tank came to an abrupt halt. "We hit something."

"Drive over it!" Romero ordered. "Or around it! C'mon!"

In response, the driver shifted the twin Cadillac engines into a low whine, backed up and tried again. And again the tank came to a halt.

"See anything down there, Sloan?" the sergeant asked. "All I got is dust."

Looking through the observation rectangle, Sloan saw the angular outline of some apparently manmade object. "Can't really tell—"

"Well, try it again, Corporal!" the sergeant ordered. "This here's the tank that won the war! You gonna let her get bogged down by some lil' Nevada sand dune? Let's get *traction*!"

Suddenly the whine from the engines increased in pitch as the tank vibrated ominously. "Sarge, we lost our tread."

"What?" The sergeant peeked down from the turret. "Throw it into front wheel drive!"

"Can't. It's jammed."

"Well, what the hell did we get into anyway?" The sergeant peered through the glass. "A swamp?"

"Maybe we hit another tank," Duffel suggested, folding up the map.

"Well, hell," the sergeant said, unlatching the hatch, "gotta get outta here *some* damn way—" A second later, the cabin interior was filled with a thick brown dust.

"I don't like this." The sergeant's voice was filled with regret.

Sloan climbed to the hatch and looked. Jammed up next to the tank were blistered metal girders, glowing and hissing amid the brown haze. Beneath them was the shattered concrete pedestal, smouldering in a sea of green glass.

He knew instantly where they were.

———

"There was a *what* in that last blimp?" Colonel Thorne snarled at the artillery spotter.

"A naked woman, sir. Naked as can be."

"Uh, huh." Thorne paced back and forth in front of the enlisted man. "So that's why you missed it. You thought there was a naked woman in it."

"Yes, sir." The enlisted man offered his binoculars. "You could see them."

"See *what*, Corporal?"

"Er, breasts, sir. Both of them. And she was waving her arms."

"Uh huh. And was she saying anything, Corporal?" Thorne asked drily. "I mean, anything that you could, you know, *hear*? Was she *calling your name*?"

"No, sir."

"Tell me, Corporal," Thorne growled, "how much coffee did you drink before you came here this morning?"

"Five cups, sir."

"Well, that's probably more than enough. Your system can't take it."

"Yes, sir."

"All right." Thorne picked up the walkie talkie. "All units. Listen up. We've been able to get two of the targets. There's only one to go. Last seen, it was drifting north through Reveille Canyon. Track it down, then shoot it down. That's an order."

———

"Flying up a godforsaken canyon in the middle of nowhere—chased by a mushroom cloud and forty or fifty tanks!" Marienfeld's wife stormed. "I really hate this!"

"It's not your average date, you'll have to admit," Rhinehart said, looking out the window. "You know, either we're moving faster, or those rocks are getting closer. I think we're losing altitude." He leaned out the window. "Bullets must have pierced the helium bag."

"Are we gonna crash?" Marienfeld's wife looked out of the window nervously.

"I doubt it," Rhinehart said. "We can go down the rope ladder and jump just before we touch down. Then, with the blimp lighter, it'll probably float another hundred miles."

"Just wish I knew where we were," Marienfeld's wife groused. "Probably heading for Idaho or Montana somewhere. Maybe the damn North Pole—"

"Not that far," Rhinehart said, putting on his trousers. "But I'm sure we've probably left the test site."

"Then why is that cloud still back there?" Marienfeld's wife asked, pointing out the window at the ominous ball of brown haze following them through the basin.

"I dunno," Rhinehart shrugged. "I was under the impression those things never strayed too far from home. Guess I can't know everything."

"Look, I really don't want to spoil your fun, but we gotta get out of here." She tapped her bare foot nervously against the wall of the gondola. "Stanley's gonna kill me. He doesn't like it when I fool around, you know."

"Understandable," Rhinehart nodded. "Just tell him it's a mistake. Tell him it was a spur of the moment thing—"

"He'd never buy that," she shrugged. "One time he saw me talking to some soldier over at Ethel's Bar. Raised all kinds of hell. Thought I'd given him my phone number on a beer can. Do you believe that?"

"I guess it's possible," Rhinehart nodded.

"Look, Rhinehart," Marienfeld's wife sighed. "We can't let anybody find out we were up here."

"Then I guess we'll have to jump before they catch us," Rhinehart said, looking out the window. "So far all they've got is tanks chasing us. We can probably make it to the rendezvous point before they send out planes."

"Rendezvous point? Planes? What are you talking about?"

"Planes," Rhinehart said, scanning the ground. "And they're probably just crawling with reporters. No, if we don't want to get caught, we'll have have to get out of here before all the helium runs out."

"How long before we hit the ground?"

"I'd guess five minutes—maybe you'd better get your clothes on."

The soldier standing next to the switch engine, an Army captain with a round boyish face, appeared both apologetic and suspicious. "Hello, Mr. Pliney."

The engineer surveyed the row of tanks assembled along the railroad tracks, then aimed a wad of tobacco toward the officer's patent leather boot. "How can I be of service, young man?"

The man took a step back. "I wonder if you could tell us if you've, uh, seen something."

"In sixty-odd years ya see a lot of things."

"Well, we're looking for something, uh, in particular," the man swallowed. "And since you were operating up here north of the target— we, uh, thought you might have seen it.

"Seen what?"

"A blimp. Traveling north. Followed by a big white cloud, hanging close to the ground. You couldn't miss it."

"Uh huh."

"Both harmless, of course," the man said. "You didn't see anything like that?"

"Yeah."

"You *saw* it?" The officer brightened.

"No," Pliney grinned evilly. "'Yeah' I *didn't* see it."

"You're sure?" the officer asked suspiciously.

"Ya wanna search th' train?"

"Uh, no—"

"That blimp *might* be hidin' under a flatcar," Pliney shrugged. "What you want it for? It break the law or somethin'?"

"Thank you for your time." The man turned on his heel and strode toward a waiting truck.

"Sonsabitches," Pliney mumbled. As the tanks pulled away, he reached back and tapped the door to the equipment room. "They're leavin'—guess you two can come out now."

13

Capon

"Hi, Dr. Linneman," the chubby blonde receptionist smiled brightly.

"Hi, Carol. Donna not working today?"

"She's taking off. I think she's showing Senator Curry around Las Vegas."

"Ah," Linneman nodded. "Is Dr. Demming in?"

"Yep. He's expecting you, isn't he?" She glanced at the appointment book. "Yep, here it is. 'Talk with Linneman.' That's you, all right."

"Wish it weren't," Linneman said mournfully.

"Well, he'll be a few minutes," she said, still smiling. "He has Stanley Marienfeld on the phone. He seemed to be really mad about something. Want me to listen in?"

"No, no! That's all right." Linneman reached for an old copy of the *Saturday Evening Post*.

"So when are you taking me to Doom Town?"

"Oh, uh, I don't know," he said, turning the page. "It's dangerous out there. Maybe you should think about going to Las Vegas instead."

"Nah." The girl dropped her head until her long blonde hair all but covered her eyes. "If I was gonna go anywhere, it'd be to Rhode Island. You ever been to Rhode Island, Dr. Linneman? It's really a beautiful place."

"I've been there a few times." He looked at his watch. "Uh, did Donna say when she's coming back to work?"

"Next week, I guess." The girl looked down sullenly.

"Carol," the intercom squawked suddenly, "tell Dr. Linneman I'll be with him in a few minutes."

"Yes sir," the receptionist replied. She turned to Linneman. "You know, he does sound mad. I'd put my thoughts in order if I were you. I've found that's the best way to live around here. To have your thoughts like little ducks."

"Excuse me?"

"My dad always told me, he said, 'Carol, you've got to keep your thoughts like little ducks. In a row.' You want to borrow my brush?" The girl suddenly reached into her desk and handed him a huge pink brush shaped like a penguin. "Maybe if you do something with your hair you won't look so scared. It's bettern' nothing."

"I don't think so—" Linneman said, handing the penguin back.

"Okay, but I know *I* look better when my hair is brushed." The receptionist stuffed the brush back into a drawer. "'Course, people like Donna don't have to do that—they look great *all* the time. Guess that's why they hired her."

"Carol," the intercom squawked again, "send in Dr. Linneman."

"Sit down, George," Demming said, as Linneman closed the door. "I want to discuss something with you."

"Sure." Linneman collapsed into the low chair in front of Demming's desk.

"George." Demming removed his glasses. "How do you feel about management style?"

"Style?" Linneman gulped. "Why, I've never given it much thought."

"Apparently not." Demming tapped his glasses on the desktop. "You know, very soon now, your staff is going to have to come up with some designs for atomic bombs—"

"Meghalty and Uborka are working on that," Linneman interrupted. "I'm sure they'll have a finished blueprint in, oh, about a week. Maybe even sooner—"

"I'm not concerned about them, George." Demming leaned back in his chair. "I'm concerned about the other people on your staff. And some of the things that have happened recently—the general tells me that during the test one of his men saw a—well—*naked person* in one of the blimps. Would you—"

"I don't know anything about that."

"Stanley Marienfeld thought one of your men might be involved."

"I'm sure they're not," Linneman replied, chewing his lip nervously. "There's no reason for any of them to go up in a blimp."

"So you think Stanley was misinformed?" Demming raised his eyebrows. "Do you think he could be wrong?"

"I'm sure he is, Dr. Demming," Linneman nodded. "Yes, I'm *sure* of it. Rhinehart wouldn't do anything like that. I mean, he was locked in his dormitory room throughout the test. I had the key in my pocket."

"Rhinehart?" Demming stopped. "Did I say Rhinehart?"

"No," Linneman said, "but—"

"George, let's get one thing straight. Your job is to make the laboratory run as efficiently as possible. And from the looks of things, that hasn't been happening. Scientists blowing themselves up, disappearing. Running around proclaiming they're the deity. And now you have one who takes blimp rides with—with *nude persons*."

"I really don't think that was Rhinehart—"

"Quiet, George," Demming barked. "Very soon now, we will be making and testing practically *all* the army's tactical nuclear weapons. All eyes are going to be on us. That means reporters, politicians and little old ladies who bitch about bright lights in the middle of the night and fallout killing their pets. Now, we've been trying our damndest to sell the idea that atomic bombs are essential, and that we have a certain measure of *competence*. We want people to think we know what we're doing." Demming leaned forward menacingly. "Am I clear?"

"Yes, sir."

"Now I know we've had our differences, I know you've had trouble as a manager," Demming smiled. "There have been times when I've suspected you were promoted beyond your ability. But I'm going to give you an opportunity to prove me wrong."

"Oh?"

"There are only three more shots scheduled in this test series. I want them to go off without a hitch. No suicides. No rumors of *naked people* in blimps. No adverse publicity. Nothing that will upset me or the

Atomic Energy Commission. Nothing that will upset Dr. Trumbo."

"No sir. I mean, of course, sir."

"I don't want her here in Nevada—at least until the *Vulcan* test . . ." Demming paused. "Because, George, if something happens to embarrass us—and Dr. Trumbo gets involved—"

"Yes, sir."

"*You* will answer for it."

Stanley Marienfeld returned to the corner booth with his sixth drink of the afternoon and distributed his 6'2" frame evenly inside the cubbyhole. Here he was, the Director of Public Information. The second most powerful person at the nuclear test site, saddled with a wife who— according to rumor— had displayed her tits to a thousand dusty marching *enlisted men*. Common soldiers. It was almost as bad as when he had caught her with that math professor, doing algebra on his grandmother's quilt.

No, it was worse. Then there had been no nuclear cloud, no tanks, no shells to call attention to the goings-on. Now he had to contend with a Movienews reel of his naked, grinning wife hanging from a gondola. He felt like a goddamn capon. All because of that horrible Rhinehart. If the bastard wanted to kill himself, why didn't he just jump in front of a truck or something? No, he had to gum things up on the way out, screw somebody's wife inside a blimp. And then deny it had ever happened. Claimed he was in the dormitory the whole time. *Asleep.*

Marienfeld shook his drink and watched the surface of the foam for a stem. He hoped Roy had remembered to add the maraschino cherry. If it didn't have one, he'd demand his money back. Perhaps he was thinking about the blimp incident too much. Maybe he should stop thinking about it. It was making his drink taste bad. Yet the vision wouldn't go away.

"Where did you get that sunburn?" he had roared.

"You got me, I've been home all day," she said. "Watering the plants."

"Well, *somebody* was up there with—with big tits!" he sputtered. "And everyone said it was you!"

"Nope," she had said, rubbing on the calamine. "I was here. Just me and the plants."

Marienfeld checked his pulse. Yes, he must try to think of something else. He would think about getting drunk. Like a buzzard watching a swamp for signs of death, he scrutinized both the surface of the beverage and his watch. He had been here an hour and he wasn't even tipsy. "Roy must be watering the drinks again," he muttered under his breath. "That sonofabitch. Ought to have his license yanked for a few months. Put him and his ugly wife on the street." That's it, Marienfeld nodded. Show them they can't trifle with the second most powerful man at the test site. *He would close Ethels down.*

No, he decided after a moment, he would probably have to put up with it. One of the compromises the truly powerful have to tolerate every day. Glancing around Marienfeld noticed a dark object hovering above him, pointing straight toward the center of booth. Probably the Sword of Damocles, which hangs over the head of every man in power. Looking up, he saw that there *was* something above him. A warhead. Or more accurately, a warhead-shaped object. It was a lamp shade, another of Roy's bomb items, a souvenir from some long-forgotten fizzle. Marienfeld noticed that, for no good reason, the black shade had been wrapped in Christmas tree lights and covered with bits of trinitite—molten glass foraged from one of the GZs. Roy's wife had probably done it—dressed the bomb so that it didn't look particularly dangerous anymore. What was the word? *Festive.*

Women didn't understand bombs, didn't belong at the nuclear test site. It was a job for *men*. Tough men. Men like Demming and the general. Men who weren't afraid to discuss yield estimates or kill ratios. Men who weren't ashamed to say they worked for the Atomic Energy Commission. Removing a nail file from his vest pocket, Marienfeld offhandedly stirred the meringue atop his brandy Alexander, then poked around the bottom of the glass, hoping to harpoon the maraschino cherry loitering there. Nothing. Maybe there was no cherry. After another stab and miss, he replaced the nail file, still wet with foam, in his vest pocket.

Shaking his head to remove transient images of Marsha and Rhinehart, Marienfeld cast about for more comfortable thoughts. Specifically, thoughts about his ascent to power at the test site. He credited his position to an early keen lack of interest in other people, especially females. He liked watching them, liked reading about them in *National Geographic*, but that was as close as he dared get. Even as a child, Marienfeld knew girls were a different species altogether—whining, sneaky little creatures with shifty eyes, sharp little teeth and voices so shrill they made your ears hurt.

Marienfeld spun the drink. Still no sign of a cherry. As early as the fifth grade, he had made a conscious decision to distance himself from women, to work toward a *man's* profession, one where only the strongest and the fittest survived. A calling where things were logical and totally bereft of the vagaries and flufferies associated with the female gender. Then, the very day after he obtained his doctorate in psychology, he was sitting in that Boston saloon when his life plan crumbled. *She* walked in. Blonde, long-legged, knowledgeable, *extremely* agile, standing there in tight denims asking for directions to Beacon Hill. Marsha.

Scrunching his shoulders like a scoliotic vulture, Marienfeld thought about her. Smartmouthed, ambitious, competitive. *So* competitive, in fact, that the Atomic Energy Commission sent her all the promotions, let her meet with all the bigwigs from Congress. Thank God he was a man, Marienfeld brooded. At least he was *paid* better. And she still had to do the cooking.

"Hey, Stanley!" someone shouted at him. "Aren't you going to the meeting?"

Marienfeld looked up blearily, then hunched closer to his drink. It was Groder. Little red-headed weasel Groder. By some misprint in the organizational chart, he was one of the few people the Office of Public Information had no control over.

"Rhinehart's supposed to give a talk. It's about keeping abreast of fallout."

"What?"

"Keeping abreast of fallout," Groder repeated in a loud voice. "Bet it's real interesting. No one really knows where that nuclear cloud will go. I mean after we set 'em off, it's out of sight, out of mind. Right? So Rhinehart's offered to give a talk about it. He says he followed this one cloud—"

"Shut up!" Marienfeld snapped, spilling the drink.

"You really ought to go," Groder shrugged. "I hear your wife's gonna be there."

"Where's a phone?" Marienfeld rose to his feet in a rage. "I want a telephone!"

"Pay phones on the wall," Roy said from behind the counter, "right next to the rest rooms."

Shoving Groder aside, Marienfeld rushed to the black pay phone, his pudgy fist full of dimes.

"Look, if you want a copy of the speech," Groder said, "I'm sure I can get you one."

Muttering under his breath, Marienfeld fished around inside his jacket for a moment, then produced an address book. "Hmmmm. Let's see," he grumbled, flipping furiously through the pages. "Ah, here we are. Atomic Energy Commission—Operator! Get me Washington DC!"

"You know, if you're calling the lab, I doubt if anyone's there," Groder said, shuffling over to the phone. "I think Linneman gave 'em the rest of the day off—"

"Shut up!" Marienfeld barked, stuffing dimes into the slot. "And get out! Or I'll have you fired!"

"No more drinks for him, Roy," Groder said, returning to the bar.

And no more waiting, Marienfeld decided, dialing the number. No more waiting for Rhinehart to dissolve himself, no more putting up with the incompetence of *any* of those people over there. He'd show them, hurt them worse than an atomic bomb could. He would *take away their jobs*!

"Atomic Energy Commission." The receptionist's voice.

"Hello!" Marienfeld slurred. "I want to speak with Dr. Trumbo."

"Dr. Trumbo has left for the day."

"Oh, is that right?" Marienfeld growled. "Does *anybody* work in this goddamn organization?"

"Well—"

"You tell Dr. Trumbo that she better get her *big fat ass* to the test site, because it is *out of control*!"

"I'm sorry. I didn't get that—"

"I said it's out of control! Bombs that don't work! And there's naked people running around—*screwing* in balloons—"

"May I say who's calling?"

"Yes!" Marienfeld screamed. "I'm—a—a— *concerned citizen!*"

Then it was over. He had done it and he felt good. Blown the whistle. Thrown the switch. Kicked ass. Soon, the vicious, powerful head of the Atomic Energy Commission would come roaring in and set things straight. Maybe even hand out a few promotions to deserving supervisors. But most importantly, Rhinehart and those other incompetent smartasses over at the lab would be *out in the street*, tin cups in their hands.

He downed his drink in one gulp. There was no cherry.

"Well, Joe, here we are." Hendrix slowed the pickup to a halt and shut off the engine. "Ground zero's up ahead. Better get the mask on."

Joe Bob wiped a trace of perspiration from the corner of his eye, adjusted his respirator and climbed out of the truck. Feeling another drop of sweat form on his forehead, he twisted his neck and wiped his brow against the rough-textured hood of the radiation suit. Ramey hated the suit. It was made from cotton, but had a sealant stuck between the weave that kept any air from getting in. Half a day in a rad suit could make a man a candidate for heat stroke.

As Hendrix unloaded equipment from the back of the truck, Joe Bob paused at the edge of the GZ and looked at the terrain. All around was standard Great Basin geography—flat expanse of alkali surrounded by a gruff array of alluvial fans, ridges, gullies and ravines. While the GZ itself was devoid of vegetation to six or seven hundred yards, the area outside the ring of fire sported a surprising variety of plant life—clumps of yellow wheatgrass interspersed with tall, frothy green stands of greasewood. Farther out, short round balls of creosote bush dotted the hillsides like spots of light green ink amid the darker blotches of the yuccas.

"Hey, see that?" Hendrix stopped and pointed at a small furry object on a nearby hill. "Jackrabbit."

"Wonder if he's radioactive?"

"Well, some of the reptiles around here are." Hendrix handed Joe Bob a field pack. "Deckman killed a sidewinder awhile back up on one of the north targets. Left it lay on a photographic plate for an hour and *damned* if it didn't fog that thing up. I gave the rattles to my oldest girl. She sewed it on her baseball cap. Calls it her lucky charm."

"Don't you think that's a little risky, Don? I mean, after all—givin' your kid a radioactive snake?"

"Oh, the rattles were clear," Hendrix replied. "Most of the pluto-nium was in the fangs."

"Sure hate to get bit by one of *those*," Joe Bob laughed. "Just about ruin your whole day."

"Radioactive venom," Hendrix gave a muffled laugh from behind his mask. "That's really an *awful* insult."

"You just *know* it'd hurt."

"Heck, I bet after something like that, a man would glow all over. His wife could use his wangus for a nightlight."

Joe Bob chuckled as he followed Hendrix into the inner circle of the target. The area was slightly depressed and covered with a crystal froth of green glass over a layer of white ash. At the center, a mound of shattered and fused concrete supported a 12-foot sculpture of melted metal. "Looks like a piece of art, doesn't it?" Hendrix asked.

Probably ought to box it up and send it to Washington," Joe Bob nodded. "Put it out in front of the AEC's office. Maybe in the lobby."

"Looks like my film badge is fogged already," Hendrix said. "What's the meter say?"

"Looks like 600 millirads. Still kinda' hot."

"Let's don't go any farther. We'll come back after it's cooled down some—hey, look at this. Tank treads." Hendrix pointed his glove at a wide set of parallel tracks that meandered in from the northeast, crossed the outer periphery of the central depression and ended up squarely at the base of the demolished tower.

"George told me one of the tanks ended up here. They had to put the crew in the hospital."

"I don't doubt it. But take a look—there's tracks going in, but not back *out*."

"Maybe they backed it up," Ramey shrugged. "I've spent some time in tanks. They all have reverse gear."

"So this guy backed up *exactly* the way he came in, huh? Good trick." Hendrix shook his head. "No, something came in here and *got* that tank. Picked it up, hauled it out of here—and didn't leave a mark. That's really something."

Joe Bob studied the tracks. Hendrix was right.

"Damn military," Hendrix shook his head. "You never know what to expect from 'em. They're not even supposed to be in this area yet, and they come in and get a tank! Well, the GZ is still too hot. Maybe we can take some soil samples next week."

"Yeah." Joe Bob stared at the wide set of tracks ending at the ruined tower. "Next week."

14

The Ground Zero Effect

V incel Puhl squeezed his hand into the jar of Vienna sausages. "We sure appreciate you drivin' us out here to the restaurant this afternoon, Lieutenant Perkins—'specially since your recent experience at ground zero and all."

"Well, the doctor said I was fine," Perkins smiled. "And you *did* pull me out of that trench. So bringing you fellows here is the least I can do."

"I hear stayin' at ground zero makes a man hard as a rock," R.W. Doggett commented under his breath. "In the, uh, *romantic* sense. There any truth to that?"

"You'll have to excuse R.W. here," Vincel smiled apologetically. "He's always interested in anything that will help his chances of a good *presentation*. If you get my drift."

Doggett nodded soberly. "Captain Wanker said that after a man's been to ground zero the women can't stay away from him."

"I really wouldn't know about that," Perkins grinned sheepishly. "It hasn't worked for me."

"See, R.W.," Vincel said, turning to Doggett, "the lieutenant here has been in the hospital for over a week. I mean, he ain't exactly had a chance to, uh, show off any particular talents." Vincel paused, leering across the table at Perkins. "Unless, of course, there was some *nurses* hanging around that infirmary."

"How about it, Lieutenant?" Doggett leaned over the table. "Did bein' at the ground zero help you in the *nurse* department?"

"Nope," Perkins said. "Sorry."

Doggett leaned back against the booth and stared slackjawed. Vincel maintained his position against the table's surface, looking like a fat sea turtle someone had snagged and laid out. "C'mon, Lieutenant," he said, his eyes narrowing to slits, "there's just me and R.W. here. An' we ain't no generals or anything. We're jus' two small town boys. You can tell us."

"Look. Being at ground zero doesn't, uh, *affect* things like that." Perkins felt like he was being cross-examined by a marmot and a weasel.

"I think we better ease off, Vincel," Doggett said. "I bet the lieutenant just ain't tried it out yet."

"Look," Perkins said, nervously stirring his iced tea, "all that stuff's probably just a rumor. The only thing being at ground zero did is give me a touch of the flu."

"Yeah, like Sloan," Doggett said. "Got stuck in a tank at the GZ 'an got hisself exposed again. Had to put him in quarantine."

"I hadn't heard that." Perkins was relieved that the subject had shifted from romance to disease.

"Some say he done it on purpose," Vincel whispered. "To help his chances with the ladies."

"We heard some candystripers got ahold of him the last time he was in—an' he had to escape fer his life." Doggett nodded. "True story."

"It was leave or die," Vincel intoned.

"Hey, look fellas," Perkins said finally, "I really don't think being at ground zero affects a man's, you know—his—"

Vincel turned to Doggett. "R.W., it appears we have yet another officer who feels that information of an important nature is still off-limits to the common enlisted man. I suggest we repair to the *games*."

A minute later, Perkins was left alone in the booth. Watching the burly Vincel slam his hand against the pinball machine, Perkins wondered if he should have taken them out to lunch in the first place. Of course, the Pig 'N Bun couldn't really qualify as a real *restaurant*, but it was the closest thing to it in the general vicinity. And damned if he'd take anyone down to Las Vegas for steaks just for pulling him out of a trench.

Perkins took a drink of the tea and stared across the floor, but the scene that reached his eyes was a thousand miles away. A place of clear skies and warm sunshine on upholstery in the back of his parent's Ford. "Tell me something," she had asked.

"What do you want to be told?" he said, going after her bra.

"Why are you joining the army, Will?" She looked straight into him. "Don't you want to settle down, have kids?"

"Officers can have kids, too," he replied, or something like that. Then she had gone and written him some damn poem about wings across rooftops and the color of the wind. Just the kind of thing a woman does to get you to stay.

"Ain't I anything to you," she had asked, "don't you like me beneath the covers?"

What a question, Perkins thought, looking out onto the dusty street. Of *course* he liked her beneath the covers. Middle of the night with the radio playing Ebb Tide. Rain coming down, her parents on a vacation somewhere in Arkansas, no exams for another week. In the morning— the mornings at home were softer than here—he would wake first and watch the shadows from the venetian blind cross her body, striping it like a zebra.

At boot camp, when everyone sat around telling what they missed about the civilian world—haircuts, parking meters, women taking off their underwear—Perkins told them he missed his freedom. But that wasn't true. What he really missed were the venetian blinds in Amy's bedroom. And the radio playing "Ebb Tide."

"What you two doin' in the coin box?" the tall, angular man behind the counter growled at Vincel and Doggett.

"Sorry, sir. The little door musta' swung open."

"Well, swing the goddamn thing back shut!"

"Yes, certainly. Our apologies."

Perkins stared out the window and looked through the tunnel of the next several years, the next decade—a broad green military haze of canvas and dust and bombs and metal, and people barking orders. No *wonder* she'd left him.

Outside the wind was picking up, sending dust devils of fine white alkali fluttering and spinning down the street. In the distance, the blue-grey peaks shimmered in the midday sun like the landscape of a Bob Steele western.

As Perkins stared morosely out the window, the door clattered open and a small, slim woman came in, her short blonde hair exploding from beneath a red baseball cap. "Lester, fix me up a nice, big ol' milkshake and a cheeseburger. Drag it through the garden. Cheese, mayo and double onions. Extra ketchup. Okay?"

"Sure thing, Bobbie." The counter man disappeared into the back of the kitchen.

"And make that a strawberry milkshake."

"Gotcha," the man called out.

"Use *real* ice cream, Lester," she warned. "I'm no damn tourist. Las' time, you gave me some goo I really couldn't call ice cream. An' I didn't pay for it, did I?"

"No, I don't recall you did."

As Perkins watched, the little blonde hopped atop a barstool and plonked her elbows down on the counter. She was maybe in her late twenties, but Perkins was astonished by how much she reminded him of some of the women back at college—chambray shirt, tied at the waist, Jane Russell style, separated from the baggy rolled-cuff blue jeans by a fraction of an inch of skin. Tennis shoes were missing, though. In their place were two of the scruffiest cowboy boots he had ever seen. Here was a genuine, honest-to-God Nevada cowgirl.

The woman glanced in Perkins's direction. "Won't get no real ice cream here 'less you ask for it."

"Here you are," the counter man said, handing the woman a large waxed paper cup. "That'll be a quarter."

"Here's a dollar, Lester." The blonde scooted the bill across the counter top. "Need some change for the jukebox. Wanna hear Hank sing?"

"Sorry, Bobbie. Had to take him off."

"What! You took off *my Hank Williams*?" the woman asked, eyes wide. "What the hell for?"

"Had to," Lester said. "Playin' that thing three, four times a day, you just wore him out. 'Tween you and Sue Colter, that record looked like somebody took a plow to it. Had to put somethin' else on."

"It better be good," she grumbled, striding over to the cream-colored Wurlitzer. "What the—! *Doggie In The Window*? What the hell kind of song is that? And what's this—*Mambo Italiano*? Where the hell is your *mind* Lester? Where's th' *Tennessee Waltz*? Where's *Cattle Call*? Ya ain't even got anything here by Hank Snow, for cryin' out loud! What the hell kind of a place is this anyways?"

"It's a restaurant," Lester said stubbornly. "With music."

The blonde slapped the side of the jukebox. *"Earth Angel, Cryin' In The Chapel?* What's this place turnin' into? A *church?"*

"It's the latest music and the tourists from California like it," Lester said defiantly, "and they buy a lot of hamburgers and milkshakes."

"This world could use an engine overhaul," Bobbie Jean mumbled, shaking her head at the play list. "Lessee . . . *Hi Lilli-Hi Lo?* Baby talk! Lester got nothin' but foreign crap, church music and baby talk on this thing! I just can-*not* believe a reasonable human bein' would want to listen to baby talk. . Hey you! You like listenin' to crap like this?"

Perkins slowly looked up from his iced tea.

"You listen to baby talk?" she asked, walking over to the booth. "Or you the kind that wants to hear church music?"

"Oh, I sorta' like, uh, Hank Williams . . ."

"Hey! Now, you're talking *real* music," the woman said, extending her hand. "M'name's Bobbie Jean Barnett. I own a flying service over't the airport."

"Will Perkins. I'm stationed at Camp Sagebrush."

"Sagebrush, huh?" The woman slided into the booth across from him. "I'll bet you have somethin' to do with the bomb tests. Right?"

"Yeah." Perkins stirred his iced tea. "Sort of."

"So what you doin' here on a Friday afternoon? Thought you guys worked on weekdays."

"Aw, we maneuvered last night, so today our platoon took a few hours off," Perkins grinned.

"Those two with you?" Bobbie Jean asked, nodding toward the two soldiers rattling the pinball machines.

"I brought 'em over here today, bought 'em lunch. I owed them a favor."

"Must not a been a real *big* favor," Bobbie said, slurping her milkshake.

"It wasn't." Perkins glanced over his shoulder at the pinball machine. To his horror, he saw the enlisted men walking toward the booth, both smiling broadly.

"Well, Lieutenant, we couldn't help but notice you had company," Vincel leered. "Perhaps you would care to introduce the lovely lady to your military colleagues."

"Yeah, you gonna introduce us, Lieutenant?" Doggett asked accusingly. "I mean, you already got the advantage of a—"

"Uh, Miss Barnett," Perkins interrupted hastily, "this is Vincel Puhl and his cousin, Robert Wayne Doggett. They're in training for the Atomic Brigade at Camp Sagebrush."

"Here's to us." R.W. Doggett slid into the booth, his glass of beer raised in a toast. "Most dangerous brigade on the face of the earth."

"That right?" the woman asked. "That's real impressive."

"Yes, ma'am," Doggett said, after finishing his beer. "Out on th' test site we got enough A-bombs on *one train* to blow up, heck, I don't know, *any place.*"

"Uh, by chance did the lieutenant inform you that we saved his life?" Vincel asked, winking at Perkins.

"These guys saved your *life*, Mr. Perkins?" the blonde asked admiringly.

"Wasn't much, ma'am," Vincel said, smoothing back his hair. "The lieutenant just stayed in the trench a little too long. Probably had too many things on his mind—of a *technical* nature, of course."

"Technical?" The blonde looked approvingly at Perkins.

"Well actually," Vincel arched his eyebrows pensively, "that effort was top secret, now that I recall. My apologies for bringing it up, Lieutenant. Little slip of the tongue there."

Doggett shook his head, his long face the picture of seriousness. "To tell the truth, we're not even allowed to *think* about it."

"A terrible responsibility," Vincel sighed.

"Uh, you guys want to play another game of pinball?" Perkins asked finally.

"If it was all the same to you, Lieutenant," Vincel winked broadly, "I'd rather listen to a little music—Hank Williams maybe."

"Th' *Tennessee Waltz* is my favorite," the blonde said. "I could dance all night to that one."

"Yes, a wonderful song," Vincel nodded sadly. "Even if it is about a place I've never cared much for."

"You don't like Tennessee?" Her eyes narrowed.

"The state carries unhappy memories for R.W. and myself," Vincel explained. "The result of a few simple misunderstandings."

"We borrowed a car without the owner's written permission," Doggett nodded at his empty beer glass. "It was a misunderstanding."

"A technicality, actually," Vincel sighed. "They called us an incorrigible burden on the courts." He shook his head. "An embarrassing designation, that. But it did offer us the opportunity of travel."

"The judge told us, it's either jail or the military," Doggett added. "So here we are. In the army, waltzin' around ground zero."

Vincel leaned toward the blonde. "I guess the lieutenant here explained how bein' around ground zero can *affect* a man?"

Perkins quickly reached into his pocket and produced a five dollar bill. "Maybe you guys want to play the pinball machine again . . ."

"Sure Lieutenant," Vincel took the money. "Me an' R.W. can just vanish for awhile. Good luck."

Bobbie watched the two enlisted men walk back to the pinball machine, then turned back to Perkins. "How come he winked at you?"

"He didn't wink, did he?" Perkins shifted in his seat.

"Sure he did." Bobbie knitted her brow. "What's that stuff he was saying about ground zero?"

"Nothing," Perkins shook his head. "It's nothing."

She paused for a moment, then leaned forward over the table. "Ya know, I have this little flyin' service. Tourists come up from Vegas. Want to see a real atomic bomb. Most of the people around here—the ranchers and all—are used to it, but those mushroom clouds still bring in the tourists."

"You actually fly *over* the test site?"

"Sure!" She broke into a huge smile, crinkling up all sorts of little laugh lines around her eyes. "Me an' Albert—that's my airplane—me an' Albert'l take 'em up north 'round Hiko, circle around a little bit, then zip in over the line."

"Cheeseburger's up, Bobbie," Lester yelled.

"Be back in a minute." The blonde got up from her seat and retrieved the cheeseburger from the counter. "Put it on my tab, Lester." As she returned to the table with the cheeseburger, Perkins noticed that she shuffled and wiggled herself around in a little circular motion, polishing the vinyl bench seat. "You want some of this?" she asked.

"Uh, no thanks." Perkins caught himself staring at her shirt.

"Well, suit yourself," she said, taking a bite. "Damn this is good. Sure you don't want some?"

"Now, you said you fly over the test site?" Perkins asked. "Isn't that kind of *illegal*?"

"Not as far as I can tell," the woman shrugged, her soft denim shirt moving like jello. "Anyway, nobody's said anything. I ain't been shot outta the sky or nothin'."

"Huh." Perkins scratched his head. "I always thought it was illegal."

"So you're an atomic soldier, huh?" The woman smiled again. "What exactly do *you* do out there? On the test site, I mean."

"Well," Perkins began, choosing his words carefully, "we perform maneuvers, advance on the enemy position, attack ground zero. Those kinds of things."

Bobbie Jean leaned forward, the front of her shirt pressed against the tabletop. "Lemme get this straight. You go out there and set off the bomb, then you run around attacking things."

"Enemy positions."

"But you just said you attacked ground zero." The woman leaned back. "Look, if I'm getting this wrong, just tell me."

Perkins took a deep breath.

"Ya know," she shook her head, "I've always wondered what the hell goes on out there. Who plays the enemy? You go out to ground zero and choose up sides, like shirts and skins or somethin'?"

"Nobody plays the enemy," Perkins said. "Least as far as I know."

"All right. So you set the bomb off, then run around attacking an enemy that isn't there. What good does *that* do?"

"Look, I don't know," Perkins shot back. "I've only been on a few tests—and besides, you said you fly over the test site all time. You tell *me* what they're doing out there!"

"I don't have the slightest idea." The woman shrugged and took a huge bite of burger. As she did, a fat slice of tomato slid from the sandwich and splattered onto the table, followed by three huge pieces of pickle.

"Come to think of it," Perkins wagged his finger, "I'll bet it *is* illegal to fly over the Nevada Test Site."

"Mnf. Mnf mfn mn," she replied. Despite the growing puddle of food on the table, the blonde still held the collapsing burger at face level.

"You ever been arrested for that?" Perkins leaned forward.

"Nope. I know the general."

"What?"

"I know General Umber. He and my dad were real good friends." The blonde wiped her face with a napkin. "Back before the general got his star, he and Pop were pilots at Indian Springs. I remember when I was in high school old *Hank* would come by for barbecue." She held out the cheeseburger. "Sure you don't want some of this? It's gonna be gone in a minute."

Perkins shook his head. "I didn't know his name was Hank."

"Not many people do," the blonde shrugged.

"And he doesn't care if you, er, take *tourists* over the nuclear test site?"

"Nah. I've seen him lots of times—flyin' in that big Mojave helicopter. He just smiles and waves. Nice as you please. Real friendly." She finished off the cheeseburger. "If you ask me, I think he gets a kick out of it. Heck, *you* must know him. What do *you* think?"

"Actually, I haven't met him yet," Perkins admitted.

"Mebbe if you took a ride over the test site with me," she slurped the last of the milkshake, "you'd get your chance."

"Flying?" Perkins looked up. "In an *airplane*?"

"Not scared, are ya?" She leaned forward.

"Scared?" Perkins tried to smile.

"Scared." She nodded. "I can tell. I been flyin' since I was twelve. I know candy-ass when I see it. I bet you get a nosebleed when you look up."

"What?"

"Bet you get within ten feet of an airplane your knees knock," the woman said. "Bet the dimes rattle in your pockets!"

"Hey!"

"Bet we couldn't get you *inside* a plane, even if it was sittin' on the ground!"

"Look, that's silly." Perkins picked up his glass for a drink. It was empty.

"Thirsty, ain'tcha?" Bobbie grinned. "See? Just *talk* about gettin' off the ground and you get dry as a bone. I seen it before. Thing that tipped me off was the fact you're a ground-pounder."

"What's that got to do with it?"

"Infantry types want to stay as close to the ground as they can. Ground-pounders *like* diggin' trenches an' crawlin' around on their bellies."

"I'm not afraid of flying!" Perkins barked, his face warm. "I've been in a plane before."

"Uh-huh." Bobbie folded her arms and smiled. "Okay then. There's this little grass field just south of Indian Springs. Junction of I-95 and State Road 52. There's an airstream trailer with a Ford parked outside. It's mine. An' here's my phone number," she said, stuffing a piece of paper into his shirt pocket. "Next week some time?"

"I think there's a test scheduled," Perkins stammered, looking at the piece of paper. "Friday. Might have to maneuver."

"Well, after that you can give me a call," she said, getting up from the booth. "That is, if ya don't chicken out."

"Why don't they come over here?" Sloan looked out the hatchway of the tank through the dust cloud at the smoldering metal object, at shapes moving through the haze. "It's been an hour now. Don't they see us?"

"These'll make *great* photos!" The reporter edged past Sloan, then squeezed off shots into the murk. "It's just so damn dark. Wish I'd brought more flashbulbs."

That had gotten their attention. A few minutes later, white-suited men wearing respirators were banging on the lid of the disabled tank, dragging them out through the hatchway one by one. "What the hell are you doing here?" one had asked in a hard voice. "Where did that light come from?"

The scene shifted sideways and Sloan remembered the trip back to the camp—riding in the dark room, feeling as though someone had tightened a metal band around his waist. They seemed to hit every bump.

Thinking back, he remembered the chaos—Sgt. Romero, the tank commander, curled into a tight ball, the reporter scurrying around the corrugated metal floor, then falling over like a rag doll. The driver, the gunner.

Sloan opened his eyes, and the blurry, bare walls of the hospital room slowly came into focus. Flexing his right arm slightly, he felt the sharp pain of the needle. Darn it, he thought, they have an IV in both arms. Can't write to Cathy. Well, she would never believe it anyway.

Closing his eyes, he imagined a conversation sometime in the distant future, perhaps to his youngest: "You're too sick to go to school? Ha. You don't look sick to me. Your dad was sick one time. *Really* sick. They had him in the hospital, blood and things going into *both* arms." Along with the images of his future son, Sloan saw the upstairs room, the four-poster bed, the quilt his mother had tried to give him when he left for the army. "They won't let me keep this stuff, Ma. They'll give it away."

"Fort Lewis is cold in the winter," she'd said, looking up at him with that worried expression. "And what if they send you to Korea or somewhere. I heard they sleep on the bare ground there, with stones as their pillows—"

"I'll be all right. Besides, the Korean war's over."

"Here, Cathy," he heard his mother's voice, "this was his quilt when he was a boy. He'd have wanted you to have it."

"Er, excuse me? Mister Sloan?"

Sloan opened his eyes. The tall, scraggly-looking man was in the room. The fellow with the British accent.

"I happened to by strolling by," the man smiled, "and I saw that your door was ajar. I trust you're on the mend—"

"I think I'm the same," Sloan croaked. "Feels like I've swallowed broken glass."

"Oh, yes," the man nodded. "I suppose it does."

"How long does this last?" Sloan asked. "How long am I supposed to stay here?"

The man looked perplexed. "Oh, I'm afraid I couldn't answer *that.*"

"Thought you said you were God," Sloan smiled.

"I must say I'm somewhat new to the business." The man shook his head sorrowfully. "Very much like being required to captain a ship, when all you know how to do is, well, *mop the galley.*"

As silly as the conversation was, Sloan got a kick out of talking with the old guy. He never knew what kind of answers he'd get.

"Did you sleep well?" the man asked, after a pause.

"My dreams are getting longer," Sloan replied.

"Oh, yes," the man nodded. "I suppose they will, I'm sorry to say."

"That's okay," Sloan said. "Don't have to put up with all these aching bones and this sore throat. Wish they'd have given me a different room. I always get the same one."

The man looked around. "Yes, it *is* somewhat drab."

Sloan smiled. Years before, attending catechism classes, he and his friends had pored over the same old questions. For example, the question about the Holy Trinity—how could God be three people all at the same time? That was a tough one. "You know," he croaked, looking at the man in his room. "I have this question for you."

"Certainly."

"What's going on out there?" Sloan asked. "And why do I always end up here—no matter what I do, I seem to end up here—"

The man nodded. "That seems to be the case, doesn't it?"

"But why?" Sloan asked.

"It's the way our part of the world is, right now." The man reached up and tapped the wall. "Suppose there is a bubble of air under the wallpaper here."

"Okay," Sloan nodded sleepily. In his mind he pictured the wallpaper in his room at home—blue with a pattern of tiny white dots forming a soft gridwork from side to side. "I can see it."

"Now, suppose I were to give it a gentle push." The man paused. In his mind, Sloan could almost see the bubble move. "Same pocket of air, you see? Now, if one were to *strike* the air pocket—" the man gave the wall a sharp rap, "one would have an abundance of smaller bubbles, broken away from the larger one. Islands, really."

Sloan watched the bubbles retreat from the center of the wall, like mercury on a tile floor. He closed his eyes and the image faded, then reappeared. As though in slow motion, he saw the man strike the wall again, this time in the center of the largest bubble, tearing an ugly gash in the wall, ripping it from top to bottom. Then the gash became a line, like a string of freight cars, then a fissure in the ground—a trench, with lightning crackling from wall to wall. Looking up, Sloan saw the huge cloud, a roaring gray cylinder, roll over their position. Walking through the dust storm toward the center of the target, he looked in amazement at the small thunderheads roaring past his boots, tiny anviltops no more than a foot high flowing along the ground away from the mushroom. Cathy, he thought, you'd never believe this.

And, just as before, the film caught in the sprockets, the scene turned dark and burned away. Okay, he thought, looking at the screen. I want to see Cathy now. And our kids someday.

Instead, he got that autumn day when he was ten. Bright blue and lonesome as a block of eternity, that day flattened out the universe and placed it folded on the grass, brought the austerity down from the sky and set it on the ground before him. Looking up, he watched the clouds racing west, high and cold. Shivering inside his dream, he wondered: Is this the one? Or am I going to wake up again? And where is God?

"Are you still in pain, Corporal?" It was Dr. Bartholomew, peering over the bed, his thin mustache the only thing in focus. "Last night we increased your medication. You're coming along quite well."

"Where's the man who was here? I want to ask him something."

"Have you talked to anyone?"

"He was right there."

"Nurse, this man is to have no visitors. Post a guard."

Sloan noticed there were two people in the room, both dressed in white—with darker forms milling around just outside the door. Waiting.

"Do you recall anything else about what you saw out there?" Bartholomew asked. "Did you tell anyone about our little agreement?"

"There were clouds everywhere," Sloan said.

Dr. Bartholomew backed away from the bed. "Nurse, discontinue the sedatives to this patient. Be prepared to move him to isolation."

"Uh, Doctor," Sloan croaked, "I'm real sorry about the wall."

"Excuse me?"

"I'm sorry about the wall. It was an accident. He tore a hole in it but he didn't mean to."

"Yes." Bartholomew turned back to the nurse. "Keep an eye on him. If there's any change in his condition, notify me immediately."

With a supreme effort, Sloan raised up in bed, paused for a moment on the edge of the room, then fell back into the tunnel of his dream.

15

Chrome

"Emil, we're in a real pickle barrel." Uborka stared at the blank paper before him. "No bomb design and only one day to go."

"I still think we should pack in the lithium fusion fuel," Meghalty said, slapping the desk. "Make our very first project thermonuclear! Who would know?"

"Who would know?" Uborka looked up, his eyes wide. "Everyone would know! H-bombs *look* different! They make a bigger clouds, they make a bigger holes in the ground! Nooo! If we added lithium deuteride to our bomb, Dr. Linneman would kill us!"

"They want us to make a bomb, but they don't want it to *do* anything!" Meghalty folded his arms stubbornly. "Twenty or thirty kilotons. Ha! A little cloud that goes up a few thousand feet and then blows away with the breeze. I vote to add the lithium."

Uborka shook his head. "If we put it in, someone will see it. All you have to do is open the lid and there it is. They would say—'Emil, Eduard come here. What is this? Lithium deuteride? This isn't supposed to be an H-bomb.' Then what would we say?"

"They don't have to find it!" Meghalty brightened. "We can sneak it in. Just a few thousand grams of lithium would make our bomb bigger than any of those pipsqueaks Los Alamos sends us. We design little nooks where we can squeeze in the lithium and no one would be the wiser!"

Uborka produced a pencil from his pocket. "Then here. Draw our bomb for me—and don't forget the nooks."

"I can't draw anything." Meghalty handed the pencil back. "*You* draw it."

"It's *your* idea!" Uborka threw the pencil on the table. "How can I design nooks when I don't even know what you're thinking!"

"Maybe I should get someone else to help me with this," Meghalty sniffed, "someone who isn't a big sissy about H-bombs. You're too afraid of excitement, Eduard."

"I'm not afraid of excitement," Uborka replied, looking hurt. "I just don't think we can sneak it in. If Joe Bop Ramey inspects it, he'll find it in a minute. He looks at everything!"

"We have to think of something." Meghalty tapped the table. "George Linneman wants to see our finished design tomorrow—"

"Why don't we get someone to help us with it?" Uborka suggested.

"Who?" Meghalty snapped. "Joe Bob Ramey won't let us put in the lithium—and Arthur Flagmeyer is always afraid of getting into trouble—"

"I know just the person," Uborka said, picking up the phone. "Someone who isn't afraid of *anything*."

Rhinehart leaned back in the chair and lighted his cigar. "So why are you two asking me?"

"You are a very creative person, Rhinehart," Uborka smiled.

"True." Rhinehart blew a stream of smoke into the air. "After all, I created you two guys."

"He's crazy, Eduard," Meghalty grumbled. "Maybe we should do it ourselves."

"The first problem I see with your design," Rhinehart said, tapping the blank sheet of paper, "is that it lacks *flair*. You bring this in to George tomorrow and he'll hand the project over to somebody else."

"Okay, then." Meghalty handed Rhinehart the pencil. "What do you suggest?"

Rhinehart took the pencil and quickly sketched a cylinder with fins. "First off, this is what you *don't* want. Your standard iron bomb certainly isn't going to get anyone's attention. George Linneman might like it, but the American public will *yawn*." Rhinehart wadded the paper and threw it into the waste can. "Now, if you *really* want to score some points, you need a bomb that is more acceptable. Friendly."

"Friendly?" Uborka asked, a blank look on his face.

"Friendly," Rhinehart repeated, quickly sketching a design on the paper. "We could stick some padding here, put on some fins up *here*— and if we wanted to, even paint some eyes on it."

"It looks like a teddy bear," Meghalty said sourly.

"Exactly," Rhinehart nodded. "A round bomb could hold the plutonium in a spherical configuration. The ears would double as tail fins and the arms could conceal the radar antennae.

"I don't think we should have a bear." Uborka clouded over. "A bear sitting on a tower waiting to explode—it doesn't look right."

"How about a bunny?" Meghalty suggested. "There's this bunny, see. . .! Bunny and Fudd! They had a—"

"Okay. No bears. No rabbits." Rhinehart wadded up the paper. "Public would never go for it. They want something friendly, yet powerful. Maybe with a lot of *chrome*."

"A bunny with chrome?" Uborka asked.

"We could throw in some stabilizer fins with chrome accents," Rhinehart said, sketching a new design. "Attractive and rust-resistant. Here we can throw in some forward fins with lights on the end—"

"Lights?"

"If the bomb is dropped from a plane, you'll want to see it fall, won't you?" Rhinehart took a puff from his cigar. "A few bumper pads, an air intake grille and ribbed canvas over the instrument panel will add a *graceful* look that will beat the bulging smugness of the earlier models."

Meghalty stared at the paper.

"And last but not least," Rhinehart said, finishing off the drawing, "a single high-intensity lamp in the nose will direct the bomb toward its destination—creating a circle of light at ground zero that grows smaller and brighter until detonation. Gentlemen, my only condescension to the purely aesthetic."

"It—it—," Uborka stared at the design, "it's a *car*!"

"Not just *any* car," Rhinehart smiled. "You're looking at a 1953 Cadillac Eldorado convertible."

"But where will we put the plutonium?" Uborka asked.

"Anywhere you want," Rhinehart shrugged. "Those caddies have plenty of room in the trunk."

"Linneman will *hate* it!" Meghalty said.

"But the public will love it," Rhinehart replied. "And if the University of California won't build it for you," he said, getting up from the table, "you can always call Detroit. Or go to a junkyard."

"I don't know," Meghalty whined, looking worriedly at the sketch. "What if we get fired?"

"Forget it!" Rhinehart said, walking toward the door. "This is a *great* idea—those guys at Los Alamos will be green with envy. The public will love it and Linneman will love you guys for it. Trust me."

———※———

Linneman slowly rose from behind his desk. "You have designed a *what?*"

"A Cadillac," Uborka smiled weakly.

"Convertible," Meghalty added, wiping perspiration from his brow. "Do you like it?"

"I ask you to design a nuclear weapon and you give me a—a— *luxury automobile*." Linneman looked bewildered. "I don't believe this."

"I kind of like it." Flagmeyer studied the drawing. "Especially the nose light."

"What color you plan to paint it, Ed?" Joe Bob Ramey asked.

"Tan, with maroon accents," Uborka replied. "It would match the whitewalls."

"This is ridiculous—ridiculous!" Linneman stormed. "They want us to make a bomb and we give them *this*! Demming will fire us all!"

"I dunno, George," Ramey said. "You gotta admit it's different. Probably catch the public's attention."

"That's right," Hendrix nodded, lighting his pipe. "Demming is real sensitive about the public mood lately. This design might be just the thing. Besides, with those wheels, you can roll it right out of the bomb bay."

"Demming will fire us." Linneman sank back into his chair.

Hendrix got up. "I have to get back to the Control Point, but if I were you, George, I wouldn't worry about it too much. Compared to

Stan Marienfeld's latest idea, it's not bad at all.

"*What* idea?" Linneman looked up.

"Didn't you know? Marienfeld wants Demming to authorize public tours of Doom Town."

"Public tours of Doom Town?" Linneman asked, a blank look on his face.

"Yep." Hendrix smiled at Linneman. "With Rhinehart as the tour guide."

"He's right," Ramey said as Hendrix walked out the door. "The car bomb *is* a better idea."

⚒

"Good afternoon, Donna," Linneman smiled as he peeked into the waiting room. "Is Dr. Demming in?"

"Have a seat, George," the receptionist said in a flat voice. "He's expecting you."

"Er, I didn't see you here the last time."

"Nope." The woman flipped through the pages of a photo magazine.

"I heard Dr. Demming was considering, uh, *tours* to Doom Town . . . before they blow it up, that is. Er, did you ever wonder what it's like out there?"

"Nope."

"They're going to blow it up in a few weeks," Linneman continued. "Might be sooner than that. Won't be there after a few weeks."

"Good riddance." The woman turned another page.

"Donna," the intercom squawked, "send in Dr. Linneman."

For the next twenty minutes, Linneman watched Demming silently study the schematic of the car bomb. The only sounds in the office were the occasional crisp snap of the huge sheet of paper, mixed with the whirring of the air conditioner and Demming's dyspeptic rumblings. Linneman watched Demming's complexion change from a perplexed white to a flushed pink. Finally, he looked up.

"This is very nice."

"Very *nice*?" Linneman gulped.

"It is a very interesting design. Very modern," Demming nodded. "But it had better work. Senator Curry will be here, the press will be here. I understand Dr. Trumbo may even show up. Do you think it will work?"

"Yes, yes. Oh, absolutely," Linneman said quickly. "No question about it."

"Nice big fireball, eh?" Demming narrowed his eyes. "The public likes big fireballs. Mushroom clouds that *soar* up into the air. Think your little bomb can do that?"

"Of course," Linneman smiled. "There's plenty of room for plutonium in it. Plenty of space under the hood. Right behind the grille—"

"Behind the grille?" Demming asked suspiciously. "What do you mean *behind the grille*?"

"It's a—er—figure of speech. The *bomb* there is perfectly capable of—er—blowing up. The uh, *nuclear weapon* will work fine."

"Fine, George. See that it does." Demming relaxed his brow. "I suppose you've heard of Stan Marienfeld's little proposal—the Doom Town tour?"

"Uh, yes." Linneman hastily stuffed the schematic for the car bomb back into his briefcase.

"As you know, we've had some problems with community relations." Demming tapped his pencil on the desk. "Stanley thought we might open part of the test site specifically for a tour of Doom Town."

"Open to the public?" Linneman asked.

"No, no," Demming chuckled, "not the public. To people of substance and *influence*. Congressmen, businessmen, that sort of thing. We can give them tours of the targets." Demming steepled his fingers. "Show them the craters. Let them take home souvenirs from ground zero. In fact, Stanley even suggested we open up a gift shop. Great way to clean up the targets *and* turn a tidy profit."

"But that stuff is radioactive—isn't that dangerous?"

"Of course it is," Demming said. "But that's not the point. The point is, we want to improve our standing with the people who count. If the press and the politicians ever changed their attitudes about atomic testing—well, we'd be out of our jobs. Do you want that?"

"No, of course not." Linneman shook his head. "But I heard Dr. Marienfeld suggested Carl Rhinehart as a tour guide."

"Heh, heh," Demming chuckled. "That was one of his *many* suggestions for Dr. Rhinehart. Actually, I think that old train engineer would be better suited for the position. What's his name? Pliney?"

"Yes, I think so . . ."

"Yes," Demming smiled, "I think he would do just fine. Of course, if we use the Atomic Express as a target, he'll be out of a job anyway. He *does* know how to drive a bus, doesn't he?"

"I suppose," Linneman nodded.

Demming stood up, a huge smile across his face. "Well, if he doesn't, he'd certainly better learn."

16

Portal

"Anybody home?" Joe Bob knocked on the office door, then peeked inside.

"Sure, come on in." Don Hendrix was scribbling furiously in a notebook. "Coffee's on the hot plate. I'll be with you in a minute."

Joe Bob retrieved a cup from the file cabinet. "What did you think of Uborka's car bomb?"

"Classic American design," Hendrix chuckled, peering at his slide rule. "I'm surprised two guys from Budapest, Hungary came up with it."

"Yeah, well, I think I saw another influence," Ramey laughed.

"Like Carl Rhinehart, maybe?" Hendrix smiled, jotting down numbers. "One of these days Carl is gonna give ol' George Linneman his tenth nervous breakdown—if Demming doesn't do it first."

"Yeah," Ramey nodded, "since Wiggers's little accident, he's been sorta' on the edge—say, whatcha workin' on?"

"What does it look like?" Hendrix adjusted his slide rule. "We have another military test scheduled Friday. Thirty kilotons."

"That right?" Joe Bob set his coffee cup on the desk. "Nobody told me."

"It's an unannounced test. Demming didn't want the press to know until the last minute. You'll probably hear about it tomorrow morning." Hendrix placed the slide rule on the table and reached for his coffee cup.

"Demming." Joe Bob shook his head. "My daddy always said all the federal government amounted to was secret deals among sonsabitches in high places."

"Your daddy was a smart man."

"I think I'm gonna quit and be a sheep farmer," Joe Bob sighed.

"Not anytime soon, I hope," Hendrix said. "Your name's down for the bomb inspection on the next three shots."

"Yeah?" Joe Bob squinted at the memo. "What ornery sumbitch did that?"

"You're looking at him," Hendrix shrugged. "I don't trust anybody else. Especially with that goofy car bomb thing that Meghalty and Uborka are putting together."

Joe Bob took a drink of coffee. "Aw, I don't think they're gonna have any trouble. It'll work."

"Oh, I'm *sure* it'll work," Hendrix said. "I'm just afraid it'll work *too well*."

"Afraid they'll try to sneak in some lithium?" Ramey grinned. "Worried we'll have a *thermonuclear detonation* out there on the test site?"

"Laugh if you want to, but I know 'em. Uborka likes H-bombs and they don't call Emil 'Megaton Meghalty' for nothing."

"Nervous about the thing goin' *big*, huh?" Ramey chuckled. "Afraid that lithium'll catch the air on fire and embarrass everybody? Heck, Don, if that thing Elmore Wiggers made didn't blow everybody up, nothin' will."

"They'll sneak lithium deuteride in that thing, I guarantee it," Hendrix said.

"I'll watch for it," Joe Bob said, getting up from his chair. "Hell, even if they *did* add a little lithium—it'd just make a bigger bomb—it's not like it's gonna cause any major damage or anything." Ramey shook his head. "Sounds like you been listenin' to Dr. Jeff or somethin'—or mebbe Elmore."

Hendrix looked up from his desk. "Don't forget, Joe. Elmore doesn't work here anymore."

"Loper Infirmary." The voice on the phone was crisp, efficient.

"Good afternoon. This is Captain Jake Stein. I'd like to speak to a Corporal Andy Sloan. He's a patient there and—"

"Which ward, sir?"

"I don't know. I was told he was injured in a tank accident and was sent to the infirmary. He's in training for the Atomic Brigade."

"I have to know the ward number before I can transfer you, sir."

"Well, he was in one time before." Stein paused. "I think it was ward 10. Could you check to see if—"

"There is no record of a Corporal Sloan in ward 10."

"Well, he was there just a week ago!" Stein snapped. "He's in my training company, and I want to know how he is!"

"We can't give that information out without his doctor's orders."

"Who is his doctor?"

"I'm sorry. We can't give out that information."

Stein slammed the phone onto the hook. Then, after a moment, he took a deep breath, picked up the receiver and dialed another number.

"Jupiter Weapons Laboratory."

"I'd like to speak to Dr. Joe Ramey."

"He isn't in right now, can you leave a message?"

"No," Stein paused. "I'll call some other time."

From the green haze of a troubled dream, Sloan opened his eyes. Bright lights had suddenly replaced the smoking metal of his nightmare. He was out of the tank and back in the hospital again. Listening to the hum of the air conditioner he closed his eyes and tried for a more peaceful dream. He felt the huge dark sheets of sleep begin to rumble through his brain, black clouds moving across a twilight land. The outside sounds dissolved as Sloan settled in to watch the show.

First came the images of his girlfriend back home in Seattle—Cathy with her ice-cream cones and impossible demands . . . blond-haired kids with big soft eyes, playing with their store-bought balloons. Hot chocolate mornings with nothing to do but watch the frost melt from the rooftops, squeezed inside an apartment with the hot showers and brick walls. A good, solid place and time. He'd have to visit more often—

"Get your coat, boy, you're going home."

"Good idea," Sloan said, dropping from the envelope of his dream. But instead of touching down on the cot inside his familiar barracks, he felt the screen stretch like a film of saran, then separate, depositing him in the hard, sterile room of the quarantine ward. A dream within a dream.

"If you want to go home, you better get awake. Train's leavin' any minute."

Sloan opened his eyes and looked across the white, blurry room to a smiling, red-headed figure crouched at the door. "Remember me? Hugh Duffel," the man said genially, throwing his raincoat onto the chair. "I was in the tank with you."

"Huh?" Sloan tried to focus his eyes.

"Where's your suitcase? You have a suitcase?"

"In the closet," Sloan mumbled.

The man opened the door and removed the canvas bag. "Wow, they sure don't let you keep much, do they? Of course, there's no place to go. Except the mess hall, I guess."

Sloan waited patiently for the blur to clear up. Instead, it was joined by a headache and a dull ache in his muscles.

"I've always wondered," Duffel pitched the canvas bag onto the bed, "in an army hospital, do they call where you eat a mess hall or a cafeteria?"

Sloan sat up in bed and rubbed his eyes. "Mess hall. But I've never been down there."

"Mess hall," Duffel nodded solemnly, stuffing clothes into the bag. "Then this place is run by Army doctors. Civilians would call it a cafeteria—I can never get this army stuff straight. How do you feel?"

"The doctor said I have a low-grade blood count."

"Low-grade, huh?" Duffel took Sloan's neatly pressed dress-green army jacket, balled it up and stuffed it into the bag. "I always get a kick out of medical talk. Low-grade headache, low-grade fever, low-grade everything. You gonna get dressed?"

"What for?" Sloan asked.

"Like I said, you're going home—well, back to the barracks."

"Doctor Bartholomew said he was gonna send me to the quarantine ward," Sloan explained. "Did he change his mind?"

"You said it. The doctor changed his mind." Without looking,

Duffel tossed a set of fatigues on the pillow. "No quarantine, no sick list. You're free to go. Hurry and put these on."

Sloan slowly slid his feet to the floor. Despite the heat in the room, the tile surface seemed surprisingly cold. He felt the chill percolate through his body like ice water through a sponge.

"You know, I was real impressed with how you did up there in that tank," Duffel said, helping him on with his shirt. "Calm as a block of granite. Sorry about the little business with the directions. Can you see well enough to walk?"

"I guess," Sloan said.

"You're lucky," Duffel said, retrieving combat boots from the closet. "The rest of the tank crew is in quarantine."

"They are?" Sloan asked.

"That's right," Duffel nodded. "The sergeant, the driver, the reporter—what's his name—*Batman*?"

"I don't remember."

"Yeah, he's feeling better, but they won't let him out unless he promises not to squeal about the goofup. Here, put these boots on. I couldn't find your socks—what's wrong?"

"Me leaving the hospital like this . . . is it all right with Captain Stein?" Sloan pulled on the boots.

"Who?" Duffel turned. "Stein? Sure. Me and him are old pals. Go way back. He's gonna let you be my assistant for a while. I'm gonna make you a *cinematographer*. Whattaya think about that?"

"Sure, that's fine with me. I guess." Leaving the room, Sloan followed Duffel into the dim, empty corridor.

Art Flagmeyer slumped into his small den of an office, closed the door and sulked. Eduard and Emil were good scientists. Reputable, sensible scientists. Nothing like Rhinehart, but certainly more creative than, say Joe Bob Ramey. And here they come up with the Laboratory's first bomb design and it was a *Cadillac*. How could they do it? Whatever happened to *tradition*?

Flagmeyer looked at his wall chart, a picture of the inner workings of the standard iron bomb. He knew the device as well as he knew Newton's *Principia*. Its territory was as beautifully structured as Ovid's *Metamorphosis*. Practical, clean and perfect. More than anything else, the bomb was a machine. And it should *look* like a machine. Not the reflection of some designer's aesthetic, but a practical device with countersunk screws and a smooth metal surface. Had *he* designed the bomb, it would be *real*. The nose would come to a simple point. At the rear, dark, flat fins would erupt from the skin—fins to direct the device on a path straight and true toward the target. Five hundred pounds of iron, copper, beryllium and plutonium, obeying the laws of Newton.

Structure. Structure was everything. The practical was the asthetic. Yet he knew that at the instant of detonation, things change. Mass and weight and iron become a spinning vortex of pure radiant energy so strong it can bore holes in the very fabric of space—a spinning, violent artifact set up by the detonation and shielded by the light from the disintegrating bomb. A door in a heretofore impenetrable wall, for one split-second, open. Then closed again. In an instant, space becomes flat once more and the machine is gone, become light.

One of the original scientists at the laboratory, Elmore Wiggers, had made a study of it—the energy and structure of space at the exact point and time of detonation. Wiggers was the most respected of Camp Jupiter's weapons men. He was concerned not only with the proper placement of the various gadgets inside the bombs, he was also mindful of the little quirks in quantum theory that the devices might put to the test.

Flagmeyer opened his desk drawer and extracted a faded notebook. Inside were his notes from Wiggers' final staff meeting. He remembered it perfectly. A Monday, 9:00 AM. Outside, a thunderstorm pelted the tin roof of the auditorium as the bespeckled, balding scientist stepped to the blackboard. "If space itself is gaining energy from the nuclear detonation—and this looks to be the case—then perhaps we may be inadvertently changing some very basic quantum structures. It's a finding that is both exciting and troubling." In that lecture, Wiggers had invoked disturbing images of real objects—cars, houses, people— behaving as quantum particles, appearing and disappearing as foam on the surface of a storm-tossed sea.

Later, in the hallway, Flagmeyer had his last coversation with Wiggers, had listened dumbstruck as the somber little scientist talked of "a lonely island of reality in the ocean of the universe—irretrievable, perhaps, even by God." Early the next morning, Wiggers loaded a small atomic device in the back of his pickup truck and drove to the test site. The detonation happened just before sunrise.

Somewhere out there on the desert, a door had opened briefly, then closed.

Each scientist at the lab took Wiggers' death differently. His colleague, Dr. Jeffrey Christopher, quit briefly, went to Las Vegas, had a nervous breakdown, then found religion. Meghalty and Uborka took off a week, while Ramey responded by covering himself up with work. And Rhinehart continued being Rhinehart.

Flagmeyer responded to Wigger's suicide with an almost continual reevaluation of his place at the test site. Of his place in the universe. Certainly the bombs he worked with were *capable* of twisting and wrenching the weave of spacetime, but to actually cause the fabric to unravel? No. Not in the real world.

Yet in his dreams, it happened all the time. And in the early hours before dawn, alone in his mind, he even watched it occur: deep inside the bomb, electrical circuits would close and a portal would appear—a frayed hole in space ringed by an intense binding energy. He had even been there, to the other side of the portal. And instead of the grotesque geometry of another dimension, it was always a place of soft blue skies over warm Iowa countryside, all rolling hills, farms and trees. In the distance there was a small town, with churches, old brick buildings, wooden frame houses and clothes on the line.

And there were sounds—the rustling of trees in the wind mixed with the distant calling of a mourning dove. In his dreams of the other side, something always dropped from the sky, a black teardrop shape turning end-over-end as it fell to earth. As it reached the ground, it dissolved into something else—a bird, a cloud, even a balloon—floating harmlessly above the fields. In his dream the object would be small enough to hold in his hand, yet large enough to fill the sky.

In the beginning, Flagmeyer had feared the atomic devices. But after Wiggers' death, he came to fear only the fiery threshold itself. He believed the machines he inspected simply dropped through portals of their own creation, then transformed themselves into simple things in complete harmony with the landscape. Wherever that might be.

Flagmeyer glanced up at his bulletin board. His first day on the job he had written a poem and placed it there: "To unleash the fire, to open the door—regardless of where it might lead," he said softly to himself, "or to what subtle responsibilities that might accrue."

Then he noticed that someone else had added, in tight precise script, "Where's now the great prognostic of the mind, shall from this science extrication find?" Flagmeyer felt a chill course through his body. Perhaps someone had set the thermostat too low.

17

Ethel's

his place would make a great backdrop for the *Big Picture*," Hugh
Duffel said, scanning the white expanse of desert. "You ever watch
television on Saturday afternoons, Stein?"

Stein shook his head and steered the jeep between a pair of charred
cactus. Ahead of them, a dust devil snaked briefly across their path, then
vanished.

"Yeah, you don't know what you're missing. It's the best thing on
television. My idea, did you know that?"

"I didn't know that."

"Yeah," Duffel continued, "movie screen. Anyway, I'm convinced
the public would love to see more of the bomb. Fireballs. Mushrooms.
Houses getting blown up. You ever seen Doom Town, Stein?"

"I've driven past it," Stein said, wiping his wireframe aviator's
glasses on the front of his shirt.

"How many houses they have out there? Sixteen? And a main
street!" Duffel shook his head. "Now that's something the public wants
to see! Main street going up in a ball of fire! Cars flying through the
air! Woah!"

"I doubt if they'd let you show that," Stein replied.

"Sure they would!" Duffel nodded vigorously, the sun's reflection flashing against his glasses in tiny explosions. "The public loves to see stuff like that! And how about that train! The public is *crazy* about trains."

Stein stepped on the gas and the jeep accelerated across the flat expanse of desert toward a wisp of black smoke. A few minutes later, a dark line on the ground came into view, a thin ripple on the surface of the desert. As Stein slowed the jeep, they passed a small field of pipe, all leaning in unison away from the center of the circle. The radiation meter on the floor of the jeep remained quiet, the needle resting against the left peg.

"Place looks real familiar," Duffel said. "Of course, it's been a few days since I was here. Never could figure out how they got us out of that tank."

"I was just going to ask you that," Stein said, staring at the twisted black structure in the distance. Gray smoke emanated from the object, softly ascended then disappeared in the blue haze of the morning sky.

"Really beautiful on the desert." Duffel cracked his knuckles noisily. "I love this place. It's like a second home to me."

"The desert?" Stein parked the jeep at the edge of the crater, reached down and retrieved the radiation meter from the floorboard. Strange. Even at the edge of the bomb crater, there seemed to be no radiation.

"I remember riding along in that tank," Duffel said, shaking his head, "I was thinking about what a great shot it would make and—well, the driver made a little *turn*—guess he went right over this ridge—then we hit that thing out there. Ha! Here I thought it would be some boring ride in a tank and we ended up at ground zero. You could have knocked me over with a feather."

"I would imagine." Stein climbed out of the jeep and looked at the radiation meter again. The needle remained at zero. "I want you to tell me what took place in that tank. How did they manage to end up out here?"

"Well, hey, why ask me?" Duffel asked, a hurt expression on his face. "Wasn't someone from your company in the tank? Corporal Sloan, right? Ask *him*."

"He says he doesn't remember anything." Stein examined Duffel's face closely. "I thought if you came out here, you might be able to tell me what happened."

"Well, all I know is there we were at ground zero. Happened real fast. Then I end up in this white room with people staring down my throat. Ha! What's that meter say, anyway?"

Stein removed his sunglasses and looked closely at the instrument. The needle remained firmly over the zero mark.

"No reading, huh?" Duffel said. "Clean as a Swiss hotel. Don't even need a mask out here. What say we go to ground zero—to see where that smoke is coming from?"

"It's off-limits," Stein replied. "Are you sure you don't know what happened? Somebody read the map wrong, maybe?"

"Wish I could help," Duffel said. "And believe me, I know exactly how you feel, Stein. You probably feel responsible for what happened. Yeah, it's tough. Especially when there's not much you can do about it." Duffel paused, as if deep in thought. "You know, Stein, I *can* keep some of your men out of trouble for awhile. Until they get the hang of this place."

"Oh?"

"Sure!" Duffel nodded. "Assign them to me on temporary duty. They can be my assistants. Interviews, holding the camera. Real safe."

"You sure?"

"Hey, Stein!" Duffel clapped him on the shoulder. "Right now, I have room for just one—Corporal Sloan. And the offer expires in one minute."

Stein paused. "Okay. Just be careful. He's going home in six months and I don't want him in any more tests. Understand?"

Duffel broke into a broad smile. "Don't you trust me, Stein? I'll be right there with him. Anything happens, it'll happen to me too. I know what I'm doing."

"Okay. As of today, he's all yours." Stein climbed into the seat and turned the ignition. As the jeep left zero area, the needle of the radiation monitor slowly, silently arced across to the right side of the scale.

———

Robert Wayne Doggett stared at his beer. Foam had run down the side of the glass, forming a small wet spot on the wooden bar. He lit his last cigarette and deposited the match in a mushroom-shaped ashtray marked ETHELS. "This place is gettin' on my nerves," he growled.

"You don't like my bar?" Roy glared from behind the counter.

"Nah, Roy, it ain't your bar—" Doggett began. "Your bar's real nice. It's just all the other stuff."

"Try to be more specific, R.W.," McCorkle leaned toward him. "Is it the dearth of basic facilities, the complete lack of real culture? Do you miss the ballet?"

"The ballet?" Doggett looked up from his beer. "Yeah, I sure do."

"Nearest reputable opera company is 400 miles away," Vincel Puhl nodded.

"I guess the thing that really bothers me is havin' to run around in the desert with all that gravel and stuff comin' down around my ears."

"The fallout *is* a disadvantage," Vincel agreed. "You just never know where it'll turn up."

"I don't like havin' to go out there with everything I own on my back." Doggett slowly spun around on the bar stool to stare at the desert. "I gotta carry my rain poncho, tarp, tent and candy bars—just so we can walk around in the desert. Under a damned old *cloud*."

"I never could figure out the candy bars." McCorkle shook his head. "They always melt inside the field pack."

"I hate it when the trench caves in," Wobey said. "You have to climb out of the hole with the fireball still sitting on the tower."

"Well, I don't like hiding in the trenches *at all*," McCorkle said. "It's demeaning for *anyone* to have to burrow in the ground."

"Beats having to stare down the fireball," Wobey said.

"I remember this movie once," Roy said, removing the empty glasses from the table. "There was this prospector who got caught at the test site. The fireball turned him into a hundred-foot tall *atomic brain*— looked like some kind of big, glowing beet. Kind of *scooted* out across the desert—ran over a police car. Burned some houses. Real interestin' movie."

"I guess you know," Vincel said, "that bein' exposed to the atomic bomb has its advantages. Just after Lieutenant Perkins got lost at ground zero he met up with a cute little blonde. She just walked over to him and started up a conversation."

"We saw it happen—an' she wasn't even wearin' any *you know*—" Doggett slapped the front of his shirt with both hands.

"I don't know about you gentlemen," McCorkle said, "but anything to help my chances with the ladies would be given careful consideration."

"Isn't worth the risk," Wobey mumbled. "There's no women out here anyway."

"Oh, I don't know," Vincel replied, a huge grin on his face. "R.W. tells me he met one here just two weeks ago. Blonde, long legs. He tells me she even gave him her phone number. Am I getting this story right, R.W.?"

"Hey, Robert Wayne," Wobey grinned, "tell us about it—"

"Ain't nothin' to tell." Doggett looked at the floor. "I just fixed her flat tire, and, uh, she gave me her phone number."

"That right?" Wobey asked, his eyes wide. "Wow, Doggett. You musta' been sneakin' out to ground zero or something."

McCorkle got up from the bar. "Before I know it, I'll be believing this stuff. Anyone for a game of pinball?"

A moment later, Doggett was alone with his thoughts about the blonde from Hiko. He would never forget the day he first saw her, just after that last big atomic test. Dust and gravel were still falling out of the sky, planes chasing this big old mushroom cloud, cannons and mortars still going off like the Fourth of July. And here at Ethel's, wedged into a booth between Vincel and Sgt. Quaak, he had seen her—strolling through the door like she owned the place. Tight skirt, long blonde hair down to *there*, long legs up to *here*—and covered head to toe with black soot. He would never forget her words to the bartender: "Make it a double, Roy, and don't be stingy."

It was fate. At first, he thought she might be a movie star. But then he heard Roy call her by name—*Marsha.*

Drink in hand, she had strolled over to the pinball machine. Doggett closed his eyes, remembering the scene—her left elbow resting on the glass, her right hand coaxing the nickel into the slot—the machine beeping and flashing. Then, as everyone in the bar watched in stunned silence, her hand s-l-o-w-l-y slid down to caress the plunger, her thumb moving from the knob to the spring and back. Finally, she hammered the balls into the playing area. Five at a time.

Sweating profusely, Doggett and the others had stared as the blonde fought the machine—slapping the flippers—teasing, shaking, *banging* it with her fists, at one time even *lifting* it off the floor. And then it was over. Beeping softly, the pinball machine displayed the total score—a million points. Doggett remembered her sly, appreciative smile as the onlookers applauded. And then fate played its card. Glancing outside, he noticed that the only civilian car in the parking lot—a pink Coupe de Ville—had a flat front tire. It had to be hers. So, while the rest of the bar regulars stared at her through the bonus games, he quietly sneaked out and changed the flat, trading it for the spare from a nearby truck.

In gratitude, she had given him her address and phone number—or more accurately, *left it* for him to find—secretly scrawled on a flattened beer can in the spot where the caddy had been. *Thanks. Love always. Marsha.* Doggett played the scene over and over in his mind, like a favorite movie. He was in love.

Until the day she came in with that sumbitch. Big guy with fluffy brown hair, bushy eyebrows, beady little eyes and a cocker spaniel smile.

Listening to the clang and sputter of the pinball machines, Doggett poured out a fistfull of toothpicks. He placed them in his mouth, one right next to the other, fanning them in a wide arc across his face like a small wooden duckbill.

"*Hey*, boy," Roy hollered from behind the bar. "Them toothpicks cost money!"

Doggett removed the toothpicks from his mouth and laid them in a row on the bar. "There they are, Roy. I was just borrowin' 'em for a minute—they'll be dry in no time."

Roy scooped the toothpicks off onto the floor, then carefully swept them into a dustpan. "If yer that *hongry*," he said, "mebbe I can get ya somethin'. There's a special on Gamma-burgers. Comes with cheese an' chili peppers."

"No thanks, Roy," Doggett said mournfully. "I was just thinkin' about what I'm gonna *do*. There ain't nothin' here for me. No women, no future. And truth to tell, this ain't much of a job. Nah, I'm getting damn *tired* of it all."

"Ya thinkin' about *suicide*?"

"Thinkin' about runnin' away. Vincel and I got this aunt Louise in Acapulco." Doggett paused to pour a few more toothpicks on the bartop. "She used to be a teller at the savings and loan. She said if we ever needed to get away from the authorities, to come visit."

"Well, if yer gonna run away, I suspect there are worse places than Acapulco." Roy leaned on his broom. "Think ya can find a job down there?"

"I figure we can lay on the beach all day," Doggett said. "Maybe sell auto parts. Or hubcaps. Aunt Louise says they're always runnin' short of hubcaps."

"Damn shame." Roy walked away pushing the broom.

Doggett grabbed more toothpicks, then lined them up on the table. Maybe he *could* go to Acapulco. With a little luck and some hard work, he could make a go of it. Be the hubcap king. Then he'd come back and get Marsha. Or maybe just stay down there and marry some nice senorita. Sure would beat stomping around in the desert, gettin' your oysters smoked.

He looked out the window at the alkali hills and the flat expanse of the test site. In a few days there'd be another another fireball. Another trench caving in. Another mushroom cloud. Maybe it *was* time to head south.

18

Ventral Turret

Sloan pulled the collar of his army field jacket around his ears, then stepped off the bus onto the airport tarmac. It was a strange place to view an atomic test. "There'll be this guy there to meet you," Sergeant Quaak had said. "That's all I know about it. See ya after the test."

Sloan shivered in the chill, dark air. Rubbing his eyes to clear them of sleep, he wondered who he was supposed to meet. And what he was supposed to do. At the western edge of the runway, he saw the dark shape of Ethel's Bar. In a few hours it would be open and the old bartender would be brewing up a pot of coffee. Sloan shrugged. No telling where he would be in two hours. Maybe not even on the ground.

Turning, he walked toward the huge hanger. In the dead quiet of the airport, the only sounds came from his boots clicking on the concrete. Even the wind had died down.

Then, walking around the side of the building, he saw it—a B-24 bomber. "Hey, Andy, boy!"

Sloan turned. It was the man who had rescued him from the hospital.

"This is it!" Duffel patted the airplane. "Gonna watch the bomb from way upstairs. Whattaya think of that?"

"I guess it's okay—"

Duffel grinned, pulling a small camera from his bag. "I convinced Stein you'd be perfect for the job. Ever spent any time in a plane?"

"No."

"Well, that's okay. Look it over."

Sloan gazed at the long, thin wings. Despite the big radial engines, they looked surprisingly vulnerable. The wide, flat tail section with its twin vertical stabilizers looked like two giant, flat shovels. At the center of the span was a small bubble sprouting twin machine guns. Sloan knew from basic training they were 50 caliber Brownings. Walking up to the nose of the plane, he noticed someone had painted a naked woman with big white wings and a halo. *The Lonesome Lady*.

"Yeah, quite a plane," Duffel said, patting the woman's likeness. "I've been waiting for *years* to get inside one of these. Notice the ventral turret here." Duffel pointed to a small plexiglass bubble on the bottom of the fuselage. "A lot of planes nowadays don't have the ventral turret. Replaced it with a radar unit or something. We're lucky this plane still has it. We can get down there and get some *great* film of the mushrooms. You ever get dizzy, Sloan?"

"Uh, no—"

"Well, you're lucky, 'cause I do. I'm ashamed to admit it, but I'm afraid of heights." Duffel paused. "It takes a real *man* to sit in that ball turret. Gunners had to get in there, spin around, fire those machine guns. I bet it's like being on the best carnival ride in the world. Any carnivals where you're from?"

"Yes, sir."

"Carnival is an interesting place," Duffel nodded. "You see a lot of interesting things. I'll bet you're the kind of person who would know an interesting scene when he saw it."

"Well—"

"Sure you would." Duffel patted the ventral ball turret. "And I know if you ever got a chance to take an interesting picture, you wouldn't turn it down, would you?"

"I guess not," Sloan shrugged.

"Didn't think so." Duffel handed Sloan a small, square object. "This is a Bolex movie camera. Corporal, how would you like to be an *official cinematographer* for a real television show?"

Taking an empty chair at the console, Joe Bob Ramey poured himself a cup of hot coffee from his thermos. Not far away a morose Rhinehart, his leg handcuffed to a chair, scanned the television monitors. "See anything, Carl?"

"Just the usual," Rhinehart mumbled, removing a cigar from his shirt pocket. "Soldiers in trenches, tanks, a few reporters."

"Do you see our friend Batman?" Ramey asked.

"He's still in the hospital, Joe," Don Hendrix said, pulling up a chair. "He was in the tank that went to ground zero."

"Poor bastard," Ramey shook his head. "I can't imagine what the hell they were doing out there."

"Ask the general," Hendrix shrugged, "he can probably tell you all about it."

"Yoo hoo! Any seats left?" It was Uborka, one huge hand wrapped around a cup of tea, the other holding a half-eaten doughnut.

"Have a seat, Ed." Ramey pulled a chair out from the table. "Didn't know you had Control Room duty."

"I couldn't sleep," Uborka said, sitting down. "I'm worried about my bomb design. We got the plutonium in today, but we have nothing for the bomb itself. I'm very embarrassed."

Hendrix looked up. "You mean about your Cadillac bomb?"

"It's his fault." Uborka pointed at Rhinehart. "He got us into the spot. Now our test is next week and we don't have anything yet. And a senator is supposed to watch the test, too."

"Look, Eduard," Rhinehart said, "you can put this thing together in no time. You already have the plutonium—you just need the *chassis*. Go to a junkyard."

"There's one in Beatty that specializes in luxury models." Hendrix scratched his ear. "Should be able to find an old Caddy there."

"But what about the firing circuit?" Uborka whined. "Nothing will happen without the firing circuit, and Los Alamos won't send us any."

"Hell," Rhinehart waved his arms, "you have to improvise! Get it from Roy's pinball machines! A pop bumper makes a great firing pin—and the solenoids will work with detonators."

"Sounds like he's done this before," Hendrix observed. He looked at Uborka and shook his head. "Ed, I can't believe you let him design your first device. An atomic Cadillac."

"Yes," Uborka said glumly. "I hope it rains."

"Doubt if that would help," Joe Bob shrugged. "You and Emil gonna watch it from the Control Point?"

"I'll be too nervous." Uborka poured a handful of sugar into his tea. "I'm so worried about a fizzle, I plan to be drunk. Get with Carl Rhinehart and look for women or something."

Hendrix smiled. "Better make sure Carl doesn't sneak on board the drop plane. Might want to *drive* your bomb to the target."

"No, no," Uborka said, "it's a military test. The guard will shoo him away."

"Well, I've still got *this* test to worry about, so if you will excuse me . . ." Hendrix glanced at the clock, then switched on the microphone. *"All site personnel take your stations. We have one hour to zero. Repeat. One hour to zero."*

"See this little gizmo here?" Duffel instructed, pointing to a hinge at the base of the camera. "Just fold this over before you film anything. Otherwise, it'll spin and hit you in the face. Wouldn't want you to get *hurt* doing this."

Sloan looked at the camera.

"Three lenses." Duffel pointed a stubby finger at the three cylinders protruding from the front. "Wide-angle for close-ups, telephoto for long and medium for medium. Got that?"

"Okay," Sloan smiled.

"Great. You're a natural. If you want a picture of the mushroom cloud while we're close in, use the wide. If we're out a few miles, use the medium. I doubt if we'll need the telephoto."

Sloan hefted the Bolex camera. It felt dense and solid in his hand.

"Before we get up in the air, you can take this into the top turret." Duffel motioned toward the front of the plane. "We have a few min-utes—follow that catwalk through the bomb bay to the turret. It's just behind the flight deck. You can't miss it."

Gripping the Bolex in one hand, Sloan threaded his way through the dark, boxy fuselage of the idling bomber. Inching past the open lid to the ventral plexiglass blister, he saw that the guns had been removed, but the gunner's harness remained, hanging empty against a pitch black background.

Suddenly the pilot's voice came over the intercom. "You guys strapped in? Might be a rough ride."

"We're fine," Duffel called back. "Let's go. We don't want to miss anything."

Turning quickly, Sloan scrambled back to his seat inside the weaving, roaring airplane.

"Hold tight, boys," the pilot said. "Here we go!"

As the engines revved to a high whine, Sloan hastily fastened his seatbelt, then looked outside. Through the small window he saw a flashing red reflection against the moving concrete. A minute later the cabin tipped back, and the reflection fell away into darkness.

An hour and a half later, Sloan scraped the ice from the inside of the top turret blister and looked through the window he had made. Thundering along only several hundred feet from the left wingtip was a heavy bomber, a B-36, its six powerful engines facing backward. Sloan gazed at the huge machine hanging motionless in the cold black air, its surface covered with red, green and white lights, flashing rhythmically. It looked like a big metal fish in the sky. He aimed the Bolex at the flight deck of the B-36, glowing dull red in the viewfinder. Pressing the trigger he felt the camera vibrate in his hand.

"Hey! How you doing up there!" It was Duffel, looking up at him from the mezzanine. "Can you see anything?"

"Nothing much." Sloan looked around the ice-coated blister. "It's kinda' chilly and dark."

"Yeah, I know," Duffel nodded. "Wish I had the nerve to get into those turrets. They scare the hell out of me. Don't they scare you?"

"No." Sloan broke into a grin. Actually, it was a lot of fun. Certainly more fun than hiding in a trench. He scraped more ice from the turret and looked out across the roof of the airplane, at the red glow from the running lights and beacons reflecting on the gleaming metal surface. On either side, the lights danced across the circular path of the propellers.

"Say," Duffel yelled over the roar of the plane, "you don't get airsick, do you?"

"I don't think so." Sloan looked out through the plexiglass at the B-36 and took a deep breath. It was a shame he couldn't *stay* up here. It was peaceful, and despite the thunder and whine of the engines, sort of *quiet*. Maybe he would tell his children about it someday. Or his grandchildren. Tell them he rode in a B-24 bomber at 10,000 feet—just a few hundred feet away from a real B-36. It would be a great story.

"They're getting ready for a practice run over the target!" Duffel yelled. "I want you in the turret *underneath* the plane!"

"Okay," Sloan sighed, "I'm coming down."

———※———

Joe Bob looked up from the oscilloscope. Halfway across the room two men pushed their way through a crowd of technicians toward the radar console.

"It's Spaulding and Doc Bartholomew," Hendrix mumbled, "wonder what the hell *they're* doing here."

"Maybe they're interested in the shot," Joe Bob shrugged. "Might want to see the fireball."

Hendrix eyed the men suspiciously. "When Bartholomew gets interested in a particular nuclear test, I get nervous."

Ramey returned to the oscilloscope. "Relax Don, they just want to see the shot."

"Three minutes to zero." Henderson's voice rang out from the Control Room speakers. "Ready the flares."

Hendrix glanced at the radar screen, then did a double take. There were two blips over the target. "What the hell—?" He tapped a switch on the console. "Milt. Is there another plane over the GZ?"

"Yeah," Henderson's voice came in over the headset. "I see it too. Spaulding says it's the photo plane. Estimated altitude is ten-five."

"Damn. I thought so." Hendrix slapped the console. "That idiot pilot is way too low. Stop the clock."

"Can't."

"Why the hell not?"

"Spaulding says they can get out of there in time."

"The hell they can!" Hendrix snapped. "That fireball will get 'em before they can blink! Stop the goddamn clock, Milt!"

"Can't, Don," Henderson replied. "This one is out of our hands."

———※———

Sloan settled into the harness of the ventral bubble. Unlike the frost-coated top turret blister, the plexiglass here was completely free of ice.

Panoramic. Perhaps *too* panoramic. He felt as though he were hanging in midair *beneath* the bomber, approaching a glowing gridwork of lights on the desert floor below. Above him, the bottom surface of the fuselage stretched forward toward the nose, a wide, riveted expanse of dark metal. Twisting around to face the underside of the B-24 just ahead of the blister, he placed the camera between his knees, released the lock switch, and set the lens to telephoto.

"Hey kid." Sloan looked up. It was Duffel. "See anything yet?"

"Not much yet," Sloan replied. "Just a few lights down there. When's the bomb going off?"

"We got plenty of time. Another ten minutes at least. Now, if you're worried, I can give you some dark glasses . . ."

"Nah," Sloan said. "We got another ten minutes. Then I'll put them on."

"See everything okay?"

"Yeah. It's really great." Sloan looked straight down through the plexiglass. The lighted grid had begun flashing in slow, deliberate intervals. For the first time, he saw the center of the area—a surprisingly large circle of light in the shape of a target. He put the camera to his eye, pulled the trigger and felt the vibration as the film threaded past the lens.

Then he felt a tap on the shoulder. "Here put these on." Duffel handed him a pair of sunglasses.

"What?"

"Guess I was wrong about the time," Duffel said, closing the lid. "Hope you get the picture."

Looking down, Sloan saw that the ground below had gone completely dark.

"I can't believe they're still there!" Hendrix stared wide-eyed at the radar screen.

"*Twenty seconds and counting,*" Henderson's voice crackled from the loudspeakers. "*Eighteen, seventeen—*"

"Calm down, Don," Joe Bob said, "ten thousand feet is enough altitude. I've been closer than that myself."

Hendrix slumped back in his chair.

"*Fourteen, thirteen—*"

"Everybody wants to see how close they can get," Hendrix said, irritably. "Hell, all they have to do is use the target cameras. Then they can see the damn fireball from ten feet away!"

"I guess." Joe Bob glanced at the timer. Eight seconds. Seven . . .

"On the *Windstorm* shot we had five cameras mounted," Hendrix said. "Four on the tower and one in the bunker itself."

"Windstorm was before my time." Joe Bob returned to the oscilloscope.

"*Two, one—Fire.*"

Joe Bob saw the quick blip on the oscilloscope, followed by a bright green line arc,, a glowing electronic spike signifying a sudden electrical disturbance in the atmosphere. Fourteen miles north of the Control Point, at the top of the shot tower, a fireball was forming.

———※———

Sloan had just fitted the dark glasses on his face when the star appeared directly beneath him. In an instant it grew to surround the bubble, the plane. Everything.

Inside its brilliance, Sloan curled in helpless defense, an embryo rolling beneath the dish of the sky. Then, as the light subsided, came outlines. As colors rushed to fill the void, Sloan became aware of the blue static discharges dancing inside the plexiglass bubble, a smell like that of an overheated motor. Below, the star had become a chaotic ball of flame, growing inside a series of expanding circles—waves rippling outward from the center like bores on a frothy storm-tossed lake. All in a perfect austere silence that, for a moment, extinguished all other sounds.

His hands and face flat against the surface of the bubble, Sloan watched the turbulence unfold. Despite shouts from the cabin, the muffled roar of the engines, the creak of the cables—the plane was motionless. Suspended in the air, helpless. Then, like a fiery, raging river, the cloud rushed up to engulf them.

19

Bobbie

Y ou want a *duffel*, sir?" The clerk looked up from his sandwich.

Stein leaned across the desk. "His name is Captain Hugh Duffel. He's supposed to be staying here in the Bachelor Officer's Quarters. I want to know what room he's in."

"I'm not sure we have that information." The clerk leaned back in his chair.

"I'm sure you do," Stein said menacingly.

"Uh, yes sir." The man carefully placed his sandwich on the desk and removed a small folder from the file. "Okay. Duffel. Captain. With the Signal Corps Pictorial Center. Temporary duty from Fort Monmouth to work on a television film—"

"That's him," Stein nodded. "What's his room number?"

"Maybe you should wait until Colonel Storax gets back—"

"What's his room number!" Stein barked, the veins pulsing in his neck.

"Room 225. Do you want a key?"

"No." Stein climbed the stairs two at a time, then strode down the darkened hall toward the room. The emergency room medic had made the identification—Sloan had been brought in by a fast-talking red-headed man wearing an Hawaiian shirt. No question who it was.

Reaching the door Stein paused, then knocked. No answer. "Duffel!" Stein pounded on the door. "Open up!"

Nothing. Reaching into his pocket, Stein removed his set of lock picks, jammed one into the keyhole and felt for the tumbler. Seconds later the door swung open. The small gray room was completely empty.

═══〰〰═══

Tugging at the zipper of his leather jacket, Perkins found it wouldn't move. Stuck. The slipstream of chill early morning air past the Chevy's window was making the drive damned unpleasant. As if the purpose of the trip weren't bad enough—going for a ride in an airplane.

Still, it was a perfect Saturday morning. Ahead and to the south were the bare foothills of the Spring Mountains, their light brown color masked by the shades of dawn. Halfway up the ridge, purple scud clouds drifted slowly by, obscuring the blue-black fuzz of juniper and pine. "I've been in Nevada too long," Perkins said aloud, "this place is beginning to look kinda' *nice*."

As he came over a hill, Perkins searched for the turnoff. Bobbie Jean had said she lived in a trailer next to an airstrip. At the top of the hill, he spotted a tall pole with a faded red rag on top. A windsock. Then he saw the airplanes—single and double-engine planes of every shape and size, lined up in neat rows, facing north. And to the east, amid several rectangular aluminum boxes, looking like an elongated metal egg with windows, was the Airstream trailer. Behind the trailer sat a morose, bullet-nosed Ford. She was home. Perkins considered turning his Chevy around and heading back to Camp Sagebrush, back to the security of his barracks. Far from dangerous airplanes and crazy women.

Then he thought better of it. After all, he was training as an officer in the atomic army and this crazy woman was on a first-name basis with the general. As he pulled to a stop beside the trailer, he noticed a shadow behind the venetian blinds. Had she been serious about the invitation? Maybe she'd forgotten. Maybe she getting ready to go to work or *fly* somewhere. Maybe she wasn't wearing anything.

Perkins shifted into reverse. At exactly the same time, the trailer door opened and small blonde appeared, wearing a red bandana over her hair. It was her. Bobbie Jean Barnett. "Glad you could make it,

Perkins," she said, tucking a khaki shirt into her denims. "Had breakfast already?"

"No, uh, I don't usually eat anything in the morning—"

"Ya ought to," she smiled. "Keep your stomach settled. Don't want you to go throwin' up all over my plane. C'mon in."

"Fine," Perkins said, getting out of the Chevy. "You talked me into it."

Inside, he found a compact metal and wood environment that served as kitchen, living room and—judging from the striped pajamas stuffed into a corner of the couch—sleeping area. Next to the couch and opposite the kitchen was a smallish table, supported on one side by twin brass hinges and on the other by two wooden legs.

The kitchen itself was nothing more than a small gas range fitted between a stubby refrigerator and a sink. On the ledge over the window sat a diminuitive brown radio playing a slow country song. Perkins surveyed the objects stacked across the ledge behind the couch—a ragged teddy bear, a stack of notebooks and a hi-fi phonograph surrounded by record albums. Ernest Tubb, Hank Williams and Patsy Cline.

"The climate here bother your records?" he asked, after a long, awkward silence.

"Sure does," she said, cracking an egg into the skillet. "You oughta' see my Little Jimmy Dickens record. Last year it got up to a hundred and thirty in here and that pore little thing about melted. Ya ever try to play a melted record? The grooves sort of *seal up* or something. Coffee's on the stove, make yourself at home."

Perkins poured himself a cup of coffee and sat down at the makeshift table. He was surprised how much like his own home the place seemed—the static of eggs in the pan, steel guitar twang pouring from the radio. He began to relax.

"Those two soldiers at the cafe said you'd been to the GZ." The blonde paused to flip an egg. "What's it like? All smoky and stuff, right?"

"It was dusty, I'll tell you that." Perkins stared at the table. "You have any, uh, cream for the coffee?"

"Sure," she said, producing a milk bottle. "Cream's on top. Just spoon it off."

"Uh, okay." Perkins stared at the bottle.

"Did ya see the death bunker?"

"The *what?*"

She flipped another egg. "You been to ground zero—you *must've* seen the death bunker. It's right up next to the tower. Where they do all those Civil Defense experiments and stuff."

"Well, it was kind of dusty—" Perkins spooned the cream from the bottle.

"They put all kinds of things in there," she said, slapping an egg onto a plate. "Bicycles, candy bars, silverware, television sets. Kind of like Doom Town, only it's right up close to the tower, y'know?"

Perkins shook his head. "I didn't really see much out there."

"I heard it just melts the hell out of everything." She handed Perkins a plate of fried eggs. "'Course, it doesn't take a genius to figure that out, right?"

"Guess not," he said, staring at the greasy eggs.

"Yeah, that test site's quite a place. Want some more coffee? Don't want you to go to sleep in the plane, ya know."

A half hour later, Perkins found himself in a place he feared almost as much as ground zero—an airport. Surrounded by airplanes and loaded with greasy fried eggs and two cups of strong coffee, he knew he was headed for disaster. What had he been *thinking?*

"Pretty nice old birds, aren't they?" Bobbie Jean grinned. "Fly like the wind, every single one of 'em."

Perkins stared at the nearest plane, a ragged wreck covered in tattered yellow cloth.

"These are fine old birds," she nodded. "Great place for 'em too. Dad picked it. The ridge over there keeps the winds down. West of here, around the entrance to the test site, I've seen it get so dusty they had to close the highway. 'Course, when you get above the dust, you're fine."

"I see."

"Yeah, it *really* gets dusty when they test one of those bombs," she laughed, scanning the group of planes. "And it's even *worse* north of the test site. I got this friend of mine, Harold Frye—has a ranch just outside the Gunnery Range. About two hours after the shot, you'll see that ol' cloud come roarin' through the canyon. Looks a lot like fog or somethin'. Only thing is, it'll give you a hell of a sunburn. You get sunburn when you went to the GZ?"

"I don't remember. Uh, are we *really* going to fly over the test site?"

"Well, *sure!*" The blonde laughed. "I was thinkin' of taking you over Doom Town. Ever seen Doom Town, Perkins? They got all kinds of things there—houses, cars, sidewalks. There's even a water tower out there. I've seen it from the air. Now why the hell did they put up a water tower, if they're just gonna blow it back down? I'll show ya when we fly over."

He looked at his watch. "I really don't know if I'll have time for Doom Town."

"*Sure* we do—it's Saturday. Nobody works on Saturday," she said, walking over to a silver airplane. "We'll take the ol' 170 here. 'Course, we could take th' Champ—" she pointed to the tattered yellow airplane. "Take the side door off and it's just like flyin' a chopper."

"Helicopter?"

"Only thing is, it's slow. Takes forever to get up to altitude." The woman's voice dropped, as if she were talking to herself. "Nah, th' Cessna's a lot less scary. Yeah, we better take the Cessna to Doom Town—"

"I really don't think we have time." Perkins took a step back.

The blonde turned and scowled at him. "You ain't afraid of heights, are ya? Afraid you'll get a nosebleed or somethin'? Damn. I knew it!"

"I just don't think we have time to, uh, fly over the test site. Doom Town."

"Th' general don't like mud puppies either," she nodded. "I remember him comin' over to the house, bitchin' and complainin' about the quality of his officers. He'd sit there with a beer and he'd say, 'B.J., what in the hell am I gonna do with my men? Not a single one ever been inside a plane. All of 'em chickenshit of gettin' up in the air.'"

"General Umber said that?"

"He'd say, 'B.J., give me one good infantry officer—even a lieutenant—who ain't afraid of flyin', and I'll punch his ticket all the way to the top.' Next time he comes over here for barbecue or somethin', I'll give you a call."

"Barbecue, huh?" Perkins turned to look at the plane. It resembled an aluminum coffin with wings.

"'Course, I'll let him know you've been flyin' with me," she smiled, opening the door. "Hop in."

Perkins climbed inside the cramped cabin, wedging himself into a seat that looked like it belonged in a carnival. He began to perspire.

"Just make yourself at home while I do the preflight," Bobbie called from somewhere behind the plane. He heard a splashing sound. Gasoline?

"I've gotta bleed the tanks," she yelled. "Every now and then the gas'll have *water* in it. Gets into the carb and the engine quits."

"Oh Lord," Perkins mumbled. It *was* the carnival. The beginning of his nightmare about falling. While the rest of his family boarded the whirling, spinning instruments of nausea, he had sensibly stayed on the ground, working his way through sno-cones and cotton candy. But when he reached the fifth grade, a girl cousin talked him into what she claimed was the "most romantic" of all serious carnival devices—the Ferris wheel. Against his better judgement, he bought the tickets.

He remembered sitting on the tiny, swinging bench, remembered the thin wooden bar being placed in front of them. "We could slide out the bottom," his cousin had warned. She was right. Then the engine roared, the wheel clanked and the ground fell away. They soared upward, *backward*, two sets of untied tennis shoes hundreds of feet from the ground. His arms, hands, and legs were weak and useless, his spine tingled in helpless, dizzy fear. He remembered begging his cousin to please, please, *please* don't rock the seat. And he remembered her determined *wiggling*, pushing and pulling on the wooden bar until the bench started to tip *backwards*. A second later, the reliable Midwestern horizon had come unhinged. One minute the sky was there, the next minute the carnival grounds, then even *more* sky. He remembered people below shouting at them.

When they reached the top, his cousin tilted the seat until he was staring straight ahead, up into the very *top* of the sky, his back to the center of the huge metal wheel. "Here we go—" she screamed in his ear. "Upside down!"

It didn't happen. But he did throw up every lunch he had ever eaten—all over himself, his cousin, the Ferris wheel, the carnival, the entire town.

Suddenly Bobbie climbed in and pulled the door closed. "I like to check everything. Cotter pins, cables, control surfaces. Can't be too careful."

"Can't be too careful," Perkins echoed. He was so scared his brain had resorted to the cheap trick of *repeating* the last four or five syllables he'd heard. He had become a parrot.

"See that thing?" Bobbie pointed to a tiny metal ring at the corner of the door. "Looks like a hand grenade pin? Don't pull it."

"Don't pull it," Perkins repeated. "Why?"

"The doors'll come off," she said, starting the engine. "This plane's rated for aerobatics. Something goes wrong and you want to get out quick, you pull that pin. then bail out."

"Doors come off.?" Perkins checked his pulse. It was too fast to count.

The woman taxied the plane to the end of the runway, then, in a deft motion, spun it around. "Sure you ain't got time to see Doom Town?"

"Uhhhh-" Perkins pointed to his watch.

"Well, too bad." She shook her head and eased in on the throttle. "How's that breakfast treatin' ya?"

"Breakfast." In a flash Perkins thought of the eggs. Greasy, slippery eggs. And that coffee. And, and—the horrible sight of the milk bottle with its plug of congealed cream—

"Ready, Perkins? Well, let's go!" The blonde jammed the throttle to the firewall. As the engine screamed, the tachometer flipped over toward the far end of the green line and the plane moved forward, tipped up, skipped a few beats, then jumped into the air.

———⟆———

Linneman opened the door to Demming's office and peeked inside. The receptionist of the day was the chirpy, chubby blonde, Carol, reading an old copy of *The Saturday Evening Post*. Taking a deep breath, he quietly closed the door behind him and took a seat.

"Hi, Dr. Linneman," she said after a moment.

"Hi, Carol. Tell Dr. Demming I'm here."

"Yeah, he'll see you in a minute," she said, turning the page. "The Marienfelds are in there, both of them. And the head of Camp Jupiter security, too!"

"Vernon Fogler?" Linneman asked, surprised.

"Yeah, and he's awake!" Carol smiled brightly. "So I guess it must be real important, huh? Have any idea what it is?"

"No," Linneman admitted, "I'm usually the last to know anything around here."

"That's what Donna always says."

"She's not working today then?"

"She took the week off." Carol returned to the magazine. "Said she needed a vacation. Said she might take a look at Doom Town before they blow it up." The receptionist set the magazine aside. "I think she's gonna take one of her boyfriends out there. Have you ever been to Doom Town, Dr. Linneman?"

"Uh, yes," Linneman mumbled. "I helped wire the transformers."

"Wow!" The blonde's eyes widened in amazement. "For the whole town? Maybe you can take me out there sometime."

"I don't know, Carol. It's a dangerous place—" Linneman thought he saw a trace of anxiety in the hazel eyes. For a brief instant, she looked almost fragile.

"Yeah, I want to see what the construction guys do with those mannequins." She looked around, then leaned forward. "I heard they strip 'em down—put 'em in all sorts of cute positions, then sell the clothes at the pawn shops in Las Vegas."

"I hadn't heard that, Carol."

"It seems a shame to waste good clothes on a dummy though, 'specially if you're gonna blow him up, right?"

"I suppose so." Linneman glanced at the cover of the magazine she had been reading, a mushroom cloud, sprawling orange and lazy toward the zenith. Across the face of the photo, were the words, *Bomb Rips Desert, Troops Maneuver.* And beneath that, in smaller print, *Great Recipes For Your Summer Cookout.*

Suddenly the intercom came to life with Demming's familiar whine, "Carol, send in Dr. Linneman."

As Linneman entered Demming's drab office, he saw both Stanley and his wife, sitting at opposite sides of the desk. The half-asleep Director of Security slouched in a chair nearest the coat closet, his glutinous frame molded to the leather like a huge cantaloupe gone bad.

"Take a seat, George," Demming smiled. "Vernon says we have a problem, and I thought you might be able to help us out."

"Problem?" Linneman turned to Security Director.

"There has been a breach of security," Fogler said, shifting to a more upright position in the chair. "Foreign agents, communists, maybe—and I'm getting a committee together to study plans for an investigation—"

"Someone recently phoned the national office of the AEC," Demming interrupted, irritation in his voice. "They phoned Dr. Anna Faye Trumbo. The call was traced to Ethel's Bar at Camp Sagebrush."

Linneman looked around the room. Everyone was staring at him—Demming, Fogler, the Marienfelds.

"The caller, who identified himself only as a 'concerned citizen'," Demming continued, "said that things here were going straight to hell. Or words to that effect. And that there were naked people running about."

"Naked people?" Linneman leaned forward. *"Naked people?"*

"The caller disguised his voice with a drunken slur," Fogler added, his eyes narrowing like two tiny beads in a mound of dough. "Either that, or he was a foreigner. You have foreigners in your section, don't you Dr. Linneman? And people who *drink*?"

"Well, we have two *Hungarians*," Linneman nodded, "but I can't imagine Uborka or Meghalty doing anything like that."

"Now I am aware that there is some *dissatisfaction* in the ranks," Demming said, a thin smile on his lips. "Some here don't like our work week, don't *like* getting up in the early morning to monitor the tests, don't like coming in on Saturdays—"

"*I* don't mind coming in on Saturdays," Stanley Marienfeld interjected.

"George," Demming continued, "Anna Faye Trumbo gave me my first job with the government. We're old friends. And frankly, we both found this little mystery phone call *amusing*. But continued trouble of this sort can adversely affect the nation's defense—"

"We know it was someone who works here—" Fogler interrupted, "someone familiar with Dr. Trumbo's, er— *appearance*."

"Well?" Demming asked, staring at Linneman. "Your men are known to frequent the bar where the phone call was made. Do you think one of them might be *disaffected* with my policies here? Dr. Rhinehart—"

"I can't imagine Carl doing something like that," Linneman shook his head. "He would have identified himself—."

"But he's disaffected, everybody knows that!" Marienfeld interrupted. "And he drinks! We've *all* seen him drink!"

"No, Carl Rhinehart wouldn't make a call like that," Linneman continued. "He, uh, thinks he *created* everything and, um, *everybody*, so I really doubt if—"

"If *what*?" Demming leaned forward.

"If he would, um, make *disparaging* comments about any of his—" Linneman gulped, "—er, *handiwork*."

Demming stared.

"It's what he thinks," Linneman shrugged helplessly. "It has to do with quantum mechanics."

"Rhinehart believes he *created* Anna Faye Trumbo?" Demming peered over his glasses.

"It's his religion," Linneman nodded. "Or something. I'm not really sure."

"What about those two foreigners then?" Stanley Marienfeld asked. "And what about that little guy with the crewcut?"

"Uborka and Meghalty are working on the lab's first bomb design," Linneman replied. "They wouldn't cause trouble, especially now. And I can't imagine Joe Bob Ramey doing anything like that. Or Art Flagmeyer either." Linneman paused to gauge the effect of his denials. Demming was staring at the surface of his desk, while Vernon Fogler appeared to be scanning the interior spaces of his brain for a stray thought. Marsha Marienfeld was absentmindedly sliding a pen back and forth under her nose, like a Cuban testing a cigar. Her husband Stanley, on the other hand, looked as blotchy as a bag of overripe tomatoes. Linneman knew where the next attack was coming from.

"I *know* Rhinehart did it," Marienfeld suddenly barked, rising to a half-crouch. "I'll *always* think Rhinehart did it. He wants to discredit what we're doing here. He wants to discredit me personally."

"But I don't think he *knows* you, dear," Marienfeld's wife said.

Linneman smiled gamely at Marienfeld. "I don't think Carl Rhinehart would stoop to an anonymous phone call. His activities take place on a somewhat *broader* scale."

"George is probably right, Stanley," Demming smiled. "I don't think Rhinehart or any of the other weapons specialists were involved."

Marienfeld deflated into his chair, for the moment beaten. Linneman took a deep breath and began to relax.

"It *had* to be Rhinehart!" Marienfeld screeched suddenly. "Nobody else would do a thing like that!"

Demming glared at the agitated Marienfeld. "Whoever it was, Stanley, we'll find out soon enough. They made a tape recording. And Anna Faye will probably bring it with her when she comes down."

"Anna Faye Trumbo is visiting the test site?" Linneman asked.

"Yes," Demming said, "she wants to oversee the Vulcan energy test next month, and I know she'll want to talk with the 'concerned citizen' while she's here."

Linneman nodded.

"Dr. Trumbo has quite a temper." Demming looked around the room. "We'd better identify this phone caller before she arrives. Find him and *squelch* him."

"Yes, of course," Linneman sighed.

"Meantime, Stanley—" Demming turned to the still blotchy Marienfeld. "I want Senator Curry insulated from this. Try to keep him busy somehow. Give him a tour of the desert. Take him to Doom Town."

"Me? Doom Town?" Marienfeld's eyes widened. "I think I would do better trying to find the phone caller—"

"I'm leaving that to Marsha," Demming replied, turning to the drowsy Fogler, "and to Vernon here. At least *they* aren't falling apart at the seams over this."

<hr />

Marienfeld buried his head under his jacket, his eyes sqeezed shut. Four inches away, the foam from the Brandy Alexander flowed down the side of the glass, formed a wet circle of merangue on the tabletop, then coalesced into a river that eventually reached his nose.

"Want another drink, Marienfeld?"

"Beat it, Roy," he snarled.

"I don't know what you're doin' under under that coat, and I know it ain't my business," Roy continued, "but your drink is about to run off onto the floor."

"Leave me alone!" As Roy's footsteps faded away, Marienfeld opened his eyes and tried to focus on the drink, but perspiration kept getting in the way. He was in deep trouble.

And it was all because of women. Sneaky, screechy, unfathomable, hormone-sensitive women. If Trumbo had been a *man*, he would have seen the outburst as, well—just one of those things. Might have even laughed it off. But no. Anna Faye Trumbo was a woman. A woman with a PhD in nuclear physics who had spent six years in the Marines. And he had phoned her, *insulted* her, said something about her *big fat ass*.

Marienfeld took a drink, tried to line up his alibi. After all, it had only been a euphemism, a joke, a casual remark— No. She wouldn't buy it—she was too mean and smart to buy it. After all, she was the goddamn head of the Atomic Energy Commission. She doubtless had dozens of people listening to the tape recording for any nuances, any *inflections* that might identify him.

Marienfeld took another drink and pulled the jacket tighter around his head. His career was ruined. He had tweaked the nose of a banshee and he was going to pay *big*.

20

Dr. Jeff

Joe Bob followed Hendrix through the dark steam tunnel connecting Camp Jupiter and Loper Infirmary, then up into the basement through the boiler room past the locked quarantine ward. It was a long, byzantine route, that neatly bypassed the guard station. "If we get caught in here, just say we're looking for a radiation leak," Hendrix chuckled. "That always gets them."

Joe Bob carefully negotiated the darkened staircase. "Does he still think he's God?"

"Oh, yeah. Sure." Hendrix opened a door into the corridor. "But it's not like he's obsessed with it or anything."

"That's good," Joe Bob mumbled. "I'd have a tough time talkin' to God." He looked warily at the drab brown walls of the darkened hall. He hated hospitals, even in the middle of the day. They smelled like antiseptic, wax and death. "How many times you been in here to see him?"

"A couple." Hendrix paused at a hallway intersection. "I've been sneaking him equipment. The guards usually won't question me—just figure I'm going to the lab or something. It's real easy to find your way around this place. Follow me and act like you know what you're doing."

Ramey looked over his shoulder at a group of doctors milling around a bulletin board at the far end of the hall. He hated doctors. He hated being here and hated even more seeing an old friend who'd gone over the brink.

"Here it is, Joe," Hendrix motioned toward a darkened corridor. "He's in the fourth room from the end—room 137."

Ramey looked down the bleak, empty hallway. "Where's the guards?"

"At lunch. This place is always empty around lunch." Hendrix smiled and stepped up to the wooden door. "You haven't visited him here, so don't be surprised at what you see. Like I said, I've sneaked him some lab equipment. The doctors don't seem to mind—it keeps him busy."

"Hold it," Ramey said. "Before we go in there—"

"Yeah?" Hendrix asked, peering over his glasses.

"Is he, you know—still crazy?" Joe Bob whispered nervously. "I mean, I don't know how to deal with crazy people. I won't know what to say."

"You'll be fine," Hendrix said, tapping on the door. "Dr. Jeff? It's Don Hendrix."

"Come in!" The voice was thin, high-pitched, crisp.

As they entered the room, Ramey's jaw dropped. The place was a mess—a galaxy of wood, glass, metal and paper. In the center, where one would normally expect a bed, was an empty chair facing a roll top desk, its surface absolutely clean. Surrounding this nucleus was a maze of tables and surfaces supporting the clear glass and hard gray steel of physics equipment—scintillation counters, amplifiers, rheostats, potentiometers, galvanometers, electronic boards of every shape and size, all connected by a tangle of wires and cables. It looked like a junkyard. And in the middle of the junk was a slender middle-aged man with a huge hooked nose and pale blue eyes. Dr. Jeffrey Christopher.

Ramey was mildly surprised that the physicians had let the patient retain his working clothes. Instead of a hospital gown, Dr. Jeff wore his signature outfit—a yellow bow tie, wrinkled white shirt and brown plaid slacks held up by both belt *and* suspenders. As usual, his shoes were scuffed to the point of being almost unrecognizable.

"Did you bring me the oscilloscope, Donald?" the man asked, peering at the smiling Hendrix.

"Not this time, Dr. Jeff—"

"Well, please try to get me one," the man said, putting on a pair of rimless glasses. "I think the electron is becoming quite uncertain again. They're going to rip another hole, I know it!"

"I brought along—"

"Joe Bob!" the man said, adjusting his glasses. "Good to see you! It's been months!"

"Don sneaked me in past the guards," Ramey smiled, gripping Dr. Jeffrey's calloused hand. Despite his stooped appearance, the man's handshake was healthy and firm, his pale blue eyes clear. "How're ya feelin'?"

"Fine, fine," Jeffrey smiled. "Very fit, ready to go back to work—soon as they let me out."

"Uh, yeah," Joe Bob looked around the room. "All this lab equipment—looks like you've made yourself right at home."

"Yes, yes," Jeffrey replied, "Thanks to Elmore and, of course, Donald here. He's been bringing me the equipment I need. Must continue the research, you know."

"Research? Here?" Joe Bob shot a quick glance at Hendrix.

Jeffrey patted a rectangular-shaped box. "I've been watching the charge of the electron."

"Well, good," Joe Bob said, starting to relax. "How's it goin'?"

"Why, I'm *concerned*!" Jeffrey leaned forward, his voice a whisper. "The universe is loosening up again. The rivets are weak."

Joe Bob took a step back.

"The charge on the electron is becoming very unstable." Jeffrey turned to Hendrix. "Did you bring me a newspaper, Donald?"

"Not today." Hendrix smiled gamely.

"It's been in the news, you know. There in the background chatter and no one's noticed. Last week the newspaper made mention of the word *vulcan*. Not once, but twice. One, in a want ad, the other in a travel article—"

"The *Vulcan* test is on schedule for July 4, Jeffrey," Hendrix said patiently. "It's the energy experiment. It's been on the schedule for months."

"It was just like it was in 1945 before the Trinity test," Jeffrey continued. "In newspapers all over the world—words like *gadget* and *fire* and even *Trinity*, popping up weeks before the test. One was in a cartoon the day *before* the test. Did I ever show it to you, Joe?"

"I'm sure he's seen it, Jeff," Hendrix said. "Actually, we don't have much time—we just wanted to stop by, see how you were doing—"

"Donald," Jeffrey turned to Hendrix, "you must find Elmore. I'm certain he's behind this. He thinks he's doing the right thing, but he's all wrong."

"Elmore is dead, Jeffrey."

"Oh, of course," Jeffrey nodded, "but he's *still* involved."

"Involved?" Joe Bob shot a quick glance at Hendrix, then back at Dr. Jeffrey. "Involved with *what*?"

"The irregularities!" Jeffrey hammered his fist on the desk. "Now, they're beginning within a hundred hours of each atomic test—the variation is always commensurate with the yield! Can't you appreciate that?"

"We haven't had the time to look into that, Jeff," Hendrix said. "The schedule keeps us pretty busy."

Joe Bob felt his throat tighten up. Why had Hendrix brought him here anyway?

"The fine constant of the universe is losing stablity," Dr. Jeffrey continued. "The nuts and bolts holding our part of the universe together are *dissolving* from around us. We are becoming *disconnected* from the rest of the cosmos, and I can't do a thing to stop it."

"Even God can do only so much," Hendrix offered.

"Perhaps. But I'm at least *partly* responsible for this. And it's beyond my capabilities." Jeffrey sat down in the wooden desk chair. "You can't imagine how that makes me feel. Impotent, that's what."

"I'm sure it's tough," Hendrix nodded, stealing a quick glance at Ramey.

Jeffrey shook his head. "It's embarrassing. The entire test site is starting to behave like a subatomic particle; we'll be here one instant and gone the next!" After a pause, he looked up at Ramey. "Are you sure you haven't seen Elmore?"

"No one's seen him for months, Jeffrey." Hendrix patted his shoulder. "Not since the accident."

"That wasn't an accident, and I know he's behind this." Jeffrey knotted his brow in a moment's thought. "He just can't expect to bring us back to the fold in—in—*fits and starts*!"

"Of course not," Hendrix said gently.

"It's way too difficult for those people—killing them first."

Jeffrey's blue eyes began to cloud. "And who knows what will happen to them then?"

"If I see him, I'll talk to him, I promise." Hendrix patted the man's shoulder, then stepped to the door. "Maybe first thing next week."

"That will be too late, Donald." Jeffrey looked up, tears in his eyes. "I'm sure of it."

———≈———

"You know, Joe Bob," Hendrix said, pushing open the double doors into the Emergency Room corridor, "I thought he'd be getting better. Thought maybe seeing you might get him back on track."

"Well, you were damn sure wrong on that one," Joe Bob mumbled. "One minute we were talkin' about how nice a day it was, the next thing I know the universe is unravelin' or something . . ."

Hendrix shook his head. "Last time I was there he didn't mention *any* of that business. Asked how Amanda was, how the kids were doing—"

"Kinda' wish he'd made more sense in there. I didn't know what to say." Joe Bob paused and looked up at the dark ceiling of the narrow hallway. "Felt like a damn fool."

"Look," Hendrix said, "I'm sorry I brought you over here. I thought it'd help him out."

"Well, it probably didn't hurt," Joe Bob shrugged. "Th' kind of job we got, it could happen to any of us. I'm gonna run over to the cafe for a drink. Wanna come along?"

"Thanks, but I have to get another oscilloscope from the lab," Hendrix said.

"For Dr. Jeff?"

"Yeah," Hendrix chuckled, "if the universe *is* going to unravel, I want to be the first to know."

———≈———

Joe Bob stared out the window into the soft grey drizzle. Across the street from the Pig N Bun, a shopkeeper cranked down a green awning, then disappeared back inside his hardware store. A pickup truck slowly rattled up the street, swerving from side to side. Then, just as it neared

Joe Bob's Roadster, the truck swerved, sloshing into a deep pothole and spraying mud onto the front of his car—all the way to the windshield. "Dammit," Ramey grumbled. The sumbitch had done that on purpose.

At a nearby table, a burly rancher and his wiry, white-haired wife were picking at a plate of soggy fries. Stacked at the edge of the table were the crumbled, ketchup-soaked remains of two hamburgers. Ramey had seen them when he first came in, had watched them watch *him*. "One of them guv'ment *bomb boys*," the man had said, loud enough for damn near everybody to hear. It wasn't an insult, and yet it was. Ramey had heard it before and had ignored it before—and he had done the same thing today.

Sometimes he would fool them—dressed as he usually did, in levis and maybe sporting a three-day growth of beard. Then they'd come up and grin, say, "I seen you before," or "where th' hell do we know each other from?" He'd mention that he was at the town meeting a while back. That he was a government man. Made bombs for a living. They'd cock their heads to the side a bit, in that funny-suspicious way some westerners have. The smile would go hard—or maybe fade away completely—and they'd bring up how their sheep herd was losing lambs. Or that their maiden aunt had come down with some damn disease—"just about the time yer bombs started goin' off."

As though the bombs were his. And maybe they *were*. He'd seen most of the devices, stared into their sterling guts, affixed wires to the proper terminals, set the radar timers, and watched them detonate. From their black metal skin to the plutonium core, the bombs were, in a way, *his*. He and the others were responsible for them, responsible for the detonations and for the consequences. But the country needs a *defense*, didn't these people realize that? No, they probably couldn't see it.

Taking another drink, Joe Bob looked out the window at the mud splattered across his car's windshield. Should have got the license number of that pickup. Then again, maybe he should have stayed in the army and got that promotion to chief flight trainer instead of traipsing off to get those initials behind his name. Now, instead of flying Sikorskis at Fort Sam, he was sitting by himself in a dusty-assed Nevada cafe, wondering if the grief and hostility was worth it.

"You're Dr. Ramey, aren't you?"

Joe Bob turned to see a compact, dark-haired woman wearing blue jeans and a faded denim shirt. In one hand was a set of keys, in the other an iced tea. Over her shoulder was a worn strap holding a huge leather handbag. He had seen her before somewhere.

"You *are* Dr. Ramey, aren't you," the woman repeated.

"Guilty as charged," Joe Bob sighed. "What can I do for you?"

"My name is Susan Colter," the woman said, pulling up a chair. "I work for the Beatty Gazette."

"Reporter, huh?"

"Reporter, assistant editor, classified's—I do it all. It's a small newspaper," the woman smiled. "Anyway, weren't you at that town meeting last month?"

"Yeah, that was me," Joe Bob said.

"Uh-huh." She produced a small yellow notebook. "Seems your friend Marienfeld did most of the talking—"

"Yeah, somebody said it was a ventriloquist act," Joe Bob grinned, looking at her squarely. "And I was the dummy."

Colter smiled sheepishly. "Oh, who would say a thing like that?"

"Some lady reporter," Joe Bob paused. "'Bout your size."

"Probably someone from the Las Vegas Sun." Colter shook her head. "You just never can tell about them. They'll say anything—"

"Look, Miss—"

"Colter. Susan Colter," the woman smiled sweetly. "Remember?"

Joe Bob noticed that while her hair was black, her eyes were blue-gray, like hard slate. Or maybe like those little clouds that trailed a blue norther. It was a bad sign. He took a deep breath and began again. "Mrs. Colter. If you're here for some kind of interview, I'm sorry—I really can't help you much. You can call the Public Information Office—"

"Oh, I'd rather talk to you," she said, "if you don't mind."

"Well, Dr. Marienfeld pretty much deals with the press releases, Mrs. Colter—"

"It's *Miss* Colter," she interrupted him. "That's an interesting accent, Dr. Ramey. It is Alabama?"

"Texas," he nodded. "San Antonio."

"San Antone!" She brightened. "Pop spent some time there after the war. Kelly Field. Army Air Force. Nice place to spend the winter."

"Uh-huh. That's San Antone all right. Yep." It suddenly occurred to him he had been nodding his head throughout the conversation—like a poor old dray horse under a heavy load, or a gawky high school kid on his first date.

"And after that," she continued, "we moved to Carswell. Fort Worth. That's where they had all the B-36's. Biggest airplanes I've ever seen in my life."

"They're heavy bombers. They can carry a lot of ordnance." Joe Bob felt his throat beginning to dry up. "It's an *unusual* plane. The, uh, props face the *rear* rather than the front. Kind of *pushes* them through the air. Some of them have what you call a *turbo* on 'em—"

"Yes, I know," she said, still smiling. "Pop sneaked me on board for an oil burner run once. You ever ride in a B-36?"

"It's been awhile—"

"You know, the B-36 is a good plane but it handles like a lumber wagon," she shook her head at the thought. "Takes forever to trim out to straight and level, and even then you have to watch it like a hawk."

"That right?" Joe Bob discovered he was nodding his head again.

"Give me a little single-engine plane any day. Have you ever been in an airplane, Dr. Ramey?"

"Planes make me nervous. I try to stay out of 'em."

"Are you afraid they'll crash?" she asked. "I've heard there was a crash on the test site two years ago—at the *Windstorm* shot. Is that why you're afraid of planes?"

Joe Bob paused, at the top of a thought, studying her eyes. Friendly. And she still hadn't written a word in the yellow notebook. He decided to go ahead. "Okay. I'll tell you why I don't like 'em."

"Tell me." She leaned forward, her face scarcely a foot from his.

"Can't land 'em when you want to," he said, his back unstiffening a bit. "If you want to come down, you gotta find just the right place. Either a landing strip or some place that's real flat."

"Oh." Susan leaned back against the booth.

"Now, take that desert out there." He motioned toward the window. "Some of them dry lakes look flat from the air, but you get right down on 'em and there's all sorts of gullies and ravines and brush and whatnot. And by the time you see all that, you're too low to do anything about it. Now, with a chopper, you can land wherever you want, don't make much difference—"

"You ever fly in a tracking plane, Dr. Ramey?"

"A few times," he said. "How come you know about tracking planes?"

"Like I said, my pop was in the Air Force," she smiled. "He and his crew used to fly these old World War II bombers—follow the mushroom clouds across the country. He used to come home after being gone a few days and tell me how far he'd followed those things. Sometimes as far as the East Coast."

"So your dad was a cloud-tracker, huh?" Joe Bob asked. "I knew some of those guys. What's his name?"

"Charlie Colter," she said. "About your size. Black hair. Flew out of Indian Springs—"

"The name doesn't ring a bell,," Joe Bob said. "Is he still flying?"

"No," she shook her head, "not anymore.

"Retired, huh?" Joe Bob grinned. "Yeah, those guys've got it made—"

"Well, Dr. Ramey—" She dropped her notebook back into the shoulder bag and scooted from the booth. "I probably shouldn't take any more of your time. It was good talking to you."

"Er, if you see your dad," Joe Bob said, "maybe we can get together sometime—sit around and swap stories. I bet he's got a few to tell."

"And I bet you do too, Dr. Ramey." She handed him a card. "Call me sometime. I'm usually there. Maybe we can talk some more."

"Sure," he nodded. "That'd be fine—just so it ain't classified or anything."

"Don't worry," she said, hefting the bag on her shoulder. "I certainly wouldn't want to get you into trouble with your *employer*."

"Appreciate it," he said, watching her walk out the door.

Joe Bob took a deep breath. The soft, light rain had settled the dust to earth and laundered the buildings on either side of the empty street to a slick freshness. He looked at the business card for a moment. "Sue Colter, huh? Wonder what the hell she wants?" After a long moment, he removed his billfold and placed the card inside, right between his driver's licence and his Camp Jupiter security I.D.

21

Bullseye

Stanley Marienfeld rapped a plump fist against the cab window and yelled at the old man inside. "Slow the train down, dammit! Senator Curry wants a photo of the soldier trenches!"

The old engineer nodded in silent acknowledgement and rotated the throttle back. As the locomotive slowed slightly, the tall, smiling senator squeezed around Marienfeld and aimed his camera at a line dug into the earth. "How far are we from the ground zero, here, Stan?" the senator asked, winding the camera. "Five miles isn't it?"

"Two," Marienfeld replied tersely, brushing a layer of white dust from his blue sport coat.

"Two huh?" Curry exclaimed, taking another photograph. "That's really something. I'll bet those fellows get quite a view of the mushroom from two miles! Beautiful!"

Suddenly, the engine revved briefly, sending a puff of grey smoke from the side of the engine housing.

"Do you think they appreciate the view afforded them, Stanley?" the senator grinned.

"If they don't they should, Senator. After all, these are expensive—*dammit*!" Marienfeld snapped. "This—this *wretched, fucking train!*"

Somehow a spot of oil had appeared on the front pocket of his jacket, creating an angry black-and-tar smear across his family's coat-of-arms. Marienfeld scurried off the front deck of the locomotive and through the side door into the engine compartment. "Look at this! Look!" he shouted at the engineer. "Oil!"

"It's oil, all right," Pliney nodded. "Prob'ly came from the diesels."

"It happened when you accelerated out there!"

Pliney stared at Marienfeld. "Didn't do nothin' of the kind."

Suddenly the door swung open and the senator joined them in the crowded cab. "Beautiful place indeed," he said, smiling broadly. "Especially with that tower—majestic. Standing tall in the middle of desolation."

Marienfeld backed away from the engineer.

"I've had the occasion to tour this area many times, Stan." The senator slapped him on the back. "And I always wonder how the public can't appreciate what we're doing. Pliney, here, for example. You know what we're doing. And I know *you* can appreciate it."

In response, the old engineer sent a bullet of tobacco through the window.

"Yes," the senator continued, "out here in this dry, desolate place no one really wants—the arsenals of our democracy are being forged."

Pliney looked up suspiciously. "I thought they was just seein' what they could blow up."

"No, Pliney, that's wrong." Marienfeld turned to the senator. "Senator—"

"You can call me *Hodel*, Stan."

"Hodel, I'm sorry you had to hear that, but it's an example of the popular thinking out here." Marienfeld sneered at the engineer. "It's a misconception that I—as the AEC Public Relations Officer—have spent *years* trying to change."

"Yes, yes," the senator nodded, suddenly preoccupied with something out the window. "Uh, Stan, you didn't happen to bring my *rifle*, did you?"

"It's in the passenger car, *Hodel*," Marienfeld replied. "I'll get it for you."

As Marienfeld disappeared through the door, the senator turned to Pliney. "Thought I saw a jackrabbit. Old timer, you probably don't get a chance to see much out here in the middle of nowhere. Ever been to Las Vegas?"

"Nope."

"Well, that's a shame." The senator shook his head and chuckled. "It's a beautiful place. Especially when you have a beautiful woman on your arm. I don't know why she puts up with—"

"Here's your gun, *Hodel*." Marienfeld burst through the door, holding the weapon. "All loaded, ready to shoot."

"Good, good." The senator aimed the rifle out the window and sighted down the barrel. "Thank you, Stan. As I was just telling Mr. Pliney here, this desert, this test site is a laboratory where we make our weapons better and better. Democracy's arsenal."

"There's the rabbit, Hodel!" Marienfeld pointed out the window.

"Thanks, Stan," the senator said, squeezing off a shot. "Dammit."

"I suggest we take this train up to target 14," Marienfeld said. "You can find all kinds of wildlife up around those locomotives."

"Oh really?" The senator brightened. "Any deer? Elk maybe?"

"Oh sure," Marienfeld smiled. "I think Pliney here feeds them."

"We can go if you want," Pliney nodded. "But there ain't nothin' up there but those diesels—waitin' to get blown up. Seems a damn shame."

"All this is an integral part of our energy policy, Mr. Pliney." The senator squeezed off another shot, then turned back to face the engineer. "—And don't you think the nation's energy policy should best be left to those *equipped* to understand it? To *deal* with the complex issues involved?"

"The people out there have the impression we're just playing around," Marienfeld shook his head ruefully. "They seem to think we blow up trains and buildings and towers just for the fun of it."

"Ha! Ho!" The senator squeezed another shot. "Got one! This place is thumping with jackrabbits! Where do they all come from?"

"And then there's the Doom Town problem," Marienfeld continued. "I wish we'd never even told the public about it. We get letters from little old ladies, poor people—everybody wanting to know why we have to destroy those 'fine homes'—some people actually want to move out here!"

"Well, those houses *are* pretty nice." The senator ejected a spent shell onto the floor of the cab. "*Very* comfortable."

"Useless damn public," Marienfeld groused. "It can never see anything beyond its own nose."

"Well, Stan." The senator placed the rifle into a corner. "We both know the public can be a little *parochial*. But perhaps we shouldn't fault them too much." He paused to smile warmly at the train engineer. "Now, take Mr. Pliney here—a man whose waking hours are spent in honest, manual labor—he *certainly* can't be expected to take time to bother with the larger issues."

"I'd hope not." Marienfeld scowled at Pliney.

"For example," The senator rested his huge manicured hand on Pliney's shoulder. "I suspect Mr. Pliney just hasn't troubled his mind with, say, the political perspective—have you Mr. Pliney?"

Ignoring the hand, Pliney carefully bit into a plug of tobacco and chewed for a second. "I may not be able to figure out what's goin' on over there in th' great citadels a' science, but day in and day out, ferryin' people back an' forth—I get to know *this* place pretty well."

"See?" Senator Curry smiled, patting the engineer's shoulder. "Here we have a simple, insular man—a man who can't take the *time* to digest the issues. A man who requires explanations from those better informed. He does understand his place in the world—"

Suddenly Pliney fired a loose spray of tobacco out the window, dampening the senator's coat and sleeve. Stunned, the senator stared at the brown splotch for what seemed like minutes.

Finally, Marienfield blurted, "look at the desert! What a beautiful day!"

Curry looked up and cleared his throat. "Ahem. Yes. And I'll wager Mr. Pliney knows every little gully and wash out there, don't you Mr. Pliney?"

"Yep," the engineer nodded as the train rattled over a small steel bridge. "Right now, we're crossin' Achera Dry Creek."

"Named for some Indian, I'll bet," the senator mumbled, taking a handkerchief to the tobacco stain.

"Nope," the engineer shook his head, "Eye-talian. Named after th' river *Acheron*."

"Well, I certainly wouldn't dispute you." The senator picked up the rifle again. "But I've been to Italy a number of times and I don't recall any river by that name—of course, my wife and I usually go to Florence. Very good place to buy leather goods, you know."

"I'm sure it is," Marienfeld nodded.

"Think I have time to fire another few rounds, Stan?" the senator asked, aiming at a passing tree.

"Of *course*," Marienfeld said. "Slow the train, Pliney—just take your time, Hodel—squeeze the trigger—"

The senator fired off three quick shots in succession. "Ha! Ho! Direct hit!"

"Shore hope that wasn't a *Joshua* tree," Pliney said, staring straight ahead. "Th' Injuns out here consider 'em sacred."

The senator winked at Marienfeld. "What is the punishment for this offense, Mr. Pliney—an arrow?"

"Well, sir," the engineer replied, "they say anybody who shoots a Joshua tree'll fry in hell."

"Dammit, Pliney, that's not true!" Marienfeld shouted. "Everybody knows there haven't been Indians out here in—in—*years*! Apologize to Senator Curry *at once*!"

"Just givin' th' man a little local information, *Stanley*," Pliney grinned. "Anyways, goin' to hell prob'ly ain't gonna hurt his election chances—"

"Go ahead and shoot, Senator," Marienfeld said. "Shoot at anything you want. This desert belongs to the government anyway. I'm sure the Indian legends don't have any real *religious authority*."

"Heh," Pliney cackled. "You hope."

"Uh, I'm fresh out of ammunition," the senator said, setting his rifle aside.

"Got s'more right here , Senator," Pliney pointed to the box of shells on the floor. "You can only go to hell once. Right, Marienfeld?"

Marienfeld squeezed between Pliney and the senator. "Listen *you*," he hissed, grabbing the old engineer by the lapel. "This is an important man and if you upset him in *any* way, you're *fired*! Understand?"

"I hear ya," Pliney said, studiously ignoring Marienfeld's rancor. "Doom Town's just up ahead."

"And don't call it Doom Town anymore." Marienfeld brought his face even closer. "We're going to call it the 'Domicile Ignition Site.'"

Grumbling, Pliney reached for the brake lever. Up ahead, the 100-foot water tower gleamed in the bright Nevada sun, its toriod shape a perfect steel representation of the mushroom cloud. East of the tracks, Pliney saw the chalk white stretch of the "Doom Town Highway." He knew the gravel road ran parallel to the tracks for exactly two miles. If he worked it right, the engine would slow down to a crawl just as they entered the city limits of the vacant village.

A few minutes later, as Marienfeld pointed out the scenic high points, Pliney watched the backs of the various stores along Doom Town's main street come into view. He'd been here many times since their construction, and was as familiar with them as he was with the old neighborhoods along the Lakeshore line—a grocery store with a green awning, a bank, a clothing store with a huge glass window, a dry cleaners, a barber shop.

Months earlier, before the senator and other dignitaries had started showing up, Pliney had parked the Express at the depot next to the water tower and walked into town. It was a chill sunny Saturday morning in late February. Since Doom Town's main street ran north to south, only one side of the street was in the sunshine. It reminded him of his younger, rougher days during the Depression—of that early spring in '32 when he was looking for work. Bright Saturday mornings when the cold February wind cleared the dark clouds from a chill spring sky and the direct sun was the only source of heat.

It reminded him of a crisp, bright little tune from that faraway time: *On the Sunny Side of the Street.*

For some strange reason, that song seemed to fit this part of the Nevada Test Site. Friendly buildings in the middle of nowhere.

Pliney tapped the sand knob on the console and the locomotive screeched to an agonizingly slow stop, finally coming to rest at a wooden boardwalk near the water tower. At the north end of the village, near the residential houses, the sun glinted from the tops of cars parked in a huge lot. To the south were rows of red, yellow and green storefronts—the main street of Doom Town.

"There are sensors in each of those cars, you know," Marienfeld effused, his hand tentatively patting the senator's shoulder. "And multiple sensors in the houses—"

"In all the houses?" The senator appeared startled. "In each *room?*"

"No, just a few," Marienfeld said. "When the bomb detonates, we'll know immediately what happens to the structures. We'll be able to see it on television."

"Certainly a beautiful place," the senator said, stepping off the train. "Such crisp, clear air. Reminds me of a little village in Maine. Like an Edward Hopper painting . . . except for the cactus, of course. Are you a Hopper connoisseur, Stan?"

"Uh, yeah, Hopper." Marienfeld turned to Pliney. "I'm going to show him the car lot. There's a Lincoln convertible out there I think he wants."

"Guess that's why you wanted th' flatcar, huh?"

"That's none of your business," Marienfeld snapped. "Just be here when we bring that car back. I don't want him to have to *drive* it across the desert."

A few minutes later, settling back into the worn leather seat, Pliney looked east to where the tracks faded in the distance. From here, he could barely make out the dots and shapes of ground zero, the actual aiming point for the Doom Town bomb. Though there was no telling when the damn thing would actually be detonated—he was usually the last to know—it would likely happen before the July 4 shot at target 14. Probably within a month or so.

Just two weeks earlier, Demming had ordered him to bring the locomotive *Hiawatha*—along with five empty rail cars— to the target. Yesterday he had left her up there at the center of the bulls-eye, all small and quiet and alone. It damn near broke his heart.

Pliney took a deep sigh and tried to think of something else, but nothing stuck. With any luck, the bomb would go off at altitude, right overhead—blossoming like a big rose. Then, in one quick flash, it would melt the proud old girl in style. And if the wind was right, it would send her ashes east, maybe over the old rail centers, to places like Alliance, Sedalia, Burlington and Chicago.

Would it be raining over the old North Shore Line? Probably. Always rains this time of year. Might even send some dust down on the Llewellyn Park station, or maybe over the old abandoned streetcar near the cornier of Utica and Washington. Perhaps the breeze might take the Hiawatha back north, over the Milwaukee Road and out over the Great Lakes to the trackless places that had never seen rails—the sand hills of Nebraska or the wild grasslands of the Little Missouri. With luck and the right weather, the Hiawatha's remains could fall into Lake Itasca. From there, the train would begin a voyage it could never have taken as a standard iron locomotive—it would travel down the great Mississippi, past the villages of Wacouta, Pleasant Valley, Dorenna and Venice. Places he had known himself.

As for everything else, the bomb would cremate the houses and the storefronts of the nearby test village—scattering the ashes of the past into the heart and bones of the future.

"It's best," he said, taking a deep breath. "It's best."

———

"Company orderly!" Ratney Wanker yelled, bursting into the room. "Where is Stein? I want to see him *now*!"

"He's not available, sir," Vincel answered, taking his feet down from the desktop. "He left about an hour ago." Vincel looked at the clock. "He should be back in a few minutes. He was looking for that guy in the Hawaiian shirt. Then I think he was going to stop off at the hospital. Sloan's in again—"

"Again?" Wanker shook his head. "Damn! That guy is *always* in the hospital. What's he in for this time? *Raspy throat?*"

"I think he met up with the A-bomb," Vincel shrugged. "I heard he was flyin' too low during the last test and the cloud got him. Real embarrassing to the brass."

Wanker's eyes brightened. "Maybe *that's* why Thorne's been reassigned! Sure! Because of Sloan's getting cooked!"

Vincel nodded. "I suspect something like that would do it."

"I wonder who'll get his job?" Wanker's eyes glowed. "Maybe me I mean, sure! Why not? I'm the best qualified—"

"That's wonderful news, sir," Vincel yawned. "But I thought a captain had to go through major to get to colonel."

"You ever heard of a field promotion, Puhl?" Wanker huffed. "I can jump as many ranks as the general wants."

"Happy to hear that." Vincel took a candy bar from the desk drawer.

"And when I take command of this dump—well, there's gonna be some changes here! We won't just be in training for the Atomic Brigade. We'll be *better* than the Atomic Brigade."

"A sensible goal." Vincel carefully peeled the wrapper from the candy bar and took a bite.

"Instead of just getting ready for atomic tactical warfare, we're gonna *do it*! No more waiting to drop a bomb on a phony town—we'll use the real thing! Vaporize *real* stores and houses and cars."

Vincel stopped chewing on the candy bar and stared at him.

"Okay, we'll evacuate everybody first, sure." Wanker looked irritated. "But think about it, there's all kinds of towns around here that would be perfect! We could buy the place, get rid of the people and then *have at it*! You know any places we could buy, Puhl?"

Vincel scratched his head. "Well, there's this little place called Hiko. My cousin Robert Wayne said he met some woman from there. *Said* that's where she lived, anyway. Of course, she might have been just pulling his carrot, so to speak—"

Wanker shook his head. "We don't have to use *Las Vegas* or anything. Just someplace small—like Alamo. Or Pee Wee. There's not a hell of a lot in Pee Wee."

"I think there's a grocery store," Vincel pointed out.

"There's a whole lot of places around here we could use. We could drive the tanks up through the White River Valley, take out Elko, then march north toward Boise." Wanker pointed at the map. "What do you think of that idea, Puhl?"

"It's certainly audacious."

"Damn straight!" Wanker pounded his fist into his palm. "That's what maneuvers are all about! Audacity! Find and fix the enemy! Get the job done, then get your ass out!"

Vincel nodded sympathetically. "But you know, *marching* up through Idaho might present difficulties, especially under the circumstances."

"*What* circumstances?"

"Well, I've always believed that the great reticence of people to join the armed services centered around the excessive *walking* involved. Now, if the foot soldier could bring his own automobile, you'd get a lot more cooperation. And the savings in boots alone would be considerable."

"Then they wouldn't be called foot soldiers, would they?" Wanker snapped. "Damn! You enlisted men just don't know the first thing about tactical maneuvers!"

"I couldn't agree more," Vincel smiled. "Now, didn't you have something for Captain Stein?"

"I guess I can tell you." Wanker retrieved a piece of paper from his shirt pocket and handed it to Vincel. "A few days ago, Stein was over at the Bachelor Officer's Quarters asking about Captain Hugh Duffel."

Vincel studied the note.

"Well, General Umber wants him to *lay off.*" Wanker drew his finger across his throat. "Colonel Myrmidon is taking care of it, and he doesn't want any interference."

Vincel leaned forward across the desk. "Did Captain Duffel get caught stealing hubcaps from Doom Town?"

"I'd tell you, Puhl," Wanker said, "if you were an officer. But enlisted men are supposed to be kept in the dark—no offense."

"None taken."

"Just make sure Stein gets that note. He's to leave Duffel alone. Understand?"

"Of course."

Wanker started out the door, then paused. "You know, Puhl, we're not paid to *make* orders in this army. We're paid to *take* orders. Remember that and you'll go far."

"Seems like a sensible admonition," Vincel smiled, putting the memo aside. "Certainly one to keep in mind."

"Just let me know where he is, Colonel." Stein leaned forward in the chair, his voice tight with anger. "I only want to *talk* to him."

"Yeah, Jake, I bet you do," Thorne nodded solemnly. "But I can't let you."

"Why not?"

"'Cause I'd get my butt in trouble." Thorne broke into a sly grin. "I'd have to call up those people at *The Big Picture* and explain why their little fat boy is doing temporary duty in the infirmary."

"I promise I won't lay a hand on him," Stein said. "I just want to ask him why he ordered Sloan into the ventral turret. And why he sent that tank to the GZ."

"I'd like to know the answer to that myself, Jake," Thorne admitted. "But Spaulding and Myrmidon are already looking into it—"

"You trust Spaulding with something like this?"

"No, of course not," Thorne said. "But Myrmidon's another thing entirely. And the general trusts him. So as far as I'm concerned, it's being taken care of."

Stein stiffened.

"Look, I'm sorry," Thorne continued. "Duffel's a pain in the ass, and I wish he'd get the hell back to Fort Monmouth or wherever it is he came from. But I'm just the battalion commander—I can't kick him out without the general's say-so." The colonel paused to rub his forehead. "Besides, I just got my transfer to General Umber's staff. I'd sure as hell hate to muddy things up right *now*."

"Yes, *sir*." Stein got up to leave. "Thanks for your time."

"Just a minute, Jake," Thorne said after a moment. "We have another test scheduled for Friday. An airdrop, right?"

"Yes sir."

"Okay. If Spaulding and Myrmidon haven't done anything about Duffel by then, I'll talk to the general about him." Thorne smiled. "Maybe we can put his butt in a vise. Find out what he's up to. Meantime, just keep things low and slow—as a favor to me. Okay, Jake?"

"Of course."

Thorne shook his head. "God knows, this place is dangerous enough without some damn *outsider* causing problems."

Captain Spaulding shifted on his chair and glanced at the two people in the room with him. While Colonel Myrmidon appeared relaxed, Dr. Bartholomew looked as uncomfortable as Spaulding felt, crossing his legs nervously and studying the horrible furnishings of the cramped apartment.

For an officer who supposedly had a sense of taste, Hugh Duffel didn't know the first thing about interior design. His room in the Bachelor Officers Quarters was reasonably large, but the wallpaper had been scraped clean and replaced with something that looked like oxidized copper. Then there was the furniture—four metal folding chairs marked *Nevada Test Site*, around a small wooden table with an odd battery lamp like those used in Civil Defense Shelters. And the place was dark as a cave. Spaulding wondered how Duffel could stand the room, wondered how *anybody* could. "I think we should open the blinds," he said after a moment, "let some light in here."

"Let's not disturb anything," Myrmidon said, looking up from his notes. "He'll be here any minute."

"I'd feel better if he opened them up," Bartholomew grumbled. "This place reminds me of some kind of dungeon. I can't imagine how he stands it."

"There's a shortage of apartments on site," Myrmidon shrugged. "They probably had to give him an unfinished room—"

Suddenly the door swung open and a smiling Hugh Duffel, dressed in green army fatigues, burst into the room. "Hey, fellas, sorry I'm late," he said, pulling up a chair. "How long you been here?"

"Half an hour," Bartholomew said irritably. "Why can't you ever be on time?"

"Hey, I'm a busy guy," Duffel said, throwing a camera on the table. "You should see the footage I took out there. Beautiful shots around that last ground zero."

"Let's get down to business, Captain Duffel," Myrmidon said, glancing at the others. "There is a test coming up. The laboratory is going detonate its first device at Area 10—eleven miles northwest of Doom Town. There are no test bunkers in the area, so we may have to rely on you again."

"Sure," Duffel smiled broadly. "Anything I can do to help."

"Good." Myrmidon glanced at some notes. "We're primarily interested in placing test subjects in the vicinity of Area 10. Do you think you can get them there?"

"Inside the fire zone," Bartholomew added. "Preferably within two miles of zero."

"Two miles?" A look of astonishment crossed Duffel's face.

"It will be a thermonuclear device," Myrmidon continued. "Two miles will be at the edge of the fireball."

"Well, if you think two miles will do it," Duffel shrugged, "two miles it is. Of course, I *could* arrange for 'em to be right there at the bulls-eye. Think that would be okay?"

Spaulding chuckled and shook his head. Duffel was totally, completely mad. He wondered how much radiation the man had absorbed on his various excursions to ground zero. Probably more than enough to kill *ten* people. "Let's save the bulls-eye for next time, Hugh."

Duffel nodded. "So, how many do you want out there? One? Ten? A platoon?"

"We have room in the ward for two," Bartholomew said. "Two will be fine. Just make sure they're healthy to start with."

"But no one from Stein's company, at least this time around," Myrmidon added. "He may cause trouble."

Duffel rubbed his nose. "I really don't think it's gonna do you much good to have 'em two miles from the target—"

"Hugh," Bartholomew said, "we've discussed this before. How can we develop a vaccine against atomic radiation without proper testing? How can we test the effect of atomic radiation on the motivation to continue fighting? These experiments are crucial. For this shot they have to be at the two-mile marker."

"What the doctor is saying, Hugh," Spaulding added, "is that any closer than that and you'll, uh, *invalidate* the experiment. The subjects have to be *alive* after the shot."

"Two miles, huh?" Duffel's eyes reflected the light from the small lamp. Two perfect yellow discs, twin moons hovering in the darkened room.

"Two miles." Bartholomew raised two fingers. "No more, no less. It's very important."

"Whatever you say," Duffel nodded, his face an outline. "But if it were up to me, they'd be right on the bullseye."

22

Eldorado

12:02 a.m.

Joe Bob watched his screwdriver hit the tile floor and roll beneath the huge object. He wondered why Uborka and Meghalty had to build their damn car bomb so low to the ground. Pausing in his inspection job, Joe Bob stepped back. He had to admit the critter looked impressive—ten feet of smooth, curving metal painted a classy tan with maroon accents. The nose of the device, the "hood," curved back from the flashy chrome grill, then flared to accommodate the wide front fenders. From there, the chassis smoothed out until it reached the rear section, where it widened slightly to form a boxy trunk.

At the top center of the device, Uborka and Meghalty had designed a small cockpit for the timing circuits. Over that, they had placed an accordion of white canvas stretched over aluminum ribs. And the whole shebang was supported by four tires. Whitewalls. To top it off, they'd fitted the nose with a chrome hood ornament depicting an unidentifiable bird. A swan, or maybe a goose, Ramey wasn't sure.

"Ha! Joe Bop, you can't run but you can hide!"

"Hey, Joeey! How is our bay-bee?"

Ramey turned. Uborka and Meghalty stood in the doorway. "Yer baby's just fine, fellas," he said, reaching into the toolbox for another screwdriver. "All the circuits look good—"

"Did you notice the headlamp, Joe Bop? How about this chrome nose?" Uborka walked excitedly around to the front of the device. "I found them at a junkyard. From an old Studebaker."

"Pontiac," Meghalty corrected him.

"See the little chrome albatross?" Uborka pointed to the hood ornament. "My bowling team gave me that."

"Looks great, guys. One of a kind."

"The frame is original, you know—from Detroit," Uborka said. "General Motors bomb division, hee hee."

"It'll be a hit on the street." Joe Bob patted a side panel. "Now, if you fellas will excuse me, I've gotta finish this up."

"Did you look under the hood?" Meghalty asked. "There's even an engine. To drive it onto the plane."

"I took the horn from my own car," Uborka said. "And did you see the siren on the side? It will alert the troops that the bomb is falling."

"That's real considerate," Joe Bob said as he reached up behind the dashboard.

"Joey, there's a light sensor on the hood here." Meghalty pointed out a tiny glass object on the nose of the device. "Be careful not to get fingerprints on it. Hokay?"

"And be careful of the wings, too," Uborka added, patting a shiny maroon fender. "They fold out so our baby can glide to the target."

Joe Bob looked up wearily. "I really doubt if I'm gonna have time to look at much more than the circuits."

"Oh?" Meghalty asked.

"That's right. How come you guys put 'em behind the dashboard? I mean, there ain't nobody gonna *drive* this thing—"

"You don't like our bomb?" Uborka looked hurt.

"I don't know," Joe Bob shook his head. "This ain't like any atomic bomb I ever worked on. It ain't like any *car* I ever worked on either."

"The reporters liked it!" Meghalty hastily retrieved a scrap of newspaper from his coat pocket. "They said it was 'an exciting debut. A new era in weaponry. And sure to capture the attention of the American public.' Do you want to hear more?"

"Sure, sure." Joe Bob returned to the dashboard.

"This one said that 'a weapon modeled after a luxury automobile will go a long way toward changing the mistaken perceptions that the public has toward the atomic bomb.'" Meghalty paused as if to gauge Joe Bob's reaction, then continued. "He said the designers—us, of course—'should be proud of their achievement.'"

Joe Bob removed the plastic radio knobs from the dashboard. "Yeah, it's *real original* all right."

"Everyone gave us ideas at first," Uborka said. "Mrs. Marienfeld wanted us to make it like a real bomb. But with the radar pods on the tail."

"Yes," Meghalty added. "And she wanted something that would shoot sparks on the target just before the impact. To confuse the enemy."

Joe Bob nodded. "That would do it, all right."

"You should have seen the drawing she gave us," Uborka whispered, his eyes wide. "*Whooooeeeeee!*"

"Well, Joey." Meghalty clapped his hands together. "We have to go. Do you think you'll have it inspected before morning?"

"Prob'ly," Joe Bob nodded, examining a maze of wires behind the dashboard. "When are you guys gonna add the nuclear core?"

"It's already there," Meghalty said.

"*What?*" Joe Bob looked up, his eyes wide.

"It's in the trunk," Uborka said. "We welded it shut—"

"You mean all this time I've been foolin' with a *hot bomb?*"

"No, no. It's not armed." Uborka lifted the hood and pointed to an empty space near the frame. "See? We left the battery out. No electricity. Nothing."

"I don't like this." Joe Bob climbed out of the cockpit. "You're tellin' me there's an armed core in the trunk—and it's welded shut?"

"So nobody would steal it," Meghalty smiled wanly. "Plutonium is very expensive, Joey."

Joe Bob stared at the weld line across the trunk lid. He turned back to Uborka and Meghalty. "Now, there ain't any lithium deuteride in that trunk is there? You two ain't planning to turn this thing into an *H-bomb* out there tomorrow morning, are you?"

"Oh, *no*, Joe Bop," Uborka shook his head. "No. No. Noooo!"

"No H-bombs, no thermonuclear!" Meghalty shook his head vigorously. "And out of respect for that, we have hardly any plutonium in it. It will be a very small bomb."

"Very small," Uborka smiled. "So small you will barely see it. You can look at it without hurting your eyes."

"I guess I believe ya," Joe Bob sighed. "Now George Linneman gave me strict orders to finish this inspection *myself*, 'an I ain't got but another hour before they come for this thing—"

"Of course, Joe Bop." Uborka patted him gently on the shoulder. "We'll leave. We just wanted to see how you were doing. We want the best for our baby here. It's our first."

"Hell," Joe Bob grumbled, climbing back into the cockpit, "th' idea is to blow it up, not send it to private school!"

"We were talking about the fireball," Meghalty huffed. "We only want for it a decent fireball."

"If you two don't leave me alone here, it ain't even gonna get *that*," Joe Bob replied gruffly.

As the two left, Ramey removed a cover plate from the dash and surveyed the jumble of wires behind it. Just one more voltage check, and he would call the guys at the airstrip. Then, in about four hours, they'd fly over the target and drop the world's first atomic Cadillac.

3:05 a.m.

Colonel Morriss stroked his chin and stared at the object taking up most of the bomb bay. "It has wheels. The goldang thing has *wheels*."

"That's what they look like, sir," the airman nodded.

"That's the damndest thing I ever saw." The colonel squeezed his lanky frame around to the front of the device. "Whoever heard of puttin' wheels on a bomb?"

"I think it's supposed to look like a Cadillac Eldorado," the airman said. "That's what the scientist told us."

"He did, huh?" Colonel Morriss looked up, a surprised grin on his face. "Does it have a horn?"

"Yes, sir." The airman pulled back the canvas panel covering the cockpit. "If you press this button here, it'll honk for you."

"Well, I'll be," the colonel grinned broadly. "Maybe you boys ought to borrow this thing and take it down to Vegas for the weekend."

"Yes sir."

"Bet you could pick up your share of ladies drivin' this around." Colonel Morriss peered into the cockpit. "Got a radio in here?"

"I wouldn't be surprised, sir."

"Huh." Morriss shook his head in amazement. "This is the damndest thing I ever saw. You know, it's only got one headlight. How come it's only got one headlight?"

"I don't know sir," the airman replied. "I never thought to ask."

The colonel paused for a moment. "We probably should've brought in the flying boxcar. Then we could have just driven this thing out the back, ain't that right?"

"Probably."

"Well, get to your station, Airman," the colonel said finally. "Let's fire this old bird up." As the airman scurried down to the bombardier's platform, Morriss took a last lock at the device. Then, shaking his head, he headed back to the flight deck.

3:35 a.m.

"Half an hour to go!" Ratney Wanker yelled at the line of enlisted men. "Anybody out here tough enough to watch this thing standing up?"

Silence.

"Ha! Didn't think so," he growled, stalking back and forth in front of the nervous, shivering soldiers. "G'dammit men, what's a little light 'n heat? And wind? Dammit, I swear, yer afraid of yer own shadows...got me a buncha old ladies here. Is that what you are?"

"Yes, sir," someone mumbled in the darkness. "We're old ladies."

"Hell, you ain't even that! I seen some women that wouldn't think twice a' running into that cloud *head first*, no sir!"

A few minutes later Stein appeared. "Get any volunteers, Ratney?"

"Hell no, Stein, whattaya think?" Wanker growled. "This company of mine is a bunch of little girls. Hell, I'm tired of it. I had a platoon last month that went up and spit on the tower. Whattaya think of that?"

"Well," Stein shrugged, "all *my* men are in the trenches. I hear this is going to be a big one."

"So what?" Wanker replied. "Thought I'd be leading a bunch of hard-assed men instead of—hell, I don't know what they are."

"Little girls," a falsetto voice came from the darkness.

"There's a smartass hidin' in there somewhere, Stein." Wanker glared the group. "I'll find him."

Stein pulled Wanker aside. "Listen, Ratney, have you seen that officer from the *Big Picture* out here this morning? Captain Duffel?"

"Naw, he ain't here," Wanker shook his head. "Prob'ly scared too. Hell, everybody's chickenshit of a little firecracker."

"If he turns up, let me know, okay?" Stein turned to leave. "I have to get back to my men."

"Yeah, yeah," Wanker grumbled, turning to his company. "All right, goddammit. If nobody's got enough hair to face this thing standing up— go ahead! *Get in th' damn trench!*"

At that the men scrambled into the dark, narrow ditch. A second later all was quiet and Wanker was alone. "Now, don't forget to cover up yer heads!" he spat, kicking a clod of dirt into the trench. "Hide under yer damn blankets, you babies!" He turned to face the target and shook his head. "How in the hell am I gonna make general with a buncha *babies* fightin' for me? That's what I wanna know!"

<hr />

"Where are we, Eduard?" Meghalty yelled, his white hair flying in the wind, huge owl eyes squinting into the inky blackness ahead of the speeding convertible.

"Don't stand up while I'm driving!" Uborka yelled back. "What if you fall out? What would happen to my insurance?"

"We won't see them drop our big debutante!" Meghalty replied, his voice almost lost in the roar of the wind. "We'll miss it— and it will be all your fault! Stand on it!"

Uborka jammed the accelerator and aimed the Studebaker down the line of white gravel. A second later, the car hit a bump, causing Meghalty to lose his grip on the windshield molding and tumble down into the seat. "You don't know where we are!" he shouted, his feet in the air.

"We're somewhere on Base Line Road." Uborka twisted the wheel as the road curved to the northeast. "The target is just ahead."

"We'll never see the fireball."

"Of course we will!" Uborka clicked on the brights. "We will be at area 11, six miles south of the drop zone. We'll see it all."

Meghalty carefully regained his grip on the windshield molding and once again attempted to stand. Amid the rocking and bouncing, he reminded Uborka of a proud but limited maestro attempting to conduct Mahler's ninth in cut time. "I wish you would sit down," Uborka mumbled, brushing the hair from his eyes. "This is starting to make me nervous."

Suddenly it occurred to him there was no longer any gravel in the headlight beam. Somehow he had lost the road.

3:45 a.m.

"Skylight, this is Jupiter Control Point. Please stand by."

"Skylight." Colonel Morriss released the transmitter button. Waiting for the reply, he scanned the instrument panel, glowing dull red in the darkened flight deck of the rumbling B-36. "You know," he said, turning to the copilot, "I've carried many a bomb in this ol' girl—from blockbusters to that big thermonuclear sonofabitch at Eniwetok. But I've never *ever* seen one with tires an' a horn. *You* ever seen one like what we're carryin' back there?"

"Nope." The copilot shook his head.

"I wonder sometimes what those scientists are *thinking* about," Morriss growled. "A damn bomb with a chrome goose stuck on its nose I just don't know."

A second later, a tinny voice came over the headset. "We have you on radar at ten nautical miles to the Drop Point, heading 270, ground speed 280 knots. Please confirm."

"Skylight confirm, right on the dot, Control Point," Morriss replied crisply, looking out the side window. "We now have the target in sight."

"Target will remain lighted until zero minus four minutes," the voice on the radio said. "Is the bomb armed?"

"Armed and ready," Morriss said. "You swept that zone for me down there?"

"Area ten is clean as a whistle, Skylight," the voice responded. "You are cleared for the bomb run. Maintain radio silence through completion. The target will be dark for the final pass."

Morriss took a deep breath and glanced at his copilot. "Gotcha. Skylight out."

———※———

Steering the convertible across the desert, Uborka suddenly saw what he was looking for—the thin, silver glint of railroad tracks. And beyond them, a tiny flicker of light. "This is it!" he said, twisting the wheel hard to the right. "The railroad tracks!"

"Tracks?" Meghalty echoed, bouncing into the air.

"The tracks always lead past the targets!" Uborka yelled. With a bone-jarring rattle, the car bounced over the rails and landed on the other side. Shaking his head, Uborka peered into the blackness ahead of the headlight beam.

"Is this the place? Can you see anything?"

"Look for a light," Uborka replied, squinting into the darkness. "There should be a monitor station here."

"Will we get in trouble?"

"We'll tell them we got lost," Uborka said. "That's what Rhinehart always says when they catch him—hey! There it is!"

Up ahead, clearly visible against the darkness of the moonless night was a single, flickering glow. The monitoring station. They had made it. They would get to see the fireball.

3:56 a.m.

As Morriss guided the B-36 over ground zero, the illuminated bull's eye flickered briefly, then vanished. "Target lamps out," he said laconically. "That's our cue. Open bomb bay."

"Open."

Morriss felt the plane slow down, as if trying to fly through molasses. The big barn doors were open. "Alright, fellers." He banked the B-36 into a long, lazy turn. "We're in final pattern. Hang on!"

━━⟨⟩━━

Meghalty peered into the darkness, scratching his head. "The light at the monitor station just went out."

"The technician must have turned it off," Uborka said, slowing the car to a crawl. "Maybe he wanted to see the fireball."

"He could see it with the lights on, couldn't he?" Meghalty asked. "I'm sure this is close enough."

"I guess you're right." Uborka brought the car to a stop. "There's enough lithium deuteride in the trunk to make a fireball as big as a mountain. I'm sure we'll see it."

"I'm sure."

Uborka looked at Meghalty. "What if Joe Bop found the lithium? If he found it, he'll tell George Linneman. Linneman hates thermonuclear We'll get in trouble."

"I'm sure Joey didn't find it, Eduard. Stop worrying."

"I just want it to go right," Uborka said, staring out into the darkness. "What if the fenders don't fold into wings like they're supposed to? And what if the light sensor doesn't work?"

"Who cares?" Meghalty shrugged. "The light sensor was a loony idea anyway."

"It is *not* loony!" Uborka said. "It's a perfect way for a warhead to find an enemy city—just look for the lights."

Meghalty stared into the distance for a moment, then asked, "Eduard, how much lithium deuteride did you put in it?"

"You mean, everywhere? In the fenders, a bag perhaps." Uborka paused. "Maybe two bags. And in the hupcaps, each a liter maybe."

"And in the trunk?" Meghalty retrieved a slide rule from his coat pocket. "How much did you hide in the trunk with the plutonium?"

"The rest—maybe a hundred kilos."

"Excuse me." Meghalty stepped out of the car and walked around to stand in the headlight beam.

"What are you doing?"

"Calculating." Meghalty squinted at his slide rule. "By my figures, we are going to be too close."

"Are you sure?" Uborka asked, stepping from the car.

"With the lithium added, the device will be thermonuclear," Meghalty mumbled. "And with a hundred kilograms of lithium—the nearest safe place would be . . . Denver, Colorado."

"Not there," Uborka shook his head. "We would never see the fireball from there."

Meghalty tapped his slide rule. "According to this, we would."

3:59 a.m.

"The bomb is away, repeat, the bomb is away." The bombardier's laconic voice filled the intercom headset. Colonel Morriss felt the plane bounce up, three thousand pounds lighter. In a single swift motion, he pushed the throttles forward and pulled the B-36 into a tight right turn, almost flipping the huge plane onto its back.

"Make it kiss its own ass," the copilot chuckled.

"If this is a thermo," Morriss replied grimly, "I don't want to take any chances."

"Uh, sir—" It was the bombardier's voice.

"Yeah, Phil?"

"The bomb. It's not dropping."

"Say again, Phil. Over." Morriss shot a worried glance at the copilot.

"It's not dropping—it's *flying*," the bombardier replied.

"What the hell—" Morriss waited a beat, then pulled the huge B-36 into another wing-over. Leveling out, he looked through the windscreen to see something moving slowly away to the north, preceded by a bright yellow cone of light.

"What the hell is going on here? Is there a prop on that thing?"

"Nothing like that, sir," the bombardier replied. "It must be gliding."

"Well, just where in the hell does it think it's gliding *to*?" Morriss exploded. "*Idaho*?"

<hr />

"I think you're wrong, Emil." Uborka tried to wrest the slide rule from Meghalty's hand. "You must have miscalculated."

"You mean like *you* did last year?" Meghalty shot back. "You divided by zero and thought the world was going to burn up!"

"Well—"

"I'm much better at math than you and—what's that?" Meghalty frowned. "Are you whistling while I'm talking to you? Do you think this is funny?"

"I'm not whistling," Uborka said. "Maybe it's the wind. The wind whistles a lot in the desert."

"You left the radio on, didn't you?" Meghalty said disgustedly. "I don't know what you're thinking sometimes, Eduard."

Uborka felt his heart begin to race. The desert was becoming brighter. Rocks, hills, cactus that, just a moment before, had been invisible in the pitch black darkness, were now clearly visible. With a horrifying jolt, Uborka realized the landscape was inscribed within a circle of light. A *contracting* circle of light.

At the edge of the disk, hills, cactus and Yucca trees suddenly flicked from view, while at the center of the strange zone the ground became brighter and brighter. And all the while there was that strange whine—an air raid siren, or an opera coloratura singing Wagner.

Then, looking up, he saw it—a bright, whining, roaring, four-wheeled nuclear warhead—heading straight toward them.

Stein knelt on the dirt floor, waiting for the blast, mentally counting the seconds. The last sound he had heard was the voice from the loud-speaker, counting backward from ten. Then silence, nothing. Of course, that didn't mean there *wouldn't* be a detonation; the air drops were never on time. But twenty seconds late was a little unusual.

"Captain Stein, has the bomb gone off yet?"

"No, Mr. Batman," Stein replied. "I don't think it has."

"It's Batt*mund*," the reporter said, standing up.

"Please, Mr. Batman, get down—"

"I think it was a dud." The reporter rested his elbows on the ground and looked squarely in the direction of ground zero.

"When that bomb goes off," Vincel cautioned, "those light beams will bore right through your eyes and out the back of your head."

"It won't go off," Battmund barked, "because it's a dud! A fizzle! A misfire! Vaunted new weapon bombs out!" Battmund started to climb from the trench. "Car bomb forces test program off road."

Stein dragged the reporter back into the trench. "Save the headlines until you're sure."

Suddenly a shadow appeared over the edge of the trench. "Well, Stein? Where the hell is it? Isn't there supposed to be a fireball?"

"How would I know, Ratney?"

"You got friends at the Control Point." Wanker tossed a dented walkie talkie into the trench. "Call 'em up."

Stein tossed the radio back. "*You* call them up."

"Okay, I will." Wanker clicked the key. "Hello? Come in? Hey!" Wanker put the radio down. "They don't want to talk. This is a hell of a deal. Come all the way out here and the chickenshit bomb flies away. Damn sorry day when even the *bombs* are afraid of a little action!"

As the cursing, snarling Wanker stalked away into the darkness, the reporter climbed out of the trench. "The guy at the hospital said it wouldn't work. And he was right."

Stein looked up. "Wait a minute. You saw some guy in the hospital who said this shot would be a dud?"

"Yeah," Battmund nodded. "Real smart guy. He was right on the mark, too. Should have listened to him. I woulda' had a story."

"Hold it!" Stein growled. "What was that man's *name*?"

═══〰═══

Eduard Uborka opened his eyes to a flickering orange-red blur. As his vision cleared, he could see scattered patches of fire beneath a dull, smoky haze. So this was what it was like inside an atomic blast. That, or the detonation had taken them somewhere *else*. Uborka staggered to his feet. "Emil?" No answer.

Carefully avoiding the smoldering bushes, Uborka considered the implications of what he was seeing. Maybe Wiggers' theory had been right. Maybe the loops of energy *did* extend out beyond the nuclear fire, then squeeze back to pinch off sections of the universe—like ligated amoebae. The only problem was, now he was now in the ligated part.

"Emil! Are you here?" Suddenly he stopped. Something up ahead was coming toward him through the smoke and haze.

"Eduard! I thought they had killed you!"

"Emil!" Uborka breathed a sigh of relief. "You're stuck here too! Wonderful!"

"Wonderful?" Meghalty snarled, emptying dust from his shoes. "Our debutante was a flop."

"A flop?" Uborka sagged. "How?"

"You must have added too much lithium," Meghalty said. "It clogged the firing circuits."

"Me?" Uborka yelped. "It was you who wanted it to be a spectacle! You wanted it to be an H-bomb!"

"Don't start with me now." Meghalty shook his fist. "You forgot to put in the plutonium, didn't you?"

"Of *course*, I put in the plutonium!" Uborka said. "It was my bomb, too!"

Meghalty's face was red with anger. "You purposely sabotaged my project!"

"*Your* project?" Uborka yelled. "It was really *my* project! And now it's ruined because you *had* to have a thermonuclear bomb! I'm leaving you out here! Where's my car?"

"Ha!" Meghalty sneered, drawing himself up to his full height. "It's gone! Your big debutante *fell* on it!"

23

Doom Town

George Linneman had been sitting in Demming's waiting room for
more than an hour. Even though the air conditioner was running full
blast, and it was so chilly the usually cold-blooded secretary was wearing a sweater, he was perspiring. His shirt was wrinkled, his tie a mess.
He decided he looked less like a manager than something from the funny
papers. "I'm in trouble and I'm going to be fired."

"You said something, George?" the receptionist asked, staring at her
book.

"No, nothing." Linneman looked up. "Uh, Donna?"

"Yeah?"

"Want to go out to Doom Town *this* weekend?"

"Busy, George. Maybe *next* month."

"I may not be working here next month."

"That's too bad," the woman said, turning a page. "I was really
looking forward to seeing that place."

Linneman took a deep breath and sank back into the couch. After a
minute of staring at the wall clock, he decided to get to more immediate
matters. "What do you think Dr. Demming wants to see me about?"

The receptionist raised her eyes, her face a mixture of astonishment and mild amusement. "You mean *you don't know?*"

"I—well—I guess it might be about the, uh, fizzle. Right?" Linneman stammered. "Did he act, uh, *angry?*"

"I think he wants to tear your head off."

"Donna," the intercom squawked, "send him in."

"Bomb Frightened By Troops, Destroys Car." Demming shoved the newspaper at Linneman. "What a truly magnificent headline. Don't you think that's a magnificent headline, George?"

"Yes, sir." Linneman squirmed in his chair. "It's a magnificent headline."

"Those two—*scientists*—who put this thing together—did they think it was a magnificent headline?" Demming asked, rising from his chair. "Did they approve?"

"I don't think they've had a chance to read it," Linneman gulped. "They just got out of the hospital."

"Listen to me, George." Demming wagged a blunt finger inches from Linneman's face. "You and your *weapon scientists* have made us all look bad. The senator had already given his speech about Camp Jupiter Laboratory designing its own atomic bombs. About how he had confidence in our abilities to produce a truly spectacular product. Now he wants to cut our funding."

"But isn't General Umber on our side? I mean—"

"General Umber?" Demming interrupted sharply. "General Umber called the Control Point from his helicopter. He wanted to know where the mushroom cloud was!"

"Well—"

"He had about 500 troops, twenty tanks and God knows how much equipment out there waiting to charge into a mushroom cloud. And there *wasn't* one. I didn't know what to say. After all the bragging I did beforehand, I felt pretty stupid."

Linneman nodded lamely.

"And to top it off," Demming said, taking a deep breath, "I've been getting calls from Washington. From Dr. Trumbo herself, wanting to know *what the hell is going on!*"

"With all due respect," Linneman began, sitting up as straight as he dared, "it was a simple fizzle. Something that just happens. Why, two months ago, a Los Alamos device failed to fire—"

"Because one of your men was sitting next to it," Demming broke in. "Isn't that right?"

Linneman slumped back into the chair.

Demming paused and gave a brittle smile. "You know, George, I was planning to retire to some little place, perhaps in the Southwest, someplace where no one would know my name. Now, thanks to your *quirky* scientists, I have the spotlight right on top of me!"

Linneman stared at Demming's gleaming bald head.

"There is a way out of this mess," Demming continued, returning to his desk. "I've talked it over with Stan Marienfeld, and we've come up with something that might work. He's releasing a statement that the test was just a *dry run*. That the bomb wasn't *meant* to go off. It was a test of the homing device—"

"I didn't know it had a—"

"Enough!" Demming snapped. "We're going to tell the press that we'll detonate the *real* bomb this Friday. And that it will be the *real* test of the laboratory's first atomic device. Understood?"

"I—yes," Linneman nodded.

"Now, tomorrow afternoon we'll receive a proof test device from the stockpile in Denver. To keep from arousing suspicion, they're shipping it by truck."

"Truck freight?" Linneman asked. "An *atomic bomb*?"

"Stanley has offered to drive down and pick it up himself. We'll detonate it from the train. I understand there's one parked near Doom Town, isn't that right?"

"Yes, I believe so," Linneman nodded. "But—"

"As soon as the bomb is loaded on the flatcar, you send someone out there to inspect it," Demming continued. "Then we'll move it to one of the test areas. Any questions?"

"No." Linneman rose to leave. "I'll tell Dr. Ramey that another one is on the way . . ."

"Ramey?" Demming looked up. "Didn't he inspect the last one?"

"He's the chief weapons inspector," Linneman said. "He has the most experience of anybody at Jupiter, except Hendrix, of course—"

"Well, have him inspect the circuits on *this* one, too." Demming steepled his fingers and leaned back in his chair. "But I want you to be there with him. To make sure he doesn't *miss anything* again."

"But, Dr. Demming," Linneman said, "I'm an—well, I *was* an electricial engineer, not a nuclear weapons designer. Maybe Arthur Flagmeyer can go with him."

"You're his supervisor, aren't you George?"

"Well, yes . . ."

"Then it's your responsibility to *supervise him*," Demming said sternly. "Now unless you don't enjoy working here anymore, Ramey will be on the flatcar with that device, and you will be looking over his shoulder. Making sure he does things *right!*"

"Of course," Linneman nodded wearily. "We'll be there."

Leaning out the window of the locomotive, Pliney glanced back at the three shiny railcars trailing behind. He could barely make out the passengers, an embarrassing batch of uptown, self-important public officials from all over the country that Marienfeld had invited to tour the Nuclear Test Site. Pliney tested the wind and fired a plug of tobacco toward the railcars, then watched with interest as the trajectory curved back and smacked against the nearest window.

He turned to face the front, looking over his shoulder at the three men with him in the engine cab. Directly behind him, sprawled in the back right corner, his stocking feet propped against the control column, Carl Rhinehart dozed, a cowboy hat pulled firmly over his eyes.

A few days earlier, Demming—at Marienfeld's insistence, had named Rhinehart as temporary tour guide. While Rhinehart obviously didn't care for the job, Pliney found him a welcome change from the sleazy Marienfeld. The day before, for example, Rhinehart had given Pliney an "atomic cigar lighter," a curved mirror with a clip soldered to the center. "No matter where you are," he said, "if you happen to see an atomic burst, you just stick a Swisher Sweet in the end of this clip and point the mirror at the fireball. Your cigar'll be lit in no time."

Rhinehart was all right, Pliney thought. But the other two were a different deal altogether. Huddled together in the corner, reading big, thick manuals marked *Top Secret*, the hulking Uborka and the shorter, bespeckled Flagmeyer looked like trouble. They looked like just what they were—front men for the atomic bomb. "Better get yer readin' done, boys." Pliney smiled at the two men. "We're only about a mile from Doom Town."

"Thanks," Flagmeyer replied, then pointing out the window, "*Look* at all those buildings, Eduard! They can't expect us to look at all of them! What do they think we are?"

"I don't know," Uborka shrugged. "I'm just happy to be here."

"Gettin' ready for another test, boys?"

Flagmeyer glanced up but said nothing. In the corner of the engine cab, Rhinehart peered briefly from under the cowboy hat, then pulled it over his eyes again.

"I guess ya know Ramey and Linnement are out at the *Hiawatha*," Pliney pressed. "Took 'em out there 'fore I picked you guys up. Think that train's gonna have anythin' to do with an atomic test?"

"I really don't know," Flagmeyer said irritably.

"So they're *not* gonna use th' Hiawatha this time, huh?" Pliney asked.

"We're not supposed to talk about about the tests." Flagmeyer glanced around nervously.

"How's come they want to blow *that* little place up?" Pliney motioned toward Doom Town. "Seems like a waste of good lumber."

"It's an effects test," Flagmeyer answered. "They want to see what the bomb will do to residential structures."

"Well, I can understand *that*." Pliney scratched his nose with the back of his glove. "I was askin' why they have to *blow it up*."

"I really can't talk about it," Flagmeyer said uneasily.

"Suit yerself." Pliney turned back to the front. He eased back on the throttle, and the speedometer dial drifted down through 25, then 20 miles per hour.

Minutes later the train eased toward the familiar boardwalk of the Doom Town depot. "Better get ready to hop off," Pliney said to Flagmeyer. "Those *dignitaries* back there'll fall all over each other tryin' to be the first one out. It's a regular stampede."

"Thanks," Flagmeyer said, closing the manual. "What if we stand out on the catwalk?"

"I was just gonna suggest that," Pliney said as the two scientists stepped outside the cab.

"Are they gone?" Rhinehart pushed the cowboy hat back off his forehead.

"They're still standin' out there, waitin' to get off," Pliney mumbled. "Ya know, the big guy's okay, but that Flagmeyer sure is an odd duck."

Rhinehart studied Flagmeyer a moment, then nodded. "It's his glasses. Makes him look too smart."

"Think that's it?" Pliney asked.

"That, or he's had too much formal education." Rhinehart stood up and stretched. "Where's the microphone?"

"Right here." Pliney handed Rhinehart a huge heavy silver object. "Borrowed this from that teevee star, Dave Garroway. He was out here last year with his monkey. Did a broadcast from right over there by the water tower."

"We really should pry off this NBC nameplate,," Rhinehart said, examining the microphone. "It looks suspicious."

As the locomotive slowed to a crawl, Pliney noticed something moving across the landscape at a right angle to the track. A dark object, floating above the surface of the desert like a huge black wasp. "Here comes trouble."

Rhinehart shrugged. "Just the general taking his afternoon cruise."

Suddenly a bright orange flame appeared near the tracks about a mile behind the train. In the railcars, the tourists pressed their faces to the windows, mouths open.

Pliney stared as another explosion flared silently on the desert. "Dammit, Rhinehart. I wonder what the hell he's doin' out *here*?"

"Wish I knew," Rhinehart shook his head. "Sometimes my imagination gets the better of me."

"Well, seems to me you oughta' start takin' more *responsibility* for stuff you come up with."

"Tell you what, Pliney—" Rhinehart slapped him on the shoulder. "If that general and his helicopter give you any trouble, just tell me. I'll take a few tranquilizers—calm down the old imagination a bit. What do you say?"

"Good idee." Pliney watched the helicopter drone off into the distance. "We shore don't want this to get *out of hand.*"

"No, we don't," Rhinehart said, finally wrenching the NBC emblem from the microphone. "Are we ready?"

"In a minute," Pliney said, easing back on the throttle. "Looks like Flagmeyer and his pal jumped off already."

"Good," Rhinehart said, stuffing the huge microphone into his belt. "Now remember, keep it moving." As the train moved along slowly, Rhinehart stepped out onto the catwalk and climbed the ladder to the top of the engine cab. Reaching the top, he retrieved the microphone from his belt and yelled, "Okay! This is it!"

In response, fifty faces appeared at the windows of the passenger cars.

"Here we are!" Rhinehart barked into the microphone. "Doom Town USA! Remember, no photos. No pictures, no sketches, no tape recordings. Just written notes. Now everybody off! Everybody out. *Now!*"

Immediately, the faces disappeared from the windows. Seconds later, tourists crowded toward the open doors, taking with them notebooks, pencils, Bibles, and miscellaneous small suitcases. Pliney waited a second and hammered the air brake, bringing the train to a sudden, screeching halt. An instant later, the ground was covered with a pile of rolling, dusty, cursing civilians.

And cameras. Cameras of all makes and sizes, scattered over the earth, some intact, most not. Rhinehart, from his perch at the top of the engine cab surveyed the mess. At the center of the sprawling mob of angry tourists, he spotted an angry Civil Defense official with a huge blinking lens protruding from the middle of his shirt. "You!" Rhinehart shouted. "Yes, you! With that *Weno Hawkeye*! What do you think you're *doing* out here?"

"I don't know," the man shouted back.

"Is that camera *yours*?"

"No! I just found it!"

"Then give it to me," Rhinehart said sternly. "You know the rules! No photos! Now, if everyone will please leave their cameras there in a little pile, my associate will collect them . . . Mr. Pliney, the confiscatory burlap, please."

"Shore," Pliney said, retrieving a gunny sack from beneath the engineer's seat.

Rhinehart folded his arms. "Mr. Pliney, you may now retrieve the contraband."

A few tense moments later, Pliney returned with the bulging sack. "What d'ya think, Rhinehart? Not bad, huh?"

"Not bad at all." Rhinehart reached into the bag. "Lessee—a couple of Hawkeyes, a couple movie cameras . . . Hm. That little Stereo Realist should bring fifty bucks at the pawn shop, easy."

"Good, heh, heh," Pliney cackled, tossing the bag into the engine cab.

"All right, break it up, break it up," Rhinehart commanded the grumbling, angry crowd. "Taking photos at the Nevada Test Site is a crime and crime doesn't pay. Now, have a good time, but remember— no souvenirs. Those of you who want your cameras back can retrieve them after paying a small inspection fee." He took a puff from the cigar. "Train leaves in an hour."

"You gonna go with 'em this time, Rhinehart?" Pliney asked.

"Nah," Rhinehart said, watching the tourists grumble their way toward the vacant village. "I'm sure they can take care of themselves."

"Don't look like it to me."

"Yeah, I guess you're right," Rhinehart said, jumping to the ground. "Next time around, I'll try to make 'em a little more *independent.*"

Art Flagmeyer hefted the thick inspection manual and gingerly stepped from the wooden depot platform to the ground. The residential houses he and Uborka would inspect composed the eastern half of the "village," including the huge parking space devoted to test automobiles.

While he hated doing these surveys, he was always interested in the cars the Civil Defense people sent in to be blown up. They only chose the best: Lincolns, Cadillacs, Mercurys, big Pontiacs. Perhaps that was why half the cars vanished just days after arriving at Doom Town, requiring even *more* replacements. It took a lot of nerve to steal a car from the Nevada Test Site, but, despite the constant surveillance, it always seemed to happen. Flagmeyer suspected it was an inside job. Probably somebody from the military.

"I think we should have gone with George Linneman and Joe Bop this morning," Uborka mumbled, looking up the tracks toward the shot zone.

"What's the matter, Eduard?" Flagmeyer smiled. "Is this place too small-town for you?"

"Joe Bop gets to inspect a real bomb," Uborka shrugged. "*We* look at houses. I think George is angry with us."

"Could be. He's always angry about something." Flagmeyer paused and scratched his head. "Hm. There are 20 buildings in all, including six storefronts. Let's go over to the east side of town, just south of the car lot."

As they walked up the middle of the empty street, Flagmeyer felt a distinct sense of foreboding, as though he and Uborka had entered a deserted village whose inhabitants had been dissolved by some strange force. It was an eerie feeling.

Several months earlier, Joe Bob Ramey mentioned a road that had been built near one of the more remote targets. According to him, it was a two-mile stretch of highway "big as an interstate—six lanes, a hundred feet wide." And after the blast, he said that "the whole enterprise just vanished—damn highway *led* to no place, then *went* there."

Walking into the shadow of the water tower, Flagmeyer paused to crane his neck at its immense bulk. "It's full of water, you know," he said after a moment.

"Water?" Uborka asked, looking perplexed.

Flagmeyer gazed at the structure. "It'll probably be the only thing standing after the blast."

"Unless that Lincoln hits it." Uborka pointed to a long black automobile at the edge of the car lot. "A Lincoln is a lot of car."

"Yes, but it can't fly," Flagmeyer smiled. "Now, you take a Cadillac Eldorado—"

"Er, *ahem*," Uborka interrupted, "maybe we should start our inspection. We can't have all day here, you know."

Flagmeyer pointed to a small white ranch-style house. "Let's try this one."

As they walked up the sidewalk to the porch, Uborka paused. "Should we knock first? These tourists might be in there trying out a bedroom. Like Mrs. Marienfeld and the senator."

"Who told you that?" Flagmeyer asked.

"The train engineer," Uborka said, knocking softly on the front door. "Yoo hoo! Anybody home? Marshaaaa!"

"Tell her I said hello." Stepping off the porch, Flagmeyer walked around to check the foundation and siding.

He figured they could get four houses done before the train left. To complete the inspection, they would have to return to this dolorous place five times. He cursed the day he'd told George Linneman about his interest in architecture.

Pausing, Flagmeyer looked at the expanse of desert between the back of the house and ground zero. There was nothing there, only the flat horizon and a dark line that must be the target train. Last year, while inspecting an even more elaborate "test village," he'd remembered looking at the thin vertical shot tower. Despite the structure's apparent size in relation to the landscape, the immensity of its purpose caused it to dominate the entire sky. No matter where he looked, it had always been visible, tracking across his peripheral vision like a tiny malignancy in the field, a relentless icon of mortality.

Now, though, the sky over the horizon was clear, devoid of discernable manmade objects that would facilitate the detonation. This time, the devastation would come from above, blossoming at eighteen hundred feet. Just like at Hiroshima.

Flagmeyer looked around at the sensible wood-frame ranch houses. When the first Doom Town was conceived, the AEC had polled local Civil Defense officials across the country for styles "representative of American housing." And they had received plans for Virginia mansions with arched windows and Tuscan columns, Delaware mobile homes and Florida motels with plastic flamingoes out front.

The engineers and carpenters had given in and actually built one of the proposed designs—a midwestern-inspired home with multiple gables, elaborate porch supports and more gingerbread than a Swiss bakery. Unfortunately, they ran out of the thick siding boards, so they substituted thin wooden lath. After that, the carpenters apparenlty abandoned the blueprints, modifying the house to conform to some other eerie design, some strange voice speaking to them in the baroque.

As a result, houses that had started out as American Gothic became Gothic *Stick*, one of the spookiest styles ever to mar the Nevada desert— false gables, false mansard roofs, weird tiny porches that went nowhere, and huge bay windows surrounded by strange ornamentation. One house close to ground zero had even been fitted with a vast, winding staircase leading past an ornate metal ceiling into a small stuffy closet. Inside the tiny room, the floor had been painted bright yellow, the walls dark orange. Among the scientists, only Elmore Wiggers had liked the place, said he wanted to take it *back* with him.

To everybody else in the Lab, the first Doom Town was plain spooky. Though he'd never actually say so, Flagmeyer was glad the place had been destroyed. This second village, though boring, was easier on the nerves.

"Oh, Artur," Uborka said, suddenly raising a window, "I've found a defect in here."

Flagmeyer stepped inside the house and found Uborka kneeling next to a large wooden cabinet, continuity tester in hand, vacuum tubes scattered across the floor.

"The radio doesn't work," he said, looking up. "I had to remove the guts."

"I see," Flagmeyer nodded, reaching for the wall switch.

"Lights work. Radio doesn't," Uborka said. "This a *Stromberg Carlson* Model 245, made in 1936, the same year I came to the United

States from Budapest. I think it needs a vacuum tube. There's one in here that's all burned—"

Flagmeyer stroked the veneer of the wooden cabinet. "You know, you're right. It *is* a Stromberg Carlson. Back when I was growing up, I remember listening to one like this. We auctioned it off when we moved from Minnesota."

"Look at this!" Uborka pointed to a yellowed paper placard inside the cabinet. "It says, 'acoustical labyrinth—extends bass range, eliminates unnatural boominess—'"

"That's very interesting, Eduard."

"Perhaps we should remove this radio from the test site," Uborka chortled. "We don't want to eliminate any boominess."

"You work on the radio, I'll check the house." Flagmeyer took a deep breath and opened the checklist manual. The Civil Defense people wanted the Doom Town houses to reflect the average home, midcentury modern, so the Atomic Energy Commission's interior decorators had installed a short-tufted light aquamarine wall-to-wall carpet in the living room, and then added several multicolored throw rugs. The furniture was a hodgepodge of styles, from a rust-colored camel-back couch and matching loveseat to two ultramodern orange butterfly chairs. On either side of the couch were Danish design boards done in dark wood veneer, masquerading as a matched set of end tables. Flagmeyer marked the squares on the page: *Bluegreen carpet*—check.

Turning back to Uborka, he noticed that the scientist was using as a backrest an overstuffed, S-shaped hassock covered in green-and-gold tweed. *Ameboid couch*—check.

Across from Uborka and his radio, Flagmeyer was startled to see what appeared to be a dark gray eye floating against the wall. Up close, it turned out to be a Philco television set. The designers had fit the picture tube on a swivel above the chassis, and the electronics box itself was covered in gold metallic fabric. Flagmeyer returned to the list: *Philco Prototype "Predicta"*—check. He could predict how the prototype would endure the atomic test.

In the kitchen, he found an array of appliances sparkling in off-white enamel and connected by a Formica countertop with an ugly boomerang design. On the kitchen table, someone had arranged a place setting of plastic dishes. With red, green and yellow squiggles. *Poppytrail Melmac*—check. *Talk of the Town Melamine*—check. He was familiar with melamine, a urea-based plastic that tended to burn and char rather than melt. If his own kitchen had to go through an atomic attack, he would rather have dinnerware that charred instead of melted. Less mess to clean up.

The interior designers had done their jobs. Both the flimsy metal table and chairs would probably withstand the initial mach front and the subsequent shock waves. As projectiles, they were too light to be a serious hazard to the walls and structural supports, but they would kill anyone unlucky enough to be enjoying breakfast when the bomb popped. Nothing like getting speared by a metal chair leg. Of course, thermal radiation might be a problem. He envisioned a fellow having an early breakfast, reading the morning edition of the Doom Town Gazette when—click!—an intense light pours through his kitchen window, *incinerates* his newspaper, gives *him* a nasty burn, then melts the plastic seat covers, gluing him to his chair.

What a way to start the day.

Moving to the bedroom, Flagmeyer noticed something on the floor, a copper slinky toy. The imaginary family has children. Then he saw another boomerang design, this time as a set of blue ceramic ashtrays, resting on the nightstand. "Children who smoke?" he mumbled. On the wall hung a pair of fluorescent pink ceramic comedy-tragedy masks. Flagmeyer knew the fluorescent color was in response to invisible ultraviolet light from the sun. He wondered what the fluorescent paint would do in the vicinity of an atomic burst—a couple in bed reading, perhaps making love, who suddenly look up to see their wall decoration glowing. *Comedy-Tragedy*—check.

Flagmeyer opened the closet. Inside was a blue chiffon gown, a sundress with enormous black polka-dots and a strapless pink party dress. Separated by some empty coat hangers, he found men's clothes: four yellow pullovers and some Hawaiian shirts. *Street clothes*—check.

He remembered the closet at his childhood home in Minnesota that served as a hiding place for him and his younger sister. In contrast to this sparse little closet, the one in his parent's home was dark, warm, and filled with great vertical layers of fabric that smelled of pine and moth-balls. There were coats of all shapes, sizes and textures—his father's denim work coat smelling faintly of kerosene and chainsaw oil; his mother's church coat, a soft camel-colored raiment with a torn satin lining. There were cotton dresses and trousers and overalls with grease stains, there was his older brother's leather motorcycle jacket, his older sister's crisp chiffon prom dress . . . and shoes. *Mountains* of shoes, crushed and worn and twisted and defeated by years of service, too old to wear, too good to throw out. Flagmeyer remembered how he and his sister had made that closet theirs, arranging the shoes into a rough pile, a bumpy hill of hollow leather where they would sit and scheme, hidden from their older siblings, their parents, the entire world.

"Can't do much with a closet like this," Flagmeyer said softly. Closing the cover on the checklist, he decided the house looked fine. He went to check on Uborka and found the big scientist still in the front room, sitting amid a scattered assortment of radio parts. "Well, are you going to take it back?" he asked after a moment.

"No," Uborka replied. "I think I can fix it, then leave it here."

"If you change your mind, I'll help you carry it to the train," Flagmeyer said. "I'll be across the street."

Walking across the concrete pavement, Flagmeyer opened the manual. House #15. Ranch bungalow, wood, platform frame. Twenty pages per house. Tiny printed words across from little printed squares. Uborka was right. They *should* be inspecting bombs instead of houses. "Let's see," he mumbled to himself, *Foundation: Note All Cracks.* "None." *Water seepage:* "In the desert?" Flagmeyer slashed the printed squares with his pencil. Why did Linneman volunteer his best weapons scientists to be *real estate appraisers*? He and Uborka should be in air-conditioned labs, for God's sake—or at *least* at the target with Joe Bob Ramey—instead of nit-picking over the particulars of buildings that wouldn't survive the first shock wave.

He thought of what would happen to this house, to all of them, in just a few weeks. It would make whatever he did today absolutely irrelevant. First, the electrical power would be cut off, to prevent magnetic surges in the power supply. The houses, automobiles, storefronts, streets, the water tower, all would await their fate in total darkness.

Then, ten seconds later, the device would trigger, and one mile away, in total silence, the explosion would begin. Night would become day and day would become light and the light would obliterate all detail until nothing was left except a complete retina glare. Anyone standing in front of the picture window would see a river of glowing smoke and debris, thundering across the desert toward the house, pushed by the pressure wave moving at 300 miles per hour.

Flagmeyer touched the surface of the house, felt the rough texture of the painted wood siding. The thermal radiation from the GZ would reach it at almost the speed of light. Once there, it would ignite the dried paint, creating a dense layer of black smoke and causing the underlying wood to spew jets of flame back toward the expanding fireball. Just beneath the surface, the enormous heat load would cause wooden battens to sizzle, while behind them the asphalt tar paper would begin to bubble, then curl. The sheet rock behind the walls would smoulder and buckle under the thermal load, releasing thin ghosts of carbon dioxide and radon into the already tortured air.

Under the influence of the magnetic storm, the incandescent lights over the kitchen sink would flare briefly, go dim and then go out. In the bedroom, the fluorescent wall ornaments would glow eerily, silent demons of warning. And there would still be no sound, no movement other than the cacophony of clicks and creaks of a house twisting under the nuclear glare.

Then, destruction.

Flagmeyer watched the scene play across his mind: the pressure wave approaches the city, preceded by a line of dust stretching from horizon to horizon. Automobiles take to the air in a slow ballet, riding the crest of the shock front, gently pushing through the houses like rocks through balsa. Immediately behind them, a line of houses begins to disintegrate as the blast front hammers past. Windows implode, creating shrapnel that slices through the room, piercing walls like needles.

Within the structures, pine joists bend, twist, then snap; roof trusses give; sheetrock walls balloon, then rupture, spraying plaster and gypsum into the glowing air. Then the ceilings begin their slow fall into collapse, and the sharpened timbers drop to the floor, tearing through the burning carpet and smoldering furniture. Finally, with a loud sigh, the air rushes *back* toward the rising, roiling fireball, still as bright as the sun.

Flagmeyer looked out across the one-mile stretch of desert, toward the target where Ramey was inspecting the bomb. An instant after the shot, all the inanimate inhabitants of Doom Town, including house Number 15, would be gone forever.

24

Hornet

Joe Bob watched sullenly as soldiers moved a hook into position above the wooden crate. In a moment, the hoist would lift the object and swing it onto the empty rail car nearby. Then the soldiers would unpack the device, a small proof test atomic bomb from the Denver stockpile. It would be his job to wire it up, test the circuits and wait for the men in white—probably Meghalty and an assistant—to deliver the plutonium capsule. Within 24 hours the device would be armed, ready to vaporize one of Pliney's favorite trains.

During the past hour, the operation had gone from bad to worse. The old electric hoist had cables too small for the load. And none of the soldiers seemed particularly sure how to operate it. All the while, a pale, irritable Linneman scribbled furiously on his oversized clipboard. It would be a bad day.

"Look, George." Joe Bob took a deep breath. "There's no reason in the world to put this thing on the train."

"Demming wants it on the train," Linneman shrugged. "We have to do something spectacular to make up for that fizzle last week."

"I know that." Ramey paused to look at the ground. "But this little bomb barely has enough plutonium to make a decent fireball. All it'll do is vaporize a bunch of old rail cars. What the hell good is that?"

"Look, he wants it on the train. Right behind the engine. And that's that."

"We ought to just admit we had a fizzle, then get on with it," Ramey grumbled, kicking at a clod of alkali. "If Demming wants some kind of *grand production* to save face, tell him we can put sixty kilotons on a tower."

"That's not for you to decide, Joe," Linneman replied, his voice tight. "Now are you going to wire those detonators?"

"Give me the schematic," Joe Bob sighed.

"It's back at the lab."

"What?" Joe Bob pointed at the crate. "You expect me to dig around in there *blind*?"

"It's two years old—spherical configuration," Linneman shrugged. "Radar clock on the firing timer. It's no different from hundreds you've seen."

The soldiers hoisted the crate from the back of the truck, swung it through the air in a neat arc, then clunked it down on the wooden bed of the flatcar. "What's the purpose of this test, anyway, George?" Joe Bob asked acidly. "Somebody want to use locomotives as *delivery vehicles*?"

" Joe," Linneman said, "I don't know what your problem is right now, but you've picked the *worst* possible time—"

"Listen, George," Ramey interrupted, "puttin' a bomb on a train—"

"No, *you* listen!" Linneman hissed. "Uborka's little misfire nearly cost us our jobs! We are not going to screw *this* one up. If you can't get up there and do a workmanlike job, *I'll get somebody else*."

Ramey took a deep breath, slumping his shoulders. "Okay, I'll do it." He picked up his toolbox, and stalked sullenly over to the railcar where four shirtless soldiers were removing the wooden slats from around the weapon canister. In an easy motion, he jumped on board, set down the tool box and removed a ball-peen hammer. "Outta the way, fellas," he growled, "I gotta make this little sumbitch say 'ah.'"

The soldiers flew off the flatcar and scrambled away behind a flatbed army truck. Though the nuclear capsule was missing, the device *did* contain a respectable amount of high explosive. Joe Bob studied the dark gunmetal blue canister. On its side was the familiar radiation sticker and the markings LASL #04-275 HORNET. DENV. It was rated for just four-tenths of a kiloton. The old devices were as inefficient as hell, so the *actual* yield would probably be a tenth of that. Damn thing could go off in somebody's hip pocket and they wouldn't notice. Joe Bob retrieved a Phillips screwdriver from the toolbox and started to work.

The inspection plate came away easily. Inside was a confusion of wires and thicker cables—red, green, white and black. No external power would be used to fire the gadget; instead, the charge would come from an internal source. Sure enough, the bottom of the inspection cavity held a dark, cylindrical battery, black cable attached to the negative terminal, a red cable hanging from the positive terminal. Joe Bob carefully tucked the end of the red cable between the battery and the inner wall of the canister. This way, there would be no electricity to the rest of the device. No electricity, no chance of detonation. He knew most misfires in these self-contained units resulted from shorts in the battery linkup, somebody forgetting to tighten down the terminals before leaving the tower. He wondered if the *Eldorado* misfire was because he'd forgotten to tighten the battery terminals.

After briefly checking the battery, he followed the red battery cable to the capacitor, then to the fuse. Everything seemed tight. "How are you doing?" Linneman called from a short distance away.

"Fine!" Joe Bob wiped away a bead of perspiration. Normally, the desert was so dry it was almost impossible to sweat. Today, though, the humidity was up and the stinging liquid was getting into his eyes. He paused to wipe his face, then looked around to see everyone standing near the truck. Each time the weapons men made field checks, all the spectators congregated where they thought they would be safe—usually about 50 feet away. Ridiculous. If the spherical shell of tetryl explosive blew, it would shatter everything to *twice* that distance.

Joe Bob reached up and around the smooth surface of the tetryl, running his hand across the thin strands of detonator wire until he found the small rectangular shape of the firing circuit, hanging loose near the capacitor. Quickly he plugged the circuit into its receptacle atop the capacitor, effectively connecting the detonator harness with its power supply. The bomb was now partially armed. Looking inside the bomb cavity, he saw the harness assembly hanging motionless over the explosive shell like an wire jellyfish. And behind it, clearly visible on the wall of the canister, was the squarish radar clock with its tiny red light.

Ramey swallowed, wiped perspiration from his forehead. The device would be detonated by the timer—and the timer would be started by radar pulses. Stray radio signals could sometimes start the things going. He hoped no one was using a walkie-talkie in the area. Examining the cavity, he saw that the lamp was dark. So far, so good. "Is it wired yet?" Linneman called.

Reaching around, Joe Bob attached the leads from the clock into their proper receptacles on the firing circuit. "Almost there!" Perspiration stinging his eyes, the sickly sweet smell of tetryl explosive in his nose, he scanned the medusa of wires connecting the clock to the detonators. Everything looked good. He was halfway through. Now for the continuity check. Wiping dust and sweat from his eyes, he took a deep breath. This part always made him nervous—sending a small electrical signal through the firing circuit to see if everything was connected. Though it was fraction of the charge needed to detonate, it made him uneasy. He paused, his head throbbing from the heat. Removing the continuity tester from his belt, Joe Bob attached one end to the capacitor side of the firing circuit. Then, in a quick, practiced move, he connected the other end to the top of the nearest detonator. Almost reflexively, he placed his thumb on the red slider switch, preparing to send the test current through.

No. Wait a minute. He had to count the detonators first.

"Are you finished up there yet?" Linneman asked.

"Workin' on it!" Joe Bob yelled. "I just want to look at somethin' here."

Setting the tester aside, he scanned the surface of the explosive shell, counting the detonators. They were all there—32 of them—protruding from the tetryl sphere like angry bumps on a huge gray golf ball. If things worked correctly, the radar pulse would trip the clock and send its pulse to the firing circuit. Then the circuit would allow energy from the battery and capacitor to course through the wires to the detonators, which would all explode in unison. This, in turn, would set off the tetryl explosive shell, compressing the central nuclear capsule into supercriticality.

Only the capsule itself was needed now. Later someone would insert the plutonium sphere into the center of the tetryl shell through the top of the canister. Joe Bob stood up. The easiest part of his job was making sure the hatch at the top of the canister opened easily to drop in the plutonium sphere.

He inserted the screwdriver blade into one of the hatchway release screws near the top of the canister. It refused to budge. "Must be frozen," he muttered.

"What's wrong?" Linneman yelled.

"It's the capsule hatch. It's stuck or somethin'." Joe Bob wiped his face on his sleeve and peered at the seal around the lid. Suddenly he heard his own heartbeat. Something was wrong.

"What's going on up there?" Linneman took a few steps toward the flatcar.

"I think we got us a problem, George," Ramey said. The capsule hatch had been sealed with flat-head security bolts. Was the nuclear capsule already in place?

"Joe—"

"George, bring me the neutron counter. There's one in the front seat of the truck."

Linneman placed the monitor on the floor of the railcar, then took a step back. "Is something wrong?"

"Don't know yet." Joe Bob set the monitor next to the canister and switched it on. To his consternation, the needle swung to the middle of the dial and remained there. "George, there's plutonium in this thing."

The soldiers standing near the truck bolted and ran, leaving Linneman standing wide-mouthed by the flatcar.

"Yeah, it's hot all right," Ramey nodded, looking at the meter. "There's neutrons all over the place. May be near critical."

As Linneman feverishly studied his papers, Ramey noticed how stupefyingly hot it was in the desert. That, combined with the nauseatingly sweet smell of the tetryl explosive, had made him a little sick to his stomach. Maybe if he stood up, tried to catch a breeze—

Suddenly something caught his eye. Something inside the canister.

A tiny flash of red.

"George, anybody got any walkie-talkies out here?"

"I don't think so. Why?"

"Not sure yet." Joe Bob squinted at the lamp. Was it his imagination? How could the radar lamp be working if the battery was disconnected? Maybe something inside the canister was reflecting the sun. Then he saw it again, a single dull red blip. An improbable, horrible thought flashed through his brain: *Hornet* was trying to come to life.

Joe Bob scrambled to peer into the cavity. The battery cables were as he'd left them—the red wire tucked neatly between the chassis and the battery frame, the black cable coiled harmlessly around the side of the explosive shell.

Another red blip. What the hell was going on here?

Looking again, he saw the problem. The battery cables were attached to the wrong terminals. "Oh brother," he mumbled. In his peripheral vision he saw Linneman's figure disappearing beneath a rail car.

Joe Bob reached for the battery cables, then hesitated. The mixup had probably occurred hours, maybe days before, allowing the capacitor to charge up full. Pulling the wires now wouldn't do much good. In fact, the firing circuit might interpret the sudden drop in current as a go-ahead for the detonators. Hell of a deal.

Another red flash.

Reaching for his tool kit, he retrieved the voltmeter. By measuring the current buildup along the circuit, he might be able to predict how close the bomb was to detonation. Carefully, Ramey attached the alligator clips to each end of the firing circuit, then looked at the needle on the voltmeter. It was rising. The capacitor *was* charged. Not only was the little bastard armed, it was getting ready to detonate.

Joe Bob rattled through the tool box for the wire cutters. No. The wire cutters were metal. If he upset the equilibrium inside the circuit, the detonator would detect it instantly.

He had gone over this thing in his mind a hundred times, even in his dreams. And he had never won. Always he pulled the wrong wire, or bumped some weak circuit board, or just stood there and watched the firing circuit until it popped, sending the fatal current to the detonators—

Another flash from the radar clock. The signals were coming more often—one every seven seconds. There was no question, a detonation was imminent. He needed something that didn't conduct electricity. Perspiration pouring down his face, he pulled a wooden pencil from his pocket. Glancing at the voltmeter, he saw the needle resting against the far post.

It was almost too late, too much current bouncing around inside the bomb to do anything. The electricity could instantly reroute, skip the capacitor altogether and go straight for the detonators. Joe Bob felt his chest fill up, his pulse fill his ears, drowning out even the rush of the desert wind. What a stupid way to die, he thought, poking around inside a bomb with a little wooden pencil. A number two with a bitten-off eraser. Stabbing at a hornet's nest with a short stick—

"Ramey. Are you all right?" Linneman's voice. "There *is* supposed to be plutonium in it. It says right here. Joe?"

Something was drowning out the voice. A hard, distinct hum, a whine like the sound of an overloaded transformer. The sound of hornets. Ramey tried to clear his mind of the noise, tried to focus on the problem—an armed nuclear device with a circuit absolutely flooded with electricity. Where could he disconnect?

Sweat stinging his eyes, he pulled at one of the detonator connections. It remained firmly embedded in the shell. Good job, you bastards, he thought. Nice and tight. Glancing at the radar lamp, he saw the light now fibrillating into a steady glow.

Think! Why couldn't he *think*?

All he could hear was a high steady hum, blotting out the sound of the wind, fighting for the voice in his mind. He wished he could concentrate. Concentrate! Rhinehart had said the bomb hums just an instant before it goes. Electrons roaring around inside the capacitor like a horde of bees. Turbulance—

Ramey shook his head violently, trying to remove the extraneous images, only to have them come back. The sting of the Hornet. Susan Colter. Ethel's. His home in San Antonio. Something whirring and clicking in the distance. The howling wind. If he could bleed off the pressure somehow. It seemed all his senses were sending signals through one tiny part of his brain at the same time. Hands shaking violently, uncontrollably, he was blowing all his goddamn fuses—

That was it. The fuse!

Ramey grabbed needlenose pliers from his belt and scrambled, sprawled to where he could see the tiny glass cylinder—a thin bridge of filament wire that conducted the current to the firing circuit. He looked, took aim and stabbed the pliers into the heart of the bomb, aiming for the tiny wire bridge.

Contact. Pull. The crackle of breaking glass, converging on the fine wire bridge. Snapping back in stop time. The roar of the Hornet.

Click.

"Joe?" Linneman called from beneath the railcar. "Are you all right?"

Opening his eyes, Ramey saw soft white brush strokes of cirrus circling the sun in a brilliant blue sky, felt the desert breeze, now cool on his face.

———※———

"Thank you for coming in, Joe," Linneman said. "Sit down."

"What's on your mind, George?" Joe Bob asked, his eyes on the supervisor.

"I want to talk to you about the mishap with the *Hornet* device yesterday," Linneman said stiffly.

"*Mishap?*" Joe Bob sat up in his chair.

"I've reported the incident to Dr. Demming, of course."

Joe Bob watched Linneman shuffle the papers on his desk nervously, then looked around the cramped, stuffy office. On the bookshelf were Linneman's books on management. On the wall was a picture of some kind of fish.

"Demming wanted to know how it happened."

"How it happened?" Joe Bob felt a knot form in his throat.

"I recall you said you'd miswired it." George Linneman sat stock still behind his desk, his voice strained. "I heard you say that."

"I never said that." Joe Bob fought to keep his voice under control, but it came out as a low growl. "The battery cables were reversed. It was that way when I *got* there."

"So you think somebody wired it that way at Los Alamos?" Linneman asked. "And that the device spent two years in the Denver stockpile fully armed? Is *that* what you're telling me?"

"I don't know!" Ramey replied. "But *I* sure didn't arm it!"

Linneman sat back in his chair, his jaw muscles twitching nervously. Ramey had seen that twitch before, when the lab supervisor was dealing with Carl Rhinehart. It meant he was going to stubbornly stand his ground, then retaliate totally out of proportion to the offense. Sometimes Joe Bob wished Linneman would just lose his temper instead of walking around three-quarters mad all the time, looking for revenge.

"All right," Linneman said finally, "you're telling me the bomb came to the test site armed and miswired—"

"I'm sayin' it came to the target that way," Joe Bob said.

"This is the second mishap you've been associated with, Joe," Linneman sighed. "With the Lab bomb—well, I could understand your missing something. It was a new design. But the *Hornet* was a two-year-old device. You've seen—I don't know—dozens of those. Now, I'll have to explain this to Demming—"

"George, that damn thing had plutonium in it!" Ramey suddenly took the offensive. "You don't put plutonium in a bomb until just before you detonate!"

"Many of our test devices are armed in advance." Linneman paused to remove a pair of glasses from his shirt pocket, then carefully placed them on the bridge of his nose. "Joe, did you do anything with the battery cables before examining the firing circuit?"

"Sure," Ramey replied, "that's the procedure. You check to see if the positive lead is off the terminal."

"Yes," Linneman leaned back in his chair.

Joe Bob felt uneasy. Before he became lab manager, George Linneman had been in charge of Camp Jupiter's electrical systems. He probably understood batteries and capacitors better than anyone at the test site.

"You're sure you disconnected the proper cable?"

"Sure," Ramey said. "The red one."

"Now, the positive and negative terminal posts on the battery are clearly marked." Linneman narrowed his eyes. "Did you double check the battery to see if you'd deactivated the proper *terminal*?" The question hung in the air like a dark cloud.

"I don't remember," Ramey said finally. "I don't know. I just looked at the cable color."

"I asked Art Flagmeyer to look over the Hornet device, and he found the negative terminal of the battery connected to the chassis— grounded."

Joe Bob swallowed hard. He knew what was coming next.

"And the positive terminal was connected to the firing circuit. It was in the proper configuration for detonation. It looks like you went out there and *armed that bomb*."

Ramey tried to think, tried to visualize the canister with its battery and wires and cables and flashing lights. Had he checked to see if the cables were attached to the proper terminals? He had done something to one of them, but *what*? All he could remember was the blinking red light. "Okay. What about the radar clock?" he asked. "The radar lamp was flashing—"

"There are stray radio signals all over the area, you know that. One of them probably activated the countdown timer. But it wouldn't have mattered if you first hadn't connected the firing circuit."

Joe Bob felt an eerie chill spread down his spine. Linneman was right. He *had* almost caused a detonation. Out there on that flatcar, he'd been so worried about putting a bomb on one of Pliney's damned old trains that he'd almost gotten everybody killed. He felt the gooseflesh rise on his skin.

Linneman looked directly at Joe Bob. "Even if there *was* a problem with the device when it arrived, even if there *was* a nuclear core inside, the point is, *you* were inspecting that device. You should have caught the problem, and you didn't."

Ramey nodded, only half listening. All he could see was that tiny flashing radar lamp.

"I'm putting you on probation—pending the outcome of the investigation. Art Flagmeyer will take over your duties at the lab."

"Art, huh?"

"Until we clear up what happened," Linneman said, his voice softer. "For the time being, you'll be reassigned to the Control Point." He paused. "You'll be happy to know Demming changed his mind—about detonating the device from Pliney's train."

"He did, huh?"

"At least for this test." Linneman looked at a memo on his desk. "He's having the Hornet placed on the shot tower at Area 12. It's scheduled for tomorrow morning at 4 a.m. Report to the Control Point about an hour before the shot."

A few minutes later, Joe Bob stepped from the administration building into the bright sunlight. What in the hell had happened out there on that flatcar? He tried to remember, tried to recreate those horrible minutes, but all that came was the image of that flashing red light, counting the frames of his own personal movie down to the end. Joe Bob put on his sunglasses and headed for his roadster. After tomorrow morning, that red light, the radar clock, the whole damn bomb, would be out of his life, just part of a dirty pink cloud drifting east toward the sunrise.

25

Hendrix

Joe Bob looked up at the metal tower rising into the clear air. It seemed to be in the middle of a flat, dusty area. In the far distance the mountains arced above the horizon, glowing bright orange under a cloudless purple sky. But there was no sun.

Above him, high atop the tower, was a squarish building with a thin cable running from it, forming a lazy inverted parabola to a low concrete building in the distance. And there was a soft hum, a whine. Where was it coming from? Looking behind him, he saw his Dodge Roadster convertible parked next to a railcar. Had he driven here?

"Four minutes to detonation. Take your positions."

Now he knew. The hum was coming from the tower, from the bomb. He was in his car now, but it wouldn't start. Looking up, he saw a line of lights moving in a V-formation. Bombers. Cloud trackers. Waiting for the mushroom to form.

Turning, he saw someone climbing the shot tower.

"Two minutes to detonation. Fasten dark glasses and cover your eyes."

No!

Joe Bob sat up in bed, his face covered with sweat, listening for the hum. It was gone, replaced by the occasional hiss of tires on the highway outside. Embedded in darkness, the clock's luminous dial glowed softly on the dresser. It was 2:20. He'd been asleep only four hours. Pulling the curtain away from the window, he saw headlights rush past the trailer. Civilian workers coming in from Las Vegas. Rubbing the sleep from his eyes, he looked at the clock again. The Hornet test was less than two hours away.

Good, he thought. Take the li'l sumbitch out and set it off—turn its goddamned mixed up cables and blinking radar lamps into so much neutrons and electrons and radiation. Turn it into a cloud and send it east. Get it the hell *out* of here. Shivering in the chill air, Joe Bob sat at the edge of the bed and pulled on his slacks. There was no time to shower.

Whump. Whump.

McCorkle opened his eye to a glare of overhead light. At the other end of the barracks, Sgt. Quaak, cane in hand, methodically thumped the bunks. "C'mon. G'up. Les' go." Whump. Whump. *Whump*.

McCorkle reached under his pillow for his watch. 2:30 exactly. Another atomic test. He closed his eyes and pulled the blanket over his head. The sergeant usually made two passes before calling him out by name. He would get another two, maybe three minutes of sleep.

"C'mon, you too, Corkle."—*whump*—"g'dammit. G'up."

"Sure, Sarge." Shivering in the cold, McCorkle swung his feet to the floor. The place was freezing. Some fool had switched on the fan at the back of the barracks, sending chilly night air through the bay. McCorkle removed his green fatigues from the headpost and slowly stepped into them, one pant leg per minute.

"C'mon," the sergeant barked, "th' old man wants ta see ya down front in ten minutes."

McCorkle wondered where Captain Stein would take them this time. Another maneuver around the edge of the base surge? Unlike that asshole Captain Wanker, Stein never brought his troops too close to the GZ, always tried to keep them in clear air. As the men slowly, silently filed down the aisle toward the stairs, McCorkle quickly buttoned up the thick olive cotton shirt, then opened his footlocker to retrieve the mask. Oh yes, cotton for the earplugs. Didn't want radioactive dust getting inside his head. After quickly making his bed, he sat down to finish lacing his boots.

"You dressed yet, Corporal? You're holding everybody up." McCorkle looked up at Lieutenant Perkins, fresh-faced, bright-eyed, ready to go.

"Lieutenant, I am a man more sinned against than sinning."

"Yeah, okay," Perkins grinned. "Great. See you down in front."

McCorkle returned to his bootlaces. A few more months of this, then he'd be out in the real world. College maybe. He'd be there now if it wasn't for this. "A man whom fortune hath cruelly scratched," he mumbled, finishing the tie. Looking up, he saw that the lieutenant had gone. He was alone in the barracks.

McCorkle stretched his tall frame to its full height, yawned, then shuffled around the bunk to his locker. He took out the field pack and dropped it onto his back. It felt like it weighed sixty pounds. "A little heavy," he mumbled, "should have added more newspaper." Tightening the straps, he noticed a shadow move across the floor. Someone was standing behind him. "Hold your horses," he said, closing the locker door. "I'll only be a minute."

≡⊶⟊⊷≡

Joe Bob picked the most comfortable-looking chair at the monitor banks, then settled in to watch the show. Behind him, Milt Henderson navigated his bulky frame down the cramped aisle, chattering to everyone present. "Coffee's on—got three hot plates going—coffee's on. Use your own cups, please."

Sighing deeply, Ramey looked at his watch. Three-thirty. Half an hour to go. He stared at the monitor. He had chosen number nine—one of the long-range lenses mounted on the Control Point roof and aimed directly at the target. It provided a good overall picture of the tower and surrounding grounds. When it was working. Right now, it showed only static. He picked up the phone and dialed.

"Operations. Groder."

"Hi, Jimbo, this is Ramey."

"Heard about your close call two days ago."

"Yeah, yeah," Ramey nodded. "I'm over here at the station nine monitor and I'm just gettin' snow. Think you can do anything?"

"Number nine, huh? Just a minute." Suddenly the screen displayed an extreme closeup of Groder's chipped front teeth. "How's this? Better?"

"I think I'd rather have th' static," Joe Bob chuckled. "Is the roof camera on?"

"Gimme a minute." The screen convulsed to a point of light, then reappeared as a soft glow. The search lights of the target.

"Thanks, Jim," Ramey said, hanging up the phone. He would get to see Hornet's demise after all. Through the Control Point picture window he saw a flare arc into the black sky like a distant firework.

"Twenty-five minutes to zero, fellas," Henderson said, nudging his way though the aisle. "Last chance for breakfast. Only four doughnuts left."

"Here, Joe, you ought to be awake through this." It was Hendrix, wearing his plaid coat and bow tie. In his outstretched hand was a steaming cup of black coffee.

"Thanks, Don." Joe Bob locked at the oily surface of the black fluid, then set the cup down in front of the monitor.

"I heard you're *somewhat familiar* with that little fellow out there," Hendrix said, pulling up a chair. "What happened?"

"It damn near got me. *That's* what happened," Joe Bob replied. "Demming wanted that little bastard on one of Pliney's trains. They'd just put it on the flatcar out near Doom Town and I started checkin' the circuits— when something tripped the radar light. Stray radio signal probably."

"Bet that made you think." Hendrix took a sip of coffee.

"It was my own damn fault," Ramey mumbled. "Cables were reversed and I didn't even see it."

"Those things happen. But it could have been a whole lot worse," Hendrix grinned. "It could have turned into quite a *spectacle*. At least you're around to talk about it."

Joe Bob scratched his head.

"Look what happened to Wiggers. When he went he took a whole town with him."

"It was just a test village. Nobody lived there."

"Well now, it was *still* a town," Hendrix replied. "I was gonna take Amanda and the girls out to see it. What was Wiggers doing out there with that bomb anyway?"

"I dunno," Ramey shrugged. "He never said."

Suddenly the loudspeaker snapped on, and Milt Henderson's voice filled the room: "Twenty-minute flare coming up. Everybody take your positions."

"Well, that means us." Hendrix got up from his chair. "See you after the shot. Maybe we can stop off at Ethel's for some breakfast."

"Good idea," Joe Bob replied. Outside, the second flare exploded into the night sky and slowly drifted back to earth, burning green all the way to the ground.

Crouched in the cool darkness of the trench, Perkins watched the greenish ball of fire arc directly overhead, then descend to the desert floor. As the flare touched ground it disintegrated in a fountain of orange sparks. Behind it, illuminated by the floodlamps, a sinuous ribbon of white smoke drifted southeast across the desert toward the line of tanks. "There's a light breeze," he said to no one in particular.

"It's blowing our way." It was the reporter's voice. "That breeze is going to bring the mushroom right on top of us."

"I really doubt that, Mr. Battmund." Stein's voice. "But just in case it does, make sure you're wearing your respirator."

As he waited for the signal to take cover, Perkins leaned back against the dirt wall, loosened the cotton plugs in his ears and listened to the random voices in the cold morning darkness. Some had the flat tones of boredom; others carried the high, pinched tension of fear.

"I lost my earplugs." The reporter again. "Does anybody have any extra cotton balls?"

"What do you think we are," someone asked. *"Teddy bears?"*

"Here's some cotton. Don't lose it." Stein.

"Why can't I ride with the tanks again?" Battmund whined.

"You'll have to ask Colonel Storax."

"Then where's Colonel Storax?"

"I don't know."

Silence. Perkins adjusted his respirator straps, removed his smoked glasses from his ammunition case, then checked to see if his radiation film badges were all in their places: helmet, shirt pockets, hip pocket and one dangling by a chain from his belt buckle. He thought the belt buckle was a stupid place to hang a radiation film badge. When he ran across the desert it bounced against Mr. Friendly.

Suddenly he heard the reporter again. "Captain Stein, I hear they're gonna let Dave Garroway broadcast from the Control Point."

"I hadn't heard that."

"And he's even gonna bring that chimpanzee along. What's his name? Zippo?"

"It's *Zippy*," Sergeant Quaak mumbled from the darkness. "Zippo's a goddamn *cigarette lighter*."

"Five minutes to detonation. gentlemen," the loudspeaker crackled. "Troops and observers should be at your positions."

"Everybody down," Stein commanded. "Don respirators!"

"Three-minute flare," Henderson called out across the Control Room, then keyed the microphone. "H minus three minutes. H minus three minutes. Troops and observers should now be in position—"

Joe Bob leaned forward in his chair and studied the scene on the monitor. On the left, a black metal tower extended into the darkness. Except for its height, it resembled one of those old Aeromotor windmills he had seen on countless Texas farms.

"Two-minute siren," Henderson announced casually. Since the siren was attached to the shot tower, Ramey knew it would take twenty seconds for the sound to reach the Control Point.

"Capacitor charging!" Henderson called from behind the console.

Hendrix threw a switch, then flashed a sly grin at Joe Bob. "Radar lamp active. The timer is running."

Henderson nodded, then keyed his microphone. "H minus one minute."

Watching the screen, Ramey felt his muscles tense. He wondered who was monitoring the trenches, the troops. Wondered what kind of a fireball Hornet would produce. Wondered—

"Three—two—one—zero!"

Ramey stared at the screen. The scene was still there.

"Misfire! Misfire! Hold your positions!" Henderson yelled into the microphone, his voice almost shrill. As Ramey watched, the Control Room froze for an instant, then erupted into chaos. "What the hell is this?" Henderson stormed. "Where's the snag? A short in the cable?"

"It carries its own charge," someone said. "It has a battery—"

"Well—*damn*!" Henderson exploded. "Ramey! You inspected that thing! What the hell have we got out there?"

"I don't know. I—"

"I think somebody else looked at it after him," Hendrix interrupted. "Art Flagmeyer wasn't it?"

"Well, why the hell isn't *he* up here?" Henderson said, picking up the microphone. "Hold your positions! Repeat! Hold your positions!"

After the loudspeaker rattled out the misfire announcement, Perkins counted to ten, then slowly removed the smoked glass from his respirator visors. The visors were completely fogged with moisture. It was like being inside a warm car on a cold, wet spring night. This thing needs a defroster," he mumbled.

"Nobody move!" Stein yelled.

Perkins shifted to the other knee, trying to figure how he was going to clear the visors. Maybe if he loosened the strap —

"What do you think, Joe?" Henderson positioned the schematic to the center of the table. "Is it the firing circuit?"

"Dunno," Joe Bob shook his head, studying the diagram. "It's a pretty reliable design."

"I was told you had a problem with it," Henderson said.

"The battery cables were reversed," Ramey mumbled, tracing the circuit diagram with his finger. "The timing circuit seemed okay—anyway, Art Flagmeyer looked at it after I did. And Art's pretty thorough."

"Then why doesn't the goddamn thing *detonate*, Joe?" Henderson roared. "The capacitor's loaded, the timer's down to zero. And it's just *sitting* out there!"

"Okay, then. I'll go out and take a look."

Henderson paused, weighing the alternatives. After a moment, he shook his head. "No. Nobody goes out there until we know what the problem is."

"Milt." Groder held up a phone. "It's the general, hopping mad. He wants an all-clear."

"Tell him to wait—tell him I'll get back to him." Henderson turned to Hendrix. "Don, this thing has a radar clock. Do you think it could it be a stray signal coming from somewhere? A walkie-talkie? Maybe from the general's helicopter?"

"I guess anything's possible." Hendrix paused to light his pipe. "But Joe's right. The only way to find out is to *look* at it."

"Milt," Groder said, holding up the phone, "it's the general again. He wants to send in the tanks."

"Tell him no," Henderson snapped, then turned back to the group. "Okay. Who wants to kill it?"

"I'll do it," Hendrix said. "My toolbox is in the office."

"Okay, Don," Henderson nodded, "it's all yours. I'll deenergize the switchbox chassis."

"Look," Joe Bob said, "I'll go instead. I've already seen the inside of that thing."

"Sorry, Joe," Henderson said. "You know the rules on misfires. Only one on the tower at a time."

"Milt!" Groder said, holding up the phone. "It's General Umber. He wants to talk to you. It sounds like he's mad."

"Tell him we're busy," Henderson shot back.

"But—"

"Tell him to go *fuck* himself!"

———

"How much longer are we going to have to stay here?" the reporter asked.

"Not much longer," Stein replied, looking at his watch. "A few minutes ago I saw a jeep on the way to the tower. They're probably going to disarm the thing."

"Can we get up now?" Battmund asked.

"No."

"My knees hurt."

"Be patient, Mr. Battmund," Stein replied. "It'll only be a few minutes."

———

Hendrix stopped the jeep next to the switchbox and shut off the ignition. The soft breeze carried the dull drone of the gasoline-powered generators at the base of the tower, two hundred yards to the north. Probably shouldn't drive any closer, he thought. Unlike the generators at the GZ, the coil in the vehicle's ignition system was unshielded, producing a small but significant amount of radiofrequency. With the impaired radar clock—well, there was no use taking chances.

Reaching into the back of the jeep, he retrieved his tool pack and stepped out onto the hard desert alluvium. He opened the lid on the switchbox, and surveyed the column of knife switches—some dedicated to the spotlights surrounding the metal tower, others to the various experiments, one controlling the elevator. As a security procedure, the metal frame of the switchbox was usually energized by 220 volts of electricity. Not only that, there were the protruding pieces of electrified copper plates sticking out of the switchbox like a forest of metal rulers standing on end.

In theory, if anyone—Russian spies, for example—tried to tamper with the switches they would probably touch the frame or the copper plates first and be instantly electrocuted. Hendrix thought it was an incredibly stupid setup. Besides, there were no Russians in Nevada. Carefully, he touched the frame of the switchbox and one of the copper rods with the blade of his screwdriver. No sparks. Good. The security system was off. Reaching into the switchbox, he ran down the list, murmuring, "spotlight, camera one, camera two . . . military . . . military camera . . . elevator. Here we are." He closed the appropriate knife switch and heard a metallic clunk from the direction of the tower.

⚒

"He's in the elevator," Joe Bob said, watching the monitor. "It's moving up the tower."

"I really hate it when he uses the elevator." Henderson shook his head. "I'd rather he just shut down the electricity altogether—"

"He'll be all right, Milt," Joe Bob nodded. "He's done this before." As Ramey watched the long-range monitor, the other technicians in the room crowded around monitor #13, the one showing the inside of the bomb cab. Watching the group stare at the screen, he privately wished they had chosen a different number for that camera.

⚒

Hendrix glanced at his watch. 5:10 a.m. Directly overhead, blotting out the stars, was the flat black shape of the bomb cab. Hoisting himself over the edge of the platform, he peered into the dim light of the shed. A lone 60-watt bulb hung from the ceiling, creating just enough light for the television camera to record anything that might take place inside. Hendrix chuckled to himself. The camera was one of Security Chief Vernon Fogler's brilliant ideas. Each blast turned another million dollars worth of television equipment to vapor. Carefully staying out of camera range, Hendrix surveyed the bomb cab—cables lying every which way, wires of every shape, description and color. Someone had even left behind a candy bar wrapper. *Gifford's Fudge Bar.* It was Deckman's. Only Deckman would eat a Gifford's Fudge Bar.

The shot cab was a mess, like a dingy, unkempt garage.

Still, there was no need to clean up before a detonation. The fireball always took care of that.

Staying out of view of the cab's television camera, he opened his toolbox and retrieved a telephoto lens.

"Come on, Don!" Henderson growled, hitting the console with his fist. "Say something!" Then, turning to Groder, "Are you sure he's up there?"

"There's nothing on the monitor yet," Groder answered, his face inches from the screen.

"Come *on*!" Henderson hit the console again.

"Easy, Milt," Joe Bob said. "He's good. He'll get to it."

"Dammit, Joe, he *always* does this! Stands around scratching his ass—I wish he'd just *pull the plug!*

"It's a self-contained unit, Milt," Joe Bob replied. "He'll be careful. Besides, I've seen you do the very same thing. You hung around the Charlie device for half an hour before you disconnected it."

"That was different," Henderson grumbled. "Charlie was a much safer device."

Hendrix threaded the telephoto on the end of his camera, attached the tripod, then stepped to the door of the bomb cab. To the south, the lights of Camp Jupiter glowed soft yellow in the clear night air. Closer to the tower, the floodlamps at the army maneuver zone resembled downtown Las Vegas. Looking out over the edge of the platform, he searched the ground around the base of the tower for tire tracks. After a second, he found them, snaking along the edge of the lighted zone, leading to the darkened area east of the tower. The restricted military quadrant. The bunker.

Carefully positioning the tripod on a smooth space of the floor, Hendrix aimed the camera, and tripped the shutter.

———※———

"Mister Stein?"

"Mr. Battmund, "Stein sighed, "I know what you're going to ask. And the answer is still no."

"But—"

"We have to stay here. In the trench. Until the loudspeaker says we can—" Suddenly there was a buzz from the darkness. The communications line.

"It's Captain Wanker," Sergeant Quaak said. "He wants to move forward to the tower. He said it's been cleared with the general."

"Good for him," Stein said. "But we're staying put."

———※———

"Hey!" Groder yelled. "There he is!"

Joe Bob hurried over to the cab monitor. On the screen was the familiar small black canister. Hornet. Then a ghostly figure appeared, crossed in front of the scene and retrieved something from offscreen. The Control Room speaker gave a loud pop, followed by a soft hum. "The microphone's on!" Groder said.

"What's that humming noise?" Ramey growled.

"Cable static," Henderson replied. "—Probably."

"Can you fellows hear me?" Hendrix's voice, tinny and metallic, crackled from the loudspeaker.

"Fine. We hear you fine, Don," Henderson replied. "Go ahead."

"Everything up here appears in order. I can see that the hatch is loose. Hm—"

Joe Bob felt a chill as he watched the blurry white figure kneel in front of the canister. Still, Hendrix was the best technician in the business. His specialty was the misfire. He knew what to do.

"—I can't tell yet what caused the malfunction. Cables seem tight. Battery connections are tight. Detonator harness is wired properly. The radar lamp is on the firing circuit. Joe Bob, are you there?"

"Right here, Don."

"You've had some experience with this thing," he said. "Anything special I should know about it?"

"There's a fuse behind the firing circuit," Ramey said. "If things get mean you can always break it."

"Thanks."

"Don, this is Milt again—" Henderson began.

"Uh, Milt, excuse me." Groder held up a phone. "General Umber wants to send a security platoon to the target."

"No he will *not*!" Henderson thundered, the veins in his forehead pulsing. He turned back to the cab monitor. "Don, this is Milt. Pull the plug. Disconnect the timing circuit. That damned thing is armed and I'm very concerned for your safety up there."

"The white figure on the screen nodded. "I will in a minute. I just want to see if the receiving cable is attached to the antenna. Looks like it might be crimped." With that, the figure vanished from the screen.

"Wish the hell I could see what he's doing up there." Henderson shook his head. Then, picking up the microphone, "This is the Control Point. Remain at your positions. Repeat. Remain at your positions."

"Milt," one of the technicians yelled from across the room.

"What is it?"

"We notified the radar plane of the misfire, didn't we?"

"Of course!" Henderson said, his face tense. "Why?"

"The shot cab receiver is getting a signal."

———※———

Hendrix peered inside the canister. Everything was intact. No crimps. No breaks. Everything, even the antenna cable, was intact. It defied reason. There *had* to be something wrong here.

Suddenly, an agitated voice broke through the headsets. "Don, this is Milt. I don't want to alarm you, but we're picking up some kind of radar signal. Is the lamp flashing?"

Hendrix looked at the small black box. Nothing. "Milt, you're probably picking up a signal from the television monitor. I'm not real worried about that."

"We're also getting some sort of hum on the cab mike. Do you hear anything?"

Hendrix removed the headset. To his consternation, there *was* some sort of a buzz, a low whine—like being too close to a beehive. Replacing the headset, he took a deep breath, then spoke into the microphone. "There does seem to be an audible signal here."

"Unplug the detonator harness, Don. Shut it down. *Now.*"

"Good idea." Hendrix reached into the machine. Suddenly he stopped, frozen. There was a shadow. Someone was in the bomb cab with him.

"Don! What's going on up there!"

Moving only his eyes, Hendrix looked toward the shadow. Inexplicably, an image came to mind, the time his father had caught him and his brother in the garage smoking. Slowly turning his head, he half expected to see the old man again.

Nothing. Only the dull metal of the bomb cab wall. Slowly releasing his breath, he turned back to the detonator harness. Then he saw something else, this time real: a distinct blink of red light. The radar lamp. "I may have a problem up here."

"What?" Henderson's voice.

"The radar clock is running," Hendrix said, staring at the flashing light. "It's too late to pull the detonator harness."

"Don," Joe Bob's voice. "Break the circuit fuse. Use your pliers."

"Where is it, Joe?" Hendrix peered into the device.

"It's up behind the wiring harness." The voice in the headset was calm. "On a black cable linking the firing circuit with the capacitor. It runs along the chassis. Do you see it?"

Hendrix brushed the wiring harness aside. Sure enough, at the back of the weapon, clipped to the inside wall of the canister was the black cable, connecting the fat, cylindrical capacitor to the firing circuit. But there was only a long, continuous length of black cable.

"Do you see it?" Joe Bob's voice.

"No," Hendrix replied,, his throat tightening. "There is no fuse."

In the Control Room, Ramey heard Hendrix's voice and felt the blood drain from his face. "It's got to be there! It's a glass fuse—"

"No fuse, Joe," Hendrix voice was distant. "There's no fuse."

"Then *cut* the cable, Don. It's your only chance!"

"It's a double-reverse, Joe. It would fire anyway." Hendrix said. "I'm sorry. Tell Amanda I love her, love the kids—"

"No!" Ramey screamed.

Around him, the Control Room was chaos. Henderson, yelling to kill the power, Groder opening knife switches, Meyer's voice through the loudspeakers. "Get down! Get down! Get down! Burst imminent! Repeat, burst imminent!"

Echoes in memory, time approaching a solid wall, getting nearer—just another minute—

"Don—"

"Goodbye, J—"

Static, like lightning.

Then, silence.

Joe Bob felt the knot in his throat, the muscles convulse his face, shattering it into tears, streaming down his face uncontrolled, onto his shirt, onto the desk. He would not look at the television monitor. As he sat there, shaking with sobs, his face in his hands, he heard the buzz of the Geigers recording the passage of the radiation. Through the detectors, through the room, through all of them.

26

Anna Faye Trumbo

T here it is, Joe," the pilot's voice crackled in the headset.

As the top of the mountain ridge dropped away, Joe Bob took a deep breath and stared through the sand-blasted bubble at the basin below, a glistening green star on a lake of white sand. All that was left of the area nine tower.

"You want to take it, Joe?" the pilot asked.

"Yeah, sure." Joe Bob fitted his boots onto the rudder pedals, his hands around the control sticks. Gunning the throttle briefly, he lifted the helicopter level, then nosed it into the basin. As they floated down the side of the mountain, he scanned the desert floor—a lone, determined part of him looking for signs that might tell him something, any shred of evidence he could use as a shield against logic that would tell him Hendrix was still alive somewhere. Hurt maybe, but alive.

"You see any tracks, Earl?"

"Just the ones we saw yesterday, Joe. I don't think you're gonna find anything."

"Well, I just want to look." Joe Bob eased the chopper over the glassy surface of the huge dished-in area—the central imprint of Hornet's fireball.

"Remember, this was a military test," Earl said. "If we see any planes—"

"We'll be all right," Ramey muttered, staring at the seared desert. "I doubt if they're even flying today." Then he noticed a wispy set of lines beginning near the shattered remnants of the instrument bunker and trailing away toward the south. Double tracks. Too big for a jeep. Maybe a deuce-and-a-half.

"See anything?"

"Not really," Joe Bob shook his head.

"Maybe we better be getting back, Joe," the pilot said. "This place is still off-limits."

"Give me another minute, Earl." Ramey stared at the remnants of the tower. He wanted to stay, just for a while longer, flying over this cemetery in the desert. Trying to say goodbye and failing miserably.

After his father died, Joe Bob had dreamed about him for years— talked to him, joked with him, fought his final battle with him, over and over and over. And there were days on the street when he would see his father's face in the crowds, if only for a moment. In some deep, illogical part of him, he felt his father had never really died, he had just moved away—had taken a step aside—maybe into some nearby dimension. Perhaps if Joe could only take that step, or do the exact right thing, he would see him, see that lopsided grin that he missed more than anything in the world. And they would embrace, shake hands, laugh.

That same illogical sense forced him to return to the blasted-out crater, to look for a set of jeep tracks that never were. Don Hendrix never made it out. Not in this world, not in any world.

"There's nothing here, Joe," Earl said finally.

"Yeah, you're right," Joe Bob mumbled. "You want to take it?" As the helicopter lifted away toward the north, he took a deep breath and slumped in the seat. The world had gone flat, and he was watching it as a spectator in a movie. Someday he would grow tired of watching it, get up and walk outside into the sunlight.

"I'm gonna take this up around the north side of the mountain," Earl's voice crackled in the headset, "then down over Papoose Lake, just like we came in. It's restricted, but it's a real pretty part of the test site."

"Fine." Joe Bob gazed at the hills, at the alluvial fans and bajadas rising up to become chalky, dusty peaks dotted with cactus, yellow-green specks against the brown desert. In the basin below, patches of fluffgrass and silver sage mottled the surface, with occasional splashes of purple sage. On the debris slopes at either side of the basin, Ramey could see stands of trees—blackbrush and greasewood and yucca, rustling in the hot desert wind. Yucca Flat. As Earl guided the helicopter down toward the alkali surface, Joe Bob dropped his gaze to the dry lakebed, watching the shadow of the helicopter grow and move sideways to meet them. As they droned above the desert, he watched the sinewy motion of the tire tracks below, watched them weave, flash, then disappear. "You know," he said after a moment. "They never found his jeep. He *coulda'* got away."

═══≈w≈═══

"Dr. Linneman, when are they going to blow up Doom Town?" The receptionist smiled shyly, twirling a strand of hair with a pencil.

"You mean the *Moriah* shot?" Linneman looked up from his newspaper. "I think it's sometime early next month, Carol. Why?"

"Oh, I thought maybe we'd get a chance to go out there and see it . . . before the bomb went off and all."

"I thought you'd been out there already," Linneman smiled, turning the page. "Donna said you've been all *over* the test site."

"No, just to Shoshone Mountain. Never did get to Doom Town.

"Well, there's really not much to see."

"That's not what *I* heard." The receptionist leaned forward conspiratorially. "Donna says it all depends on who you're with."

"Guess so," Linneman nodded.

"I hear they've got *televisions* and *dishwashers* and things out there. Seems to me that instead of blowing all that up, they ought to give it to the Indians. Those poor Indians living on the test site could use that stuff."

"There are no Indians living on the test site, Carol." Linneman turned another page.

"*Sure* there are!" the receptionist nodded. "You know the bomb that was shaped like a car? I heard they found an arrow sticking in it. That's why it didn't go off."

"I didn't know that."

"The Indians are trying to stop the tests. That's why Dr. Trumbo came down from Washington."

Linneman dropped the newspaper. "Anna Faye Trumbo is here—at the Nuclear Test Site?"

"Sure!" she continued. "That's why Dr. Demming asked you to come in this morning. To see Dr. Trumbo. She's in his office right now with Marienfeld and some army people. Dr. Linneman, do you feel all right? You sure don't *look* all right . . .

"Carol," the intercom squawked, "send in Dr. Linneman."

Linneman closed the door behind him and flashed his best bureaucrat's smile. In the aftermath of Hendrix's accident, he had expected maybe two safety officers from the AEC, a representative from Los Alamos—

Instead, seated in a row of chairs was Stanley Marienfeld, Captain Spaulding, a few other military brasshats and—standing flat against one wall, Davis Demming. Turning, Linneman saw that Demming's desk and chair was occupied by a burly, middle-aged woman in a white lab coat, her thick, muscular arms resting across the desktop.

"Anna Faye, this is Dr. George Linneman," Demming said in a strangely choked voice. "He's in charge of our weapons section. George, this is the Chairman of the Atomic Energy Commission. Dr. Anna Faye Trumbo."

"Sit down, Linneman," the woman rasped.

"Sure," Linneman smiled. "But there doesn't seem to be one left—"

"Find him a chair, Davis," Trumbo said.

"Yes, Anna Faye. Of course." Demming moved briskly for the door.

Linneman studied the woman behind the desk. He had never met the AEC boss, but he had seen photos, mostly taken from afar—Anna Faye Trumbo, big and solid as a boulder, shaking hands with an anemic-looking president; Anna Faye Trumbo, towering over a university nuclear physics class; Anna Faye Trumbo, planted on a ship's deck like a massive shell, observing a thermonuclear test. But he had never seen her up close. Until now.

Anna Faye Trumbo in person looked as though someone had taken a huge peach and attached a pug nose with a pair of case-hardened eyes from the shark section of the toy shop, and then topped it with a blond duster from the closet. The effect was unsettling—like a pixie haircut on a bulldog.

Linneman quickly scanned the room, saw the brass visibly cowering against the wall. He couldn't understand the reaction. Despite her fearsome reputation, the woman was just another bureaucrat. In fact, she was probably here to learn what had happened to Hendrix—maybe help them determine where that radar signal came from, find out why the bomb detonated. After all, she *was* a nuclear physicist.

"So you're Dr. Linneman," Trumbo smiled, picking up a sheaf of papers. "I've heard a lot about you."

"Thank you," Linneman nodded. In response, the woman paused and looked up from the memos. Had he said something wrong?

"Were you in charge of the Hornet device?" Trumbo asked. "The one that killed one of the technicians?"

"Actually, no," Linneman said, relaxing a bit. "Two of my weapons specialists said there was a fuse on the firing circuit, but Hendrix said he didn't see one. We plan to investigate—"

"A fuse?" Trumbo glanced at Demming. "*What* fuse?"

"There was a fuse on the firing circuit cable," Linneman continued. "The cable *could* have been replaced just before the shot. Also, there was a problem with a spurious radar signal that was somehow picked up by the radar receiver on the device. Which in turn—"

"Davis," Trumbo interrupted, looking over Linneman's shoulder, "what is this man talking about?"

"Nothing, Anna Faye," Demming said. "It's an investigation into a mishap. Routine. Nothing you would have to be concerned with. We're taking care of it."

"The press doesn't know anyone is missing," Marienfeld said.

"*Missing*?" Linneman turned in his chair. "Hendrix isn't missing. He's dead. He was *killed* out there."

"We have to classify him as *missing*, George," Demming said nervously, "until we have undisputed evidence to the contrary."

"The body, for example," Marienfeld added.

"So, for one thing, there's the problem with the fuse," Linneman continued, turning back to Trumbo. "And secondly—"

"Dr. Linneman," Trumbo interrupted again, "I really am not interested in fuses."

"But it was a mishap and—"

The woman smiled and held up her hand. "Please let me finish my sentences."

"Of course," Linneman nodded. "Sure."

Trumbo's smile vanished as she continued. "What happened to that technician *may* have a bearing on why I'm here." She steepled her fingers, looked around the room, then returned her gaze to Linneman. "Not long ago, my office received a phone call from someone who had intimate knowledge of the Nuclear Test Site operations. Claiming to be a concerned citizen, the caller mentioned, among other things, 'bombs that don't work.'"

Linneman felt the room go warm.

"This latest mishap is just one of many that have occurred here lately." Trumbo narrowed her eyes. "For example, I've heard you have a scientist in your group who believes he is the deity?"

"That would be Dr. Jeffery Christopher," Linneman nodded, choosing his words carefully. "It happened after Dr. Wiggers disappeared, and uh, actually, he's getting much better. The medication appears to be helping."

Trumbo nodded slowly.

"Then there's Dr. Rhinehart," Linneman continued. "Now, while he's never actually *claimed* to be, er, the deity, I think he also believes he is—but only in the quantum sense."

Trumbo stared at Linneman.

"I don't know how to explain it. Myself, I was raised a Presbyterian—"

"Dr. Linneman," Trumbo interrupted, "what are you talking about?"

"The deity," Linneman responded, his throat dry. "I was explaining about, um, Dr. Jeffrey. And Rhinehart. They think—"

"I'm not interested in what they think," Trumbo growled, pushing a newspaper across the desk. "What I am interested in, is how did *this* come about?"

Linneman stared at the headline: *Bomb Frightened By Troops, Destroys Car.*

"Well, the bomb simply didn't go off," Linneman replied as evenly as he could. "We investigated, and it seems there was no plutonium in it. There was lithium deuteride that shouldn't have been there—"

"What's wrong with lithium deuteride?" Trumbo asked suddenly. "Do you have a problem with thermonuclear weapons, Dr. Linneman?"

"No," Linneman shook his head. "It's just that from what little I understand about the law, we're prohibited from detonating thermonuclear devices on the Nevada desert—"

"Very good, Dr. Linneman," Trumbo smiled. "The next time I need a legal opinion, I'll seek your advice. Now, getting back to that phantom caller." Trumbo gazed at the others in the room. "I don't know who he was, maybe even one of you here today. But frankly, he performed a service. We *do* have a problem here." She returned her stare to

Linneman. "And I suspect much of that problem is sitting in front of me now."

Linneman flinched.

"What do you think I should do about someone like you, Dr. Linneman?"

"I—I don't think that—," Linneman swallowed hard. "I mean, I don't know—"

"You don't know." Trumbo paused for a moment. "Well, *I* know. I'm going to relieve you of your supervisory position. And from here on out, you're back at your old job—whatever that was."

"He was an electrician," Marienfeld said.

"Electrical *engineer*," Linneman mumbled.

"Don't take this too hard, Linneman," Trumbo smiled. "Now you have an opportunity to do something you enjoy. You obviously don't care for management, do you?"

Linneman sighed, getting up from his chair.

"No, no. You stay right there," Trumbo growled. "I want you to be here to meet your replacement."

Joe Bob blinked and rubbed his eyes. Still the blur remained, like a greasy windshield in a slow drizzle. Two hours flying over the desert, then another four or five staring at the same film over and over. He focused on the screen, watching a jittery blur of black and white images, a sequence from one of the photo planes. Darkness, then suddenly a concentric wave of energy expanding in all directions, spreading toward the periphery of the target area. "That was no small bomb," Ramey mumbled as the screen went white.

Suddenly the phone rang. Probably Groder again. "Yeah?"

"Joe, hurry up with that film. If Demming hears I've let you in here—"

"Five more minutes," Ramey said, replacing the phone on the hook. As the scenes flashed silently, violently on the screen, he threw the toggle switch on the tape recorder. The slow motion sequence was next. There had to be a clue.

"Uh, the radar lamp does appear to be on the firing circuit." Hendrix's voice, cool, calm. The image of the tower flashed across the screen, a spotlighted framework against the black background. In the foreground was the jeep, parked next to the switchbox. Off to the side, barely visible in the shadows, was the flat instrument bunker.

"Don, this is Milt—" Henderson's voice crackled from the tape recorder. The day after the accident, he'd taken sick leave, then vacation.

A closeup from the telescope camera atop the Control Point. The shot cab in the crosshairs. Frame. A light in the cab. Detonation. Again.

"The radar clock is running." Don's voice. Ramey tensed as the chilling words came, "I can't pull the detonator harness. I don't know what to do—"

Where was the radar coming from? An airplane? Some damn military experiment? Joe Bob rolled the film back, then forward again. Frame. On the screen, the walls of the cabin glow—frame—then dissolve. Instant by quantum instant, the cab disintegrates, flames reaching from its sides in frozen time. And on the audio tape, "Do you see it?"

"There is no fuse."

Frame. The cab is engulfed inside a cloud of fire, lightning bolts jumping from its grainy surface to some point outside the photograph. Why had Hendrix missed seeing the fuse? The light was certainly bright enough. It was in plain view. Even Art wondered the same thing.

"Tell Amanda I love her, love the kids—"

"No!" Ramey jumped at the sound of his own voice on the tape. In the background he could hear Meyer screaming into the microphone, "Burst imminent! Repeat—"

Frame. The cab atop the tower had become a foam-covered globe, its cratered surface sprinkled with debris. With a quick motion, Ramey switched off the tape recorder. In silence, he watched the fireball consume the tower rung by rung, all the way to the ground.

Joe Bob rubbed his hand across his face. Stubble. Since the accident, he had gotten maybe ten hours of sleep. He had visited the GZ, listened to the tapes, scrutinized the blast from every conceivable angle. And had gotten nowhere.

Suddenly the door opened. It was Groder. "Demming's receptionist just called—the meeting's almost over!"

"I just want to look at the—"

"Scram, Joe!" Groder hissed. "Now!"

Linneman tried to swallow, but something seemed stuck in his throat. No tears, he thought, certainly not over something as unimportant as a job. But then a job is a life. Maybe if he held his breath the tears wouldn't flow. It had worked when his wife left him.

"Davis," Trumbo was saying, "until we get this Hendrix mess cleared up, I want you to take over management of the Control Point operations."

Demming jotted down a note. "Uh, where should I transfer Milt Henderson—"

"Milton Henderson is no longer working at the nuclear test site," Trumbo replied. "His paperwork is being processed and he'll receive his pink slip when he returns from vacation."

"Of course," Demming nodded.

"I want to move the Doom Town shot up to next week. Then we can begin preparation for the Vulcan experiment."

"Yes. Next week?" Demming mumbled, returning to his notepad.

"Marienfeld," Trumbo turned to the public relations man. "You're to continue your job as liason for Senator Curry. But there are no reimbursements for these hotel bills."

"Hotel bills?" Marienfeld asked.

"Is there some problem?" Trumbo looked up, her eyes hard.

"Uh, I—er—believe you have the wrong Marienfeld," Demming sputtered. "Senator Curry was obviously referring to, um *somebody else*. Incidentally, Stanley's wife also works for Public Information—"

Trumbo looked squarely at Marienfeld. "Well, I see no need to have two people in *that* office. Pending further review of your performance, Stanley, you're transferred to the lab train. As tour guide."

"*Tour guide*?" Marienfeld screeched. "But I have a *PhD*!"

"You're a tour guide with a PhD," Trumbo said. "You have a problem with that?"

"No," Marienfeld gulped.

Trumbo turned Demming. "Davis, did you happen to bring along your security man? What's his name— Fogler?"

"Ahem," Demming flushed. "Vernon is, er, checking the fence line around the test site. The periphery. There have been some reports of airplanes flying overhead and—"

"He's your son-in-law, isn't he?" Trumbo interrupted.

"Well, yes," Demming gulped, "but that—"

"When he gets back from *riding the range*, have him cordon off Hendrix's office. I don't want anyone in there until I've had an opportunity to look at it. In fact—" she paused, "tell him to bring to me everything that's there."

"Yes, of course, certainly." Demming scribbled furiously on the notepad.

Linneman took a deep breath. Bureaucratic hell was breaking loose and he was in the middle of it. He wished he could find a way out. Maybe go into the desert. Visit the trains before they melted them down. Maybe he could take that cute blonde receptionist, Carol—

"George!" Demming barked. "Dr. Trumbo is asking you a question!"

"What was Dr. Ramey doing near the military bunker?"

"Ramey?" Linneman looked up. "At *what* military bunker?"

"It seems Dr. Ramey had one of the pilots fly him over a restricted zone," Demming shook his head, exasperation in his voice. "George, you *know* we're to stay out of the restricted zones!"

"I'm sure Joe Bob had a good reason for it—"

"Everyone in this room, listen up," Trumbo interrupted. "I will *not* tolerate any abuse of the AEC's contract with the army. Unauthorized flights in the restricted areas are prohibited. Violators will be brought down." She glanced around the room. "Any disagreement on that?"

"None at all," Spaulding smiled.

"Good," Trumbo said, "now, before I close this meeting, I'd like to introduce George to his new supervisor." She tapped the intercom. "Send him in." A second later, the door opened and in walked the new chief of the weapons section, a smiling, confident Arthur Flagmeyer.

27

War

Ratney Wanker roared into the small company office and hovered over Stein's desk like a lightning storm. "The general's moving up the tests! Doom Town next week, the Vulcan shot the week after that. We gotta get ready for it!"

"Why the rush?" Stein asked calmly. "Are we at war?"

"Well, yeah! Russian bombers could be coming in over Alaska!" Wanker paced back and forth in front of the desk, dust falling from his flak jacket. "That almost happened once, you know. Caught us with our pants down."

"I don't remember that," Stein said, reaching for a pen.

"I bet Moscow's listenin' to us right now! Probably got some kind of microphone stuck up under something somewhere." Wanker aimed a finger at the desk. "What're you doin' Stein? Signing another sick leave? Pretty soon you're not gonna have a company left!"

"Sloan's in quarantine," Stein said, scratching his name across the paper. "The hospital keeps sending this form over for signature."

"Quarantine, huh? Probably chicken pox. You really got a bunch of weak sisters, Stein." Wanker shook his head. "And you know why? You're too easy on 'em."

"Heard from Colonel Thorne lately?" Stein asked, signing his name across another line. "How's he like working for the general?"

"I haven't seen him," Wanker shrugged. "I don't think he's right for the job. Too soft on the troops. Worse'n a mother goose."

"That's *mother hen*, Ratney," Stein corrected him.

"Did you know Colonel Storax is gonna let me organize the next maneuver? The one where they blow up Doom Town. Whattaya think of that?"

"Good for you," Stein said, thumbing through the sick leave requests.

"I might get to direct the charge from the general's helicopter! Did you know that thing has four 50-caliber machine guns?" Wanker pulled up a chair. "Tell me what you think: A hundred planes."

"A hundred planes?" Stein looked up.

"Bombers, fighters, helicopters—we could even get some of those Northrup flying wings in here too! They could circle the target while the tanks came down on the GZ. We could fire the guns before the bomb goes off—knock the tower right on its ass!"

"Ratney," Stein leaned forward in his chair. "*Why?*"

"To knock it on its *ass,* dammit!" Wanker looked incredulous. "This is a military maneuver! Everything's fair game."

"No one has ever been attacked by a tower, Ratney."

"Listen," Wanker leaned over the desk. "I have this plan . . . we knock over the shot tower and the bomb falls off, see, and bounces! We might get a full bounce before it goes off. . ."

"What if it bounces toward the trenches?"

"Hell!" Wanker slapped the desk. "There's risks in everything! Besides—if the troops see it coming, they can *run* or something—"

"The Doom Town shot is an airdrop, Ratney," Stein said. "No tower. Sorry."

"Maybe we can shoot down the plane! Knock it out of the sky—right on its ass!" Wanker's eyes gleamed. "The pilots got parachutes! They could, you know, *dive out* before we hit it."

Stein shook his head.

"We might even use the atomic cannon—smack the drop plane with an atomic shell—then we'd have *two* atom blasts! Wow! Duffel would love that!"

"Duffel?" Stein looked up. "What's Hugh Duffel have to do with this?"

"Look, Stein," Wanker glanced at his watch, "I've gotta get ready for those practice maneuvers. Be sure your troops are ready 'cause it's gonna be a rough one—"

"I want to know where you ran into Hugh Duffel," Stein said. "I need to talk to him."

"Look, I've got work to do," Wanker growled. "Besides, if I were you, I'd leave Duffel alone. He's a close personal friend of the general's. So just forget about him. *Especially* if you ever want to get promoted out of your little training company."

Stein nodded slowly, his eyes fixed on Ratney. "I'll keep that in mind."

As Wanker stalked out of the office, Stein absently ran his fingers across the scars on his face, then picked out the latest TDY request from the "in" box. Perkins. Another one transferring to Myrmidon's battalion. That would make six in just one week. Maybe Wanker was right. Soon there would be no one left. Thumbing through a sheaf of forms, he glanced at the names—Sloan, McCorkle, Wobey, Perez— Colonel Myrmidon was getting all his best men.

With a sigh, Stein retrieved Perkins' request form and prepared to add his own name to the forest of official signatures across the bottom. He would agree to the temporary duty assignment.

Then he noticed something in the REQUESTING OFFICER block. In place of Myrmidon's lean, precise script was a series of thick, unintelligible spikes like the recording of an earthquake. He had seen it somewhere before. Where? He glanced at REASON FOR REQUEST line and saw Perkins' rounded, friendly handwriting: *To help make a movie.*

Movie?

Stein grabbed the stack of forms from his desk and quickly thumbed through them. Finally he found it—Sloan's TDY request. It was for the photo plane assignment. He carefully removed the form from the stack and placed it alongside Perkins'.

The signatures were the same: Hugh Duffel.

═╼╢╾═

"Vrrmmmmmm. PFFFT—BOOM! Ka-Blam! Pow!" Ratney Wanker raced the tank over the top of the ridge, then stopped. To the west the Soviet forces were lined up, ready to take the town, maybe even the shot tower. The attack on Nevada was in full swing. "The tanks can't make it in time, General!"

"It's all over, Captain Wanker. The Russkies have taken Nevada."

"Wait, sir! I'll bring in the artillery!"

"I'm counting on you, boy!"

Ratney grabbed a handful of tanks and scooted them across the felt surface toward the new battle zone, a plaster ridge marked *BELTED RANGE*. Just south of there, at target 14, Soviet infiltrators were already starting up locomotives. "Call in the air strike!" Wanker yelled. "Target 14!"

Suddenly he heard the door open behind him. Someone was in the planning room with him.

"Ratney, I want to talk to you about something."

"I'm busy, Stein." Wanker positioned a toy tank on the side of a plaster hill. "I'm workin' out my maneuver plan!"

"I was going through the leave requests—"

"A line of Chaffees will drive east across Yucca Flat," Wanker said, picking up a toy tank. "Then, down through the center with the armored personnel carriers—"

"I saw Hugh Duffel's signature on a TDY form, Ratney—"

"See, the big guns are down *here*, at Frenchman's Flat," Wanker continued. "I can lay down a destruction barrage along a line from Papoose Lake to the shot tower—illuminating, chemical and high explosive—the whole works. Might even slip in a nuclear round. Hell, nobody'd know the difference, eh, Stein?"

"I want to know why."

"Why *what*?" Wanker looked up.

"I want to find Hugh Duffel. Where is he?"

"It's none of your business. Besides, I don't know." Wanker placed a line of tiny atomic cannons on the felt surface. "You know, I can lay a concentration barrage on Doom Town itself. Deny the enemy the objective."

"Ratney—"

"I said, it's none of your business!" Wanker hunched his shoulders over the mock-up table. "Now, either help me with this or leave me alone!"

Stein's footsteps trailed away to the door. Then, the sound of the latch turning.

"Pffff-boom," Wanker said softly to himself, pushing the toy tanks toward a tiny plastic shot tower. "A coupla' nuclear rounds from the cannon would finish off that—"

Suddenly, a scarred hand appeared and grabbed a fistful of shirt. An instant later, Wanker found himself hoisted off the floor, his back slammed against the wall.

"Ratney," Stein growled. "Let's talk."

28

Night Flight

Hugh Duffel peered through the windshield of Perkins's Chevy. "So this is the airport, huh? Doesn't look like much. Not even a control tower, ha, ha."

"This is it, all right." Perkins wheeled the car into the gravel driveway and stopped in front of the Airstream. "It's almost dark already. I don't see how you're gonna take pictures of the test site at night—"

"Not *pictures*, Wilbert, *movies*." Duffel slapped the side of the Bolex. "Remember *Citizen Kane*? That whole movie was shot at night. They used the same kind of film as we're using tonight."

"Hey, Perkins!" Bobbie Jean, smiling brightly, looked just as she had the last time—wearing worn-through denims, wrinkled work shirt, scraggly brown boots and red cotton bandanna. As she strode over to the car, Perkins also took note of the other familiar thing about her, visible even at dusk: her breasts—moving softly like liquid beneath her shirt. He would give up his favorite Chevy to see this woman without clothes. "Thought for awhile you weren't gonna make it," she smiled, wiping her hands on a greasy shop rag. "It's almost dark."

"Bobbie, this is the guy I was telling you about—the photographer for the *Big Picture*—Captain Hugh Duffel. Hugh, this is Bobbie Jean

Barnett. She'll be flying the plane tonight."

"You can call me B.J.," Bobbie Jean grinned, extending her hand. "I understand you know the general too."

"We're old friends," Duffel said. "Met in the Pacific. He was in charge of putting pigs on boats at Eniwetok. I got a lotta film out of that, but nobody'll watch it. You ever heard of the *Big Picture*?"

"Yeah, it's on right after 'Sky King,'" she nodded.

"So you're flying us tonight, huh?" Duffel edged close to Bobbie Jean.

"Nah," she shook her head. "Suze Colter is. She's got better night vision. I'm riding shotgun and you guys get the back seat. Either of you get airsick?"

"Not me," Duffel said, picking up the movie camera. "I just need a good view."

"Well, you'll get that," Bobbie Jean said, stuffing the shop rag into her hip pocket. "We're taking Albert. He's m'plane. Cessna 195. Rides good but kinda hard to handle sometimes." She paused to grin at Perkins. "Real bad for folks prone to gettin' airsick—'specially if they're ridin' in the back seat. Rocks up and down, like ridin' an *eel*." She snaked her hand through the air. "Some people get sicker'n dogs. Want to go out to the strip?"

"Uh, sure," Perkins nodded. As they walked toward the planes, he noticed Duffel was keeping a few paces behind them, eyes glued to Bobbie's hip pockets.

"Hey Suze!" she called. "You got th' plane ready?"

"Just about." The voice came from the direction of a stout silver and cream airplane parked on the grass at the edge of the asphalt runway. From behind, the plane looked like an enormous, hunch-shouldered bird.

"Come around here and meet our passengers."

At that, a petite, smiling woman stepped around the side of the plane. In the gathering darkness, Perkins could see that she was a few inches taller than Bobbie Jean and maybe a little older. She wore a dark cotton jacket over a white shirt tucked into faded jeans, rolled at the cuff exposing sneakers and white socks. She didn't look like his idea of a pilot, even a lady pilot.

"Susan Colter," the woman said. "I'd shake hands with you but they're covered with oil—you got a rag, B.J.?"

"Yeah, here." Bobbie Jean pulled the cloth out of her hip pocket and tossed it to the woman.

"My name is Duffel." The red-headed officer extended a pudgy hand. "Captain Hugh Duffel. I'm shooting locations for the Department of Defense."

"Suze," Bobbie interrupted, "have you propped Albert yet?"

Colter shook her head. "Not yet. You want to do it?"

"Sure," Bobbie said. "Why don't you give Frye a call, ask him to leave his runway lights on. We might need 'em—in the meantime, I'll show these guys something about a Cessna 195."

As Susan ran back to the trailer, Perkins followed Bobbie around to the back of the big, bulky airplane. He stopped to look at the Cessna's huge tail. The substantial vertical section curved at the top like the dome of a puffy cumulus cloud. The horizontal components, on the other hand, resembled the fragile wings of an insect.

Bobbie Jean smiled. "Albert has a cute butt, doesn't he?"

"Uh, I guess." Perkins cleared his throat and thought about *Bobbie's* tail section. Round. Like two tiny perfect cumulus clouds. Yes, he would give his car *and* half his possessions to see her naked.

From the front, the plane seemed to be all nose. Beneath the silver dome of the spinner, at the bottom of the engine cowling, Perkins noticed a small upturned oval aperture. Backed by the dark criss-cross of a metal grille, the opening formed a purposeful, heroic smile—making the plane look like a steadfast metal cyclops. "What's this for?" he asked. "An air vent?"

"Carburetor intake," Bobbie Jean said, pulling the propeller blade down. "Albert's a good plane, but these updraft carbs'll catch fire sometimes. That's why I like to hit him with two or three licks of primer before I start him up."

"Uh, is that what you're doing now?"

"Nah, I'm hand propping him. In a radial engine, the bottom two cylinders are always upside down. When he's just sittin' here, oil leaks down through the valves and rings, and those two bottom jugs fill up."

"Jugs?" Hugh Duffel appeared around the side of the plane, winding his movie camera.

"Cylinders," Bobbie Jean corrected herself. "Anyway, if I start the plane with oil in these two cylinders, the pressure'd knock 'em right off the pistons—prob'ly screw up the crankshaft and throw those jugs out on the ground."

Turning, Perkins saw Duffel aiming the camera at the front of Bobbie's shirt. "My Bolex is getting some footage of your cylinders,"

Duffel said, as the camera whirred.

"If I was you, I'd save yer *Bollux* for the test site," Bobbie Jean growled. "Otherwise, somethin' might *happen* to it."

"All ready, B.J.," Susan called. "Frye said he'll keep the light on for us."

Bobbie opened the door to the cockpit. "Let's hope we don't need it. Alright, fellas, climb in."

Inside, the cabin had a musty-acid smell, a combination of gasoline, pesticide and the upholstery of an old car. Perkins knew he was going to be sick, either from the odor or from simple fright.

"Either of you gotta pee?" Bobbie asked from the front seat.

"I do," Duffel replied. "Where's the powder room?"

"Ladies room is in the trailer," Susan said, standing by the door. "Men's room is the next airplane over—behind the red Stinson."

"We won't look," Bobbie Jean said.

"I'd better get behind a bigger plane," Duffle chortled, scurrying toward a nearby fuselage. "Twin engine maybe—"

"B.J., did you hear that?" Susan shook her head. "He said the same thing Frye always does."

"Yeah," Bobbie Jean laughed. "I heard a tourist from Cincinnatti say that, too. Needed a bigger plane to pee behind. I told him to go behind that Piper Cub—say, Suze, you want to pull the prop through one more time?"

"Sure." Susan walked around to the front of the plane.

"Yeah," Bobbie Jean glanced over the seat, "this engine throws a lot of torque on takeoff, so it's real easy to ground loop. Make sure you're wearin' your seat belt." She scratched her nose, then continued. "Albert's a good plane, though. I got his starter out of a Cadillac."

"Do we *have* to take this plane?" Perkins asked. "What about the one we went up in the last time?"

"The One-seventy?" Bobbie Jean asked. "With your friend on board, I doubt if it'd clear the runway. Duffel looks like he's been storin' up for a real long winter."

Cinching his seatbelt tighter, Perkins looked around inside the plane. Facing the two bow-tie-shaped steering wheels was a confusing assemblage of knobs, switches and dials. He placed the palm of his hand in the center of the side window, noticing that his finger tips easily touched the frame. Small windows.

"Everybody ready?" Susan asked, clambering through the door.

"Duffer's still out there somewhere," Bobbie Jean said.

"Probably behind one of the spray planes," Susan said, fastening her seat belt.

Suddenly, Duffel squeezed into the door and flopped into the seat. "Sorry I took so long. Too much coffee."

"Clear!" Bobbie yelled out the window. Susan pulled a switch, and the engine rumbled to life. Looking through the small side window, Perkins noticed that the scenery had taken on a deep purple cast. In a few moments it would be dark. "Real pretty out here, ain't it?" Bobbie yelled over the roar of the engine. "Night flyin' scares me to death."

"Me too," Susan grinned, lining the plane up with the runway. "I just hate it."

Perkins gave an involuntary shudder. What the hell was he *doing* out here? After all, he *hated* airplanes. As the plane jumped ahead, an unpleasant queasy feeling grew in the center of his stomach. Maybe he would throw up. No, he had to be positive. He was with a professional cinematographer and up ahead were two competent pilots. And all three knew the general. Perkins took a deep breath and tried to relax.

"Anyone like a cigar?" Duffel suddenly asked, pulling a pack from his pocket. "If you've got the light, I've got the Havanas."

"Sorry," Bobbie Jean said over her shoulder, "the cigarette lighter doesn't have a fuse. Kept catchin' fire, so I yanked it out."

"Do we *really* have to take this plane?" Perkins mumbled, his voice lost in the roar of the engine.

Exactly two hours later, Perkins turned from the dim, warm glow of the cabin to look out the window. The sky had long since turned from deep blue to black, while the landscape below had taken on an eerie silver cast, probably a reflection from the full moon. The somber grey mountains seemed to float on the desert like huge battleships on a metal sea. It looked peaceful, as in a dream.

Suddenly, the cabin began to rattle and shake, like a truck driving over a corduroy road. Then it stopped. "Night thermal," Susan said.

"We *hope*," Bobbie replied, attaching a headset over one ear. "Hear anything, Suze?"

Susan shook her head. "Channel's still clear. Looks like the chopper's not flying tonight."

"The chopper?" Perkins leaned forward. "*What* chopper?"

"Th' general," Bobbie replied. "Ol' *Hank*. He flies a Mojave H-37 with four machine guns and a rotary cannon. I hear he can pulverize a boulder with that thing. Hey, see that little patch down there?"

"Where?" Duffel aimed his camera.

"Just east of the road—prob'ly can't see it at night. Anyway, there's a spring down there. Good place to skinny dip. 'Course, some of the springs around here are so hot you come out *broiled*. But that's a good one. Not hot at all. Just right."

Just right, Perkins agreed. He wished he were there now, skinny dipping with Bobbie Jean. At night.

"Great place," she continued, "but kinda' hard to get to."

"I like to go up on Mount Charleston," Susan replied. "Get away from the desert heat."

Suddenly the cabin dipped like a boat on the ocean, leaned sideways, then back. "Here we are," Susan said.

"Welcome to the Nevada Test Site," Bobbie said. "We'll just switch off the runnin' lights for the time bein'—makes it easier to see in the dark."

"Dark's fine with me," Duffel said, pressing his face to the window.

Shifting nervously in his seat, Perkins took in the view—the black underside of the wing blocking out the sky, the tiny plump tire suspended in the air and, far below, the black and silver panorama of mountains and valleys and dry lakes. Suddenly it occurred to him that the cabin was stifling. "Excuse me," he said, gently tapping Bobbie Jean on the shoulder, "is there any way to, uh, turn down the heat?"

"Wish there was," Bobbie shrugged. "The oil tank's right behind this instrument panel—five gallons of oil at 120 degrees. That's why it's hot in here. If we was to kill the engine, the instruments'd get too hot to touch."

"Well, don't kill the engine," Perkins said.

"We ain't gonna do that," Bobbie Jean laughed. "Albert's so slick, he'd drop like a bucket of bolts."

"We could open up the paratrooper door," Susan suggested. "That would cool things down."

"Paratrooper door?" Perkins asked.

"Right next to where you're sittin'," Bobbie said. "Ol' Albert spent some time in the military, so they gave him an extra door. It's hinged at the top. You can prop it open with your foot—"

Perkins recoiled from the cabin wall. Sure enough, there was the distinct outline of a large door—just a few inches away.

"If you want, I can pull th' *panic wire*," Bobbie grinned. "It releases the cotter pins and the door falls right out—don't even have to kick it loose."

"Uh, you don't have to do that," Perkins replied quickly.

"It would cool things off," Susan smiled.

"I'm fine," Perkins nodded. "Really I am."

"Hey!" Duffel exclaimed suddenly. "When are we gonna see some targets, huh? We've been out here now for over an hour already. What are we doing, flying in circles?"

"We're just bein' careful," Bobbie drawled. "We don't wanna *advertise* the fact that we're here."

"I thought the general didn't mind," Perkins asked quickly.

"Oh, I'm sure he doesn't," Susan replied. "But we don't want to *bother* him."

"Nice ladies," Duffel nodded. "Very thoughtful."

"If anybody sees anything, let me know," Susan said over her shoulder.

"What are we looking for?" Duffel flicked a switch on the Bolex. "Mushroom clouds?"

"Lights," Susan replied, gently easing the Cessna into a shallow right turn. "Lights that move."

"Okay, Duffer." Bobbie Jean tapped the side window. "There's the target."

"Should be able to see the bullseye." Susan pulled back on the throttle and the engine's whine dropped to a low rumble.

Perkins pressed his face against the window. Far below, the cool, moonlit desert basin shone like a huge mirror. And in the center of the mirror was a series of four concentric circles. Rising from the center was a thin steel tower supporting a tiny squarish object. The shot cab.

"Careful, Suze, you don't wanna smack into those guy wires."

"We're okay," Suze said calmly. "I'm watching the altitude."

"Look real close, guys," Bobbie Jean pointed. "See those lines on the ground? Trenches! And the bunker ought to be on the north."

"Hey, this is great!" Duffel said, aiming the camera at the ground. "Yeah, there's the instrument bunker. Wow! Think we can *land*?"

"Forget it," Susan said. "Just take your pictures."

"And remember," Bobbie Jean added, "we get a copy of everything."

Perkins looked outside at the approaching landscape. Slowly moving past, almost directly beneath the plane, was a dark square rectangle. Nearby the thin line of the shot tower slowly tilted past, the small shot cab clearly visible, almost even with them.

"Hey, I know!" Duffel exclaimed. "Let's go to Doom Town! It's just a few miles south of here."

"Sure." Susan eased the throttle forward and the engine responded with a low whine.

"Uh, Suze." Bobbie Jean pointed out over the dash. "I thought I saw something out there—against the mountain. You getting anything on the radio?"

"Just static," Susan said, adjusting the headset. "Think they're using another channel?"

"I dunno. Whattaya say we leave?"

"Good idea." Susan hammered the throttle into the firewall and the roar of the engine rattled the cabin.

"Take it due north over Papoose Lake!" Bobbie yelled over the engine noise, "then up through Emigrant Valley—keep your hand on the landing lights—I don't wanna whack the side of a ridge—!"

"Hey! What are you talking about?" Perkins yelled. "Whack *what* ridge?"

"—When you see the ridge directly under the wing, change to a heading of 40 degrees—"

"Hey!" Duffel said. "What about Doom Town?"

"B.J.," Susan said, looking out the window. "We've got company."

"Cut him back to cruise speed for a minute," Bobbie instructed. She looked over her shoulder. "You guys tucked in?"

"What's going on?" Perkins asked. "Did you see anything?"

"Uh, oh," Bobbie said. The interior of the cabin had begun flashing a bright red. Something was outside the left window, just beyond the wing. And whatever it was, it was big. Then Perkins became aware of a sound. Overriding the dull drone of the Cessna's radial engine was a thundering resonant vibration, shaking the plane's entire fuselage.

"Maybe it's the cops," Duffel said, waving his hand.

"Yeah, right," Susan growled, giving the wheel a hard twist to the right. Suddenly the cabin tilted onto its side and the flashing light vanished beneath the frame of the window. An instant later, bright bolts of orange fire flashed past the window leaving green streaks in Perkins's field of vision.

"Look!" Bobbie yelled. "He's using the cannon! That sumbitch! *Wingover*, Suze!"

The plane dipped slightly, stood on its tail, then somehow returned to level flight. Looking out the window, Perkins saw a huge shape, gleaming in the moonlight. Whatever it was, it was big as a locomotive. And it was after them.

"Hammerhead, Suze!" Bobbie Jean yelled. "Stand him on his tail!"

"This is *great*!" Duffel laughed, handing Perkins the movie camera. "He's on your side. You mind getting a shot of this?"

Gripping the camera, Perkins looked outside. Sparks skittered over the trailing edge of the Cessna's wing. Were they on fire?

"Flash the tail spot, B.J.," Susan said. "Let's see what he looks like."

"Smile, you sumbitch," Bobbie said, throwing a switch.

Behind them, a light appeared, and the object came into view—the biggest helicopter Perkins had ever seen—an impossibly huge mass of metal suspended beneath an enormous, thundering rotor. Perkins looked through the telephoto lens of the Bolex, studying the rivet-studded monster. The fuselage was a dark metal cone, its globular front bay tapered to a narrow span of metal, then angled up to a wide flat tail. Reflecting against the angry red beacon, the rotor blades inscribed a circle in the air like a flashing crimson buzzsaw. At the front end of the helicopter were two twin pods on either side of a front bay. Turbines. Small wind tunnels drawing air into the massive, thundering engines. Perkins pressed the trigger of the camera and felt the vibration as the film threaded behind the lens. Duffel was right. This *would* make a great picture.

"Get a shot of the guns!" Duffel yelled excitedly.

"You are ordered to land."

"Who said that?" Perkins asked, lowering the camera.

"Guess!" Bobbie shot back. "Wag the wings, Suze. Like we're givin' up. Then let me take it."

Amid the thunder filling the cabin, Perkins heard the voice again, flat and metallic. "You are ordered to land. Or be shot down." Looking around, he saw that the helicopter was behind them.

"The tail's in the way." Perkins twisted in his seat. "I can't get a good picture—"

"Here, let me help." Duffel reached over and unfastened his seat belt.

"Hold tight!" Bobbie yelled. The cabin tilted back, like a car falling backward down the side of a hill—off a cliff, into space. Perkins felt the anvil of G-forces slam into his chest, felt the springs in the seatcushion dig into his back, the eyepiece of the Bolex hammer into his cheekbone. Then, horribly, his back began to slide up the seat—toward the ceiling.

"Hey!" Duffel laughed "Whatcha doin' up there, Perkins?"

The Cessna creaked and groaned like a wounded bird, rolled onto its back, then corkscrewed toward the ground.

"I thought—the general—*knew*— you guys—" Perkins squeaked. There was an anvil on his chest again, driving the breath from his body.

"You are ordered to land or be shot down!"

Perkins opened his eyes. Somehow, they were level again. Then, through Duffel's window, he saw it—the dark nose of the helicopter hanging motionless in the air, facing them. It was flying through the air *sideways*. Then a brilliant ray of light poured into the cabin—a dazzling, blinding glare. "Nuts!" Bobbie's voice. "He threw the spot on us!"

"Why don't we land?" Perkins suggested, between clenched teeth.

"Perkins, you've got *just one second* to find that seatbelt," Bobbie yelled.

"Take the picture! Take the picture!" Duffel screamed. "I'll get an Emmy!"

"Everybody tucked in?" Bobbie's voice again. "I'm gonna give 'em a little surprise."

Perkins felt the cabin tilt back, heard the roar of the engine. No question about it, he thought. They were all going to die up here. He listened to the sound of a chain being pulled, like the trapdoor beneath the hangman's noose.

Snap!

He felt so dumb. Scared of heights, so he joined the Army.

Pop!

Wanted to be a general and he wound up here—over the nuclear test site, being chased by a helicopter—

Clang!

The cabin walls moved, shook, then disappeared to the rush of wind To his absolute horror, Perkins saw there was nothing to his left. No upholstery, no smooth cabin wall. Nothing except the cold, screaming wind.

"Take the picture, Perkins! Here's your chance!"

The cabin tipped back like a Ferris wheel, then wobbled sickeningly and tipped forward—straight down. As the wind rushed into his mouth, all his fears returned at once, stampeding through his body, taking away his breath.

"Did we get 'em?" Susan's voice.

"No, dammit!" Bobbie growled. "Missed."

As the horizon rotated outside the window, Perkins felt the ceiling spar jam and ripple beneath his back, his feet splayed helplessly toward the floor. He was on the world's biggest roller coaster, at the top of an outside loop, aimed straight for the surface of the earth. Just then, the plane tipped sideways, spilling maps, paper cups, and a thermos out the open door, into cold black space.

Perkins loosened his hold on the movie camera to get a double grip on the seat supports. Hanging out through the door, his hands locked onto the thin metal brace, he watched the Bolex spin and twirl across the floor of the cabin—an expensive, whirring, determined little ballerina— taking movies of terrified passengers in a doomed airplane. Then, as if pulled by an invisible cord, it bounced offstage, out the door and into the void. Perkins, his feet kicking only air, his fingers stiff, his voice gone, could only watch it go—a tiny metal dot sailing away.

Toward the searchlight.

Like a bomb.

Then he saw sparks, like a rock smacking into a pile of hot coals.

"Did ya see that?" Bobbie yelled. "Direct hit! I think he got the left engine nacelle!"

Immediately, the Cessna roared into a dip and climbed to yet another peak—a rollercoaster in the sky. Perkins felt that he was lying on top of the plane, hanging headfirst through a trap door.

"Is he in yet?" Bobbie asked.

"*Help meeeee*," Perkins squealed, peering down into the cabin.

"Let's get the hell outta here." Colter said.

"Nooooo!" Perkins shrieked. "*Wait—*"

"Wow!" Duffel said, pulling him inside. "That was great! You really gotta be more careful, though. Those cameras are expensive."

29

Amanda

J oe Bob pulled up in front of the small mobile home and shut off the engine. The Dodge Roadster sputtered for a moment, then died. He looked at the mailbox: S. Colter. Out front were two vehicles—a late model Chevrolet sedan and a weatherbeaten Dodge pickup. Did she own both of them? Or did one belong to some Nevada sheepherder boyfriend? Ramey decided he wouldn't stay long.

Stepping out of the car, he walked over to the pickup. At one time the vehicle had been bright red, but the desert sand had removed most of the paint and worn holes through the metal. In the truckbed was an old gray tarp and a ten-gallon water can. No license plate.

"Want to buy it? I could make you a good deal."

He looked up. There she was, jeans over boots, white blouse—no, a man's shirt—rolled up sleeves, black hair in curls and those same slate-gray eyes. And the first smile he'd seen from anybody in weeks. "I had a truck just like this once," he said.

"Sorry to hear that," she laughed. "Would you like to come in?"

Stepping into the trailer, he expected to see a dusty, rough-hewn cowboy sitting on the couch. Maybe chewing on a toothpick. But no one was there. "That your truck outside?" he asked.

"No, thank heavens. Would you like to sit down?"

He pulled up a chair at the kitchen table, noting that Susan's trailer was completely different than his own. For one thing, everything seemed to be in its place. The flowers on the table were fresh. The books on the shelves were all the same size. On the coffee table was a photo of a man in an army uniform.

"I was a little surprised to hear from you," she said with a wry smile. "I didn't think you scientists at Camp Jupiter were allowed to hobnob with the locals. Especially reporters."

"I thought it was the other way around."

"I think the newspapers are pretty friendly to the test personnel," she shrugged. "After all, they gave this army brat a job."

"Say, that's right," Joe Bob nodded. "You told me your dad was in the air force. Cloud tracker, right?"

Susan nodded. "Yes, he flew the photo plane, tracked the clouds, did it all. Would you like tea or coffee?"

"Coffee would be fine," he said. "Black."

She took a cup from the shelf, but it slipped from her hand and clattered to the floor. "Hm," she said, retrieving the cup. "Good this is plastic."

Joe Bob watched her wash the cup in the sink. "You'll have to excuse me, Dr. Ramey, I haven't had much sleep." She rubbed her eyes. "I had some problems with an airplane last night."

"What kind of problems?" he asked. "Engine trouble?"

"The doors fell off." She poured the coffee. "Tore up the vertical stabilizer. And something put some holes in the fabric. Anyway, we had to leave it at an airstrip north of the test site . . . I borrowed that truck out front and drove all the way back in the dark."

"In the dark?"

"Headlights don't work," she smiled wanly. "Good thing there was a full moon." She sat down at the table. "So what brings you out here this afternoon, Dr. Ramey? Is it business? Or should I consider this a social call?"

"Uh, most of my friends call me Joe. Or just *Ramey*," he replied. "You can call me what you like." It had been too long since he talked with women this nice. He wasn't doing good at all.

"Well, Joe," she smiled. "You can call me Susan. Or Suze."

Joe Bob looked at the woman's eyes. Slate blue. *That's* why he was so nervous. All dark-haired women with blue-gray eyes were pretty—

but it always seemed like they were looking right *through* you.

"There was a fatal accident last week at the test site."

He looked up. How did she know that? There was no press release—

"Did you know him?" she asked softly.

Joe Bob looked at the floor. "I really can't—"

"Do they know how it happened?" she asked.

"No." He drummed his fingers on the table. "Nobody knows for sure what happened— yet."

She nodded. The silence hung in the air like an incompleted sentence, yet all he could do was look at the pattern on the kitchen floor.

"You know, something, Joe," she said after an eternity. "I know what the press release will say—it'll say it was a simple human mistake. A technician error. Some poor guy way *way* down on the ladder did something he shouldn't have."

Ramey swallowed hard.

"And you know something else?" She got up from her chair. "These investigations all turn out the same. The bomb never kills anybody. The government never kills anybody. They're all just simple, honest mistakes." She poured her coffee into the sink and looked out the window. Silence again.

"Guess I better be heading back."

She turned and looked at him. For the first time he noticed her blue eyes were lined in red. "Joe, I really *do* apologize—I guess you caught me at a bad time." A smile. "Too much coffee."

"That'll do it," he attempted a grin. "I had a friend once who made coffee so strong the cup would explode. Fly right out of your hand. We were gonna use the stuff as a replacement for plutonium."

She raised one eyebrow. "Is that classified information? Or can I put it in the newspaper?"

"Go right ahead."

"You know, when it comes to the test site," Susan said, "we reporters have to get our information where we can."

"Yeah, I guess." He scratched his head. "'Course, *you know* I can't tell you anything—"

"Oh, I don't expect you to. You have a job to think about." She paused, appraising him for a moment, then quickly reached to a nearby shelf and produced a small notebook. "It's surprising what you can learn just by being observant." She opened the book. "For example, right after that last fizzle, the test site received a freight shipment from Denver. The crate was four by six, and had film badges taped to the outside. The depot manager was told it was a refrigerator."

Joe Bob felt his face flush.

"And after the last test, the head of the Atomic Energy Commission arrives at the Las Vegas Airport—and the next day three top people are transferred to new positions, Davis Demming, Stanley Marienfeld and George Linneman. Anybody you know?"

"George Linneman was *transferred*?"

She flashed a sly smile. "He lost his reserved parking spot at the front gate."

Ramey stared at the notebook, wondering if his own name was in there somewhere.

"Joe," her gray eyes suddenly humorless, "I don't know what you think about all this. But when people die in that place, the public has a right to know *why*. Don't you think that's fair?"

He took a deep breath and studied his hands for a moment. "The place is a nuclear test site," he began slowly, carefully choosing each word. "We design and test weapons that are a part of our national defense. We can't just tell everybody what's goin' on in there."

"I understand that. But someone died in the last nuclear test—"

"I don't see how you can say that—" he attempted.

Susan narrowed her eyes and continued. "—and I'll bet that man's wife *still* doesn't know how it happened."

"How do you know he was married?" Joe looked up, surprised.

"Because, Dr. Ramey," she said, her voice flat, "Don Hendrix was a friend of mine, too."

"Hello, Carol." Arthur Flagmeyer smiled at the chubby blonde receptionist. "Real nice morning, isn't it?"

"Yeah, I guess so, Dr. Flagmeyer," the girl responded.

"Is everybody already here?"

"I suppose."

"Good." Flagmeyer turned to one of Demming's dog-and-pheasant pictures and examined his reflection in the glass. The haircut was a success. With his newly-purchased horn-rim glasses and dark tie, he looked the perfect supervisor. He especially liked his new lab jacket.

"Your shoes need polishing."

"Excuse me?" Flagmeyer turned back to the girl.

"I said, your shoes need polishing. They're all scuffed up."

Flagmeyer stared down at his brand new penny loafers. "I just bought them yesterday."

"Then they sold you scuffed shoes," the girl shrugged.

"You don't know what you're talking about," Flagmeyer said gruffly. "Please tell Dr. Trumbo the new weapons lab supervisor is here."

The receptionist clicked the intercom. "Dr. Trumbo, *Flagmeyer* is out here waiting to see you."

"Send him in."

Opening the door, Arthur saw the scowling Trumbo facing a small group of people—among them Marienfeld, Demming and Demming's son-in-law, Security Chief Vernon Fogler. For some reason, the corpulent Fogler was surprisingly wide awake. Sitting straight as a bolt in a highbacked leather chair, his bloodhound eyes as wide as saucers, he resembled a beagle waiting to be spayed.

"You're late, Flagmeyer," Trumbo growled. "Sit down."

Arthur found an empty metal chair directly in front of Marienfeld and quickly took a seat.

"Please continue, Mr. Fogler," Trumbo said. "Tell us what happened last night."

"Uh, nothing happened overnight."

Flagmeyer stared. It was the first time he had ever heard Vernon Fogler speak. In fact, it was the first time he had ever seen Vernon Fogler awake.

"Nothing happened?" Trumbo glanced at a military officer standing near the door. "No one from the army contacted you about anything that might have happened at the test site last night?"

"Well . . ." Fogler paused a moment, apparently deep in thought. "The sewer in one of the barracks is backing up."

"Do you think that's a security matter, *Mr. Fogler*?"

"No," Fogler smiled sheepishly.

"Davis," Trumbo said, turning to Demming, "how are things at the

Control Point? Do you think your people can pull together three nuclear tests in a week?"

"Well, *ahem*." Demming cleared his throat. "As I've mentioned before, Anna Faye, the schedule calls for one every two weeks—"

"I know what the schedule *calls* for," Trumbo cut him off. "I'm asking you to schedule three nuclear tests next week. Beginning with one tomorrow night."

"Ahem, *ahem*—" Demming sounded like he had caught a bad cold.

"I want the Jangle device air dropped tomorrow evening over target eleven. At 8 p.m. sharp."

"It will be wonderful publicity," Spaulding said. "People can park their cars along the road and watch. I'll send an announcement to the radio stations!"

"It's settled then." Trumbo paused to scribble a note. "And on the following morning at 4:30 a.m. will be the Moriah shot—the detonation over Doom Town. As for the Vulcan experiment, I believe we can trigger that on Friday."

"That's awfully soon, Anna Faye, uh, Dr. Trumbo," Demming stammered. "Also the lithium deuteride hasn't arrived—Dr. Flagmeyer here hasn't seen the schedule, and Dr. Jeffrey Christopher still won't cooperate. He's adamantly against the test."

"Put Wiggers on it, then," Trumbo shrugged.

"He's not, uh, on the staff anymore," Demming said. "We think he's dead."

"All right then," Trumbo said, turning to Flagmeyer, "maybe *you* can do it, Arthur. You're not frightened by thermonuclear bombs, are you?"

"I—no—" Flagmeyer said quickly.

Trumbo returned to Demming. "Fill him in on the plans after the meeting."

"Of course," Demming smiled weakly.

"This is going to be a strenuous test series, Arthur," Trumbo said. "It's going to involve a very big thermonuclear burst. Do you think your staff is up to it?"

"Well, let's see," Flagmeyer scratched his head. "Dr. Meghalty and Dr. Uborka aren't afraid of, er, that sort of thing. Rhinehart isn't afraid of *anything*. Ramey is okay—"

"Okay?"

"He's taken a few days vacation because of the accident last week." Flagmeyer shifted in his chair. "Actually, uh, George Linneman sort of put him on probation so he took leave. I think."

"What are you having George Linneman do, Arthur?" Trumbo asked.

"I put him on his old job, checking the terminal switch boxes at the targets," Flagmeyer said. "I don't know if he likes his new job or not." Flagmeyer looked down at his shoes. "To be perfectly honest, he's a bit difficult to work with."

"Dammit, Flagmeyer," Trumbo snapped, "of *course* he's difficult. You took his *job*. If he gives you any trouble, fire him." She shuffled some papers and looked around the room. "Now. A while back, I said I was pleased that a concerned citizen made that call to me. The one that called attention to the mismanagement here at the test site."

Flagmeyer heard someone behind him clear his throat. Marienfeld. Perhaps he had caught Demming's cold.

"— I've given it some thought and I've decided to modify my opinion somewhat." Trumbo removed her glasses. "I've decided this sort of behavior is something of a security risk—and the person who did it should be brought in for questioning."

Flagmeyer suddenly heard Marienfeld cough, choke, then sneeze, dampening the back of his new haircut.

"— To that end," Trumbo continued, "I've asked the security director to perform an investigation to determine the identity of this *phantom concerned citizen*. Mr. Fogler, I believe you have some information to share with us?"

"I've located the man who made the phone call," Fogler said. "We traced him down to the phone booth at Ethel's Bar."

"Who was it?" Trumbo asked.

"The man who made the call?" Fogler wheezed.

"Yes, who was it?"

Silence.

"*Well?*" Trumbo leaned forward.

"Whoever was in the phone booth at the time."

"Which was . . .?"

"Whoever made the call."

"That's what I *asked*." Trumbo's voice was low and flat. "Who made the call? What was his *name*?"

Fogler blinked like an old, fat beagle caught in the headlights of an oncoming truck. "We've narrowed it down to whoever was in Ethel's that day."

"Which was . . ."

"A lot of people," Fogler nodded. "You see, Roy serves breakfast all day—"

"You're fired, Fogler. Pack up and get out." Trumbo turned back to the blond army officer. "Spaulding—you take over security until after the Vulcan test."

"Yes, sir!" the officer replied excitedly. "Does this mean I get to use my weapon?"

"What do you mean, Spaulding?"

"Every officer in the infantry is issued a weapon," Spaulding said. "A forty-five caliber service automatic. Will I be able to use my weapon—on security violators?"

"You can use your *dipstick* for all I care." Trumbo scanned the room. "I want you to all understand one thing. This test program is important to the AEC, it's important to the Atomic Brigade and it's important to me *personally*."

Flagmeyer looked around him. Despite the cool, dry air everyone seemed to be drenched in perspiration.

"And I want you to make sure," Trumbo continued, in a low rumble, "that *nothing* will be allowed to stop these next three tests. All of you got that?"

"Yes, sir—I mean, ma'am," Flagmeyer croaked under his breath. "Nothing."

═══◦◦═══

Joe Bob stepped onto the newly-painted wooden porch and knocked on the screen door. Inside the house, a television was on. A children's program. Loud. They probably couldn't hear him. Rubbing his hand over his burr haircut, he glanced at the suburban street, oddly quiet for a Saturday morning. Just two children playing near the curb. They didn't look like the Hendrix kids. Amanda would never allow them near the street.

He knocked again. A second later a plump, dark-haired woman appeared, drying her hands on an apron. "Mornin' Joe Bob, come on in," she said, a bright look on her otherwise tired face. "Janeen saw your car parked over at that reporter's place. Thought I'd write you a little note."

"Lucky I got it," he said, stepping inside. "It almost blew off my windshield."

"Windshield?" She shook her head. "I told her to leave it on the floorboard. That girl—"

"Prob'ly couldn't get into the car. I've been lockin' it lately."

"Well, that's smart, with everything happening around here." The woman walked over to the television and lowered the sound to an electric murmur. "I've been leaving the television on all the time. Keeps me from thinking."

"I've considered buyin' one myself," he nodded.

"I was going to drive out to Indian Springs and leave a note on your trailer door," she said, walking into the kitchen. "But you know those security people—" She paused, then went on in a low voice, "I think they've been listening on my phone. My youngest found a place out back where somebody's been digging in the ground. Have a seat, I'll get you some iced tea."

"Probably just a dog or something, Amanda." Joe Bob pulled up a chair at the kitchen table. "I don't think anybody's gonna tap your phone. Besides, you know that anytime something—bad—happens, the AEC has people watch over th' family for awhile."

"Well, Joe Bob, we don't need any kind of government protection. What we need is somebody to buy this house." She paused to wipe a dishrag across the kitchen counter. "You interested?"

"Don't think so," he smiled. "I got enough problems with m'trailer."

"You need to get out of that thing, Joe." She removed a pitcher of dark tea from the refrigerator. "You know, you can't start a family in a tiny trailer."

"Yeah," he said, scratching the back of his neck, "guess you're right—"

"Twenty-five hundred and this place is all yours—you don't take sugar, do you?"

"Nope."

Joe Bob watched the woman bustle around the kitchen, removing tumblers from the cabinet, pausing to wipe a dishrag over the sink. She seemed constantly in motion, trying to keep one step ahead of something. As she poured the iced tea, he noticed for the first time the streaks of gray in her dark hair, the puffiness of her face, the lines near her eyes. Though she was an attractive woman, she seemed to have aged since the funeral.

"Has a nice yard out back, kids don't have to play in the street. You ever going to start a family, Joe Bob?"

"Maybe. Never gave it much thought."

"Well, you should. You're a fine and decent man. Don always thought a lot of you." For a moment it looked like she would cry. "He always was talking about you two quitting the government and going into business together."

"Don was a good man, Amanda," Joe Bob said. "I really miss him."

"He always told me, 'Joe's too decent to work for those people.'" She stirred her tea then stopped. "I just hate this place."

He considered touching her hand, but thought better of it.

"Nevada is cold in the winter, hot in the summer—dust gets into everything. No trees, can't grow a decent lawn—" She took a drink of tea. "Don always liked the desert, liked the people out here. He always got along with everybody. Everybody came to the funeral." She looked out the window. "Tuesday morning, I'm packing up the kids and leaving for Portland. I have a sister up there and she says I can probably find a job teaching school. My kids are almost old enough to take care of themselves . . ."

"If there's anything I can do—"

She smiled. "You can buy this place."

"Well—"

"The reason I asked you to stop by wasn't to sell you a house . . ." She got up from the table and walked over to the pantry door. "After the security people went through Don's desk, there wasn't a single thing left. They took everything. Pictures, notes, even his slide rule." She reached deep into the pantry. "They took everything—except—this." With a tug, she retrieved a cardboard box from the shelf.

"Let me help you." Joe Bob got up from his chair.

"I can manage," she said, bringing the box to the table. "This was Don's. I'm sure he'd trust you with it."

The box was sealed with a thick strip of government-issue nylon tape. On the side was scrawled in Don's handwriting, CUPS AND SAUCERS. "What's in here, Amanda?"

"I don't know," she shrugged. "Some things from his office. The security people missed it. I don't want it around here."

"But—"

"If it has to do with the test site, I don't want to fool with it," she said, shaking her head. "Don't want it in the house."

He picked up the box. "Okay, I'll take it back to the office—you say you're leaving for Portland Tuesday?"

"Bright and early," she said.

"I'll stop by before then. If I change my mind about this house, I'll let you know." He leaned over and kissed her cheek.

"Take care of yourself, Joe Bob Ramey," Amanda said, a worried look on her face. "This is an uncertain world anymore."

"Yeah. It's startin' to look that way, all right."

30

Station Zero

Rhinehart folded back a newspaper. "Listen to this, George: 'The purple and white cloud punched the dark sky like a stormy fist, then like a chrysanthemum from the world's biggest senior prom, unfolded into the now-familiar atomic boutonniere of doom, a lethal corsage of destruction in America's lapel.' I helped Batman write that. What do you think?"

"I don't know." Linneman morosely picked through the want ads. "See any openings for over-the-hill electrical engineers?" He ran his fingers down the column. "You'd think *somebody* would want an electrical engineer." Linneman folded the paper. "Here I've given the best years of my life to this place—my career —and it goes up in smoke."

"It's just your imagination, George," Rhinehart replied. "Actually, it's *my* imagination, so I guess I should apologize."

"No quantum mechanics this early in the morning," Linneman mumbled into his coffee. "I have to go out to the desert and check switchboxes for that test tonight. Why did Trumbo want to drop the bomb *tonight*? Nobody tests bombs at night!"

Rhinehart shoved a beer bottle at Linneman. "Have some breakfast, George, and tell me about it."

"About what?" Linneman pushed the bottle away.

"About getting canned by Trumbo." Rhinehart retrieved the bottle and took a drink. "She's really something, isn't she? *Meanest* thing I ever created. Sort of like a crocodile. I should apologize for her, too. My imagination just ran away with me."

"I don't know what you're talking about," Linneman shrugged. "I just got demoted to electrician. Maybe that's what I'm really good at—"

"You're just an average manager but you have a kind heart," Rhinehart nodded. "Sort of. Just wish I'd given you a sense of humor. My one big mistake—besides Demming and Trumbo, of course."

"Look, Rhinehart," Linneman sighed, "you don't really believe you invented all this? It doesn't make sense."

"Of course it does," Rhinehart said. "In quantum mechanics it makes perfect sense. Nothing exists unless you see it. When you look at life that way, it's on your terms."

"Your terms?" Linneman looked up from the paper. "Then why were you trying to kill yourself—climbing that tower like you did— waiting for the bomb to go off?"

"I wasn't trying to kill myself, George," Rhinehart shrugged. "I was testing the quantum theory."

"Look," Linneman said irritably, "whether it's quantum mechanics or religion or whatever, we'd all like to believe we have a say in what happens. But we don't. If I had my way, I'd have my old job back—"

"George," Rhinehart interrupted, "look out the window."

Linneman glanced out the window. Across the tarmac from Ethel's Bar was the Yucca Flat airstrip with its contingent of aircraft. Beyond that, toward the northeast in the direction of Doom Town was the broad expanse of Emigrant Valley. The early morning sky was slightly over-cast, diffusing the light, making the scene appear *flat*, photographic.

"Tell me what you see," Rhinehart demanded.

"Just the desert," Linneman said. "Looks like rain."

"You didn't mention the most important thing out there," Rhinehart said, "that big shiny B-36 bomber. Fresh from Kirtland Air Force Base. And you also missed the soldier standing guard with his little carbine. And you didn't mention the bomb-bay door. And what's *inside*—"

"Look, Rhinehart," Linneman said irritably, "what am I supposed to do, describe *the entire state of Nevada* for you? I have to catch the train to target 11. Those switchboxes—"

"Can wait." Rhinehart paused to light his cigar. "If I'm going to all the trouble to create this place, the least you can do is pay attention. Now, what's inside that bomb-bay?"

"A bomb," Linneman sighed, "the Jangle device. For tonight's airdrop."

"Exactly," Rhinehart said, blowing a puff of smoke. "And I think we should pay it a visit."

———※———

"Corporal," Rhinehart said, quickly flashing his ID badge at the young soldier, "my name is Dr. Demming. I am the boss of everybody at Camp Jupiter and I'm not in a good mood today." Rhinehart patted Linneman on the shoulder. "This is my associate, Dr. Marienfeld."

The guard looked suspiciously at Linneman.

Rhinehart took a step closer. "We have come to inspect the weapon."

"I can't let you do that, sir," the guard said, standing his ground. "This is a military effects test. The bomb is military property."

"Harumph!" Rhinehart swelled up. "What is your name, Corporal?"

"Weiner, sir."

"I thought so," Rhinehart growled. "Well, let me inform you, my little Weiner, that this plane may be the property of the military and *you* may be the property of the military but, son, that goddamn bomb in there is *mine*. And I want to inspect it. *Now*."

The guard took a step back. "I don't think I can let you in there."

"*Corporal*, are you telling me I can't see my own bomb?"

"Well, uh, you would really have to get authorization from the general—"

"The general? *The general?*" Rhinehart bellowed. "Goddamn general answers to *me!*"

"Uh, maybe we better go," Linneman said, tugging on Rhinehart's shirt.

"Wait a minute!" Rhinehart roared, his face purple with rage. "Weiner here wants to be a fucking corporal the rest of his life. He apparently doesn't know who in the hell we are!"

Linneman winced as Rhinehart positioned his face just inches from the guard's nose.

"Let me explain something, *Weiner*," Rhinehart hissed, aiming a skinny finger at the guard's nose. "Unless you let us on board that plane, you are going to be in the deepest shit imaginable. And I have an *immense* imagination!"

"You and Dr. Marienfeld can board," the guard gulped, backing away.

"Thank you," Rhinehart said, suddenly clearing up. "Thank you very much. Come with me, Dr. Marienfeld."

Linneman followed Rhinehart to an orange scaffold parked under the huge gray plane. "I'm getting an acid stomach."

"Wait here," Rhinehart instructed, "I need a few things from the shop."

As Linneman stood beneath the open bomb bay doors, Rhinehart strolled toward an orange maintenance truck. Moments later he was back, carrying a red tool box. "We've got some work to do," he smiled.

Inside the plane, Linneman followed Rhinehart through a dark, narrow corridor past the galley and into the expanse of the bomb bay. Stopping at a door marked *Maintenance*, Rhinehart reached in and retrieved a cart with two large gas cylinders.

"What are you going to do with acetylene?" Linneman asked nervously. "There's no reason for acetylene in here—Rhinehart?"

"Relax," Rhinehart said over his shoulder. Suddenly he stopped and pointed at a cylindrical metal object resting on a wooden pallet. "Well, here it is—our tedious little baby."

Linneman stared. It was an atomic bomb, about half the size of the one that had killed Hendrix.

"Poor thing is kinda *insipid*, isn't it?" Rhinehart surveyed the airplane's interior. "You know, George, this old bustard has a gross of about 160 tons and can carry two *grand slams*. And here it's obliged to haul around *this* sorry little guy. Two hundred pounds soaking wet."

"It says 30-kiloton on the side," Linneman observed.

"Obviously an inflated figure." Rhinehart retrieved the welding cart. "I'd be surprised if it made a decent fireball."

"Look, Rhinehart, the nuclear capsule is already in this thing," Linneman said nervously. "I really think we should leave—"

"Can't leave now, George." Rhinehart grabbed the welding torch and turned on the acetylene. "We have a job to do."

Linneman gave him a blank look.

"Didn't Demming want us to design a bomb the public would like?"

"Let's leave."

"George, fetch me some tin snips," Rhinehart said, lighting the welding torch. "We're gonna make this drab little sucker a *star*!"

Three hours later, Linneman wiped the sweat from his eyes and surveyed their handiwork. Under Rhinehart's direction, and with the help of a torch, tin snips, wire cutters and three cans of paint, they had transformed the bullet-shaped nuclear device into something entirely different. Two of the four rocket-shaped tailfins had been removed and the remaining ones snipped, torched and rounded into circles. The square barometer on the side of the bomb was fitted with a round metal sphere, then painted. Rhinehart had used the leftover fins to fashion long, rectangular wings, which he reattached to the fuselage just below the external radar unit. At the end of each wing he glued a white plastic electrician's glove, "to help with flight stability." The renovation was topped off with three cans of black, white and red paint.

"He may not be pretty," Rhinehart nodded approvingly, "but he looks a hell of a lot more friendly than before."

It was true, Linneman had to admit. In only three hours, they'd turned a 30-kiloton nuclear device from a drab, sinister weapon of evil into—Mickey Mouse.

"I like the bow tie, don't you?" Rhinehart asked.

Linneman shook his head. "It's smiling. Bombs aren't supposed to smile. And he has an antenna sticking out of his head."

"Here, Mickey." Rhinehart grabbed the antenna and broke it off.

"Wasn't that the radar receiver?" Linneman chewed his lip. "How are they going to track the bomb without an antenna?"

"Hell, George, all they're going to do is *drop* it." Rhinehart stooped to lift up the bomb. "Here—help me put it on the rack."

"Aren't we going to leave it on the pallet?"

"Bad idea." Rhinehart lifted the device upright. "If we strap him on the rack he'll be looking the other way. The only thing that will look out of place is the ears. Frankly, I doubt anyone will notice"

"Okay," Linneman said, "let's put him on the rack."

"I always wanted to be a sculptor, did you know that?" Rhinehart affectionately patted the device on its metallic ear. "Now I've actually sculpted something and he's gonna blow up. Damn shame."

"I really have to catch the lab train, Rhinehart."

Rhinehart shook his head. "George, I can't do it. He's sort of like a son . . . or a pet."

"What are you talking about?"

Rhinehart scooted the device across the floor of the plane. "I bet he'll fit on this welding cart. And there's a blanket in the first-aid closet—"

"What are you going to do—steal this thing?" Linneman yelled. "This is an *atomic bomb*!"

"We're not stealing him, George." Rhinehart pulled the gas cylinders from the cart. "We're just taking him someplace where he doesn't have to explode to be appreciated."

He fitted the bomb onto the cart. "Get me that blanket. We're gonna *save* this little rat's ass!"

Joe Bob looked at the tower, at the building perched at its top, high above the desert. The shotcab. And in the door, someone waved to him. Hendrix? No. Someone else.

Suddenly he was in his car again, parked at the base of the tower, in a pool of yellow light. With a soft popping sound, the sky erupted in fireworks. The two-minute flares. Then the car started. Standing on the accelerator, he aimed the vehicle away from the tower. In the rear view mirror he saw it. The metal girders. Nothing was moving. He was standing still.

Fifty seconds to detonation.

Two—one—zero.

First the spotlight went out and the air around him turned a bright cathode blue. In the purple glow, he saw an object form at the top of the tower—a hard, bright ball of incandescent air. Sitting in his car, he felt the gamma rays zip through his body like bullets through a vacant house. Then he felt the soft punch of neutrons hitting his back. It was time to leave.

In the rear view mirror, he watched the ball grow into a monstrous sphere, searing and punching the desert in a circular line. Drawing closer and closer.

As it approached, he saw its turbulent surface, mottled with debris from the tower and the shot cab. Fifty yards distant, the shell faded to reveal the horrific structure within—a riot of curtains, veils, haze and abstract shapes, connected by bright, tenuous lines of flux—all buzzing and roaring across the desert toward him.

Then it was on him like a storm, leaving him like vapor to float above the charred earth, above the wreckage, past the thundering mushroom cloud. Moving with the wind, toward the Dakotas. With the ghosts of the trains.

Joe Bob opened his eyes and stared at the wooden panels of his Airstream trailer. Getting up from the sofa, he stepped to the sink and ran cold water over his head. After drying his face on the dish towel, he took a half-empty bottle of orange soda from the refrigerator and sat down at the tiny kitchen table. Taking a drink of stale soda, he propped his foot against something on the floor. Don Hendrix's cardboard box.

Amanda's right, Joe Bob thought, taking another drink. Damn trailer's too small. No place for anything. Scooting his chair back against the wall, he looked at the box. Maybe he would take it in tomorrow. Give it to whoever was in charge of the weapons section.

He rubbed his eyes and stared at the box. *CUPS AND SAUCERS*. Damn funny thing to put on a box of office stuff. Curious, he took a steak knife from the kitchen drawer and, with a single stroke, cut the nylon tape across the top.

He stopped, then slowly laid the knife on the table. The box was filled with manila folders, yellowed envelopes, loose documents. Sifting through, he picked out a blue binder. *AEC Research. Camp Jupiter 1952*. Opening it, he looked at the table of contents: "Combat Effectiveness Following Total Body Irradiation—Liver Function Among Combat Personnel—Blood Charges After Administration of PU-239."

"What the hell is this?" Ramey picked up another folder: "Figure I-1: Station zero. Buster Delta: Windstorm."

"Station *zero*?" Joe Bob asked. "There ain't no damn station *zero*. Where did Hendrix get this stuff?" He replaced the binder and picked up a thick manila envelope. Inside was a set of photographs of nuclear detonations, bright glowing shapes rising from the desert, rockets trailing smoke on either side. He had seen most of these pictures before—Marienfeld handed them out to high schools as promotional shots. Still, some of the photos didn't look like much. Many resembled a field of dense fog. One picture riddled with radiation haze viewed the mushroom from beneath, like the underside of a fog-enshrouded water tower.

In another envelope were more violent scenes, probably the ones Marienfeld *kept* from the public. A photo of a roiling explosion spreading across the desert. A closeup of the stem, with veils of dust falling back toward the ground. The detonation from directly above the GZ—an orange cloud ringed by concentric circles. To one side, just inside the frame, Ramey could make out the series of slashes on the desert floor. The volunteer trenches. He wondered if this was the shot that had caught Stein.

Looking up, he saw that it was already 4 p.m. Only four hours before tonight's detonation. He replaced the photos into their folders and carefully closed the box. He would look at this stuff later.

———※———

"Well Spaulding," Trumbo glared. "Have you found it yet?"

"No, sir, uh, ma'am." Spaulding cleared his throat, then continued. "We can't even pick up the radio signal. Whoever took it knew what they were doing."

"You're saying it was a professional job?" Colonel Storax asked. "Spies or something?"

"Who the hell *else* would steal an atomic bomb!" Trumbo thundered. "*Burglars?*"

"We have every available man policing the area," Spaulding continued. "All exits to the test site are blocked, surveillance planes are in the air and a team from the criminal investigation division is interviewing the guard."

"Who had access to the bomb?" Trumbo asked.

"The usual people—the flight crew, the military guard, the civilian inspection team from the lab. They presented the proper ID."

"They did, eh?" Trumbo's eyes narrowed menacingly.

"There was just one guard there. But he was a very good guard. Very efficient. He never would have missed anything as big as an atomic bomb, I'm sure." Spaulding paused to catch his breath.

"Get me the names of those lab people." She turned to Colonel Myrmidon. "Did the radiation monitors at the gates pick up anything?"

"No activity at either gate," Myrmidon replied, glancing at Spaulding. "We have reason to suspect the device is still at the test site."

"You know, the bomb could have been *misplaced*," Spaulding smiled weakly. "Who knows? It might even still be in the plane."

In response, Trumbo stared at Spaulding for a long awkward minute, then turned to Myrmidon. "Does Bartholomew know about this?"

"Yes," Myrmidon answered, "he's at the Control Point with the general."

Trumbo nodded slowly, then turned to Colonel Storax. "All right. If the gate monitors didn't pick up radiation, then that means the device is still on the test site. Detonation is scheduled for 8 p.m. It's 5:30 right now. Your men have just two hours to find it. And they *will* find it. Understand?"

"Yes. Of course," Storax nodded.

"This test," Trumbo said, looking around the room, "is going forward *on schedule*."

31

Windstorm

Awright, men!" Wanker yelled. "Somewhere on this base is an *armed nuclear bomb*! Set to go off! Yeah!"

"Think you should tell them that, sir?" Sergeant Quaak muttered. "They look scared."

"Well, they *oughta* be scared!" Wanker barked. "If these *girls* here don't find it real soon, it's gonna go off! Probably kill *everybody*! Let's get out there and find that goddamn thing."

Watching the troops scatter, Quaak shook his head and tapped his cane on the ground.

"Really got 'em excited, didn't I?" Wanker huffed. "Look at 'em run!"

"They're all headin' for the gate," Quaak observed.

"The bomb *might* be there, you never know," Wanker said.

"Stein's sent a platoon over there already."

"Well, I hope he doesn't turn up anything." Wanker reached down to pick up a dirt clod. "If I find it, I might get promoted to major. If Stein finds it, nobody gets promoted at all."

"*He* might."

Wanker put the dirt clod into his pocket. "Naah. They're not gonna promote Stein. I don't think the general likes him. In fact, I bet he could save the general's life and the army wouldn't promote him."

"Neither would I, come ta think of it," Quaak mumbled.

"Yeah, it's like a big Easter egg hunt." Wanker rubbed his hands together vigorously. "And if I find the egg, I get the prize! Major Wanker!"

"Ya mean like Spaulding?" Quaak grinned. "I heard they promoted him to head of camp security. He's gonna skip two ranks and go right up to bird colonel."

"Spaulding?" Wanker asked, eyes wide. "*Bird colonel?* They can't do that!"

"Henh. They can do anythin' they want."

"But Spaulding's a *recruiter* or something!" Wanker stormed. "All he knows how to do is stand around and smile and lie!"

"Mebbe that's what they want."

"I bust my butt out in the hot sun and Spaulding gets the promotion!" Wanker snarled, throwing the clod on the ground.

"Damn shame. Henh." Quaak shook his head.

"I'm goin' for a drink," Wanker snarled. "If they ask, tell 'em I'm looking for the bomb."

Wanker slammed on the brakes, vaulted from the jeep and stormed onto the front porch of Ethels. Let somebody else find the damn bomb. Let that asshole *Spaulding* find it. "It's not what you do but *who* you do," he grumbled, stomping into the bar.

The place teemed with officers taking a break from the heat of the search activity. "Howdy, Rat," Roy said from behind the bar. "What d'ya think a' my *saloon* doors? Just put 'em in."

"They're *stupid*," Wanker groused.

"I saw a lotta yer troops out there scratching around," Roy said. "Prob'ly gonna work up a real thirst. Ya gonna let 'em come in here after ya find that thing?"

"If I get a free beer out of it," Wanker said, stalking toward the rest room.

"Natcherly," Roy said, polishing a glass. "Say. Ya want to see my new addition? Real nice souvenir—"

"No!"

"Well, all ya gotta do is look up."

"Damn *stupid*—" Wanker paused and shot a quick glance overhead.

There was *something* hanging from the ceiling. Pointed directly at the top of his head.

"Holy Jesus, Mary, Mother of God."

"Yeah, ain't that somethin', all right?" Roy laughed, showing his gold tooth. "Even got blootonium in it—I call it th' a-tomic mouse."

Wanker froze, staring at the ugly concentric circles on the nose, the four thick black fins—like pikes impaling—what? Shoes and—and—a person's *hands*?

"Yeah," Roy said, "I prob'ly shouldn't of hung it up in front of th' rest room, but it was th' only place I could find fer it. Ethel thought it'd be in the way over the bar."

Behind the grotesque limbs, a bulbous black knob jutted from the body like the Sphere of Evil, a dull red light in its twin nacelles blinking ominously.

"I'd a stuck it out on the front porch, 'cept I know somebody'd run off with it. It ain't every day ya get to hang up a *real a-tomic bomb*."

Above the dark knob, someone had painted a sneering, leering monster, its twin black eyes between saucerlike wings seemingly alive, tracking its target. And it had sighted him.

"That leetle thingamabob on the side is givin' me fits." Roy shook his head. "Keeps hummin', botherin' th' customers—I prob'ly oughta' ask Rhinehart about it—say, Rat. D'ya know ya just peed yer pants?"

Wanker tried to move, but for a long instant, his muscles refused to work. From the corner of his eye, he saw that the bar had cleared out. Except for him, Roy and that *thing*.

"Yep. When I fust laid eyes on it, it skeered me too." Roy picked up a broom. "But it ain't so nefarious when you get used to it. Hey, where ya goin'? Didn't ya want that free beer?"

Joe Bob guided his Dodge Roadster up the narrow dirt road. "You sure we're not lost?"

"I know this road," Susan said, leaning into the turn. "I come up here almost every time there's a test. You get a real good view."

"What d'ya drive?" Joe Bob laughed. "A tank?"

"My Chevy," Susan said. "Goes up hills like a mountain goat. Maybe we should have brought it instead."

"We'll be fine." Joe Bob guided the convertible over the top of a small rut, the wheels straddling the meandering channel.

"I really shouldn't have suggested this shortcut," Susan said, looking worried. "I don't think your car likes it—see, the temperature gauge is reading hot—"

"Been like that for a year," Joe Bob said. "Needle's probably stuck." Privately, he guessed he would be lucky to get his roadster back home in one piece.

"You told me you flew helicopters once," Susan said after a moment. "Seems kind of strange for a weapons engineer—"

"Learned to fly in Korea," Joe Bob replied. "When I came back home, I finished off my graduate degree at Texas A&M. Always been interested in physics."

"Oh?"

"Then I got a job with the AEC." He twisted the wheel to the left, barely missing a small tree. "They sent me to Los Alamos, then out here to Nevada."

"Flying helicopters?" Susan smiled.

"Nah. When I first came here, my official title was weapons yield specialist. I inspected the devices coming in from Los Alamos and calculated the projected energy equivalent."

"The what?"

"How big the fireball would be," he smiled. "All kinds of things go into the yield calculation. Amount of plutonium—the core configuration, everything. It's tricky."

"I would imagine," Susan nodded.

"Anyway, I'd come up with the yield figures and th' army would use that information to place the trenches. They wanted 'em far enough away from the GZ so the soldiers wouldn't get hurt, but close enough to make it *realistic*. Had to keep 'em out of the heat and radiation, but still inside the blast zone. "

"Sounds like an important job."

He nodded. "A whole lot of soldiers depended on the yield calculation bein' *accurate*."

"I'd imagine so." Susan pulled on her corduroy jacket. "You can't afford to be wrong."

"Well," he said, staring ahead into the darkness, "one time I *was*."

— ⦿ —

Uborka eased his huge frame from the jeep and swallowed hard. Above their heads, the light from Ethel's neon bomb-sign flashed and flickered, turning their white radiation coveralls a lurid orange. "Are you sure we can handle this, Emil? We've never defused a bomb before."

"We don't have to defuse it," Meghalty shrugged. "We just have to take it back to the airplane. Then they can go out and drop it. Simple."

"But the pilot said it was armed. I think we should call Joe Bop. Or Flagmeyer."

"Artur was the one who called us!" Meghalty said, pushing open the saloon doors. "Quit worrying. I know this design—it will be easy."

"Howdy, boys," Roy greeted the scientists. "Guess this is what yer lookin' fer."

Uborka and Meghalty stared. The bomb rested on a wooden table, a smiling black bullet with arms and legs, its eyes wide in an expression of surprise. "It's *Mickey*," Uborka whispered.

Roy scratched his head. "Prob'ly shoulda called ya sooner, but I never figgered 'im to be *wanted by th' authorities*, ya know."

"Pliers!" Meghalty snapped. "And the screwdriver, number four Phillips."

"They're in the toolbox," Uborka said, staring slackjawed at the scene before him.

"Yeah," Roy shook his head, "when I heard they was lookin' fer a blootonium bomb, I didn't think they was talkin' about him. Here I was, harborin' a derned *fugitive*."

"Open it up," Meghalty commanded, shoving a screwdriver into Uborka's hand. "Then attach the voltmeter to the capacitor lead. I'll monitor the charge."

"Of course, of course," Uborka nodded, peering at the bomb's bulbous nose. "Should I maybe go in here?"

"That's where the timing circuit is. The timing circuit is going to have to be clipped, Eduard."

"You know Emil," Uborka said, removing the screws at the base of the nose, "I'm not familiar with this design at all. For example, why is the bomb smiling?"

"You fellers gonna do somethin' with that nose, huh?" Roy said, pulling up a chair. "I don't blame ya. A real mouse ain't got a nose like that. Looks like a big ol' eggplant or somethin'. And there's that thing in there that keeps blinkin'."

Uborka stopped. "Blinks?"

"Yup. Ethel seen it first. Now, if yer gonna make somethin' that looks like *that*, ya shouldn't have a damn light in his nose that blinks—"

"Blinks *what*?" Meghalty asked, his eyes wide.

"I just told ya—the damn nose *blinks*!" Roy said, annoyed. "Ya get down along his *muzzle* there an' you can see it. Leetle ol' red light, blinkin' on and off. An' just about an hour ago, it commenced to hummin'. After so long, that noise is real bothersome."

Uborka quickly checked the grill on the underside of the huge metal bulge. And there it was—steadily flashing through the grating—the tiny red radar lamp. "It's blinking!" he gasped. "Is there a radio signal in the room?"

"Got the Philco here." Roy reached up to a small yellow radio on the shelf and flipped the switch. "It'll take a minute to warm up. You boys like country?"

As Roy spoke, the radar lamp went from a slow blink to an angry staccato glow.

"Oh my God!" Uborka gasped. "That radio turned on the lamp!"

"I'll just change th' station—" Roy twisted the dial. "How 'bout some Benny Goodman?"

"Eduard!" Meghalty pointed to the voltmeter. "The voltage is rising! The capacitor is charging!"

"Wire cutters!" Uborka demanded.

"No, no!" Meghalty yelled. "I know this design! It's a double-reverse! You cut any of the wires and it will explode with us!"

Uborka pulled his hands away from the humming bomb, his face pale. "How much time do we have?"

"Ten minutes," Meghalty replied. "The way the voltage is rising, maybe less."

"Does it contain lithium?" Uborka asked.

"The lithium is at the target," Meghalty said.

"Good," Uborka sighed. "At least it's not an H-bomb. I'd hate to be killed by an H-bomb in a—a—*saloon*."

"Hey!" Roy straightened up, a hurt look on his face.

"We have ten minutes or less to make it to the gate!" Meghalty scrambled to his feet. "Come on!"

"Do we have time to stop by my room?" Uborka shuffled rapidly toward the door. "It won't take a minute—"

"Roy?" Meghalty asked.

"Go on," Roy said, picking up a broom. "I'll stay behind t'clean up the mess."

Susan pointed over the windshield. "Here's the road you're looking for."

Joe Bob shifted into low gear and steered the Roadster onto another dirt trail. Like the last one, it was flanked by sagebrush, scrub oak and pinion—all soft-edged shadows in the blue evening haze. By now, the turpentine smell of the foothills had given way to the clear, gin-infused scent of altitude. It reminded him of his first month back from Korea, spent in the Guadalupe Mountains doing nothing, just *breathing* the air.

"This has grown up some since I was up here last," she said. "But it's a real road."

"If you say so." He listened to the hiss of weeds brushing past the convertible. After a sudden bump, the tires touched smooth asphalt. They had come to a stop crossways in the middle of the highway, the roadster's big round nose pointed out over a sheer precipice.

"Here's the main road," she smiled. "The lookout point isn't far from here."

"Some short cut," Joe Bob said, throwing the gear into reverse. "We'd better get outta the road before—"

Just then an enormous flatbed truck appeared from around the bend. Before Ramey could hit the accelerator, the vehicle swerved around them, horn blaring. On the bed of the truck, protected by high wooden rails, was an assortment of waving, hooting children.

"Sightseers," she said. "This is a popular place to watch the tests."

"Thought we were gonna be the only ones here," Joe Bob grumbled, pulling the convertible back onto the pavement.

"No," Susan laughed, "you'll see all kinds of cars—there's even a tour bus—*Luxo Atomic Tours*. There's photographers from Los Angeles, soft drink and hot dog vendors. It's like a big party. Everybody wants to see the bomb go off."

As they followed the asphalt up the mountain, scrub oak gave way to pinion and juniper. To the northwest was an immense panorama of hills and valleys, silent in the purple shades of evening. Joe Bob checked the clock on the dashboard. Almost 7:45 p.m.

"So what happened?" she asked suddenly.

"What d'ya mean?" He glanced at her.

"Awhile back you mentioned something about your calculations." She looked at him. "About the soldiers depending on them."

"Yeah," he nodded.

"Did something happen?" She turned in the seat to face him.

He felt her eyes on him. Ahead the road wound around the mountain, a flat snake with a white line down its back. He took a deep breath, exhaled slowly. "I made a mistake. And some people got hurt."

"How did it happen?"

"It was a new configuration I hadn't seen before. Didn't have much plutonium in it—about two kilograms. So I went to the slide rule an' figured the efficiency. Came up with just under eight kilotons. Fireball a little over two hundred yards wide." He hesitated as the memory played across his mind. The schematic of the bomb, the formulas.

"What happened?"

"The damn thing almost went big," he replied softly. "Nobody knows why—but those two kilos of plutonium made a fireball more'n a quarter of a mile wide. The thermal wave nearly took out the volunteers."

"Was anyone killed?"

"No, but some of the men were hurt pretty bad. One of 'em was a good friend of mine."

"I'm sorry."

"I always felt responsible," Joe Bob said, his voice gruff. "Then this thing with Hendrix—" he paused and shook his head. "It was just one more thing."

She touched his arm. "Would you like your jacket? It might get cold."

He forced a smile. "Want me to put the top up?"

"I'm fine," she said, her hand still on his arm. "I just didn't want you to catch a cold."

———❦———

After the scientists left, Roy walked out on the porch. The flashing glare from his neon mushroom cloud reflected against the wooden floorboards and the surrounding desert, coloring it yellow-orange. It was quiet, not a soul in sight. Nothing between the front porch and the cold lights of the Camp Sagebrush Motor Pool, a few miles to the south.

To the west, across the highway, Roy saw the dim lights of Camp Jupiter. Hard telling what they were up to. Probably cleared out, just like the army. Scanning the purple horizon to the east, he noticed that even the big plane was gone from the runway. Got the hell out, too. Of course, a person couldn't *blame* it. No use gettin' melted for no reason.

Roy looked back through the saloon doors at the bomb. How long did those scientists say it would be before it blew up? Ten, fifteen minutes? They had high-tailed it at 7:45 or so. Now it was almost 8 o'clock.

Stepping off the porch, he walked a few yards across the ground, then turned to take a last look at the flashing neon mushroom: ETHELS. It had been a hell of a profitable enterprise. Good food, good clientele.

Damn.

———❦———

"Hey, there's a place." Susan pointed toward a notch amid the parked cars. "And the view is perfect."

Joe Bob maneuvered the car into a small rectangle of asphalt with a ragged edge overhanging the cliff. After turning off the engine, he switched on the radio, then casually rested his arm on the top of the seat, his hand just an inch from the wrinkled corduroy collar of Susan's jacket.

"Good evening. This is Dick Benedetto with the news on the hour brought to you by Charlie Short Dodge."

"It's almost time," she smiled.

"—And for you bomb watchers, Test Site Chief Anna Fay Trumbo has just announced that the atomic test this evening will go off as scheduled, but at a *different* section of the test site. Observers are asked to look a bit further *south* near the vicinity of Yucca Lake. In other news—"

"Yucca Lake?" Joe Bob asked. "Hell, that's right up next to Camp Jupiter."

"He probably got it wrong," Susan said. "You know radio people."

"I sure hope so." Joe Bob turned down the volume, then opened the glove compartment. "Got some dark glasses in here. Probably better wear 'em for the shot."

"I carry my own." She produced a pair of sunglasses. "Dark Wayfarers. Almost perfect."

"If you're fifty miles away," he said.

"From up here, it looks like the sun," she said, looking out over the basin. "It makes everything go bright for a few seconds. Then you see this red fireball shoot up into the sky. After a few minutes, it goes out and all you have is the mushroom cloud surrounded by a purple glow."

"Ionized air," Joe Bob said. "The radiation strips off the electrons. Can't see it in the daytime."

"Pop talked me into watching an afternoon shot once," she said in a small voice. "Years ago—just after he got his assignment here. Me and Mom came up here and brought a picnic lunch. It was a cloudy day, kind of cool. October, just before Halloween. We were parked over there, right where that hay truck is."

Joe Bob set his goggles aside and looked at the truck, a group of children scattered around it.

"Mom gave me this chicken sandwich, but I was too excited. Pop said he was going to fly over and wag his wings." She was silent for a moment. "Then this twin engine bomber flew over. It was really something—it came over the top of the mountain and right overhead. Looked like it would take off the tops of the pine trees. And you know what?" She turned and smiled. "It wagged its wings. Mom and I both waved back. We knew it was him."

Joe Bob smiled.

"I watched that plane until it was just a speck over the basin out there." She stopped for a moment. "Then everything went white. The ground, the sky, everything. There was this big bright ball just hanging in the air. Right where my pop's plane had been."

Joe Bob saw the light of the car radio reflected against the sunglasses, heard the gentle sawing and chirping of crickets and tree frogs.

"I saw this puff of white smoke rise up," she said after a long moment. "It was a dome-shaped cloud. And I thought about my pop in that little airplane. Because I couldn't see it anymore. All I could see was this big dome-shaped thing. Leaning toward us."

More cars were arriving. It was almost time for the test.

"That night," she said quietly, "I had this nightmare. I dreamed the bomb got my pop and was gonna get the rest of us—my Mom, my sister, me." She paused and looked away, toward the darkness. "I dreamed it followed us home, got into the house and even came into my room. Made everything white—hazy like death. It was getting all of us. And there was nothing I could do about it."

The glow from the radio illuminated her face as she stared out toward the test site, watching the bomber.

Roy walked back into the bar and looked at the bomb. The light was still flashing. Then he noticed a piece of white cardboard sticking out beneath it— *Today's Special: Neutron Ham 'n Eggs.* "Dammit," he muttered, "never got around to changing that menu." With a sigh, he turned and walked over to the line of pinball machines—the Majestic, Ace High, and Uborka's favorite, Dragonette. Of course, half of them didn't work—Uborka kept coming in and stealing parts for his bombs. That atomic mouse might be half pinball machine.

Roy took a deep breath, settled down on a bar stool and looked at the bomb. "Still flashin', ain't ya? Ornery little sumbitch." He wondered if he had time for a drink.

Then he saw something through the front door. Someone was standing—actually kind of *hovering* on his porch, just outside the saloon doors. Tall, dressed in black. "Huh." Roy checked under the bar for the baseball bat. If it was the grim reaper, at least the sumbitch could wait until after the bomb went off.

Then a man pushed through the doors.

"Understand you got some kinda' *trouble* in here."

"It's that damn little knick-knack ya sold me, Rhinehart." Roy pointed the baseball bat at the table. "It's all set to blow up."

"That *right*?" Rhinehart asked, ambling over to the bomb.

"Uborka and that other guy said it was set to go." Roy looked at the clock. "I figger we ain't got but five minutes. I was gonna call Ethel, but she's down at Vegas on a shoppin' spree. She'll shore have a big surprise when she gets back. Think you can do anything about it?"

"Maybe." Rhinehart glanced around. "Did they leave any tools behind? Screwdriver, pliers, hammer?"

"They took 'em when they left." Roy shook his head. "I never saw a fat man run so fast in my life."

"Can't do much without tools," Rhinehart shrugged. "How about a can opener?"

"Got one right here. Kinda rusty, but it oughta' work—here, catch."

Rhinehart snagged the opener without looking up, then began working on the side of the bomb. "Kind of like surgery, Roy. The circuit's sitting right above the hatch, so I'll have to make a little incision here. You know, this casing is as thin as *paper*. Always surprises me how poorly these things are designed."

"Thought you was r'sponsible for all this," Roy said, leaning against the bar.

Rhinehart ripped at the metal skin. "I can't keep track of *everything*."

"Sorry," Roy nodded dolefully, "didn't mean to get all metaphysical on ya."

"I'm used to it."

"Want me to fix ya a drink?"

"Rhinehart pulled out a pocket knife. "Tanker's punch."

"I'm all outta' orange juice. How about a beer instead?"

"Carling Black Label." With the pocket knife, Rhinehart reached inside the hole made by the can opener.

Roy set the beer on the table. From where he was standing he could see the red light flashing.

"Put your finger on this," Rhinehart commanded, pointing to a small black box just inside the hatchway."

"What is it?"

"It's the firing circuit. Put your finger on it. Hold it tight."

"Won't shock me now, will it?"

"Maybe."

"Well, it better *not*." Roy squeezed his hand through the hatchway until he found the box. It was warm, like a hot plate ready for use. Not only that, it was vibrating. "Hey, ya know, I bet this is where that damn buzzin' noise is comin' from."

"Close," Rhinehart said, his left arm around the side of the bomb. "Just hold tight and don't move. It'll all be over in a minute."

"This thing goes off here, it's gonna be hell for business. Make the whole damn place *radioactive*—how much time we got, Rhinehart?"

"We don't. This is it."

"Well, I sorta thought—"

Suddenly a flash. Then nothing.

Roy opened his eyes. He was flat on his back, trying to catch his breath. A grinning Rhinehart stood above him, a fistfull of wires in his hand. "Detonators," he said triumphantly. "I had to pull 'em all at the exact same time—hey, are you all right?"

"Can't breathe," Roy gasped, holding his side. "And m'boots are gone!"

"Over there." Rhinehart pointed at two smoking objects lying against the bar. "Sorry. That firing circuit carries a punch."

"Damn right about *that*," Roy wheezed. "When am I gonna be able t'*breathe* again?"

"Couple of minutes." Rhinehart stuffed the wires into his pocket. "Half-hour maybe."

"Shore hate to wait that long." Roy picked himself up and staggered to the bar. Then, opening a Carling, he poured beer onto his smoldering boots, sending a cloud of acrid smoke through the building.

———✦———

"Repeat, the bomb test has been canceled. This is Dick Bennedetto for KTST news and Charlie Short Dodge—" As Joe Bob switched off the radio, the parking area exploded in the bright glare of hundreds of headlights. An instant later the lot was a blaring, glaring traffic jam.

"No test." Joe Bob tossed his dark goggles into the back seat. "Something must have happened."

Susan placed her sunglasses in her pocket and looked around. "This place always reminds me of the fairgrounds after a ball game. Maybe we should stay here until it clears out."

"Want to step outside for a walk?" he asked.

"Ticks," she smiled. "This place is loaded with them. And there's coyotes up here, too. Want some coffee? I brought a thermos."

"Sure." Joe Bob watched as she retrieved a thermos and two Dixie cups from her pack. "So your dad was a pilot at the test site, huh?"

"He was a real good one," she said, pouring coffee. "Flew the lead plane. Sometimes they'd get up to 20,000 feet and follow the atomic mushroom. Even in the winter. He said it was colder than a welldigger's butt in the Klondike."

"My dad used to say somethin' like that too," Joe Bob laughed, taking the coffee.

"He'd always complain how cold it was following that thing. He'd tell how the windows frosted over because they wouldn't let him pressurize the plane. He said the mushroom was like any other cloud except it was dark. And full of sand." She took a sip of coffee. "He'd follow those things all over the country." Tracked one all the way to Maine or somewhere. He said the cloud would disappear after a hundred miles and you'd have to follow the radiation."

"Is your pop retired from the service?"

She paused. "His plane went down after the one of the tests. Two years ago."

"I'm sorry."

"About an hour after the shot, the plane went off the radar scope. It was never found." She looked out into the darkness. "At least that's the story we got at first."

"What do you mean?"

"Well," she looked at him, her eyes hard, "I don't believe it happened that way."

"Why not?"

"Just didn't make sense. A big twin-engine plane doesn't just *disappear*—not over some of the most barren country on the continent. I couldn't believe they weren't able to find the wreckage."

"You know, the desert *is* kinda' rugged," Joe Bob said. "The plane could've gone down and then got covered up with dust."

She shook her head. "Joe, the military doesn't lose bombers. Not at the Nevada Test Site. I don't think I'm getting the full story."

"You think they found him and they're not telling you?"

"I don't know *what* to think, I just know something's not right." Her voice had become almost inaudible, even in the silence of the empty parking lot.

"Look, I don't think—"

"About a week before it happened," she said, "Pop told me he was going to retire. Was going to start up this flying service." She took a deep breath and continued. "He told me he was going to get a lot of money from the government—for taking part in some kind of study. He never would say what it was about."

Joe Bob finished his coffee, then carefully placed the empty cup in the back seat. "Look, I really don't think th' army's tryin' to keep anything from you—" He paused. "But every now and then, I get a chance to go through the old bomb reports. They might have something about that test. If I see anything, I promise I'll let you know—providing it's not classified secret or anything."

"Could you do that?"

"Sure," he nodded. "Do you remember the name of that test? The date—?"

"I'll never forget it," she said, looking out into the darkness. "July 5, 1954. The test was called *Windstorm*."

═══◦◦◦═══

Throwing open the door to his trailer, Joe Bob pulled the box from beneath the table. Windstorm. He'd seen that name somewhere in the documents. Ripping open a manila envelope, he spilled photographs onto the floor—eight by ten black and white glossies. Groups of soldiers walking resolutely through the dust toward the mushroom cloud. Troops huddled together, facing away from an immense glare. A shot from inside a trench, blurred, probably from the impact of the detonation. A photo of an enlisted man staring at something, his eyes wide, blank. "Marienfeld prob'ly didn't send that one out," he muttered, throwing it back into the box.

In the next photograph, vibration had caused the soldier's corneas to form little dancing stars on the print. Looking closer, Joe Bob saw that the jaw was slack in awe. And fear. The mouth, in fact, seemed to be nothing more than a grey-black hole on the print, an artifact against the magnificence of the event. What in the hell had Hendrix been doing with these pictures?

Joe Bob picked up another photo, this one taken minutes after detonation. Here, soldiers were rising from their trenches, marching lockstep toward the light. Frozen in stoptime somewhere below ground zero. Most of the prints carried a patina of radiation haze, making them appear old and faded. He stared at the photos. Massive radiation had fogged the negatives, splotching them in nonuniform patches and spots, searing across like bolts of thick lightning. Behind the haze, the marching soldiers faded to lines of grey men moving inside a luminous fog, dust devils plainly visible through their rank and file.

Pulse racing, Ramey scanned a small stack of color photos—images of a world where things were not acting as they should, a place that seemed to defy the laws of physics. Clouds on the ground. Soldiers waist-deep in thunderheads. Roll clouds with flashes of orange fire visible through the turbulence.

Another photo, another angle. Closeups of charred boots, stepping across a ground encrusted with glass foam. Then a photo taken at the center of the thing itself—a smoking, yawning metallic object charred black against a gray blast zone—a ruptured earth criss-crossed with stress fractures and craters. Here and there, objects that at first appeared ordinary became, upon closer examination, something else entirely.

Sifting through the photos, he came to one that was almost completely white, except for a fuzzy object in the bottom right quadrant. Holding it closer, he saw that the image had a texture. Someone had taken a photo of a cement block wall. Shrugging, he pitched it into the box. Oddly, the next photo was the same. And the next after that. The fourth photo, though, was different. At first he thought the texture of the print had changed. But no—it was the subject of the photograph. While the object in the corner remained the same—fuzzy and indistinct, something was taking place on the wall.

With a shock Ramey realized the photo was in color. Bursts of blue had appeared, like splashes of ink on a white tablecloth. In the next photo, he saw that the wall itself had begun to take on a uniform red glow. And in the corner of the photo was that same object, flat and unmoving. Still out of focus.

He picked up the last photograph. The wall had changed, the texture had dissolved into a uniform white, while at the top corner, where one of the blue splotches had been, was a grainy turbulence. Something had come through the wall. Turning the picture over, he saw, in faded print: *Camera 19. 7-5-54.* Windstorm.

He stared at the photo, at the cardboard box of documents, at the dark rooms of his aluminum trailer parked just thirty miles from Camp Jupiter, fifty miles from the nuclear targets. What, in the name of God, was going *on* up there?

"She's here," Demming whispered, motioning toward the door. "I hear her footsteps." Captain Spaulding jumped up from the conference table to open the door.

"Make way," Trumbo said, rumbling past him to take a seat at the head of the table, next to a nervous Arthur Flagmeyer and a taciturn

Colonel Storax. "Gentlemen," she began, "tonight's test *was* going to determine how the atomic fireball would interact with a lithium target—information crucial to our Vulcan experiment. But somehow, instead of the bomb dropping on a railcar loaded with lithium, it ended up in a saloon—looking like a mouse." She paused and glared at Demming. "How do you explain that, Davis?"

"I'm not sure I can." Demming turned to Flagmeyer. "Perhaps Arthur —"

"No, Davis," Trumbo interrupted. "I'm asking *you*. You were in charge of the Control Point."

"Actually, I think Rhinehart had something to do with it."

"Rhinehart?" Trumbo leaned forward. Marienfeld tried to move his chair away from Demming.

"As near as I can tell, he pulled the plug," Demming said nervously.

Trumbo picked up a blueprint of the device and shoved it across the table. "Says here there was a double-reverse on it. It should have detonated."

"I know." Demming looked at the blueprint. "But it didn't. I don't know why. If it had, we probably wouldn't be sitting here now, heh, heh. Ahem. When I asked Dr. Rhinehart how he managed, he, uh, said it's because he's—well—"

"What?"

"Actually, I don't recall exactly *what* he said," Demming smiled wanly. "Some metaphysical mumbo-jumbo."

"No doubt," Trumbo observed "Did he explain how a 30-kiloton warhead came to look like a mouse? Was that part of the philosophical discussion too?"

"I—I didn't ask him that," Demming stammered.

"You know what I think?" Trumbo smiled grimly. "I think it would have been better if that thing *had* detonated. Right there in that stupid little saloon." She looked around the table. "It would have made it a lot easier to start over—with a real laboratory and *real* managers. Now I'd like to reschedule the test. Just take the damn thing out there and drop it."

"Of course," Spaulding smiled. "Good idea."

"But I can't." Trumbo glared. "If the newspeople hear we're painting *faces* on our bombs—"

"You're right," Spaulding nodded sagely. "The public would never stand for it."

"Shut up, Spaulding," Trumbo replied. "I've given it some thought, and I want to go ahead with the Doom Town shot. Keep the schedule for Tuesday morning. Then, two days later, I want twelve hopper cars of lithium deuteride at target 14."

"*All twelve of them?*" Flagmeyer blurted.

"You have a problem with that, Arthur?" Trumbo asked.

"Twelve hopper cars of lithium deuteride parked at the base of the shot tower—that's a lot of lithium."

"That's the idea," Trumbo nodded.

"But if a simple 20-kiloton atomic bomb can be boosted to a 20-*megaton* thermonuclear bomb just by adding nine kilograms of lithium—"

Trumbo clouded over. "Are you *lecturing* me, Arthur?"

"No," he shook his head. "It's just that twelve railcars of lithium is—is—over a *million* kilograms. The fireball would take out the entire state—maybe the whole western seaboard!" Flagmeyer looked around the room, his eyes wide. "It might even become self-sustaining!"

"That's what we're counting on," Trumbo said. "A self-sustaining nuclear fire at target 14."

"A permanent energy source," Demming nodded.

"But that's—that's—*speculation.*" Flagmeyer shook his head. "There's so many uncertainties in nuclear energy. Why, these calculations—"

"Are *mine*," Trumbo interrupted. "And they tell me the fireball will be contained. Are you having second thoughts about our mission here?"

"No," Flagmeyer stammered. "But—"

"Look," Trumbo smiled, "why don't you go back to your lab and think about it. We'll talk later."

Flagmeyer slowly got up from the table and left the room. Trumbo looked at Demming and shook her head. "So *that's* your best nuclear scientist, Davis?"

"Well, George Linneman was always opposed to testing the big bombs," Demming said. "Maybe some of his attitudes have rubbed off. And, besides, we really don't know if it will work—"

"Of course it will work," Trumbo replied. "But we'll discuss that later. Right now we have to deal with our security problem."

"Security problem?" Demming asked.

"Less than a week before the Vulcan test," Trumbo said, shaking her head. "And we've found what may be *foreign agents* here at the test site."

32

Trapped

Spaulding turned off the room lights and switched on the projector. After a short countdown of numbers, the screen became a moving image of violet and gray.

"Here is where we first made contact with the aircraft—directly over one of the shot towers." Storax aimed a wooden pointer through the projector beam. Streaks of orange light raced across the screen from right to left. "These are tracers from our 50 millimeter cannon."

"Where did this film come from?" Demming asked.

"We're getting to that," Storax answered. "Now, you'll see that the picture jumps around. Apparently, the pilot is trying an evasive maneuver—"

Spaulding watched the screen. The projector was threading properly. It was a good presentation.

"More evasive maneuvers," Storax continued, leaning forward in his seat. "At this point they jettisoned the doors." On the screen, images of faces in an airplane flashed by. "Stop the film!" Storax commanded.

Spaulding punched the pause switch, and the projector emitted a low whine. The blurry image of a chubby, red-headed man filled the screen. Demming sat upright and stared.

"That's Captain Hugh Duffel," Myrmidon said, glancing at Spaulding. "He's a junior grade military officer on temporary assignment from Fort Monmouth. And this—"

On cue, Spaulding tapped the pause button and the screen jumped, then froze again. Another face, eyes wide, mouth open, hair blowing in the wind.

"—Is Lieutenant William Perkins," Myrmidon continued, "permanently assigned to the Atomic Brigade Training Company."

"Where did you get this film?" Demming asked.

Myrmidon held up a battered, shredded piece of metal. "It's a motion picture camera. Military-issue Bolex."

"It fell from their plane and lodged in our engine housing," Storax said. "The impact ruptured the fuel line and we were unable to pursue the aircraft." He smiled. "But we found who it belonged to. It's registered to a local pilot—Roberta Jean Barnett."

"She owns a flight service near here," Myrmidon added.

"Uh, excuse me." Spaulding pointed to the image on the screen. "Do you want me to continue with the film? It has to, uh, keep moving, otherwise—"

"Tell me, Colonel Storax," Trumbo asked, "does the general know about this?"

"He was piloting the helicopter when we made contact."

Trumbo nodded. "So instead of shooting the spies, he took their picture."

"He didn't take a *picture* of them—" Storax said gruffly.

"No, the spies took pictures of *themselves* and threw you the camera. Very helpful." She got up. "First you tell me you'd captured some spies, now it seems you just have a little *home movie*. Heh. Nice show." She shook her head. "Come on, Demming, we have work to do."

Demming jumped up from his chair.

"But—" Storax began.

Trumbo paused at the door. "Looks like things are getting out of control on your side of the fence, boys. I'd do something about it if I were you."

As the door closed, Storax drummed his fingers on the table, his face a mixture of anger and vengeance. After a long second he looked at the screen, then at Myrmidon. "I thought you told me Duffel was working for you! What the hell was he doing in that plane?"

"We'll find out," Myrmidon said cooly.

"Actually," Spaulding added, "Captain Duffel was helping recruit radiation cases for Dr. Bartholomew. We really didn't have that much to do with him. I hardly know the man."

Myrmidon glanced at the screen.

"Uh, Colonel Storax—" Spaulding said, "do you want me to advance the film? That projector light is kind of hot. I think it might melt something."

After an eternity, Colonel Storax spoke, his voice cold and dead as iron. "I want them arrested. Those soldiers. The woman that owns the plane. *All* of them."

On the screen, the image of the screaming Perkins began to char around the edges—then with a convulsive hiss, the picture rippled, blackened and burst into flame.

"Captain Stein." Vincel Puhl closed the door behind him. "There's a gentleman here to see you."

"If it's anybody less than a colonel—I'm busy," Stein growled. "We have a maneuver in the morning."

"He appears to be a *civilian* of some sort," Vincel said.

Stein sighed, motioned to the cluttered desktop. "I have to complete all these before I send you people out there tomorrow. I just don't have time to talk to anyone."

"He says his name is Ramey."

Stein looked up. "Oh. Send him in."

Vincel opened the door and a short, wiry man in a khaki shirt and denim jeans crossed the room. "How ya doin' Jake," he said, his sunburned face creased in a familiar lopsided grin.

"Joe Bob! It's been awhile." Stein gripped Ramey's hand in a solid shake, then waved him toward a worn leather chair.

Ramey pulled up the chair and sat down. "Been busy the last couple months. They have us designin' weapons now, ya know."

"Didn't you guys make that car thing? A Pontiac, right?"

"Cadillac Eldorado. Rhinehart had somethin' to do with it. Can't believe they didn't fire him."

"He's a very creative man," Stein smiled. "He should join the army.

He'd make a great officer."

Joe Bob nodded at the pile of paper on the desk. "Looks like you got some work to do."

"Test tomorrow morning," Stein said. "Your boss moved the schedule up. I have to order film badges, set up the decon units, arrange transportation to and from the trenches—"

"You're not taking the train?"

"It's being used somewhere else. This morning I saw it bringing in railcars to the north target."

"Yeah." Joe Bob hesitated for a moment, and the only sound in the room was the gentle beat of the ceiling fan. "You've been out of the hospital now, how long?"

"Two months," Stein said, "almost three."

"Looks like the burns are healin' up pretty good."

"They don't bother me." Stein glanced at the white scars across the back of his hands.

Joe Bob shifted in his chair. "Ya know I gave up on the yield calculations after that happened."

"I told you before, it wasn't your fault," Stein said. "It was just one of those things."

"Guess you heard about Don Hendrix," Joe Bob said.

"Yeah," Stein nodded. "I didn't know him too well—he was married, wasn't he?

"Yeah. Had three kids. The youngest one's only eight years old. His wife told me they're gonna move to Oregon. In fact, they're leavin' tomorrow."

"How did it happen?"

"Don't know for sure. It was kinda unusual," Joe Bob said. "Seems like the device was already armed when we got it. Then when we put it on the tower, it misfired."

A convoy of olive green trucks rumbled down the street outside, leaving a swirling trail of dust. "Hendrix drove out to the GZ to see what was wrong," Ramey continued, glancing out the window. "After he got on the tower, something happened—th' device picked up a stray radar signal or something." He shifted in his chair. "Anyway, the clock started running and he couldn't stop it. It was over in about a minute."

"That's strange," Stein said. "The Control Point is usually careful with its own people."

Joe Bob looked up. "What d'ya mean by *that*, Jake?"

"I'm just surprised it happened. You usually keep those tests under fairly tight control."

"Like I said, the bomb had a radar clock," Joe Bob said. "We checked and the signal didn't come from the Control Point antenna. And the planes were in radio silence. It had to come from somewhere else."

"Any ideas?" Stein asked.

"No, but I thought you might have one."

"*Me*?"

"I been thinkin' about it ever since it happened." Joe Bob leaned forward, his voice tense. "Look. The Control Point antenna was silent, the planes were silent, there were no signals picked up at the perimeter antennas. That signal had to come from inside the test site."

"So?"

"There are military bunkers under almost all the shot towers." He hesitated. "I was wonderin' if any of those experiments might involve radiofrequency. A television signal or something—"

"Are you asking me for classified information, Joe?"

Ramey stopped, the hurt look on his face soon replaced by a familiar expression of resolve. "*C'mon*, Jake. We've known each other for years."

"I can't give a civilian classified information, Joe. I'd be court-martialed."

"We're workin' for the same damn government!"

"Sorry," Stein allowed a smile. "There aren't that many Jews in federal prison—and even fewer in Leavenworth, Kansas. I'd be the only one at Synagogue. Just me and the rabbi, looking at each other."

"Jake, I *have* to know where that radar signal came from. A friend of mine got killed out there." Ramey's jaw tightened defiantly. "I think that bunker had something to do with it."

"You think the military killed your friend?"

"No, dammit!" Ramey said angrily. "But there's somethin' not right out there! And I think I got a responsibility to find out what it is."

"Responsibility? No, no, wait a minute," Stein said. "Let's get it right, Joe. Radar didn't kill your friend, your atomic bomb did. He just happened to be too close when it went off."

"*My* bomb? Just a minute—!"

"You're the atomic weapons specialist aren't you?" Stein continued. "You check those bombs over, send them out to the target and throw the switch. The army has nothing to do with it."

"At the military's request, Jake. Those things are *military weapons*."

"So it's the army's responsibility, eh?" Stein leaned back in the chair, folding his arms across his chest. "After a bomb leaves the laboratory, you're not accountable. Is that it?"

"That bomb killed a man out there," Joe Bob replied, his face still flushed, "and I want to know how it happened."

"Nothing *happened*," Stein said quietly. "The bomb did exactly what it was *supposed* to do. It killed somebody. Just happened to be somebody you knew this time. If it had been anybody else—somebody you don't know maybe—I doubt you'd give it two thoughts—"

"Jake, that's a damn lie and you know it!" Ramey hammered the desk with his fist. "How d'ya think I felt when I saw that fire headin' for your trench? I *told* the military liaison the damn bomb was unpredictable. And the trenches should be a minimum of seven miles from the GZ. You know what he told me, Jake? He said the army would take full responsibility. That's what he said. Full fucking responsibility!"

"Convenient how that works out, isn't it?" Stein replied cooly.

"Listen to me, Stein," Joe Bob said in a tense, low voice, "I'm a nuclear weapons man and I'm proud of what I do. But get this straight—I don't send those people out to the trenches. You and yer goddamn *army* do that. I'm sorry about what happened to you an' your men. But I'm not gonna take the blame for something I don't have any control over. I'm leavin' that to the military."

"That's our job," Stein said. "Congress makes the war, the scientists make the weapons and the military takes the blame. Any soldiers get burned out there, it's their own fault. It's the army's fault I got burned, it's the army's fault half my men are in the quarantine ward." He paused. "It's the army's fault every time something happens around here. Is that about it, Joe? Or am I missing something?"

Joe Bob was silent, staring at the wooden floor, his face clear of color and the grin slowly returning. After a moment, he looked up. "Time was, we'd settle this in the street."

"Yeah," Stein nodded, smiling.

Outside the headquarters, another truck rolled by, this one loaded with soldiers. A small dust devil skidded after the truck, whirled, then dissolved in a cloud of fine sand.

"So you're not gonna help me out?" Joe Bob asked.

"You have your job," Stein said evenly. "And I have mine."

33

Premonition

Robert Wayne Doggett sat on the barracks steps looking at his watch. 11:30 p.m. Tomorrow was another atomic test. Another morning of stuffing a bedroll, tent, boots, galoshes and a change of clothes into a 60-pound field pack, then lugging it into a mushroom cloud. An awful way to start the day.

He removed a wad of chewing gum from his mouth and pitched it into the street. He didn't feel good about this test. Nothing particular, just a nagging feeling that he would walk into the cloud and not come back. Here one minute and gone the next. And just after he'd met the woman of his dreams.

Sighing miserably, he looked up at the sky. Dimly visible beyond the glow of the porch light were stars. Damn. The only reason they ever called off a test was rain, and the sky was clear as a bell. Tomorrow morning he was going to get cooked, like some Dairy Pride broasted chicken sandwich. Or get lost. Or take sick, like Sloan. He was going to get A-bombed and he'd never see the blonde again. Even if he *did* have her phone number. He reached into his pocket and removed the flattened beer can he had found after he fixed her tire. The words were still there, scrawled in the side—*thanks, love always, Marsha*. Then, the all-important phone number scratched on the other side. "Seven-something-something-five-nine-something-something," he said softly to himself.

No, he would probably never see her again—he'd probably march into the cloud and get radiated. Maybe even turn into a monster like something in the movies. Big and squirmy and glowing in the dark. Crawling across the desert toward Las Vegas. Doggett carefully inserted the flattened can into his shirt pocket. Maybe after he got radiated and turned into something slimy, they'd find the can with the number scratched on it. "Ma'am? You remember that gentleman you saw at Ethel's? Well, we had to shoot him with the bazooka. He turned into the *Atomic Brain*."

"Sure is a beautiful night." Robert Wayne turned to see a huge, burly figure in the doorway, dressed in a torn tee shirt and grease-stained army fatigues.

"Vincel, what are you doin' up?"

"I was in the latrine. I experienced a little difficulty with some beer I purchased earlier." He sat down, shaking his head. "I couldn't determine if it was the brand or merely the excessive quantity."

"I'm real surprised at you, Vincel," Doggett said. "We're not supposed to drink before maneuvers."

"Well, over the past few weeks, I've regained the habits of my youth." He produced a bottle of Carling Black Label from inside his tee shirt. "Here, courtesy of Sergeant Quaak."

"He bought this for us?"

"No, R.W." Vincel pried the cap from the bottle with his teeth. "He bought it for himself."

Robert Wayne nodded.

"So what brings you out here tonight?" Vincel smiled, his grease-slick pompadour gleaming in the yellow porch light.

"I just don't feel like *discussing* it right this minute."

Vincel draped his arm over his cousin's shoulder. "Listen, R.W., ain't we always been close? Grew up outside the same town, bought the same car together?"

"It was a good car, Vincel," Robert Wayne nodded. "Until you threw out the rods."

"Nothin' lasts forever, R.W."

"You know," Vincel knitted his brow, "looking back on our salad days, I'll have to admit, we sure were a team. Got arrested together. Got kicked out of school together, got arrested together *again*—was asked to join the army together, now we're gonna be in the A-tomic Brigade." He paused, a thoughtful look on his face. "I don't know about you, but this sure exceeds most of my previous goals."

"Well—" Doggett took a drink, "I think I'm gonna get my li'l squirrel cooked out there tomorrow."

"Just pre-maneuver jitters," Vincel smiled broadly, taking the beer. "It'll pass."

"I don't know, Vincel," Doggett said mournfully. "Besides, there's this woman I met. Marsha. Met her at Ethel's. You was playin' the pinball and she was talkin' to some sumbitch. But I think she smiled at me."

"That's real romantic, R.W.," Vincel said, scratching under his tee shirt.

Doggett nodded. "She drives this big pink Caddie. That's how I met her the first time. I fixed her flat and she gave me her phone number. Roy told me she lives in Hiko—a little town just north of here."

"Sounds like a good start, R.W.," Vincel nodded.

"I just wanted to see her before I got barbecued by that atomic fireball tomorrow morning."

"Well, that certainly is no problem." Vincel squinted into the darkness toward the parking lot. "I'm sure if we put on our thinking caps, we'll arrive at a means of getting there."

"*We?*"

"Sure!" Vincel said. "Ain't you gonna introduce her to your cousin? Heck, R.W., maybe she has a sister."

"But we ain't got time to visit Hiko!" Doggett said. "'Sides, we're confined to the post until after the test tomorrow."

"R.W., did I hear you say Hiko was *north* of here?"

"Well, yeah . . ."

"Right now, I can see a map of the entire state of Nevada," Vincel said, staring into space. "I see the test site—Camp Sagebrush where we are—and I see Hiko!" Vincel pointed to a spot in the air. "Right here!"

Doggett looked. There was nothing there except a single moth, buzzing in a confused circle beneath the pole lamp.

"Now, as I see it," Vincel said, "Hiko is *north* of the camp—on the other side of the test site—I would guess, oh, about forty miles."

"That's a long ways."

"Sure is, if we was to take the *conventional* route up there." Vincel rubbed his huge hands together. "But since our objective is on the *other* side of the test site, we can save considerable mileage by merely *cuttin'* *through*! First we borrow a likely vehicle from our motor pool over there—"

"Hey, you ain't gonna *hot wire* anything are you?"

"—Then proceed out through the back entrance where there ain't no guards. After that, we just drive northeast until we get there."

"Are you sure we can get back before wakeup call. It's only another three hours—"

"It's almost midnight now." Vincel stood up. "We can proceed to your ladyfriend's residence, you get your *socializin'* done, and then we come *back.* I'll wager the entire matter can be consummated in the space of an hour."

"You think so?"

"Sure!" Vincel said, lumbering toward Sgt. Quaak's jeep. "All we have to do is obtain some *transportation.*"

Joe Bob walked over to his tiny range and poured himself another cup of coffee, black, his fourth in a single hour. It was already midnight, but there was no way he was going to sleep tonight. Since his argument with Stein he'd been a jumble of nerves. And what in the hell was he going to do with those photos? They were clearly classified top secret. Setting aside the coffee, he scooped the photographs into a pile on the table. On top was the stoptime picture of the bomb cab disintegrating, surrounded by little globes of fire. He shook his head. Did anyone *really* know what went on with these things? Maybe Dr. Jeffrey was right. Maybe each nuclear burst dissolved space a little, allowing whatever was on the other side to come through.

Ramey picked up the photograph and placed it in his shirt pocket. He knew what he would do. He would call Flagmeyer, offer to work on the Doom Town shot, then bring in the photographs. Maybe he could say he found them somewhere in the Control Point.

No. He was never good at lying. He would have to tell him the truth. Joe Bob reached for the phone and dialed the lab.

"Camp Jupiter Laboratory. Dr. Flagmeyer."

"Hi, Art, this is Joe Bob. Wondered if ya needed any help on this shot—"

"Aren't you still on leave, Joe?"

"Yeah," Ramey said, looking at the box of photographs. "But I thought maybe I could run the monitors for the test. I kinda' hate to miss the last shots of the series—"

"I'm sorry, Joe," Flagmeyer said, "but you missed all the meetings. They've assigned Groder to the monitors. Marienfeld's going to help out."

"Marienfeld?" Joe Bob laughed.

"That's right. Demming wanted him at the Control Point. I'd like to put you up here, but you're not on the schedule." Flagmeyer paused. "I could have you help George Linneman. He's checking switchboxes for the Vulcan shot."

"Nah." Joe Bob drummed his fingers on the table. "Guess I'll pass that up." He replaced the phone on the hook. Glancing a moment at the box of photos, he redialed the phone.

"Control Point. Groder."

"Hi, Jim. This is Joe Ramey. Ya got a minute or two?"

"Things are still quiet—only a few people here," Groder said. "You comin' in for this one?"

"Don't think so." Ramey paused. "If you're near the library, I'd like you to do me a favor, okay? Look up the *Windstorm* shot. July 5, '54. This guy I used to know flew the tracking plane on that one."

"Be right back."

Joe Bob pressed the receiver to his ear and stared at the ceiling. He was never good at lying. He'd make a terrible politician. After an eternity, Groder returned to the phone.

"Your friend might have flown a tracking plane, but not on July 5, '54."

"What do you mean?"

"Windstorm was an unannounced test," Groder said. "No tracking planes were sent out."

"Are you sure?" Joe Bob asked.

"Positive. I'm looking at the test report right now," Groder said. "No question about it."

"Say, Jim, d'ya think you can hold onto that for awhile? I'd like to take a look at it."

"Sure, I'll leave it on the table."

Joe Bob hung up and looked at the clock. It was 12:15 in the morning. He wondered if Suze was still up.

Shivering in the cold night air, Robert Wayne peered through the windshield at the desert. Vincel had picked a jeep without a top, sides or, for that matter, doors. He was afraid he'd shiver himself right out onto the road. Except, of course, there *was* no road. His cousin's shortcut to Hiko so far consisted of a blind stab at the vast Nevada desert. All he could see in the headlights was the cracked alkali flat. "Vincel," he said, holding onto the seat, "are you *sure* you know how to get to Hiko?"

"Don't worry, R.W.," Vincel grinned, his greasy hair waving in the wind. "It's merely a matter of direction. If we travel northeast we can't help but hit it—probably drive right down main street. Just keep your eye peeled for gullies. A gully in our path can seriously undermine the mission."

"Maybe you oughta slow down then," Robert Wayne said, gripping the seat.

"I've got it under control, R.W., don't you worry. Just hold on tight, we'll get you to that little blonde acquaintance of yours—in no time flat!"

"Skylight, this is Jupiter Control Point. Come in."

"Skylight," Colonel Morriss keyed the microphone. "That you, Groder?"

"Yep. We have you on radar at 38 nautical miles, 045 degrees, heading of 270. Please confirm."

"Skylight confirm."

"Please maintain radio silence until over test site."

"Will do. Skylight out."

Colonel Morriss took a deep breath and scanned the instrument panels, glowing dull red in the darkened flight deck. Every one of these airdrops went the same damn way. Loiter over the target like a bored buzzard for two, sometimes three, hours. With an armed bomb. Reaching down, he flicked the intercom switch. "Tom, we're in radio silence. If they call, *you* talk to 'em."

"Sure."

Morriss turned to his copilot. "Bill, take over a minute. I'm goin' back to the bay." He opened the door leading to the corridor and stepped past the radio operator. Just ahead of him, in a plexiglass blister, sat the bombardier. Morriss stuck his head into the cramped enclosure. "See anything down there, Phil?"

"Target at eleven o'clock. Got a bright patch next to the GZ grid. Is that another display area?"

"Gonna blow up some houses," Morriss said. "I think they got a train parked down there, too."

"Hey, that's great," the bombardier said. "I always wanted to blow up a house. Yeah, I—wup—hold it."

"See anything?" Morriss asked.

"Thought I saw a light moving down there, right below the plane."

"Well?"

"I guess it was a reflection off the cloud layer. Sorry."

⟞⟝⟞

"How come we stopped, Vincel?"

"I believe we have misplaced our location," Vincel said, thoughtfully stroking the stubble on his chin. "This isn't entirely *unexpected*, R.W. The white desert sand is something of a hinderance to a man's night vision. The headlights reflect back and—"

"What're you gonna do now? Drive in th' damn dark?"

"A sensible suggestion if there'd been a full moon," Vincel nodded. "Of course, as you can see, we've wandered beneath a blanket of clouds. Which sorta compromises our ability to know precisely where we are."

"*Our* ability?" Doggett stormed. "Damn it all, Vincel, when your directions was workin', it was *your* ability. Now you don't know where in th' hell we are it's suddenly *our* ability! A few hours from now, they're gonna drop that bomb and here we'll be. We'll probably visit the stockade for this one."

"Well, now, little cousin, I rather doubt that," Vincel said, removing a bottle of beer from beneath the seat. "Just allow me a little concentration time, and I'll have us out of here in a jiffy. Besides," he squinted into the darkness, "I believe I see some lights up ahead. Just to the left over there. See?"

"Sure do!" Doggett yelped.

"I just hope your girlfriend's home," Vincel said, aiming the jeep toward the glow. "Cause tonight she's gonna have a little *company*!"

1:45 a.m.

Colonel Morriss peeked into the bombardier's compartment. "Did ya ever see that light again, Phil?"

The bombardier shook his head. "We're over a cloud deck. Probably just reflection from the running lights."

"Hope so." Morriss peered down through the fuselage toward the bomb bay. There he saw the dark teardrop-shaped device attached to the bomb rack, strapped in place with two thick cables and a logger's chain. Sitting nearby, to make sure the bomb reached the target, were two weapons men—a big hefty man and a shorter fellow with wild gray hair. "Hey fellers," Morriss yelled. "Think that little bomb's gonna do the job?"

"Ja, sure," the men nodded. "Yeah, easy."

"You the guys r'sponsible for that Caddie we dropped outta here last month?"

In response, the short one blinked and scratched his head, while the bigger one with bushy eyebrows merely shrugged and looked out the window.

"Prob'ly can't speak English, can ya?" Morriss grumbled. "Ain't met a scientist yet that could. Well, ya shoulda seen it. Damndest thing *I* ever seen. Even had a horn. Ha. Didn't blow up or anything, so I guess you could say it was a dud."

The two scientists looked at their shoes.

"But it sure was pretty—had a real nice paint job." Morriss got up and started back to the flight deck. "You fellers keep up the good work."

"Dead center perfect!" Vincel yelled as the jeep entered town. "I swear, R.W., I don't know how I do it."

Robert Wayne looked around. "You *sure* this is Hiko?"

"Must be. It's the only town for miles."

Doggett stared at the deserted streets. "But I thought Hiko would be on a highway or something. This is in the middle of the desert!"

"You can't expect to find roads way out here like we have back home. It's the nature of the local geography." Vincel slapped him on the back. "Well, now that we're here, I guess it's time to get down to th' business of *romance*. Let's see that phone number."

Robert Wayne removed the flattened can from his shirt pocket. "Pull over under that streetlight so I can read it."

Vincel took the can and studied it closely, his huge sausagelike fingers turning it over and over. "I don't know," he said finally. "I can make out a nine and a seven, but that's all. Either this is a language of some foreign persuasion, or—" He paused, his brow knotted in thought.

"Or *what*?"

"Truth to tell, R.W., a fair judge would prob'ly call these numbers just *meaningless little scratches*."

"You callin' her a liar?"

"Now, don't get all fired up," Vincel said. "Maybe in the excitement of the moment she forgot how to write. But regardless of her intentions, we can't make out what it's supposed to say."

"Guess you're right," Doggett sighed, tossing the can into the street. "Damn. Drive all the way to Hiko and we don't know how to get ahold of her."

"You said she drives a pink Cadillac? Now, ask yourself the question, R.W.—how many pink Cadillacs can there be in a town of this size?"

"You're right!" Doggett brightened. "Heck, I bet there's not a dozen houses in this rinkydink place. We'll find that Caddie in a minute!"

Vincel pulled away from the curb and aimed the jeep down a gravel road past the water tower. Suddenly before them was the biggest parking lot Doggett had ever seen.

"Little cousin," Vincel said in a hushed whisper, "I believe we've stumbled onto a gold mine of opportunity."

2:30 a.m.

Like a tall, plump buzzard, Marienfeld stalked up the stairs to the Control Room bay and hammered on the door. After a few minutes, a freckled face appeared at the small square window.

"Who's there?"

"Who in hell do you *think*?" Marienfeld snarled. "I'm supposed to watch the monitors this morning."

"I thought you were in charge of public relations," Groder said, opening the door.

"Get outta my way!" Marienfeld pushed past Groder. "Where's the goddamn televisions?"

"Yeah," Groder said, "ever since Dr. Trumbo took over, everybody's had their jobs switched around. Demming's running the Control Point, Linneman's doing the electrical work here—they have me talking to the drop plane, isn't that something? Who's in charge of public relations now?"

"My *wife*," Marienfeld snapped.

Groder took a step back. "I'll bet she does a pretty good job. Demming always said she gave a pretty good job—uh, a full day's work—uh—"

"Where *is* Demming?" Marienfeld snarled. "I don't have to put up with being a—a—roustabout! I have a PhD! I deserve some respect!"

"Dr. Demming is in a meeting with Dr. Flagmeyer," Groder lowered his voice. "It's real high level—what do you want to talk to him about?"

"What are you?" Marienfeld flared. "His goddamn *receptionist*?"

"As a matter of fact," Groder smiled, "the blonde quit and the brunette got fired. Why don't you wait in this room here—" He hustled Marienfeld to the back of the Control Room, to a closet-sized cubicle littered with unused electronic equipment: wires, cables, soldering guns, broken oscilloscopes, headsets and television monitors with cracked picture tubes.

"Ha! That's right!" Marienfeld barked. "Put me in the junkyard! The one who had the guts to call attention to this mess. This is the thanks I get, cast aside like a used—" Marienfeld turned. He was alone.

Sitting down in a coffee-stained chair, he buried his head under his jacket. If only he had a drink right now—a brandy Alexander would be perfect—he would pour it on Demming. Right on his pants. Right in front. All these years working for the AEC, of lying to the public—and here he was. In the junkyard. Hiding under his coat.

Marienfeld cursed softly. He would probably never get his old job back. The AEC had decided the public wasn't all that important anyway. Marienfeld pulled the coat tight around his ears. Maybe he could go to work for a tobacco company, or one that made chemicals. A company that needed a professional liar to keep the public off its ass. He'd find a job. And it would be better than this place—out in the middle of nowhere—

Suddenly he heard something. A tiny buzzing, followed by a burst of static. Laughter, like a mechanical Tinker Bell. Pulling the jacket from his head, Marienfeld looked around. Where was it coming from? The headsets. Reaching up, he pulled them over his ears and settled back. Someone at one of the monitors had left the microphone on. Poor security. Maybe if Trumbo knew about this—

"—Las Vegas?" the voice said. "Ha-*haaaa*! You should have seen what they were doing at Doom Town!"

"Marsha and the senator at Doom Town? I thought ol' Stanley was the tour guide."

Marienfeld squeezed the headset closer to his ear.

"—Naaa! They didn't go out there on the train, stupid! They drove out in his car! While everyone else was looking at the storefronts, they were trying out the beds! All 32 of them—if you count the kid's rooms!"

"And the couches?"

"Rumor is, she took the senator out there tonight! Wanted one last bump before the big one hit."

Marienfeld gulped. Marsha? At Doom Town? With that sleazy, slimy *senator*? He shot to his feet, ripping the headset from his ears. Roaring past the banks of television monitors, past the staring technicians, past the dust-covered Linneman, into the parking lot, he found his car keys, his Ford, the gravel road down the mountainside, the railroad crossing, the Jupiter Highway to the targets, and finally, in the middle of the night—with the radio blasting—the road to Doom Town.

34

Airburst

2:45 a.m.

Groder settled back in his chair, took a drink of coffee and scanned the television monitors. Arranged in a row across the control panel, they provided twelve different images of ground zero and nearby Doom Town. To the far left was the telephoto of the target taken from the Doom Town water tower. Next to it was the photo taken east of the bullseye from a camera mounted atop a railcar, probably the last one in line. In the foreground was a wide-angle view of the train all the way to the locomotive. The lights of the target grid glowed steadily in the background. At detonation, this monitor would probably be the first to go blank.

Groder took another sip of coffee and glanced at the other screens, mostly mundane black-and-white views of storefronts in the nearby test village, house interiors, mannequins sitting at the kitchen table, arranged on the bed, a big guy kneeling at the side of a car, removing a hubcap—

He spilled his coffee. Somewhere inside Doom Town, a half-mile from the detonation point—someone was stealing hubcaps, knocking them off and pitching them into the back seat of a Pontiac Chieftain. Groder rubbed his eyes. The man was still there, now carefully pulling the wire wheels from an unidentified sports car. "Where's Demming!" he yelled. "We gotta stop this test!"

―――⚙―――

"Well, little cousin, it appears we're all loaded up."

"Y'know, Vincel," Doggett said, "I been thinkin'. We got in trouble for this kind of thing once before. Maybe we ought to just hightail it back to th' barracks."

"Well, I hate to disappoint you, R.W.," Vincel said, looking at his watch, "but I don't think we have time. It's already a quarter to three. Fact is, I suspect th' rest of the company is on the way to the trenches."

"What the heck do we do now?"

Vincel shrugged. "I suppose we could cut cross-country an' meet 'em at the trenches. You'll have to admit, we know the desert pretty good by now—"

"Oh, sure!" Doggett waved his hands in the air. "Drive up to the trenches in a stolen Pontiac full of hubcaps! How the hell do you think *that* would look?"

"I'll admit, little cousin, you have a point," Vincel nodded. "This is going to require some thought." He scanned the car lot, finally resting his gaze on a small black box atop the pole lamp. A camera. "You know, R.W.," he said after a moment, "it occurs to me we may need a complete change of *career*."

"What d'ya mean?"

"Tell you in a minute, R.W." Vincel squinted at the pole lamp. "But right now, I'd like you to fetch me some *rocks*."

―――⚙―――

Groder rushed to the Control Point manager's office and threw open the door. Inside, a scowling Demming was going over some papers with an intense Arthur Flagmeyer. "Dr. Demming—Dr. Flagmeyer—you have to see something—"

"Groder," Demming growled, "get back to work. Anna Faye will be here any minute."

"We have to stop the test! There's somebody at Doom Town!"

Demming turned to Flagmeyer. "See what he's talking about, Arthur."

"I didn't believe it, I really didn't." Groder led Flagmeyer through the technicians toward the monitor bank. "There was this big fat man— he was in there with the cars—"

Flagmeyer looked at the monitors. "Which one was it?"

"This one, number—" Groder stopped. The screen was blank.

"There's nothing on that monitor, Jim," Flagmeyer said. "It's not being used."

"Yes it is!" Groder said helplessly. "It's the car lot camera! Dr. Linneman wired it up yesterday." He shook his head. "It was on just a minute ago."

Flagmeyer stared at the blank screen. "Linneman probably screwed up the wiring. We don't need it anyway. Watch the other screens and send me a report after that test."

"But I think there's somebody out there—"

"Sure, Groder, sure," Flagmeyer mumbled, hurrying back to his office. "Just go find another monitor."

3:30 a.m.

Marienfeld looked at the lights ahead, then down at the speedometer. Breaking the speed limit, it still had taken him the better part of an hour. The shortcut had been a washout in the literal sense, but had allowed him to elude the guards. And that was the important thing. Now he could drive into Doom Town, catch his wife and her paramour *en flagrante* and beat the daylights out of at least one of them. "Shouldn't put up much of a fight," he muttered, aiming the Ford up the steep incline of the railroad crossing. "They're probably not wearing anything."

That awful picture firmly in mind, Marienfeld stomped the accelerator. As the Ford rocketed over the hillock, he looked around to get his bearings. Yes, he was just on the outskirts. The car slammed back to the gravel road in an explosion of dust and grit, and Marienfeld wrenched the wheel to the left, skidding the Ford around the last bend in the road to the target village. As he cruised down the deserted main street, Marienfeld glared at the fake bank, the fake barber shop, the fake grocery store, all illuminated by a dull yellow glow from the street lamps. If the pavement had been brick, it would have looked like the set from 'Singing In The Rain'. "Real romantic," he grumbled. "Probably took a little *stroll* through here before they hit the sack!"

Passing the dark somber structure of the water tower, Marienfeld stuck his head out the window and looked up. Along the side of the tank, near the top, he could just barely make out the television camera. He would have to be careful. If the camera spotted him, all sorts of sirens would probably go off, and his wife and the senator would have time to get away. Cursing, he headed the car for the houses—the houses and the bedrooms. Looking at the shadowy, silent buildings, he knew that somewhere—somewhere—was his wife, with a member of the U.S. senate, doing who knows what—and on government property. "Said she was visiting a friend," he grumbled. "Ha!"

Marienfeld drove south until the pavement ended, then turned west. No sign of his wife's Cadillac. No sign of the senator's car. After stopping at an intersection, he turned back north, passing directly through the darkened village. No vehicles of any kind, anywhere. Marienfeld pounded on the dashboard until his hand hurt. He'd missed them; they had already come and gone.

Spaulding pulled the jeep to a stop in the nearly empty lot behind the Bachelor Officer's Quarters. Shutting off the ignition, he turned to Myrmidon. "Do you think he's here?"

"He'll be here," Colonel Myrmidon said in a bored voice. "Did you bring your sidearm?"

"Yeah." Spaulding patted his holster. "I just think we should have called in the MPs. I mean, if the guy really is a spy—"

"You developed the film yourself. You saw him in that plane." Myrmidon shrugged. "And as for the military police, what if he starts telling about getting volunteers for Bartholomew? What kind of answer are you going to have for that, Spaulding?"

"Well, I still think we should have told the general about him." Spaulding climbed out of the jeep. "What if he has a weapon or something? Why don't we arrest that other guy first, Perkins?"

"Perkins has already been taken care of. Bartholomew has him. And you—" Myrmidon turned to stare at Spaulding, his eyes like steel bearings. "Are you sure you want to be an officer in the Atomic Brigade? Or would you rather be a volunteer? I'm sure we could arrange an extra place in the bunker for you."

Spaulding looked at his watch. "Well, if we're going to arrest Duffel, we'd better hurry up."

Myrmidon silently stepped from the jeep and walked around to stand next to Spaulding. He drew his service automatic from its holster and jammed the metal bullet clip into the handle. "You think you can do this?"

"Uh, yes sir," Spaulding nodded.

"Let's hope so." Myrmidon turned and stalked toward the building.

4:10 a.m.

Sloan watched the lights burning past overhead, ivory reefs fronting dark pipes and girders. To each side the streams of light would briefly illuminate vast, deep corridors containing people dressed in white, masks over their faces. He had been here earlier, though he wasn't sure when. Maybe when they moved him during the night.

He liked the hospital best at night. All soft glow and occasional steps on the tiled floor. He closed his eyes and heard the clink of the IV bottle banging against the metal pole. Then he felt something pull the skin across his chest. More wires. Another exam. If this were played on a stage now, I would condemn it as an improbable fiction. McCorkle always said that.

"Hey!" the orderly said, stopping the forward motion of the gurney. "This guy's away."

Or did he say "awake"?

Sloan stayed still, heard the rhythmic clank of another cart, like a silent train passing in the middle of the night. Suddenly the man in the other bed sat up, grabbed the orderly by the shirt. "*No person*, you sonofabitch, shall be held to answer for a capital or otherwise infamous crime—*unless* on a presentment or indictment of a grand jury—"

"Doctor!" the orderly yelled "This one's up too!"

"I *told* you to strap him down!" A man's voice echoed from some-where behind the bed.

Sloan watched as the orderly pushed the other patient down. Look-ing up, he saw two people hovering near his own bed. The doctor. And with him, a large, square man with a rippled face.

"Just a minute, doc." The man walked over to the other patient. "Son, you only got it *partly* right. No man shall be held *except* in cases arising in the land or naval forces. Or in the militia. When in actual service in time of war or public danger."

"We're not at war, *jackass*."

"You're pretty goddamn smart, soldier," the man said, then turned back to the doctor. "I want the camera on *this* one, Norm. I want him closest to the west wall."

"Yes, sir."

Sloan closed his eyes, felt the bed move again—through the hall and down the stairs. Off the ramp and into the brightness, dust, thundering roar and whirling scythes of the big helicopter. "This guy is still awake!" the orderly yelled above the din.

"I'll take care of it," the doctor said. Sloan liked the voice, heard it every day. It was warm, reassuring. Even if it always meant the arrival of the needles.

"Amytal?"

"Full dose—IV push. Let's get 'em out there!"

Sloan felt the icy chill run up his arm.

Then, nothing.

4:15 a.m.

Senator Curry watched the deserted storefronts glide past. Up ahead, the water tower stood tall, partly shrouded by darkness. Turning the wheel, he aimed his Lincoln Continental toward the residential section.

As the car slowly coasted toward the houses, Curry smiled and turned on the dome light. Hair combed, teeth brushed, nails manicured. And his best suit, right down to the silk underwear. It would be a night to remember—deliciously daring and certainly more fun than a hotel suite over a loud casino. The message she had left with the bellhop had been explicit: Meet me at Doom Town for one last go. Bring the handcuffs. Love Marsha.

Curry chuckled to himself. He'd roll around with the lissome, muscular Marsha in their favorite house, on their favorite bed— then, with just fifteen minutes to zero, they'd throw their clothes into the car and head for some remote hill. There they would sprawl naked on a blanket in the desert and watch the fireworks.

She would be waiting in their favorite house, tucked beneath the covers, supple and frisky as a Maryland teenager. And as for that little red-headed bellhop—well, maybe he could make him a congressional aide. The senator stopped the car beside a darkened house on the eastern edge of town and looked at his watch. 4:15. Forty-five minutes to zero. Plenty of time. Stepping outside the car, he remembered what the bellhop had told him: "She's in house number 15. It has a mirror on the ceiling."

The senator opened the front door and called. "Oh Marsha!"

Silence.

Smiling broadly, he tiptoed through the darkness into the next room. The kitchen? Why not? Walking to the kitchen window, he pushed back the curtain. Oh God. There was something in the back yard. A camera rack? Sighing with relief, he saw that it was a child's swing set. And near it, a tricycle. "Marsha! Are you here?" Suddenly the lights came on. He whirled. "Playing hard to get, eh?" He tiptoed into the bedroom. "Marshaaa! Come out, we only have a few minutes!" He looked at his watch. 4:15.

Still forty-five minutes to go.

＝〰＝

Spaulding followed Myrmidon through the musty, dimly lighted lobby of the Bachelor Officer's Quarters. Ahead of him, the tall, thin officer suddenly turned and nodded. Spaulding placed the clip into his service automatic. With a quick snap, he cycled the slide, propelling a cartridge into the chamber. Loaded. Seven bullets.

As they climbed the stairs to the second floor, Spaulding reviewed the plan—sit Duffel down, extract a confession. Probably wouldn't have to use force—the guy would tell everything. Then Myrmidon would haul him over to Dr. Bartholomew's quarantine ward, and that would be that. Of course, if Duffel tried to run, he would have to contend with a .45 caliber slug. And a 15-foot drop to the ground.

Spaulding watched Myrmidon walk down the hall ahead of him softly and deliberately as a cat. Not even the boards creaked, as though the man had somehow become weightless. At room 225, Myrmidon paused for a moment, then shattered the silence. "Open up! Now!"

The door opened and they stood face-to-face with a smiling, freckle-faced man in a Hawaiian shirt. "Hey, fellas, what took you so long?"

＝〰＝

The senator stalked into the bedroom again and threw open the closet. "Marsha, get out here! We don't have much time!" Did he have the wrong house? No. It was number 15, their favorite. He shook his head. Maybe she got the house wrong after all. He decided to look for her.

Returning to the street, he jumped into the Lincoln, closed the door and turned the key. The starter made a slow grinding noise. "Probably flooded." The senator held his foot on the accelerator for a few seconds.

and turned the key. Again, the grinding noise—then nothing. Throwing the door open, he stepped out of the car and gave the door panel a swift, glancing kick. "*Start*, blast you!" he yelled. Jumping back into the driver's seat, he again tried the ignition.

Silence. Only the gentle whine of a distant airplane.

"*Fords*!" he roared. "I *hate* Fords!"

Turning on the dimly flickering dome light, Curry checked his watch. It was 4:15. A dead car and only 45 minutes before the bomb dropped. Maybe Marsha had a car. He looked around. What if she'd already *left*? Did the houses have basements? No. But they had something better—telephones! Flying up the steps of the nearest house, he rushed inside and frantically searched for a phone. None in the kitchen, none in the bedroom. "What kind of a place *is* this?" he screamed, running out the door. "No phones—I cannot believe this!"

Running, falling, sliding across the grass lawn, he climbed the concrete steps of the next house. For some reason he felt like he was back in Georgetown again—home late from a clandestine rendezvous—running pell-mell through the front door to find the wrong people there. Then it had been the wrong house. Now it was the wrong town. Where was Marsha? Where were the blasted *phones*?

Spaulding and Myrmidon strode into Duffel's apartment. The room was like none he had ever seen. The wall opposite the door consisted of a wide set of windows covered by wooden venetian blinds. The other three walls were overlaid with an expensive wood veneer. And the floor was covered with maroon carpet. On a small television set in the corner was the image of a man with a wooden duck. "Say the magic word and win a hundred dollars—"

"Turn that off!" Myrmidon commanded.

"Hey," Duffel protested, "it's a great show. Ever watch it? Great theme song." He turned to Spaulding. "You'd like it."

"Do as he says," Spaulding snapped.

Duffel switched off the set, then waddled over to the couch. "If you came to watch the show, you couldn't have picked a better place. Front row seats. You'll love it. Say, would you mind putting that gun away?"

"What were you doing in that airplane?" Myrmidon asked. "We asked you to get us recruits, not spy on the test site."

"Yeah, I guess you got me," Duffel said agreeably. "I *was* taking pictures out there. Quite a place, ground zero. It's going to be part of the *Big Picture*—"

"That's a lie," Spaulding broke in. "We called the Army Signal Corps. They say they've never heard of you."

Duffel shrugged. "I really *do* work for the *Big Picture*. You just need to talk to the right people. Say, is that gun loaded?"

"Your friend Perkins has already been arrested," Spaulding said. "If you don't talk, I'm sure *he* will."

"Well, I really doubt he'll have much to say—he hasn't been to the target yet," Duffel said.

Myrmidon glanced at Spaulding.

"Fascinating place, ground zero," Duffel smiled. "You guys really should visit there sometime."

"You have a choice." Myrmidon released the safety. "Either you tell us who you really are, or we kill you here and now."

"You wouldn't do that, would you?" Duffel asked, a surprised look on his face. "You wouldn't just shoot an innocent guy like me? Ruin this nice shirt?"

Myrmidon smiled and nodded.

"Well," Duffel shrugged, "if you're gonna do it, at least let's step outside."

"What?" Myrmidon asked, startled.

"Yeah," Duffel said, motioning to the door. "I'd hate to mess up this nice interior. You can't believe how much trouble it is to keep *clean*."

"There it is." Colonel Morriss heard the bombardier's voice in his headset. "The lights are on."

"Great," Morriss yawned. "Anything from our escort service, Tom?"

"The C-47 photo plane is at altitude, the B-25 tracker is over Elko and the flying wings are maneuvering into place."

Morriss fitted his hand around the control yoke. "Approach to final."

"Heading at two-seven-oh," the copilot droned. "Airspeed 280. Doom Town in sight. Target train in sight."

"Those scientists outta the bomb bay?"

"They're with me," the radioman said. "Glasses fixed."

"Here go the barn doors." Morriss punched a switch opening the bomb bay. The extra drag made the plane weave like a car driving through deep mud.

"Bomb bay open," the bombardier's voice came over the headset. "Aiming point in sight. Radar clock running. Watch for the three-minute flare. Doom Town will be dark during final minute."

"Three-minute flare sighted."

"Entering final pattern."

=≈≈⋙⋘≈≈=

The senator rushed from the kitchen back into the living room, almost falling over an ugly, S-shaped green and gold couch. Backing up, he stumbled against another object, a huge floor radio—its electronic guts spread over the carpet in a neat pattern. Nearby were two orange butterfly chairs, a television set, an empty soda bottle and an ancient half-eaten sandwich. But no phone.

His heart pounding, he checked his watch—4:15. Forty-five minutes to find a phone. Racing into the bedroom, he suddenly saw it, resting quietly on the nightstand, beneath a pair of pink fluorescent comedy-tragedy masks.

"A phone!" the senator shrieked. Pressing the receiver to his ear, he listened for the tone, then shakily dialed the number to the Control Point. Busy.

Outside the window a flare flashed red. What was going on here? It was only 4:15. Looking closer at his watch, he saw something else. The second hand had stopped. His fingers shaking furiously, the senator tried to dial once more. Still busy. Standing up, he glanced in the mirror—at a tall, distinguished man with thick, sandy hair, tie bent out of shape, a white shirt. The senator set the receiver down and smoothed his tie. Still electable. In the background, from somewhere on the desert, another flare.

Then the house went dark.

=≈≈⋙⋘≈≈=

That's it!" the bombardier's voice snapped in the headset. "She's on her way! Forty-three seconds to go."

"Let's take her outta here, boys!" Morriss firewalled all four throttles and the B-36 screamed into a hard climbing right turn, fighting to get away from the burst zone.

—⟶⟩⟨⟵—

"Well, let's get it over with. I'm a busy man." Duffel shook his head and opened the door.

"Fine," Myrmidon smiled. "You first."

Watching Myrmidon follow Hugh Duffel through the door, Spaulding felt a chill. Something wasn't right. His knees suddenly weak, Spaulding slowly walked over to the door and looked. The dark hallway was no longer there. Somehow, the grinning Duffel and a stunned Myrmidon were standing flat-footed on some kind of balcony. Or something. Suddenly, a red fiery streak shot into the black sky, then arced back to earth. A flare. Why were they firing flares at Camp Sagebrush? And where were all the barracks? All he saw through the open door was a dark, dimly lit landscape of sand and Joshua trees with a row of lights in the distance. Was there a small town behind the bachelor officers quarters? What was going on here?

"C'mon, Spaulding!" Duffel said. "You don't want to miss this! It's the chance of a lifetime!"

His legs like rubber, Spaulding stumbled through the door onto the hard, sandy ground. The desert. Not only that, somebody had parked a line of rail cars behind the barracks. Only when Spaulding turned around, he saw there *were* no barracks. Just a derelict train of some kind. Then, he heard the drone of an approaching plane.

Suddenly the lights of the nearby town winked out.

"Hold onto your hats, guys!" Duffel shouted, pointing to the sky. "Here it comes!"

—⟶⟩⟨⟵—

The senator strode to the kitchen, then into the darkened bedroom and closed the door behind him. Suddenly, it occured to him he was no longer an esteemed member of Congress, no longer chief of the Joint Committee on Atomic Energy, no longer the greedy recipient of Marsha Marienfeld's charms. In the space of a few minutes he had been reduced to a curious night creature inspecting a vacant house in the Nevada desert. And he had seen enough airdrops to know there was probably an atomic bomb headed his way. The senator wondered if he would see it. Or would it kill him before the light got to his eyes? Taking a step toward the living room, he decided to at least get a glimpse of it—

Then something caught his attention. A light had appeared on the bedroom wall, bright pink surrounded by a halo of blue. The fluorescent masks were glowing. At the same time, a shaft of brilliant white light appeared beneath the door. He opened it. Daylight. Something had happened directly overhead.

The sun was dropping to the desert surface. Thick beams of light like dense yellow girders crowded into the room—blanking out the chairs, couch, radio—turning the objects into simple geometrical shapes. Nearby, jets of blue flame burst from the deformed, curving walls. And through the melting windows, a wall of smoke and fire rushed toward him, a thundering tidal wave consuming the car lot, the water tower, the vacant lot next door, the yard outside—then the room.

***

Joe Bob shut his eyes against the glare, opening them to watch the fireball leap from the purple expanse of desert into the sky—a bright, roiling torus of smoke and flame. Then, moments later, as the thunder rumbled over the parked cars at Lookout Point, the fire became a diaphanous mushroom cloud, leaning east with the wind, colored pink and orange by the rays of approaching dawn.

"You know, Suze, you're right." He placed his arm around her, drew her close. "It does look a lot better from up here."

35

Thermo

7:00 a.m.

George Linneman steered the pickup truck around the final curve at the northernmost stretch of Jupiter Highway, then west onto the gravel road. Straight ahead was the target 14 shot tower. Guiding the truck over the railroad crossing, he saw a bright glint of metal at the base of the tower. No one had ordered the trains moved. They were still here, waiting to be melted down, just like the one at Doom Town.

Linneman pulled the truck to the side of the road and switched on the Geiger counter. Nothing. No fallout from the Doom Town shot. He took a last look at the cloud hanging over ruined village like a solitary thunderhead. Two hours after the shot, the classic mushroom shape was still recognizable, a dark corkscrew chimney reaching from the earth to a ragged dome, everything tinged orange by the sun. Beneath it, thin curtains of pink and blue, like wisps of rain beneath a summer cloud. Radioactive dust.

Linneman shifted into low gear and returned the truck to the gravel road. At the outer circle of target 14, he steered the pickup to miss the "rail yard," the multiple sets of tracks west of the tower. At the center of the bullseye, he spotted the switchbox—the drab junction box that parceled electricity to the various motors and cameras around ground zero.

Pulling next to the box, he shut off the engine and took a deep breath. The target area smelled of creosote, turpentine, rubber and herbicide. But there was another component he could never identify—the metallic, burnt-resin, overheated-generator smell. Despite his experience with electricity, he never understood where it came from. Taking his tool box from the truck, he glanced up at the small shed atop the shot tower, a square dot against the blue sky. The Vulcan fireball would start there. An instant later, it would dissolve the tower and hammer the bullseye into a neat, perfectly round dish. The switchbox, just 80 yards from the tower, would be dissolved within the first few milliseconds.

He stepped up to the switchbox, noticing the long rectangular mound of white concrete 60 yards to the northeast. The reinforced instrument bunker. A sign that Vulcan was also a military test—classified secret.

Linneman opened the switchbox and looked at the familiar tangle of cables inside. Absentmindedly testing the terminals with his screwdriver, his thoughts drifted to less barren places. Someday soon he would take down his flounder picture, pack his bags and move back east. To Boston. Maybe he could get his old job with the transit authority, repairing cable along Boylston Street or Melnea Cass Boulevard. Or he might move to Chicago. He liked Chicago, even in the winter. He liked to watch the fog lift from the Tribune building, liked the Cubs, even liked the icy wind that blew off the lake. He paused, almost dropping the screwdriver. He was tired, so tired his heart was skipping beats.

Peering into the corner of the cabinet, Linneman located the thick white primary cable, the most important one in the switchbox. It supplied 440 volts to the top of the tower, and thus to the nuclear device itself. Reaching back into the cabinet for the main knife switch, his hand grazed the copper plates protuding from the back of the box. Had the switchbox been energized, he would have died then and there. The copper plates were part of a security system to prevent anyone from shutting off the electricity and stealing the bomb. It was simple and dangerous, but seemed to work. No one had ever stolen a bomb from the shot tower.

Linneman carefully tightened the terminal screws on the copper plates, then closed the box. Wearily walking back to the truck, he noticed that his arms felt detached from his body. He had been up now for almost 22 hours.

Steering the truck away from the target's flat inner circle, Linneman took a last look around, at the switchbox, the tower, the instrument bunker, the trains. By tomorrow morning, the passenger cars, the stolid locomotives and the drab yellow switch engines would be smoking, melted wrecks. Even the gleaming aluminum railcars that had once been part of the proud Santa Fe Super Chief. Linneman could see why the old engineer Pliney loved them.

Easing the truck over the railroad crossing, Linneman looked up the tracks to see a bright, flashing light. Pliney and his train. Bringing even more railcars to the target. This last test would be a big one.

———※———

Joe Bob steered his Roadster onto the main highway just as the sun crested the jagged spine of the Sheep Mountains. Ahead, the highway glistened, vanishing into a glowing landscape of yellow, orange and brown. A half-hour earlier, Susan had told him how she liked to watch the morning sunshine move across the valley behind her trailer. It was like pulling up a shade, she said, letting the daylight in. He had been at the test site for years and he had never seen that. He had only watched the mushroom clouds.

Joe Bob pulled into his driveway and shut off the ignition. Usually after a detonation, the air carried a yellow haze of dust. This morning seemed different, though. Crisp and clean. Perhaps the wind was in the southwest, sending the radioactive debris northeast. Pulling the keys from the ignition, he stepped out of the convertible and onto his front porch. Absently, he inserted the trailer key into the lock and turned it, realizing he had left the door unlocked. Carefully pushing it open, he stepped inside. Everything looked the same—khaki shirt on the sofa, coffee pot on the range, dishes in the sink, the empty soda bottle on the table. Yet something was missing.

Glancing at the empty floor, he knew what it was: the photos were gone.

"Control Point. Groder."

"Jim, this is Joe Bob," Ramey barked into the phone. "I want to talk to Art."

"Sorry, Joe. He's in a meeting with Trumbo. They're getting ready for the Vulcan—"

"Get him on the phone!"

"Nope," Groder said. "I'll get my ass fired. What's going on?"

"Has he sent anybody out to my trailer? Like in the last couple of hours?"

"Are you kidding?" Groder whispered. "Trumbo's on the warpath. No one's been allowed to leave the building since, lessee—3 a.m."

"You sure?"

"I'm serious. You ought to be glad you're not here. The place smells like a locker room. What's going on?"

"Nothing. Sorry." Ramey replaced the phone on the hook, then redialed.

"Company quarters." A gruff voice. Probably some sergeant.

"I want to speak to Jake Stein."

"Captain Stein is out. Shall I have him call you?"

"No."

Ramey hung up the phone, then pulled back the curtain and looked out the window, squinting into the morning sun. Finally, when his eyes adjusted to the glare, he saw it. A lone car, parked just across the highway. Facing his trailer.

<hr>

Flagmeyer glanced at his notes, then around the Control Room at the assembled crowd of technicians and officials. Real Atomic Energy Commission officials. And he was going to give them a speech.

At the front of the Control Room, Trumbo was droning on about the Doom Town test, how good it was that everyone could make it down from Washington on such short notice. Despite her gruff attitude, she seemed to be saying the right things. Most of the dour, dark-suited officials looked interested. Flagmeyer hoped they would react to him the same way.

Though Demming and most of the others were clearly frightened and disturbed by Anna Faye, he had come to respect her. She trusted him far more than Demming had. In turn, he felt more confident of his abilities, of his relationship to the immense forces science had unleashed. Perhaps he was getting closer to the military's view, the pragmatic, Newtonian attitude and easy familiarity with the lethal.

"The device detonated over a train located at area 11," Trumbo said, pointing to a wall map. "It was a preliminary test for tomorrow morning's Vulcan shot. Dr. Flagmeyer will explain the Vulcan experiment in more detail . . ."

As Trumbo continued, Flagmeyer looked at the wall map. He was glad the shot had gone well, though he felt a twinge of sadness for the objects near the drop zone—the old train, the cars, the houses. Energy from the 30-kiloton Mach front had swept through, over and past the blue chiffon gowns, the shirts, the plastic tumblers, the ceramic ashtrays on the nightstand. The beds, the rooms, the houses. Even that old radio Uborka had found, the one with the "acoustical labyrinth." The energy had swept it all away.

Ah, but *what* energy! Pure, symmetrical, pristine. Emanating from the core of the device, from the twin hemispheres of plutonium, it had formed a powerful wave rippling through the universe like a whip through thin fabric. It hammered the target like no mortal contrivance could, then raced outward in a sphere of light and pressure, cascading in all directions like waves on a beach. Flagmeyer smiled. To be oxidized by the force of pure light, swept to the winds by the most immense, unassailable power on earth—that would be an honor indeed.

"Well," Trumbo said finally, "if here are no further questions about the event this morning, I'll turn the meeting over to Dr. Flagmeyer. Arthur?"

"Thank you, Anna Faye." Flagmeyer stepped to the front of the room and turned to the audience. "The Vulcan device will be fired in the conventional way—with plutonium. The trigger will be an atomic device, placed at the top of the shot tower." Picking up two grapefruit-sized hemispheres of the warm metal, he held one in each hand. On the table nearby, a small neutron monitor began to click. The officials glanced nervously at Trumbo.

"Each of these pieces of plutonium is barely subcritical," Flagmeyer explained. "When brought together or imploded, they result in a chain reaction." As he slowly brought the heavy hemispheres toward each other, the neutron monitor erupted into an ominous buzz. "Like two half-worlds, when added together, create more than the sum of their parts."

"Enough poetry, Flagmeyer," Trumbo growled, looking bored. "Get on with it."

"Of course, Dr. Trumbo," Flagmeyer smiled, setting the plutonium aside. "Now, 500 feet beneath the atomic device will be placed 12 hopper cars, each loaded with 95 tons of lithium deuteride—"

"Dr. Flagmeyer," one of the men interrupted, turning to Trumbo, "lithium deuteride is fusion fuel. Is the Vulcan device a thermonuclear bomb?"

"Yes," Flagmeyer responded. "The Vulcan device will create a *self-sustaining* thermonuclear fire, held together by magnetic lines of flux."

Silence. Suddenly, at the corner of the room Uborka raised his hand. "Er, Artur . . ." He hesitated, looking around nervously. "That's over a million kilograms of lithium deuteride. It will be the biggest explosion the world has ever seen—"

"No, Eduard," Flagmeyer smiled, "the fireball will be contained by the magnetic field."

"No!" Uborka persisted. "The zero point energy itself only equals several kilotons per cubic centimeter. This explosion will be beyond that. It may even shift the fine structure constant—!"

"Just what is this man talking about?" an AEC official asked.

"Theoretical discussion," Trumbo said glaring at the trembling Uborka. "No relation to the business at hand."

"Why the hell do we want a permanent fireball on the Nevada desert anyway?" the man shot back. "It sounds like a lot of trouble if you ask me."

"It would be a permanent energy source," Flagmeyer offered. "Lasting well into the next century."

"Perhaps I can explain." Dr. Bartholomew stood up and turned to the group. "As a physician, I assure you there are medical applications. In addition to being an energy source, a permanent nuclear fire would supply inexpensive radiation for radiotherapy and diagnosis. It would be a boon to medical research. Many lives would be saved."

"And the fireball *will* be under our complete control," Flagmeyer added, surveying the group. He noticed that Eduard Uborka had left the room.

=◦〰◦=

Stein looked at the sky. A black pall of stratus hung over the desert. The cloud seemed to be part of the mushroom, but as his jeep drew closer to the GZ, the dusky haze became a dark ceiling supported by thin columns of smoke wafting from the wreckage. Beneath the layer, the sun was a dim yellow circle. Above, the huge black shape of the helicopter circled around to the busload of reporters following the line of jeeps. Seconds later the helicopter floated to other side of the haze curtain.

Sergeant Quaak looked at the bus, then adjusted his respirator. "Startin' to feel like a damn guinea pig."

Behind his mask, Stein allowed himself a smile. Quaak was right. The army jeeps always preceded everyone else into the danger zone.

"Captain Wanker," the radio squawked, "this is Colonel Storax. What are the radiation levels at the east end?"

"Hundred millirads an hour." Wanker's voice. "It's almost clear."

"Proceed to the train and hold your position," Storax replied. "Captain Stein, how does it look from your side?"

Stein picked up his microphone. "The same, sir. The radiation meter is holding steady at a hundred millirads an hour. We're half a mile from burst point. The news bus is 500 yards to the rear."

"Proceed into Doom Town, Captain Stein."

Stein made a final check of his respirator, then accelerated into the devastation. The well-planned tract of houses and stores was now a random collection of sticks, splinters and hollow wooden skeletons. Overlooking the rubble was the water tower, blackened, dented but still standing tall against the landscape.

A few minutes later, Stein checked the Geiger counter, pulled at his white radiation suit and exited the jeep. Then, stepping among the shredded timbers and shards of brick and glass, he shook his head in disbelief. It was like something from the war. Acres and acres of debris—once-familiar objects shattered and rendered unrecognizable by the force of the detonation. Frame buildings reduced to vacant heaps of kindling. Platforms of ragged timber that had once been second-story bedrooms now supported only by random joists and lopsided door frames. Ruptured appliances speared by huge timbers or crushed like tin cans.

He walked through the rubble, pausing to kick barely identifiable fragments with the toe of his boot. A shard of glass, a sand-scored bathroom faucet attached to a flattened length of pipe. A toilet float flattened into an awkward circle. A piece of plastic stubbornly emanating a wisp of black smoke.

"Take a look at that." Quaak pointed to a squat brick chimney surrounded by splinters and pieces of a sooty sofa. "Probably the family room."

Nearby, a car rested on its top in the midst of a pile of debris, its paint scorched to the metal, windows and headlights blackened and fused. As they looked, the sun dimmed and the huge helicopter roared directly overhead, sending the smoke into chaotic swirls. Almost simultaneously, a heap of wood and brick about 30 yards away began to creak and squeal. With a groan, a wall gave way and the entire structure collapsed into itself, sending up a thick brown cloud of dust and splinters.

Making his way through the rubble, Stein saw a group of radiation-suited men hovering around something. They weren't wearing military insignia. They had to be from Camp Jupiter—Demming's boys.

"Get Storax on the radio!" somebody yelled. "Get him down here quick!"

Stein picked his way through the debris toward the commotion. "Get security!" one of the men screamed.

"Is it a volunteer?" another asked.

"Can't be! The bunker's a mile away!"

"Cordon off the area!"

Stein saw the military escorts quickly form a circle around the shattered house, their rifles ready. Seconds later a black shape thundered down through the haze and landed between Stein and the white-suited men, filling the air with dust. Seconds later, after the helicopter roared back into the sky, the men, the escorts, whatever they had found at in the debris— were gone.

Stein sprinted back to the jeep and switched on the shortwave receiver.

"I saw the chopper," Quaak said, approaching the jeep. "What happened out there?"

"I don't know," he said, switching through the channels, "but I don't like it."

"Get anything?" Quaak stared at the radio.

Stein shook his head. "They're on a restricted frequency." He looked in the sky to see the chopper heading away toward the south. "Sergeant," he said, starting the jeep, "as of this minute, you and your men are on administrative leave."

≈⧓≈

Flagmeyer smiled at the audience, then folded his notes and placed them in his pocket. "So, if there are no further questions, we'll get to work on the test—"

Suddenly the door opened and two grim-faced soldiers stalked over to confer with Trumbo. After listening for a moment, she turned her gaze on Marienfeld. "I've just received word . . ." She paused, staring at Marienfeld "—that the chairman of the Joint Commission on Atomic Energy, senator Hodel Curry, has been murdered. We have reason to suspect foul play."

"*What?*" one of the AEC officials asked. "How?"

"He was found in his, uh, *hotel room*," she continued, "and we have a suspect."

As the crowd stared slackjawed, three black-suited men hoisted the wide-eyed, thrashing Marienfeld up out of his seat and out the door. In less than a minute, it was over.

"Arthur," Trumbo growled, "I want to see you after the meeting."

Minutes later, fists clenched, Flagmeyer strode out of Anna Faye's office and across the Control Room. It was his first perfect atomic test as weapons director and that fool Marienfield, in a fit of jealous rage had—

Just then Flagmeyer saw someone shuffle into the Control Room bay, dust trailing behind him. George Linneman, fresh from the Vulcan target. He watched his ex-manager cross the room, pause for a moment at his desk and collapse into the chair. Flagmeyer shook his head in disgust. If Marienfeld represented the nadir of human reason, Linneman represented the worst aspects of the government system—stubborn, inertia-laden bureaucrats resistant to every forward advance and dedicated to mediocrity. Afraid of the future, he had held them back. Until now.

"George!" Flagmeyer walked over to stand in front of him. "I want to talk to you."

Linneman opened two bloodshot eyes. "What?"

"Have you wired up the switchbox at the Vulcan target?"

"Sure," Linneman nodded. "I just got back in. Everything is tight. Is the test still on for tomorrow?"

"Tomorrow morning, 5 a.m." Flagmeyer paused. "We're going to use lithium deuteride."

"Lithium?" Linneman asked, his old stubborn, authoritative look surfacing. "Thermonuclear?"

"That's right," Flagmeyer put his hand on Linneman's shoulder. "For years you've prevented us from using even small amounts of lithium. Meghalty and Uborka even had to sneak it past you for their test."

Linneman pulled his shoulder from Flagmeyer's grasp.

"But, now George," Flagmeyer continued, "the Vulcan test *will* use lithium deuteride. Over a million kilograms. With a 30-kiloton atomic bomb as trigger. What do you think of that?"

Linneman stared openmouthed, shaking his head. Then he laughed.

Flagmeyer froze, watching Linneman's giggles gain strength in a smooth upward curve of intensity until the man was convulsed with laughter, tears streaming down his face.

"Stop laughing!" Flagmeyer demanded. "This is serious! You're impeding the march of science!"

"The march of science," Linneman echoed, gasping for breath.

"What is so damn funny?" Flagmeyer yelled.

"A million kilograms of lithium deuteride will blow this place," Linneman wheezed, waving his arm in a huge semicircle, "you, Trumbo, Nevada, probably the whole western part of the United States—"

"Linneman, dammit—!"

"Sky high."

Flagmeyer looked around to see if anyone was looking.

"And you know the funniest thing about all this?" Linneman continued, slapping Flagmeyer on the shoulder. "I don't care. I don't care if you turn this sorry *doomed* place into protons and neutrons and gamma rays. In fact, I think it's hilarious."

"You are way out of line, George!"

"Arthur." Linneman looked him squarely in the eye. "I quit."

"What?"

"And now, if you'll excuse me—" Linneman pushed past the confused Flagmeyer, "I have some things to do."

"Wait!" Flagmeyer barked. "You can't quit now! The Vulcan test—"

Smiling, Linneman headed for the door.

"George, you're *fired*!" Flagmeyer called. "You can pick up your paycheck—"

"Goodbye, Art," Linneman said, closing the door behind him.

After a long, horrible moment, Flagmeyer realized everyone in the Control Room was staring at him.

As he stepped into the security lobby, Linneman was surprised to see the place packed with people—mostly soldiers wearing black helmet liners, sidearms, batons and arm bands. Military police. Milling among them was a serious-looking contingent of civilians in black wool business suits. It was unusual attire for the test site, even among visitors. Linneman paused. Before a test the Control Point lobby was usually vacant. What were these people doing here? He stepped to the pay phone in the corner. No use waiting until he got to his office.

"Hello?" The voice was soft, drowsy.

"Carol, this is me. George."

"Whooo?"

"George Linneman. The guy who used to come into Demming's office all the time."

"Oh *George*! Yeah! You're lucky you caught me. I thought the phone was already disconnected."

"I heard you quit your job." Looking up, Linneman noticed one of the visitors watching him.

"Yeah, I quit," she yawned. "Couldn't take it anymore. I'm goin' back to Rhode Island."

"I just want to tell you I'm sorry about not being able to take you to Doom Town. I guess you know they blew it up this morning."

"Yeah." She paused, her voice dropping. "But that's all right. Probably wasn't much to see out there. Anyway, I'm leaving this place. Too hot. Gonna get on the bus tomorrow afternoon. Already have my ticket."

"Tomorrow afternoon?" Linneman felt a chill race across his scalp. "Can't you get away any earlier? Like *this* afternoon maybe?"

"You must want me out of town."

"No, I mean—maybe you should get a good start. There's a—"

"There's a *what*?" she asked.

Linneman looked up. The man in the suit was speaking into a walkie-talkie. Scanning the room, he noticed more people watching him.

"George, are you there?"

"Uh, yes, I'm here," Linneman said. "It's just that I'm going to New England myself, and I thought we could go east *together*. Use my car."

Silence.

"I'd pay for gas, food. That sort of thing. And get separate rooms, of course. Carol?" Linneman gulped. The man in the suit was walking toward him. "Carol, are you there?"

After an eternity, he heard her soft voice. "It wouldn't be any trouble, would it? I could pay my own way."

"No trouble at all," Linneman smiled. "Look, I'm going to clear out my office. I'll stop by this afternoon. Bye." He hung up the phone just as the man stepped up.

36

Volunteers

$\mathbf{S}$tein strode through the bright lit laboratory corridor toward Ramey's office, his combat boots clicking against the newly mopped tile floor. The hall was empty. No scientists. Where was everybody? Probably at the bunker.

Reaching Ramey's office, he found the door locked. "Joe Bob!" He hammered on the door. "It's me. Jake Stein. Open up!"

"What d'ya want, Jake?"

Stein turned. Ramey, his face drawn and unshaven, stood in the doorway to the main lab. "Th' army watchin' civilians now?"

"What the hell is going on at ground zero?" Stein growled.

Joe Bob shrugged, then opened the door. "Ed here says they're gettin' ready to blow up the world. C'mon in."

Standing at a blackboard covered with mathematical figures was the huge rumpled scientist Uborka. "Ed here was tellin' me they're trying to start something at the Vulcan site." Ramey pointed to the board. "A self-sustaining fireball. That what you're talkin' about, Jake?"

"Your lab people found something at Doom Town this morning," Stein said.

"*My* lab people?" Joe Bob looked surprised. Then turning to Uborka, "Ed, we don't have anybody out at the GZ this early do we?"

Uborka shook his head. "Flagmeyer is still in the conference and Emil's at his house. I don't know about George."

"They said something about a volunteer," Stein said. "At a bunker."

"*Volunteers at the bunker?*" Joe Bob scratched the stubble on his cheek. "If you're talkin' about the one at the GZ, it just has radio equipment or something. I can't imagine 'em putting people out there. You absolutely *sure*, Jake?"

"Joe Bop," Uborka said, pointing to the blackboard, "the Vulcan shot will create a fireball that will—"

"Just a minute, Ed." Joe Bob turned back to Stein. "Look, Jake. We've *always* been after 'em to increase the minimum distance from the trenches to the GZ. I *sure* wouldn't put 'em in the instrument bunker. That's right *at* the GZ. 'Course it probably doesn't matter." Joe Bob motioned to the blackboard. "Ed thinks we're *all* gonna be at the GZ tomorrow morning."

Uborka pointed to a series of figures on the board. "The fireball will be seventy miles wide."

"What?" Stein stared.

"The magnetic field will evaporate in a millisecond, allowing the fireball to expand," Uborka explained "It will equal 60 gigatons of TNT."

Stein turned to Joe Bob. "That's *crazy*! Why are you doing this?"

"First off, Jake, *it's not my idea*," Joe Bob replied testily. "I suspect your *general* would know more about it than—"

"It's Anna Faye's idea," Uborka interrupted, "but her math is wrong." He turned back to the board. "See, she forgot to consider the effect on the vacuum. The magnetic field will fall to zero—"

"What's this?" Stein exploded. "They're going to blow up the world tomorrow and you're doing *math*? You've got to stop the test!"

"No can do, Jake," Joe Bob shook his head. "Your army's got the whole place secured. In fact, I sorta thought that's why *you* were here."

"The fireball will kill us all," Uborka said, letting the chalk drop to the floor.

Stein looked at the figures on the board, at the pale, trembling Uborka, at the silent Ramey. "No it won't," he said finally, "because the test will *not* take place."

"What are you gonna do, Jake?" Joe Bob narrowed his eyes. "Stage a *coup d'etat?*"

"I don't know." Stein shook his head. "But we're not going to just stand around and *wait for it*." He looked at Uborka. "Are you absolutely sure of the size of that blast?"

"Absolutely," Uborka turned to the board again. "There can be no doubt."

"An' you've brought this up to Trumbo, right?" Joe Bob asked.

"She won't listen to me," Uborka shrugged. "Even Emil tried to talk to her and she sent him to his room. He's packing his things."

"Okay," Joe Bob nodded, "then Jake's right. We have to stop the test."

"And if we can't stop it, we evacuate the personnel," Stein add. "To some place where they'll be safe."

"The closest would be Denver," Eduard suggested. "Or Seattle."

Stein thought for a moment. "Quaak and the men are on leave— except for the ones in quarantine. I'll have to get *them* out—if I can get past the guards."

Ramey nodded. "I can get you in. The infirmary is connected to Camp Jupiter through the steam pipe corridor. We'll get in that way, then up to the basement and through the psych ward." He paused. "Come to think of it—"

"What?"

Joe Bob nodded slowly. "Maybe I ought to have a little talk with *God*."

Twenty minutes later, Joe Bob rapped on the door.

"Yes?" A crisp British voice came from inside. "Please come in."

After a last glance over his shoulder, Stein followed Ramey into the room. Standing in a jumble of electronic equipment, wearing a rumpled white shirt, brown plaid trousers and a bright yellow tie, was a tall, stoop-shouldered man with curious pale eyes. "Joe Bob!" he said. "So good of you to stop by—and I see you've brought your friend from the military."

"Dr. Jeff," Ramey began, "this here's—"

"Captain Stein, yes." Dr. Jeffrey extended his hand. "I've heard quite a bit about you, Jake Stein. There are not many like you on this side of the universe."

"Look, Dr. Jeff," Joe Bob said, "we have a big problem. Seems they're going to—"

"Ah, yes," Dr. Jeffrey nodded. "The Vulcan shot. They're going to rip another hole. This one will do it, I fear. We are already adrift. Sixty gigatons will complete things."

Stein felt a chill settle over him like ice fog. As if sensing Stein's unease, the old scientist smiled at him. "You're probably wondering what this is about, Stein—"

"Dr. Jeff," Ramey said, "I don't think we have too much time."

"My associate, Elmore, discovered it, you see," Jeffrey said, placing an arm over Stein's shoulder. "Quite by accident. He was calibrating the instruments for the Redwing test when he discovered an *unsteadiness* in the speed of light."

Ramey looked at his watch. "Jeff—"

"And using these figures, he concluded that the fine constant of the universe had begun to waver. The instabilities begin within a few hours of each atomic test—and the variation is always commensurate with the yield." The old scientist paused as if to gauge the reaction,. "It seems the nuts and bolts supporting our, well, *space*, are dissolving. With each nuclear explosion, we become more detached from the rest of the universe. After sixty gigatons, it will unravel completely—"

"I think he gets the point, Jeff," Joe Bob mumbled.

"Remember that conference on the matter, Joe?" Jeffrey looked at Ramey. "Arthur Flagmeyer was bored by the whole thing. *You* thought the calculation was off. Eduard Uborka thought we should put the effect to some good use—dissolving the Soviets."

Joe Bob nodded.

"And Rhinehart—" Jeffrey shook his head. "He wanted to use the bomb as a glorified subway—to hop from world to world. Well. Elmore and I discussed the matter with Dr. Demming and Dr. Bartholomew, and you see the result." He turned back to Stein. "Here I am, on a psychiatric ward. Elmore took his bomb to the desert and actually tested the theory."

Joe Bob looked at Stein nervously.

"And now," Jeffrey shook his head sadly, "he wants to bring everyone back with him . . . step by step. I told him it's a terrible thing to do. Especially to those soldiers."

"What soldiers?" Stein asked.

"Jeff," Ramey interrupted, "I thought maybe you'd come up with some idea on what we could do out there."

"You mean to stop the test?" Dr. Jeffrey asked, his eyes clear. "Why,

Joe, there's nothing you can do. Nothing either of you can do." He turned to Stein. "Of course, you will both *try*."

Joe Bob turned to Stein. "Jake, I'm goin' back to the lab—maybe Jeff can take you over to the quarantine ward."

Jeffrey looked at Stein and smiled. "Of course. I should have remembered. Come with me."

His heart in his throat, Stein followed Dr. Jeffrey down into the bowels of the infirmary, through the boiler room, past lengths of insulated piping and up a flight of stairs into a dark, brick-lined corridor. "I'm sure there was no malice behind what you will see," Dr. Jeffrey said over his shoulder. "They wanted to develop the perfect atomic soldier, immune to the ravages of the atomic battlefield. As a military man, I'm sure you can appreciate the value of such a project. The quarantine pavilion is down this hall, next to the autopsy court."

Following the man through the dim hallway, Stein became aware of the deep rumble of a nearby power plant. His childhood nightmares had resembled just this sort of place.

"This is the only occupied ward, Captain Stein," Jeffrey said, stopping by an unmarked door. "Your men are in here." Stein reached out to the doorknob, turned, pushed and was greeted by a soft, brown darkness.

"Who's there? Is anyone there?" A harsh, tortured voice.

"It's me again, old man." Dr. Jeffrey walked past Stein into the gloom. "Brought you some company."

"Ha. About time."

Stein had heard the voice before. Following the stoop-shouldered scientist between a row of beds, he stopped near a rectangle of ashen light. A bundle upon a bed, a perfectly round face, its features puffed and swollen away.

"Who is it?" the voice rasped. "That you, Jake?"

Stein felt a chill, immediately followed by heartbreaking sadness, starting at his throat and spreading up across his face, into his eyes, pulling the tears. "It's me, Thorne."

"What're you doin' here? Buckin' for a promotion, too?" The voice was an agonized whisper. "Hope you do better than I did."

"Dr. Jeffrey brought me," Stein said, his throat tight. Through the darkness and a blur of tears, he saw the twin pans of ice at either side of the bed, the IV bottle, the dim monitor recording heartbeat, the wires, the cables.

"Always good to get visitors," Thorne said, his voice now quiet as memory. "Don't get many down here on quarantine."

Stein knelt by the bed. "Why are you here, Bill? I thought you'd been transferred—"

"General offered me early retirement," Colonel Thorne responded. "Prob'ly shouldn't have done it. Didn't think it'd turn out like this."

Stein laid his hand on the colonel's arm, hot despite the icepack. For the first time, he saw that the hands in the ice were dark and swollen to twice their size. "What is this?" he asked Jeffrey. "What's going on here?"

"We have all been stricken," someone said from the darkness, "with a meandering and unfamiliar virus." Stein peered into the darkness toward a form lying in the next bed. It was McCorkle.

"Yeah," said another voice. "Now we're in the Atomic Brigade."

"We don't look so good, huh? But it's us. Your troops."

"Wobey?" Stein whispered. It *was* Wobey, like Colonel Thorne and McCorkle, bloated to twice his size, a soft, grotesque tortured caricature of a human being. The mouth swollen into a constant, painful smile, the eyes squeezed shut by folds of damaged tissue, he appeared a mocking simulation of serenity. To his deep sorrow and shame, Stein realized he could recognize them only by their voices.

"What happened?" he asked finally. "Who is responsible for this?"

"We're the new atomic army, Jake," Colonel Thorne whispered, the faint hint of a chuckle. "We're heroes."

"You should have seen it, sir," Wobey said slowly. "This big thing came through the wall and took everything with it. Came right through the wall."

"We were on television," another voice croaked from the darkness.

"But if they do it again," McCorkle mumbled, "I'd just as soon miss it."

"You know what I'm gonna miss now, though," Wobey said, trying to sit up. "I'm gonna miss all those years. Traded in for this dark business that makes no damn sense. Can't even see anymore. That's no deal."

"Science marches on," McCorkle mumbled drowsily. "We're still heroes, and that's what counts."

Stein felt alone in the darkness, helpless. He had walked through the last two years surrounded by an opaque curtain. And now the curtain had been ripped open, revealing a cyclorama of pain and horror and evil.

He watched as Dr. Jeffrey stood by Wobey's bed, his hand holding a thin glass-and-metal hypodermic syringe. "Some medicine into your IV, Mr. Wobey. This will help you sleep."

"That's no deal, is it?" Wobey mumbled as the needle punctured the plastic IV tube.

"I want to know who did this," Stein said.

"It's Dr. Bartholomew's project," Jeffrey replied. "He was curious about the amount of radiation a soldier can absorb and still function. Practical science and all that." He paused to watch the liquid enter the IV tube. "The general, of course, had a ready supply of volunteers. In return for their time, they were offered an early retirement. Technically, of course, that's precisely what they receive—starting to feel better, Mr. Wobey?"

"Yeah," Wobey slurred, "it all goes away."

"Thorazine—75 milligrams," Jeffrey whispered. "I've been smuggling them my ration."

"Did the weapons men know about this?" Stein asked. "Ramey . . . Uborka . . .?

"Oh, no." Jeffrey carefully removed the needle from the tube. "I discovered it only after being cloistered here and, I confess, I've said nothing. I reasoned if I were to cause a row, these men would be deprived of their medication." Jeffrey looked down at Wobey. "It was a terrible decision I had to make. I must say I'm not completely comfortable with it." The scientist snapped the needle against the tabletop. "But on a grand scheme, we're all to blame. I suppose Dr. Bartholomew acted for the advancement of science."

"But—"

"Invaluable information for cancer therapy—will help save thousands of lives." Jeffrey dropped the needle fragments into the trash. "Hm. Wouldn't be a bit surprised to see the results published someday. Facts will be a bit loose, of course—a sop to public sentiment and all that."

Stein looked around the room. No one was moving.

"You have found your volunteers, Captain Stein," Jeffrey said finally. "Now we should go. The doctor himself will be here shortly."

"I'll wait for him," Stein growled. "I want to meet him."

"He has a contingent of armed guards. And these gentlemen need their rest."

"Just a moment," Stein said, turning to Colonel Thorne. "Bill, you remember Lieutenant Perkins? Guy that got lost near ground zero. Is he here?"

"No."

"What about Andy Sloan?"

"Sloan? Yeah, he's here." Thorne slowly lifted a swollen hand from the ice bath and pointed toward a bed in the corner of the room. "He's in the last bunk on the right."

Stein looked. The bed was empty.

"You're a few days late, I'm afraid," Dr. Jeffrey said softly.

"As flies—" someone mumbled.

"Andy?" Stein turned to look back at the voice, trapped in the darkness. No. It was McCorkle, sitting up in bed, a shapeless mass in the lightless room.

"As flies to wanton boys are we to the gods," he continued, his voice deliberate and thick. "They kill us for their sport. Remember that, sir."

⸻⸺

As Ramey entered the laboratory bay, he saw that Uborka had company. With the Hungarian scientist was George Linneman, his red sport shirt and blue denims the only color amid the sterile gray and white. And at the desk sat Carl Rhinehart, reading a newspaper and smoking a cigar.

"Then those bastards took the keys to my desk!" Linneman shook his head. "I can't even clean out my own desk!"

"But Dr. Linneman, we have to *do* something—" Uborka said.

"If Art Flagmeyer wants to blow himself up, that's his business," Linneman said, taking a lab coat from his locker. "I don't work here anymore."

"You really should stick around, George," Rhinehart said, tapping the newspaper. "There's a great movie playing at the Beatty drive-in tonight. 'The Magnetic Storm'. Catchy title, huh?"

"Very funny." Linneman threw the lab coat into a cardboard box. "I'm heading for Rhode Island—and I've never felt better."

"If they let you out," Joe Bob said. "I hear they're cordoning off the whole test site."

"I didn't see anything unusual at the gates," Linneman shrugged. "The guard let me right through."

"Dr. Linneman," Uborka said, "the Vulcan shot will release 60 gigatons of energy. The fireball will be 70 miles in diameter—"

"Carol and I will be somewhere in Colorado by then," Linneman smiled, slapping a length of tape across the box. "We should be able to see it from there."

"You'll *feel* it from there," Joe Bob said, walking into the room. "I just talked to Dr. Jeff. He thinks this shot tomorrow morning's gonna end everything."

"See?" Uborka pleaded. "It will break down the fine structure of matter. Even Emil thinks so! He's running away to Argentina."

"Good for him. Maybe they'll understand him there."

"But, Dr. Linneman," Uborka said, "after tomorrow, there will be nothing left. Just a hole in space!"

"Space is pretty tough," Linneman growled, stacking the box on a hand cart. "It'll mend."

"I doubt it, George." Joe Bob shook his head. "According to Jeff, the works are already gettin' pretty flimsy. If this shot tomorrow *does* rip a hole of some kind, the whole thing might unravel."

"Happens all the time," Rhinehart said from behind the newspaper.

"It won't make no difference if you're in Colorado or Rhode Island, or even the north pole," Joe Bob said. "This shot is gonna take care of everything."

Linneman paused, frowning. Then he turned to Uborka. "You and Meghalty always wanted your damned H-bombs. *Now* do you see why I never wanted you to fool around with thermonuclear?"

"Gotta watch 'em every minute," Rhinehart said, turning a page.

"If I hadn't taken the plutonium out of that car-bomb of yours," Linneman continued, "this whole place would be vapor *right now*!"

"*You* took it?" Uborka asked, a hurt look crossing his face.

"*Somebody* had to have some responsibility around here."

"And we've got to stop this thing tomorrow too, George," Joe Bob said evenly.

"Count me out," Linneman replied. "I just want to leave. There's no reasoning with those people. Trumbo, Demming, Flagmeyer— they're in their own world."

"I wasn't thinking about talking to them," Joe Bob said. "But I damn sure *am* gonna stop that test."

"Joe," Linneman looked up. "There's just nothing you can do."

"You wired that switchbox out there, George." Joe Bob took a notebook from his shirt pocket. "If we can kill the power—"

"No," Linneman said. "First of all, we'd never make it. There are guards all over the place."

"We'll wait until just before the shot," Ramey said, pulling up a chair. "Meet somewhere outside the test site around midnight, then sneak in. Probably get in there through Achera Dry Creek."

"Good idea," Rhinehart said. "That's the route I usually take."

"Forget it," Linneman said. "This is a stupid idea. Now, I'm going to walk out of here right now, I'm going to get in my car, pick up Carol and drive east—as fast as I can. And I suggest you do the same."

"Then show me how to kill the power out there, George." Joe Bob handed Linneman a piece of paper. "Sketch it out. I'll be back in a minute."

Leaving Linneman staring at the sheet of paper, Joe Bob walked to his office, closed the door and picked up the phone.

"Hello?"

"Suze? It's me. Joe Bob. I've got to talk to you about somethin' *real important*."

When Ramey returned to lab, Linneman was still staring at the paper. "Well, dammit George? What's wrong?"

"I just think this is a crazy idea. I mean, trying to kill the electrical power to a nuclear test—it's ridiculous."

"Just draw the goddamn thing, okay?"

Linneman pulled a pencil from his pocket and quickly sketched a diagram on the paper. "There's a series of knife switches to the various experiments—all separated by bare copper plates. You have to be careful, they're energized by a high-voltage security line—"

"Which is the main power switch?"

"This one." Linneman pointed to the center of the diagram. "Kill it and you kill the power to the device."

"Okay."

"But, Joe, I'm telling you—" Linneman tapped the diagram with his pencil, "—in order to get to it you have to reach in past the high-voltage plates. They extend out about three inches. Very difficult to avoid touching them."

"I can do it," Joe Bob said.

"Also, when I was out there this morning, I saw a cable leading directly to the tower. It may be some sort of backup line, I don't know."

"Anything else?"

"No," Linneman shook his head. "That's about it."

"Okay." Joe Bob folded the paper and put it in his pocket, then extended his hand. "George—thanks. It's been a real pleasure workin' with ya."

Linneman gripped Ramey's hand in a firm handshake. "I hope it works."

"I'll give it my best," Joe Bob said. "And if ya change your mind— let me know. I'll be at a little airstrip at the junction of I-95 and state road 52. Look for my roadster."

"Good luck, Joe," Linneman said. Turning, he walked out the door.

Ramey looked over at Uborka and Rhinehart. "You heard it," he said. "Th' party starts at midnight."

37

Vulcan

Joe Bob looked at his watch, then across the trailer at Stein. "It's quarter past twelve, Jake. Last chance to back out of this."

Stein shook his head. "I think Perkins is in that bunker. I'm going to get him."

"Fine." Joe Bob scanned crowded trailer. "Well, guess everybody's here that's gonna be."

Uborka, holding a cup of tea, sat on the small couch across from Susan. Rhinehart sprawled in a chair and Stein sat across from him at the kitchen table, his usual khakis replaced by dark green fatigues. And at the door, arms folded, was the owner of the trailer, Bobbie Jean Barnett.

"Let's go over it again," Joe Bob said. "An hour before the shot, Jake and I are gonna sneak in to the GZ through Achera creek bed. The helicopter ought to be gone by then—Ed, are you *sure* you can get to the Control Room?"

"Yes," Uborka said. "I'll tell Artur I've had a change of heart. He'll let me in. Since Emil ran away, I'm the only one who knows anything about lithium."

"See if you can man the monitors. If they see us at the GZ, we've had it." Joe Bob paused. "Now, Jim Groder usually watches those things. I doubt if he'll give you any trouble, but if he does, try to distract him, then screw up the switchboard or something."

Joe Bob turned to Susan. "After we pull the fuse and open the bunker we're gonna have to high-tail it. There won't be any lights out there and you'll have to watch for the tower. Think you can get the plane in there and back out?"

"We've done it before," Susan nodded.

"I can vouch for that," Rhinehart said. "But the last time we did this, she wasn't able to take off in time. The bomb went off and got *everybody*."

"Who is this guy?" Bobbie Jean asked. "Some kind of scientist?"

"Yeah, sort of." Joe Bob turned to Rhinehart. "Carl, have you talked to Pliney?"

"He'll do it," Rhinehart said. "He doesn't want his trains melted down."

"Trains?" Bobbie Jean asked. "You gonna take a *train* outta there?"

"Carl here talked to the engineer of the lab train," Joe Bob explained. "While we're at the GZ, him and Pliney are gonna try to haul those lithium cars away from the tower. That way, if we—I mean, if that bomb does go off, at least it won't be thermonuclear."

"Won't help you much," Bobbie Jean said, "or Perkins either." She looked at Stein. "Try to get him, okay?"

"Dr. Rhinehart," Susan said. "Does Mr. Pliney know he can get into trouble doing this?"

"We share the same attitude," Rhinehart shrugged. "We don't care."

"Hey!" Bobbie Jean jumped. "Someone's on the porch!"

"Unlatch the door." Stein suddenly produced a .45 caliber service automatic. "Then move back."

The door opened. It was George Linneman. "Sorry I'm late. Drove past three times before I saw your roadster."

"Thought you were goin' east with your girlfriend," Joe Bob said.

Linneman closed the door behind him. "I thought about it, and you're right. The shock wave from this thing will reach way past Colorado. It'll tear up everything. I put her on a plane an hour ago."

"You coulda gone with her."

"I suppose so," Linneman nodded. "But I really didn't think you could handle that switchbox by yourself, Joe. It's more complicated than it looks."

"Never *could* delegate responsibility, could ya, George?" Joe Bob grinned. "Good to have ya here."

"Joe Bop," Uborka pointed to his watch. "It's already one o'clock. If you want me to sneak myself into the Control Room, I should go now."

"Sure, Ed." Ramey hesitated a moment. "Y'know, none of you has to do this. It's still about four hours before the shot. A person can cover a lot of distance in four hours—"

"If Vulcan is detonated above the lithium train," Uborka said, "it won't matter *where* we are. We have to stop it."

 Perkins stood at the door, waiting to step through. On the other side were the clouds and fields of home, and just a thousand feet below, more real than a dream, his very own house. All it would take is a step.

"There it is, Will." Perkins blinked. From nowhere, it was Hugh Duffel, standing at the door, his hand out. "Home. All the way down." What was *he* doing here?

"Is he awake?"

"He's moving."

"Then finish wiring him up."

Suddenly he was home again, ten years old. From the ragweeds beyond the garden he heard his cousin's shrill squeal. Then he saw her, screaming toward him, bees circling her head. Grabbing her hand, he felt the dirt slide beneath his shoes, heard the thick buzz of the bumble-bees near his ears, stabbing into his scalp.

"This one is bleeding. Damn!"

"Two more to go, Lieutenant." Bartholomew's voice, droning beside his ear. "One on each side of your head. It'll just be a minute." Two more stings and Perkins yelped, struggled to run. His cousin pulling his arm, kicking dirt and ashes into his face.

"Turn him over. Look at that. The occipital leads are loose again. Are we getting anything from the temporals?"

"Steady beta rhythm with spikes. Lots of muscle action."

Perkins pulled his shirt off and covered his head. The drone became a roar. Looking up, he saw a thundering white turbulence inscribing itself in a wide semicircle across the sky.

"Roll him onto the table. Ready—now!"

He felt the world turn, felt the tile floor as he sprawled into the kitchen, swollen from the stings. Everyone was having dinner and he was sprawled flat on his back on the floor. Naked. Why was he naked?

"Chest p.a. and lateral. And a skull series. Hurry up with it. We have to get him out there."

Struggling to cover himself with his shirt, he noticed an extra guest at the table, slightly heavy, red hair, freckles. It was Hugh Duffel. Of all the people in the world, why had his parents invited Hugh Duffel?

"They're gonna take you out to that bunker, Will," he said. "They're gonna put you right under the atomic bomb. Now, this is your last chance to go home. Whattaya say?"

"Get me out of here."

"You know, Willie," his cousin said, aiming her thumb at Duffel. "I think this guy's trying to kill you."

Now there was only Duffel—standing alongside a thin, bald little man with a sad expression. Then they were gone.

"Okay. Let's give him the pentabarb."

Icewater. Someone was injecting icewater into his arm. The light above his head flickered and shimmered like ripples on a pond. He closed his eyes, then opened the door in his mind to the big purple clouds of sleep. Sifting through the wall of night, the sounds from the outside appeared as bubbles floating past, bursting on hillsides bathed in granular darkness.

Then the bubbles vanished.

Uborka nervously flashed his identification badge at the military police-man, then guided his car up the gravel road to the white building at the top of Syncline Ridge. Five minutes later, just before the road expanded into the parking lot, he encountered yet another checkpoint. The place had been turned into an armed camp. Security for the Gotterdammerung.

"Official business?" the guard asked. Uborka saw that the MP was young, yet with a face as hard as steel. It reminded him of the ones he had seen in Budapest just before the war.

"I—I'm Dr. Uborka. I'm working on the Vulcan test. I'm supposed to be here."

"Just a moment, sir." The guard paused to dial a phone. Shivering in the car, Uborka worried that his English might fail him. When he was excited or anxious, his English was always the first to go. Quickly glancing down at the laboratory, he saw that the train was still there. Uborka shivered again as a cold wind coursed over the hillside. What if Rhinehart hadn't been able to find the engineer? What if Joe Bob and Linneman couldn't make it to the tower?

"Could you step this way, please?" The guard held out a phone receiver. "Dr. Flagmeyer wants a word with you."

"Hello, Artur?" Uborka said. "I've decided to help you."

"Eduard? You've changed your mind? Great!"

"I'm at the guard shack," Uborka said. "Tell the guard that it's okay—"

"Eduard, Dr. Trumbo and the military attache want to know if you've seen Joe Bob."

"Ahh—Joe Bop. Ja. Igen—"

"Eduard?"

"He—ah—was in the laboratory this morning. He said he was going to take another day off or something. Or other. Yes. I haven't seen him since."

"Let me speak to the guard."

After a brief conversation, the soldier nodded curtly and Uborka returned to his car. Four long minutes later, he stepped onto the hard pavement of the Control Point parking lot, carefully closed the car door behind him and headed for the entrance.

"Don't you think you should turn on the headlights, Joe?" Linneman leaned over the back seat. "I don't see how you can drive with just parking lights."

"It's not that bad, George." Joe Bob twisted the wheel to avoid a boulder. "This is a dry lake—it's flat as a board. Besides, we should be seein' Jupiter Highway up ahead any minute now."

Linneman fell back against the seat. The yellow lights from the dashboard added an eerie quality to the faces of the men in the front seat, accentuating the sharp angles and rough surfaces. The tension showed.

Half an hour earlier, they had eased out the back entrance of Camp Sagebrush, past the Yucca Lake Landing strip and onto the test range. Since then, they had driven due north, paralleling the military highway and skirting the guard stations. Now they were all scanning the landscape in the dim moonlight for a faint white line—the road that would take them to the target.

Outside, shrubs flashed by the window as dark shapes temporarily illuminated by the roadster's parking lamps. For a fleeting moment, Linneman wished he had taken the plane with Carol. They would be flying over Illinois now.

"What'd it look like at the target, George?" Joe Bob asked. "Were the trains there?"

"A few," Linneman replied. "I think the lab train is still at Camp Jupiter."

"I sure hope so," Joe Bob said, twisting the wheel again.

"How far from the tower is the military bunker?" Stein asked.

"Not very far. I'd guess about 60 or 70 yards."

"Easy runnin' distance for a tough guy like you, Jake," Joe Bob chuckled.

"Not if I have to carry somebody," Stein murmured.

Linneman leaned back in the seat, closed his eyes and listened to the rumble of the tires over the desert. Opening his eyes briefly, he looked out the window. In the west, the 3 a.m. moon was an overturned crescent, its horns pointed directly at target 14.

———※———

"Come in, Eduard," Flagmeyer said, patting Uborka on the back. "Anna Faye's been asking about you. We were afraid you left the test site. Emil quit, you know."

Uborka attempted a smile.

"—Said he was going to Buenos Aires or somewhere." Flagmeyer steered him into the Control Room. "I have an empty chair for you at the instrument panel."

"I would rather watch the monitors."

"Sorry," Flagmeyer said. "That job is taken. The general's security people are at the sensitive stations. Anna Faye thought it would be a good idea, especially after what had happened to the senator."

"The senator?" Uborka stopped.

"He was at Doom Town when the bomb detonated. Can you believe that?" Flagmeyer shook his head. "Terrible thing. According to Anna Faye, he was our biggest supporter. That's why we moved up the Vulcan test. We want to balance the bad publicity with something spectacular."

Uborka felt his pulse begin to race. "I would rather watch the monitors."

"Eduard, I really want you on instruments," Flagmeyer said sternly. "There's going to be an enormous magnetic flux from this thing, and I need someone who knows a little about that. Sit down. I'll tell Anna Faye you're here."

Uborka sat down at the instrument panel, then cautiously looked around the room, at the diagrams of the Vulcan target, at the mockup of the device and the nearby hemispheres of plutonium, at the crowd of serious-faced technicians manning the instruments. Ominously, the only face he recognized was Flagmeyer's—and Trumbo's. Where was Groder? And Demming? Who were all these other people? As Flagmeyer crossed the room with the scowling Dr. Trumbo, Uborka felt his pulse begin to race again. He should have left with Meghalty.

Trumbo walked up and hovered over the desk. "Well, Dr. Uborka. What made you decide to come in? Scientific curiosity?"

"Ja, yes," he attempted a smile. "There are a lot of interests in the, uh, magnetic pulse. I don't think it will be very strong."

"Oh?" Trumbo folded her arms.

"Yes. Also, I don't think the radiation will be sufficient to absorb the heat." Uborka fumbled for his slide rule. The chances of an uncontrolled fireball are somewhat greater than even. I think we should perhaps postpone the test until I can work out the difficulties. Maybe remove the lithium for just this one test . . ."

"You would like to postpone the test, Dr. Uborka?" Trumbo asked. "Is that what you're telling me?"

"I—yes," Uborka nodded. "Ja."

Suddenly Trumbo looked up. "What is it?"

Uborka looked behind him to see a stern-looking man in a dark suit. "Dr. Trumbo," the man said, "the general just radioed in. The plane is now over Groom Lake, heading northwest. He believes it's headed for a small airstrip just outside the northern border of the test site. He wants to know if he should intercept."

Trumbo paused then looked at Uborka. "Maybe Eduard can help us decide." She leaned forward. "You know about communists, Eduard. You know what they did to your country—"

"Ed," Flagmeyer said, his eyes wide. "What's going on here?"

"Now, we know the people in that plane are trying to stop the test. They're foreign agents. We know that now." Her eyes bored into him. "They are in the service of the enemy, Eduard."

"I—no," Uborka gulped.

"The Soviet Union. Bulganin. Mikoyan. Khrushchev—"

"Perhaps it is a tourist." Uborka glanced at Flagmeyer. "An American tourist. Or maybe a *Mexican* pilot who has merely lost his way—"

"A Mexican." Trumbo nodded. " I'm sure that's it, Eduard." After a long moment appraising the trembling Uborka, she turned to the tall man. "Tell the general to intercept. If they fail to respond, shoot it down."

"Shoot it down?" Uborka's eyes widened. "No! You cannot—!"

"Put him in room 13," Trumbo said, "until this thing is over."

Uborka shot to his feet amid the growing crowd. "We have to stop it! Vulcan will destroy everything!"

"Anna Faye—" Flagmeyer stepped forward. "Eduard *is* a competent scientist. Perhaps we should hear him out. After all—"

Trumbo turned to the dark-suited men. "Take Flagmeyer with him. Put them both in with their friend."

Suddenly Uborka felt his arm in a viselike grip. Seconds later he and Flagmeyer were being pushed through the Control Room corridor toward an unmarked door at the end of the hall. As the door opened, Uborka stared, speechless. Inside, looking thoroughly frightened, was the former Test Site Coordinator, Dr. Davis Demming.

———※———

Susan looked through the windscreen into the darkness. "The pass is just up ahead. I hope Harold's left the porch light on."

"He'd better," Bobbie Jean said. "Sure hate to land on his strip in the dark. Has three gullies in it."

"It's still better than landing at that target," Susan replied, looking out the side window. "You sure you can do it?"

"Yeah, I think so." Bobbie Jean unscrewed the top from a thermos. "If there really is a soldier in the bunker, I hope he isn't too big. Six people in an airplane is a lot of weight."

Susan looked at Bobbie Jean. "Do you really think there's someone in there?"

"With that crowd, anything's possible."

Susan nodded. "About a year after Pop disappeared, I started having these dreams. I dreamed he was on this table, tied down and there were mad scientists working on him. And I saw him with all these wires coming out of him and he was crying for help. And I would wake up screaming." She paused to look out the side window. "In the daylight, I always hoped it was just a plane crash. That the plane went down and was lost and that was it. And someday I'd find it and there'd be a funeral and I could say goodbye."

"Yeah," Bobbie Jean said, her voice quiet. "I understand what y'mean."

"Even after Don Hendrix showed me those photos of ground zero, I guess I just didn't think they had anything to do with my pop. I couldn't imagine it. It was easier to believe he *did* crash somewhere on the test site. Not killed in some—some *science experiment*."

Bobbie Jean bolted the coffee. "When it comes to scientists, I'm never surprised what those bastards do. Want some brew? Keep you awake on th' way to Canada."

"I'm fine." With her fingertips on the controls, Susan allowed the plane to settle, a foot at a time, toward the dim dot of light on the horizon.

"Take it straight in," Bobbie said. "And ya might come in a little hot. Just watch the airspeed and keep to the left a bit. That way, you'll miss those gullies. "

"I've been here before," Susan smiled, switching on the landing lights. A parallel row of lights appeared on the ground ahead of the plane. "See? He's waiting for us."

"Hope he's got more coffee," Bobbie said. "Ours is gettin' cold."

As the ground appeared, Susan held back on the yoke, then at the last minute, stall warning buzzing beside her ear, she dropped the plane to the surface of the runway.

"Nice job," Bobbie Jean said, looking out the side window. "Remember to keep to the left—oh, brother."

"What's the matter," Susan said, slowing the plane to a stop. "I missed the gullies."

"Dammit, Suze." Bobbie Jean pointed out the window at a cluster of lights approaching them from the south. "I think they got us."

━━◦◦◦◦━━

"What is going *on*!" Flagmeyer yelled at the mournful Demming. "We're scientists! We *can't* be under arrest!"

"Anna Faye has put us under detention," Demming mumbled, shaking his head. "She wants to make sure things run smoothly. This is important to her."

"But there may be a problem with the calculations," Flagmeyer said. "Eduard says the magnetic field may not contain the fireball. Isn't that right, Eduard?"

"I can show you the calculations," Uborka offered. "It's very straightforward. I can do it on the table. Do you have a pencil?"

"I'm not the one you have to convince." Demming glanced at the locked door. "I think they're going ahead. With or without us."

"But we *have* to stop it!" Uborka said. "There is a person under the tower! In the instrument bunker!"

Demming stared, his mouth open.

"Someone at ground zero? You mean right this minute?" Flagmeyer asked. "What are you talking about, Eduard?"

"They're making tests," Uborka said excitedly. "Tests with people to see how much radiation they can stand. They put the people in the bunker and set off the bomb! Dr. Bartholomew is behind it—"

"Listen, Edward," Demming chuckled, "those old rumors have been around for years. Putting soldiers at ground zero, why, that's nonsense!"

"No!" Uborka sprang to his feet. "A man named Stein saw them! Dr. Bartholomew experimented on his soldiers! That's why he's going too!"

"Going? Going where?" Demming asked.

"To ground zero!" Uborka yelled. "With Joe and Dr. Linneman. They want to stop the test!"

"Oh, my God," Flagmeyer said.

"We must get out of here!" Uborka shouted. "We must tell Dr. Trumbo to stop the test!"

"Edward, Edward, just sit down," Demming said. "There's plenty of time. I'm sure if we present this information to Anna Faye, she'll take the appropriate action."

"But we have less than an hour—"

"There's time," Demming smiled. "Now, just so I have it straight. Joe Bob Ramey, George Linneman and this Stein fellow are out there. Anyone else?"

"Rhinehart and the engineer are taking the train. They're going to drive it the long way around so it can hide from the cameras." Uborka smiled weakly. "Rhinehart said it worked the last time he did this."

"Davis," Flagmeyer said, "can't you do something?"

"Well, possibly." Demming paused for a long moment, then got up from the table and walked over to the door. "Anything else, Eduard?"

"They're going to have a plane land at ground zero and fly them away," Uborka said. "To Canada. Then they're going to tell the newspapers about Dr. Bartholomew and the atomic soldiers."

Demming nodded, then gave the door three sharp raps.

Seconds later, the door opened and a man in a dark suit entered the room. "Well?"

"Get Bartholomew," Demming said to the man. "And bring security. They know everything."

———✦———

Rhinehart lit a cigar. "How much farther, Mr. Pliney?"

"Prob'ly another couple of miles." The old engineer leaned his arm out the window. "It's hard to see with the headlight off."

"Yeah," Rhinehart nodded. "But I figured you'd know this place in the dark."

"Hell, Rhinehart," Pliney tapped the throttle with the palm of his hand, "this is all *your* imagination."

"Well, I have gone through this a few times." He blew a thin trail of smoke from the window. "But I never bothered to commit much of it to memory."

"Did we ever get blowed up?" Pliney stared into the darkness over the nose of the engine. "You know—*vaporized*."

"Every time, sorry to say."

"That security guard ya coldcocked back there in the lab depot—does he get blowed up too?"

"Yeah, him too," Rhinehart nodded. "Everybody gets blown up."

"Well, I think that's crazy as hell," Pliney said after a moment. "No offense, a' course."

"Of course not."

"Last time ya went through this, did Ramey and Linnement and that other guy ever make it to the GZ?"

"Can't recall."

"Rhinehart, yer a lyin' sumbitch."

"No, I *really* can't recall," Rhinehart said apologetically. "Going through this even a few times can be very hard on the memory."

"Yeah, guess it would be," Pliney agreed. "Next time around, mebbe ya oughta *concentrate* better."

"Maybe next time I will."

—⚜—

Flagmeyer tried to swallow, but found he couldn't. His throat was too dry. And his head ached. In the past few minutes, the small room had filled up with grim-looking civilians. As he watched Bartholomew and the security people bore in on the silent, trembling Uborka, an improbable thought flashed through his mind—the place needed windows. It was way too claustrophobic.

"You mentioned this military man. Stein was his name. Right?" Demming asked. "A friend of Ramey's—"

Uborka looked at the floor.

"Now, at the meeting you attended with them," Dr. Bartholomew leaned forward, "did you see anyone named Duffel? Captain Hugh Duffel?"

Uborka shook his head.

"Did Stein mention Colonel Myrmidon or Captain Spaulding? Do you have any idea what happened to them?"

Uborka looked at Flagmeyer, then returned his gaze to the floor.

"If you tell us what happened to Myrmidon and Spaulding, we'll cancel the shot," Bartholomew said.

In response, Uborka glanced at Flagmeyer again, fear in his eyes.

"Your friends aren't going to get out of there any other way," Bartholomew said. "The general has taken the airstrip. If Dr. Ramey was planning to escape by plane, I'm afraid he'll be disappointed."

Demming edged closer. "Eduard, about those soldiers in the ground zero bunker. Did you know they were all volunteers? They were there of their own free will—"

Bartholomew placed a hand on Uborka's shoulder. "We're trying to learn more about radiation, Eduard. We're trying to find ways to protect our soldiers and civilians from these terrible weapons. And we can't do that without experiments. They're essential for our defense."

Demming smiled. "The public doesn't understand science, Eduard. If they find out about this, they may try to close down the test site altogether. Then we would have no defense at all. Is that what you want?"

"Surely you understand, Eduard," Bartholomew continued, "medical progress is never without cost. Great advances always exact a price on some small group. If our research is stopped, we may never learn how to develop an immunity to radiation. Think of all the years of research lost. Eduard?"

Demming edged closer. "Tell us, Eduard. Who else is in on this? Who else knows about the bunker?

Uborka took a deep, shaky breath, but said nothing.

"*Damn* this!" Bartholomew shot to his feet. "We can't reason with this man. We have to get rid of them!"

Suddenly the door opened and Trumbo stepped into the room. "Davis, that locomotive is nearing the GZ. It's less than a mile from the tower."

"Let it go in," Demming replied. He looked at Flagmeyer and shook his head in disgust. "Continue the countdown."

The security man motioned at Flagmeyer and Uborka. "What do you want us to do with them?"

"Bring in a television monitor," Demming said. "Let them see what happens at the GZ."

38

The Atomic Express

3:30 a.m.

Susan scanned the room, from the face of Frye's antique wall clock, to Frye himself and to Bobbie Jean, finally resting her gaze on the tall, white-haired military officer standing by the door. Behind him, she caught the silhouettes of young men with rifles, preventing their escape.

"General, you have *no* right to be here and you know it," she said finally, her voice shaking with rage. "We have broken *no* laws, we have done *nothing* to deserve this kind of treatment—"

"Little lady, we followed your airplane through 22 miles of military restricted airspace. The nuclear test site *is* a restricted area, you know." The general's ruddy face broke into a smile, but his pale blue eyes were gunsights that had found their target.

"I told ya *I* was flyin' the plane," Bobbie Jean broke in. "An' I cut across the test site all the time."

"Even during a nuclear test?" the general asked.

"Sometimes," she shrugged. "It's been done."

"General Umber, sir." A stocky officer appeared at the door. "They're interrogating the scientist."

"Anything new?"

"No, sir. The countdown is continuing."

"Thank you, Colonel." The general turned to look at the antique clock. "That's a nice old timepiece you have there, Mr. Frye. I presume it's accurate?"

Frye responded with a silent stare.

"If it is, then there is less than 30 minutes to detonation," the general said. "You know, ladies, it's quite some distance to the Vulcan target. Even if you flew that plane as fast as you could, you'd never make it on time."

"I don't know what the hell you're talkin' about," Bobbie Jean growled.

"Nobody is going to any ground zero," Susan said. "We're just getting ready to take Mr. Frye here over to Reno. He has an appointment."

"At a hospital," Bobbie Jean added. "It's an emergency run."

The general appraised Frye, who sat scowling at the table, holding a cup of coffee. "You wouldn't want to fly a sick man through a nuclear cloud, would you?"

"Then call off the shot," Bobbie Jean said.

"I'm sorry. We can't do that."

"Why don't you people just *get out of here*!" Susan screamed. "Get out of here and leave us alone! We're not your hostages!"

"Think of us as your *protectors*," the general replied.

"Ain't no use wastin' yer breath, girl." Frye squinted at the general. "It's plain fer all t'see that th' man is simply a one-star sonofabitch."

The general turned to gaze out the window. "Your house faces south, doesn't it, Mr. Frye? I'll bet you can watch the tests from your front porch."

Susan looked out the window, past the soldiers on the porch with their rifles, saw the dark fuselage of the black helicopter shining in the yellow glow of the pole lamp.

"You know, Mr. Frye, I've always wanted to see the bombs from a distance," the general smiled. "I'm usually too close to appreciate them, flying my helicopter, directing troop movements."

"Shore wish I had some chewin' tobacca right now," Frye mumbled.

"But I hear when you see a detonation from some distance, the entire sky lights up, much like the northern lights. I suspect this one will be quite beautiful."

"I don't plan ta watch it."

"Well," the general turned, the smile still on his ruddy, wrinkled face, "I'm sure you won't mind if *I* do."

———※———

As the diesel entered the lighted target area, Pliney slowed the engine, then switched it to a side track that curved away toward the east. "Thought we'd back it into the rail yard here," he mumbled to Rhinehart. In a few easy motions, he punched the buttons on the remote switcher, then pulled the throttle to full reverse. The diesel engine stopped, then backed around the curve in the direction of the target.

Moments later, as they entered the rail yard below the Vulcan shotcab, Pliney gave the throttle a final quick burst, then applied the brakes hard, sending a metal-on-metal screech into the night. After a quick glance at the diesels and railcars scattered along the various sidings, he located his quarry parked adjacent to the tower—12 hopper cars loaded with dark, plastic-lined mounds of anhydrous lithium deuteride. "Thought yer friends were gonna be out here by now," he said, glancing toward the base of the tower. "Seems we're th' only ones who made it."

"It does seem quiet," Rhinehart nodded soberly as the diesel clanked onto the siding. "Too quiet."

Pliney watched the dark base of the shot tower drift past the window, not 30 feet away. "I'd feel better with a little more company, no offense. What time is it, anyway?"

"Half past three, I'd guess."

"Ya *guess*? Ain't ya sure?"

"I don't wear a watch." Rhinehart displayed his empty wrist. "Lost it in a blimp accident."

"Ya oughta' stay outta them damn things." As the nearest lithium car loomed ahead of the rumbling engine, Pliney tapped the brakes with his palm and the diesel came to a rolling stop. "Okay. Get on out there and see if those couplers are lined up. And don't ferget to attach the air hoses. Brakes won't do flip without air."

Rhinehart swung down the back steps of the diesel, then strolled up to the nearest hopper car. Shaking his head, Pliney realized he wasn't going to get this job done. They were cutting it too close. Suddenly he heard the popping sound of rocks hitting the engine cab. Turning around, he saw Rhinehart giving the thumbs-up.

Pliney pushed the throttle forward and the diesel slowly rumbled toward the cars. Then he felt the sharp bump that signalled connection, followed by a cascade of clicks as the line of hopper cars snapped into place. As Rhinehart climbed back into the engine cab, Pliney opened the valve. With a loud hiss, air rushed into the lines.

"Okay, Rhinehart, let's get th' hell outta here!" Pliney pushed the throttle to full forward. But instead of a relatively smooth burst of speed, the engine gave a sharp jolt, followed by an ear-piercing screech. Something was wrong. "Dammit, Rhinehart, how much time we got?"

"Twenty minutes probably," Rhinehart said.

Pliney reached for his flashlight. "Let's take a look at those brakes." After following Rhinehart up the coarse gravel roadbed, Pliney aimed the flashlight beam under the nearest car. What he saw made his heart stop cold. The brakeshoes had been welded. The lithium cars were going nowhere.

"No wonder they didn't try to stop us," he nodded. "Hell, we're gonna be in th' goddamn dead center of th' fireball."

Rhinehart pointed to a cloud of dust at the edge of the target. "Well, at least we have some company."

Steering the Roadster over the last small rise, Joe Bob headed for the flat, brightly lit circle of the target.

"There's the bunker." Linneman pointed at a dark building northeast of the tower. "It's 60 yards from the switchbox over here to the—look!"

"What?" Joe Bob asked.

"The train is still here! I thought they'd be out of here by now. And where's the airplane? Isn't there supposed to be an airplane?"

Joe Bob scanned the black horizon. "It'll be here."

"Drop me off at the bunker, Joe," Stein said, already unlatching the car door.

"No time, Jake. I'm goin' for the switchbox." Ramey bounced the car over a set of tracks, steering directly for the small white cabinet at the base of the tower. As they stopped next to the switchbox pedestal, Stein sprang from the car and sprinted toward the bunker, his combat boots kicking up puffs of dust in his wake.

An instant later, Linneman was out of the car, standing before the switchbox. "What is it, George?" Ramey shouted. "Open it up!"

"Just a minute." Linneman took a screwdriver from his pocket, then touched it to the panel. The response was a shower of bright yellow sparks. "The security system is on. It's hot."

"Think you can still do it?"

"Maybe." Linneman took a deep breath. "But in case I don't, try to get that lithium out of here. Without the lithium, it'll be just your standard 17-kiloton burst."

"That's reassuring, George," Ramey said, shifting the Roadster into low gear. "I'll keep that in mind."

═══⚓═══

As Ramey's Roadster sped away toward the train, Linneman turned back to the switchbox. When he had last seen the panel, there had been only 20 or so connections. Now there were over a hundred—all looking exactly the same and all recessed in a forest of thin copper security plates. Energized to some lethal voltage.

Then he noticed something even worse. A thin yellow cable taped to the back wall of the chassis and a spiderweb of wires emanating along its length—the classic double-reverse circuit. If he threw the wrong knifeswitch, the charge would immediately shunt to the tower and into the detonators. There would be no sound. It would be over that quick. He had to find the correct breaker. And there was only one line to the top. He glanced at the top of the tower. There it was, the single red aircraft warning light, blinking steadily. He knew the light and the bomb shared the same power supply.

Aiming the screwdriver at a random breaker, his fingers a fraction of an inch from the deadly copper plates, Linneman carefully pried the knifeswitch up past the terminals. He looked up quickly. The light was still on.

Returning to the maze of switches, he tried another. As he pried it loose from its mooring, something went dark in the periphery of his vision. One of the spotlights had gone out. And he was still alive. He aimed again, then paused. There were more than a hundred breakers. He didn't have time. It would be random. Dumb luck. Reaching in past the copper strips, he pulled another switch, then checked the light on the tower.

Still on.

═══⚓═══

The man sitting at the television bank raised his hand. "Another monitor is out!"

"Which one?" Bartholomew asked.

"It was a display of the lithium cars."

Bartholomew turned and made his way down the aisle to Demming's desk. "Someone's into the switches. I say detonate now."

"No," Demming said, "this is a normal countdown. Besides, what can they do in nine minutes?"

==—⚞—==

"Take a look at this, Ramey—" Pliney pointed to the wheels. "Sonsabitches done welded th' brakeshoes down. Can't move 'er."

"Then get the hell out of here," Joe Bob waved his arm. "Unhitch it and go! You can make it a few miles."

Pliney nodded toward the switchbox. "Accordin' to Rhinehart, if you fellas don't pull the plug on this thing, it won't make much dif'rence *where* we are."

"Yeah, I told him." Rhinehart crawled out from beneath the train. "A fireball 70 miles wide. He was impressed." He got up and brushed himself off. "Still, it's good to see you could make it here."

"It don't look good, Carl," Joe Bob said. "I think George is havin' trouble with the switchbox."

"If nobody has any objections, then," Rhinehart said, looking up at the tower, "I'll take my customary position."

"Carl, we might get out of this," Joe Bob said. "It ain't over yet."

"I'm afraid it is," Rhinehart shrugged. "I've been through this before, remember. And each time the bomb goes off. Sorry."

"Well, Carl, it was good knowin' ya." Joe Bob grasped Rhinehart's hand and shook it. "We had us a hell of a time."

"We sure did, Joe," Rhinehart grinned. "We'll get together again sometime, okay?"

"Sure," Joe Bob nodded. "Sure."

As Rhinehart walked down the gravel roadbed toward the shot tower, Joe Bob turned to Pliney. "How's it look down there?"

"Well," Pliney scratched his head, "I dunno. Mebbe I'll come up with somethin in a minute or two. And then, mebbe not."

"If it don't work out, I just want ya to know, yer a hell of a train man."

"Thanks." Pliney shook Ramey's hand. "Now get on outta here. Lemme figger this out."

As Ramey sprinted back to the switchbox, Pliney aimed his flashlight at the brakes. Then he noticed something. They were welded, but not all the way around. "Spot welds," he grinned. "Lazy sonsabitches— it's gonna *cost* 'em."

3:52 a.m.

As Ramey approached, Linneman eased the screwdriver into the switchbox and began to pry yet another breaker. "How much time do we have, Joe?" he asked.

"Not enough. How ya doin?"

"Not good," Linneman replied, easing his hand between another set of copper vanes. "Did you see Carl? He's climbing the tower."

"Yeah, I know. Guess this one's gonna finally get him."

"Probably get us all." Linneman paused. "Might as well give him a ride to the top." He carefully tapped a knifeswitch with the blade of the screwdriver. In response, the elevator at the base of the tower clanked to life. Turning, he saw Rhinehart wave, then get inside the metal lift cage.

"How'd ya figure that one?"

"It was the only breaker they left open," Linneman said. "Had to be for the lift. How much time do we have?"

"About five minutes."

As the elevator slowly moved up the tower, Linneman turned back to the panel. "You know, Joe," he said, aiming the blade toward another knifeswitch, "this reminds me of a game I got for my daughter once. Had to pull a little metal pin from a board with tweezers. If you made one slip, a little buzzer would go off. This panel is like that, only worse—"

Whump!

A fiery rocket ascended into the heavens, trailing red fire. The three minute flare.

"I've got him!" someone shouted.

Linneman turned from the breaker box. It was Stein at the door of the bunker, carrying someone fireman-style toward the car.

"Holy cow!" Ramey yelled. "Jake was right!"

"Guess so," Linneman said, returning to the maze. The intricate work had taken its toll—the muscles in his arm were beginning to tremble and shake. To make matters worse, the train was moving *away* from the lithium cars. If the engineer was trying to save his own life, he didn't blame him. Turning, he watched Ramey's convertible roar the short distance to Stein and the limp soldier. More futility. Unless he found the right circuit.

Whump!

Another flare. Two minutes.

There was only one way—the double-reverse circuit had to have a fuse, otherwise it could detonate on its own. Perspiration dripping into his eyes, Linneman carefully traced the yellow cable to a tiny glass object in the far—and inaccessible— corner of the chassis. That had to be it. Had to be connected to the tower, to the detonators. Pulling anything along the circuit would produce a 50-50 chance of detonation. But if there was a surge of current, it might blow the fuse and stop the countdown. But the charge would have to go through him.

Linneman paused, then, slowly eased the screwdriver blade deep into the panel, past the deadly stands of copper, finally making contact with the appropriate terminal. Filling his lungs with air, he deliberately tilted the metal tool toward the energized frame.

"Carol," he whispered, "don't forget me—"

"Is it Perkins?" Ramey opened the car door.

"Yeah." Stein pushed the soldier into the back seat. "Out like a light. How are we doing with the switchbox?"

"We're not," Joe Bob shook head. "George is—"

Suddenly the switchbox exploded in a flash of light. Ramey saw Linneman jerk wildly, then fall like a rag doll amid a cloud of sparks. At the same instant, the lights surrounding the target dimmed to a deep shade of gold.

"Good Lord," Ramey gasped. "He did it."

"What happened?" Stein asked. "Where's the plane?"

"Don't think it's comin'—I'm gonna get George." Joe Bob turned on the headlights and aimed his car toward the crumpled form lying near the switchbox.

—❦—

"What is going on out there!" Demming roared. "We've lost power!"

"They've got my volunteer!" Bartholomew screamed. "They've got him! Detonate! Detonate!"

"Shut up!" Trumbo turned to Demming. "I thought we put a double-reverse on that. What happened?"

"I don't know, I don't understand it—"

"Can't trust you with *anything*!" Trumbo grabbed a microphone. "Shunt the power through the secondary cable bus. When the capacitor is full charge, detonate. Don't wait for the countdown!"

"I *know* we had that wired . . ." Demming shook his head. "It just doesn't make sense."

"Get a *move* on!" Trumbo growled into the mike. "Do I have to do *everything* around here?"

Military intelligence rewired it after Linneman was there," Demming said. "They must have forgot to remove the safety fuse—"

"I can*not* believe the incompetance of this place," Trumbo shook her head. "Is the nuclear device still on the tower? Is the train still out there? They haven't run away with the train have they?"

"I don't know," a technician replied. "All the monitors are out. We can't tell—"

"Hurry!" Bartholomew screamed, his face going gray.

—❦—

Under the golden light around the target, Joe Bob jumped from the car and raced toward George Linneman's still body. Barely cognizant of Stein's presence, he hammered on Linneman's chest, then lifted the limp form into the car and placed it next to the groggy soldier. Then, willing his legs to move, his shoes digging into the sand, he rounded the front of the car. With a rush, it came to him. This was his dream.

Looking up, he saw it—the flat face of the tower pedestal, glowing like an orange bluff against a purple sky. Atop the tower, just beneath the shot cab someone was waving. Rhinehart.

"Joe!" Stein commanded. "Come on!"

In the background he saw movement as the dark, rust-colored diesel engine raced backwards toward the lithium rail cars. A loud hum filled his ears. Was it the train? No. It was coming from somewhere else. From the bomb. Time was slowing down.

"Dammit!" He felt a violent tug as Stein pulled him behind the wheel. "Let's *go!*"

Ramey jammed his foot down on the accelerator. The car fishtailed in a tight circle, then headed for the darkness just beyond the edge of the target.

"We're gonna die, aren't we?" the soldier mumbled.

"Maybe—maybe not." Joe Bob hit the dimmer switch on the headlamps and the dark landscape ahead of the car brightened.

"Probably too late for the plane, Joe," Stein said.

"I dunno," Joe Bob said. "Looks like it."

With an ear-shattering bang, the rear end of the diesel slammed into the line of rail cars, locking the coupler and forcing the entire group back several yards. In a quick, precise motion, Pliney jammed the throttle full forward and hit the traction button, dumping the full load from the sandbox. From somewhere below, the wheels screeched against the rails, then caught hold. They were moving. He had broken the welds.

As the train slowly picked up speed, he looked at the tower. The lights were back on. It must be time. With any luck, he would have the cars out of the way of the fireball.

One thing, though, was clear. He wasn't going to make it. Even with the huge engines of the Express screaming at full throttle—everything at ground zero—the tower, the diesels, the other railcars—was still within the burst zone.

This was it. In a few days he'd probably be floating up there in the stratosphere somewhere, along with the remains of his Super Chief. He and his diesel would cross over Chicago together.

"Dr. Trumbo! We have the circuit back!" someone yelled from across the Control Room. "Full charge—"

"Then detonate!" Trumbo said, her voice roaring like an approaching missile. "Detonate *now!*"

Demming reached for the knifeswitch, and in a quick motion, closed the circuit.

Suddenly, the lights inside the Control Room flickered and dimmed. On the radiation dials, the needles slammed into the far posts, then drifted back to zero. The gamma pulse.

———✻———

In the dim light of the farmhouse, Susan watched the general pace across the room, looking at his watch, humming an unidentifiable tune. The clock on the wall showed 4:05 a.m. Outside, the sky was still dark.

"Mebbe they done dropped the ball, Gen'ral," Frye grinned.

"Get Storax in here," the general barked at a nearby officer. "Call the Control Point. I want to know what the hell—"

Suddenly, the scene dissolved in a burst of light. Susan put her hands over her face, yet still she saw the silhouette of the general, his arm outstretched, a dark form standing motionless behind her closed eyes. Waiting for darkness to return, she felt the tightness in her throat. She had lost someone again.

Opening her eyes, she saw the general's smile, saw the hazy red color of the sky. In a moment, the fireball would appear over the horizon and the air would be filled with the smell of burning.

"Mr. Frye—ladies," the general said, stepping out the door, "I certainly would enjoy staying around to chat, but I must inspect the target. I'll let you know what I find."

"Leave us alone," Susan said, tears flowing down her cheeks. "Just leave."

"You heard her," Frye snarled. "Get yer asses off m'property."

The general turned back to face them, his eyes hard. "We'll be back. I still have some questions for you."

———✻———

"We got it!" Bartholomew screamed. "Open the window blinds!"

"Probably still too bright," Trumbo said, peering at the blank television screens. "Let's wait until the monitors come back. Davis, how is the magnetic field?"

"I don't understand," Demming said, peering at the bouncing, vibrating dials. "There's a strong field, but it seems to be coming in pulses—surges. I don't understand this."

"What's going on with these lights?" Bartholomew asked, pointing at the flickering ceiling lamps.

"It's the pulse," Trumbo said. "It's disrupting our power supply. It should be stable in a minute or two—have any of our monitors come back yet?"

"Yes," Demming said, his voice hoarse. "Yes, they have."

===✺===

His hands cuffed behind him, Flagmeyer stared at the flickering television screen, still white with static. At the target, the 12 railcars of lithium had by now turned to pure fusion fuel. And if so, the nuclear fireball was probably hovering somewhere above the ground, trapped by bands of electromagnetic flux. Above his head, the single ceiling lamp flashed and sputtered, dimmed, then brightened again. He felt an odd emptiness, as though none of it mattered. The science, the world, the implications. The universe. He wanted to go home. The door opened. Someone was behind him, unlocking the handcuffs. Standing up, Flagmeyer turned to see a red-haired man in a Hawaiian shirt.

"Hi guys," the man said. "Time to go. Ready?"

Nodding, Uborka rose from his chair.

"Here." The man handed Flagmeyer two hemispheres of heavy gray metal. "Got these from that little demonstration of critical mass. Pure plutonium. Barely subcritical. You know what to do."

"I—I guess so. But what—"

"Thought you would, Elmore said you were a smart guy." The man slapped him on the back. "Come on."

As though in a dream, Flagmeyer walked through the door and up the dark corridor toward the Control Room. In his hands, the plutonium seemed to grow warmer. Entering the Control Room bay, he saw that everyone was standing with their backs toward him, watching the blinds on the picture window slowly rotate to the open position.

He caught his breath. The detonation had indeed occurred—the glowing fireball was soaring toward the heavens. But something was wrong. With dawn not far away, the atmosphere should have been deep indigo tinged with blue and green. Yet the sky was a perfect black.

Except for the brightly glowing fireball and the ring of yellow fire, a veil of darkness had descended over the test site.

Moving closer to the window, close enough to see the upper reaches of the sky, he saw something moving in the heavens. Driven by the magnetic tide, a gauzy cyclone of cirrus clouds was forming above them—a great, rotating wheel of ragged, tortured phantoms circling an unseen axis. And at the center, on the ground, was the burning mushroom cloud.

Flagmeyer pushed through the silent crowd until he was the closest to the window, the closest to the flame.

"What are they doing here?" someone shouted. "I thought they were locked up!"

"It's the shock wave—look out!"

Ignoring the activity behind him, Flagmeyer watched the approach of the mach front, a thick, almost opaque ripple in the heavy air. In an ear-shattering instant it was on them, bending the window, throwing him to the floor, sending the hemispheres rattling across the tile.

"He has the plutonium!"

Looking up, Flagmeyer saw four gun barrels aimed at him. Calmly, he reached out and picked up the plutonium hemispheres, now almost hot to the touch. It wouldn't be long. But where were the others? Hadn't they followed him here?

"Shoot him!" Bartholomew commanded.

"No!" Demming screamed. "He has a nuclear core! If he brings it together—"

Flagmeyer turned back to the window, watched the approaching base surge, the turbulent palisade of fire and smoke, now almost halfway to the Control Point. Then he heard the sound of firecrackers, felt a sizzle in his arm, saw a spiderweb appear in the glass beside his head. Turning around, he saw the barrel flash. Another sizzle, this time in his other arm. Where *were* the others? Was he alone here?

No, standing beside him was Uborka. And the red-haired man.

"How much longer now?" Flagmeyer asked.

"It's time." The red-haired man said.

Flagmeyer turned. Somehow they were no longer on Syncline Ridge overlooking the test site. They were on the valley floor, with the railroad tracks leading away from the picture window and vanishing into the rapidly approaching dustcloud. Then he knew. Absolutely *knew* why they were there. He turned to the red-haired man.

"Tell Elmore we did our best—"

"You can tell him yourself.."

Not 500 yards from the face of the window, a light flashed in the dark turbulence of the dustcloud. Something was coming through the base surge. Then, as another bullet slammed into the window, he saw it—the huge sledgehammer face of the diesel locomotive, the Atomic Express, its headlight illuminating the entire Control Room.

Flagmeyer saw red blotches appear on the window, heard a snapping sound as the slug shattered his left leg. Someone fell beside him. Uborka. Spinning back, he saw the big scientist trying to rise from a pool of dark blood. "We can't leave him—"

"Wouldn't think of it." It was Elmore's voice.

"Stop them!" Demming screamed.

As Flagmeyer lifted the heavy plutonium halves, he saw the men aim, heard the report. As slugs zipped through his cheek, tore into his chest, he had the flicker of a thought—there was no pain. Just difficulty in completing the task.

He tried to push the hemispheres together, but they were gone. Bartholomew had taken them. taken their last chance. Then, his vision dimming, Flagmeyer saw the doctor shudder violently—rise into the air, then crash headfirst to the floor beside him—astonishment etched across his face, eyes staring sightlessly at the approaching disc of light.

Eduard had the hemispheres. "You wanted energy," he roared, raising them high above his head. "*Here* is your energy!"

Flagmeyer turned one last time. Just outside the window, he saw the gaping coupler of the locomotive, heading toward them.

Then, frame by frame, as the window curved, then exploded inward, he watched Uborka slam the hemispheres together, watched the familiar purple ionization glow fill the room—saw the thick flashes of lightning, saw the fire billowing from two massive hands. Even with his eyes gone he could still see it, the flames leaping through him, forming the portal of binding energy, crackling and spinning, dragging him through the light toward the hills and cornfields and meandering streams. The clouds and the wind and the call of the mourning dove.

"Did you see that, sir?" Colonel Storax pointed out over the engine nacelle. "Another explosion in the southern part of the site. That's the third so far in an hour. Maybe we should get back."

The general tipped the cyclic control to the right and the purple horizon tilted up, then returned to level. "No, we have to locate the remains. Make sure nobody escaped."

"Yes, sir," Storax nodded. "But the GZ is still hot."

"It's not *that* hot," the general said, easing the helicopter closer to the ground. "Anyway, there's too much at stake here. People can live after a hell of an exposure, Bartholomew proved that. And if they can live, they can talk. If the Pentagon hears about this I'm a dead duck."

"Yes, sir," Storax said. "But I think we should wait until it cools—"

"Wait a minute—what's that?" The general pointed at a black, smoldering object about two miles from the blackened earth of the GZ. "I believe that's it!"

"Yes," Storax said, "I think it's a car."

"Damn right it's a car! I'm landing this thing. Call the Control Point! Tell them they don't have to worry."

Smiling, the general watched though the windscreen as the downdraft from the rotors dispersed the smoke. It *was* a car—or at least it *had* been one. A convertible, in fact. Now, lying on its back, it was only a hollow shell, black smoke pouring from the burning tires, flames and white smoke billowing from the interior.

Easing down the collective stick with his left hand, Umber lowered the helicopter through the haze. A few seconds later they were on the ground. "Here we are! Let's go!"

"Here's your respirator, sir." Storax handed him the mask.

The general pushed open the door and stepped to the ground. "What's the matter, Storax, got the heebie-jeebies?"

"This place has some radiation—"

The general kicked at the smoking car frame. "Bet they weren't a mile from the shot—look! The heat even fused the glass on the head-lights. Turned 'em black! How about that?"

"I can't raise the Control Point," Storax called from the helicopter.

"Sure, I—wait a minute." The general peered at the ground. "Did you see that? Something's moving." He pointed to a patch of ground a few yards north of the wreckage. "Right over there. I'm gonna take a look."

The general strode over to the spot and paused. After a second, a small mound of dust flickered, then settled, like a spider hiding in the dust, waiting for a passing insect. A body beneath the sand, in the final throes. "Call up the Control Point, Storax and get the doc on the radio. We found 'em."

"Yes, sir."

Kneeling, he scooped away a layer of white alkali to reveal a large circular indentation set several inches into the soil. Digging his fingers down into the soft alluvium, the general touched metal. A lid. Then, before he could think, the lid moved and he found himself staring straight into the barrel of a .45.

=⚓=

"C'mon, Suze," Bobbie Jean said, opening the door of the Cessna. "Let's take Albert and go home. That general said he was comin' back "

"No," Susan said, biting her lip. "Go on without me."

"Listen, there ain't a thing we could do. Ask Harold."

"I was the one that got him into this." Susan shook her head. "Trying to find out what killed my pop. Got him interested just because of what he did."

"Aw, come on, Suze." Bobbie Jean put her arm around her. "You liked him. He liked you. He did it for you."

Susan moved away. "I used him, BJ. I really did. I tried to get that information. And then—"

"Okay. We'll talk later." Bobbie Jean backed away, then opened the door of the plane. "Let's go before the military gets back."

"You go without me. I'll borrow Harold's truck to get home. I want some time alone."

"Well, okay," Bobbie Jean nodded. "But I think—oh, no—"

"What?"

Bobbie Jean pointed to the south. Against the early morning light, low on the horizon, was the unmistakable shape of the black helicopter.

"Come on." Bobbie Jean grabbed her sleeve. "Harold's got a gun."

"Forget it, BJ." Susan watched the object approach over the fenceline, low to the ground, like a huge wasp. "You can't go around shooting the military."

Bobbie Jean reached beneath the back seat of the Cessna and produced a pistol. "Let's just see what Sam Colt has to say to them bastards—"

"Put it away, BJ," Susan said. "They've won." As she watched, the helicopter hovered briefly over the landing strip, then dropped roughly to earth.

As the engine shut down, a side door opened and a tall military man stepped to the ground.

Susan swallowed hard, tears in her eyes. It was Jake Stein.

Seconds later, another man jumped out, wearing dusty jeans and a khaki shirt. Susan ran over, ducked beneath the whirling rotor blades and wrapped her arms around his neck. "Joe—"

"Holy mother of God!" Bobbie Jean squealed. "We thought you got blown up!"

"Made it to a shelter." Joe Bob said, hugging Susan. "Shock wave just rolled over the top and that was it. Just got a few bruises is all—"

"Oh God, I thought—" Susan said, hugging him hard.

"We saw that chopper an' thought you might be somebody *else*," Frye said.

"Well, th' general and his buddy" Joe Bob grinned, "are all tied up inspecting the butt end of the fallout shelter. Stein didn't feel like kidnapping a general."

" The army frowns on that kind of thing," Stein nodded solemnly.

"Bad enough you pulled a *gun* on 'em, Jake." Joe Bob laughed.

"But what about—" Bobbie Jean hesitated, her smile gone. "Are you the only ones who—"

"There's someone in the cabin I think wants to see you," Stein said. "He's still a little woozy—and I had to extract a few wires loose from his scalp, but—"

Bobbie Jean ran to the helicopter and disappeared through the door.

"Well, gentlemen," Frye asked, ejecting the shells from his shotgun. "You just saved Nevada. An' mebbe half the continent. Can I get you anything? Coffee? A beer?"

"Yeah," Joe Bob nodded, his arm around Susan. "We'll need a sectional map of Idaho and a route to British Columbia. Thought we'd hide out there until we can get to a newspaper. Jake here wants to call the New York Times."

"Well, sure," Frye nodded, "if he reverses th' charges."

"Oh yeah, one other thing." Joe Bob turned back toward the helicopter. "We got this other guy back there who wanted to use the phone. Said he wanted to call his girlfriend in Rhode Island."

www.ingramcontent.com/pod-product-compliance
Lightning Source LLC
Chambersburg PA
CBHW020833030726
47496CB00001B/220